ROCK ISLAND LINE

ALSO BY DAVID RHODES

The Last Fair Deal Going Down

Easter House

Driftless

ROCK ISLAND LINE

David Rhodes

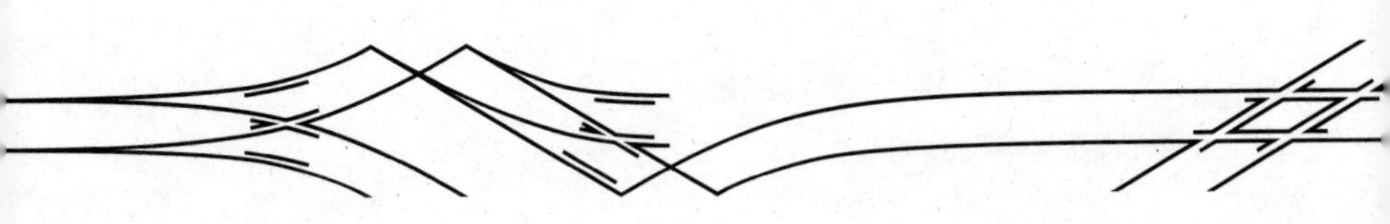

MILKWEED EDITIONS

The characters and events in this book are fictitious. Any similarity to real persons, living or dead, is coincidental and not intended by the author.

Published 2008 by Milkweed Editions
First published by Harper & Row in 1975.
Printed in Canada
Cover design by Christian Fuenfhausen
Author photo by Lewis Koch
Interior design by Wendy Holdman
The text of this book is set in
ITC New Baskerville.
08 09 10 11 12 5 4 3 2 1
First Paperback Edition

Please turn to the back of the book for a list of the sustaining funders of Milkweed Editions.

The Library of Congress has catalogued the cloth edition as follows:

Rhodes, David.
Rock Island Line.
I. Title.
PZ4.R4755Ro [PS3568.H55]
813'.5'4

74-15888

ISBN 0-06-013559-X

This book is printed on acid-free, recycled (100 percent postconsumer waste) paper.

To Nelson and Steve

ACKNOWLEDGMENTS

The *Rock Island Line* story would never have emerged without the patience, advice, and bedrock human kindness extended to me by many, many people. Although their names do not appear, their voices and spirits run like wolves through the narrative. Mention should be made, however, of my agent Lois Wallace who took the original draft to Harper & Row, where editor Frances Lindley found something worth encouraging and guiding forward. For the republication of the current edition I'm grateful to Philip Christman for his indefatigable enthusiasm, to Milkweed editor Ben Barnhart, and the rest of the Milkweed staff. They heard the wolves and understood the need to preserve the story entirely in its youthful form without the niggling intrusion of a more mature perspective. My thanks to all.

ROCK ISLAND LINE

ONE

The old people remember Della and Wilson Montgomery as clearly as if just last Sunday after the church pot-luck dinner they had climbed into their gray Chevrolet and driven back out to their country home, Della waving from the window and Wilson leaning over the wheel, steering with both hands. They can remember as if just yesterday they had driven by the Montgomerys' brownstone house and seen them sitting on their porch swing, Wilson rocking it slowly and conscientiously back and forth, Della smiling, her small feet only touching the floor on the back swing, both of them looking like careful, quiet children.

Della's hands were so small they could be put into small-mouth jars. For many years she was their only schoolteacher, and, except for the younger ones, they all had her, and wanted desperately to do well with spelling and numbers to please her. Without fail, screaming children would hush and hum in her arms. It was thought, among the women, that it was not necessary to seek help or comfort in times of need, because Della would sense it in the air and come. The old people don't talk of her now but what a shadow is cast over their faces and they seem to be talking about parts of themselves—not just that Della belonged to the old days, but that when she and Wilson were gone it was unnatural that anything else from back then should go on without them.

Wilson owned and managed a small grocery store in the middle of Sharon Center, where now old Highway 1 intersects with the blacktop to Hills at a three-way stop sign. (It has fallen in upon itself in neglect, bought finally by Eldon Sehr, an old German who would neither sell it, rent it nor use it, and who lived like a ghost in the house across the street.) The store front at that time extended by one oblong room out to the road. The Montgomerys lived in the house part in back for twenty-three years.

Della was in the store sometimes, but mostly it was just Wilson listening to his radio behind the counter. After several years he had noticed that on Saturday evening it was increasingly difficult to close the store, for the great number of people who came then to buy cereal and coffee, milk and such, and who all knew one another and were not the least hurried in leaving. They came in families. Taking note of this, Wilson hung up a new sign declaring that the store would be closed at three o'clock Saturday afternoon and reopened at seven, after dinner. At first no one would come at the later time, but Wilson had bought nearly a dozen chairs at an auction and scattered them here and there around the room and porch, and slowly those who *would* come found they could sit down and stay quite comfortably talking to their neighbors without feeling the least obligation to leave or buy anything they didn't need. And besides, Della was there too and there was always something the women would want to talk to her about, and it was so easy to lure her away from straightening the things on the shelves. Wilson too was easy to draw aside and a quick exchange with him could bring you up to date on the current events of Sharon Center and vicinity, and a lengthy discussion was maybe more than you needed to know. But mostly he was behind the counter with his radio as the talking went on farther out in the room. And it was for that reason that it worked so well, because it wasn't going visiting—imposing—it was going to the store. Yet even in winter, when only those within walking distance could really justify coming, it was just as full.

Della and Wilson had come to Sharon five years earlier in search of two of their relations—Nelson Hodge and David Montgomery, both by that time departed. It was assumed by George Barns, when he first saw them in his tiny store beside the doctor's house, that they were hoping to acquire money by inheritance, and he treated them to his usually hostile personality. He explained that Nelson

Hodge and David Montgomery, two confirmed and dedicated bachelors who had lived together for as long as anyone could remember, were dead, and that their small farm, along with whatever livestock and implements, had been sold for debt at a state auction. And if he were ever to meet them in the hereafter he might present them with an unpaid balance of $4.78 from his own meager business.

But the truth was that Della and Wilson were not after an inheritance. They were young and looking for a place to settle, and it was in their minds that their relatives might provide them a wedge for getting nestled in a new place. Neither was well traveled. Nelson and David had been their last hope of this plan's success. Of course not all their relatives had been dead, but those who were living had proved to be better as springboards for moving on than as wedges.

So with the plan dissolved, they decided to go no farther, at least for now. They visited Wilson's uncle's farm and talked to the family that lived there, who insisted that they stay, if not in the little room upstairs, then in the barn—as it was still early September and not unduly cold. So it was from these people's barn that Sharon Center began to learn of them—Della, whose soul seemed always to be reaching out, and Wilson, whose soul was like a net around the two of them, keeping hers from escaping. And by the time they rented the building from Stuzman across the road and almost next to George Barns' store and began adding on a long oblong room, many people had already heard about them. George Barns, when he learned Wilson intended to start a grocery store, told everyone that they wouldn't last long—and that even if Wilson's father *had* been a grocer, there was more to running a business in a rural community than met the eye. What he meant by that of course was that Sharon Center would not allow outsiders to come in and take money away from solid community members. But it was just that attitude—Barns' belief that everything and everyone was fixed—which made him so unpleasant; and it was more his unpleasantness that finally forced him out of business than the competition. The new couple was more accommodating. Even the meat man would rather deliver there because of the absence of complaining and because of Wilson's keen interest in fishing and politics.

Some time during those first years, before Della was asked to teach school, Wilson built swinging doors and compartments in his wagon, and a place for ice. Once a week he filled this huckster with food and delivered to nearly every house in Sharon Township, and two houses farther away (those of Floyd and Marvin Yoder). At the same time he would pick up the cream and eggs, dried beans and fruit, homemade foodstuffs like noodles and rolls, to carry back and sell. The coming of the Montgomerys' huckster was something on the order of an occasion, and the full delivery route was seldom completed until long after dark. In the winter, in order to make his stops fewer, several families would gather at one home, bringing with them their butter or eggs and cream. The children hoped their fathers would be in festive moods and buy something more than what was absolutely necessary. And though it would take a very long severe winter to daunt the spirit of those Iowa women, this once-a-week social occasion offset many otherwise lonely, house-prisoned hours, and many days wherein no confessions were held to acknowledge secret morning terrors and evening tensions, where people lived together like enraged animals and the sound of families arguing and cursing wailed unobstructed over the frozen land, howling into other homes through brown cracks in the walls.

Wilson was young then, and was never known to be quick-tempered, threatening or anything short of good-natured. In fact, it was for the reason that he seemed so one-sidedly good-natured and so very careful not to consort with any of the darker emotions that he was looked upon as a bit of a mystery by those who believed a person should be more *rounded out* in temperament and that an occasional outburst *of any kind* was a healthy thing, which in Wilson's history, so much as could be known, had happened only once, while delivering groceries in the winter.

Perry Bain and his family were being visited by relatives. A man who enjoyed nothing better than solitude, saving money and working himself into the ground, Perry found little pleasure in his new company and would have preferred walking all the way to Marvin Yoder's house to meet Wilson's huckster by himself, so that he could get down into the ditch and walk in the knee-deep snow, testing his endurance. But everyone wanted to go, and jumped at the chance to breathe fresh air; bundled up, the whole crew marched over to Marvin's to meet the huckster, despite the bitter cold. Even the two young ones came, carried by rotation from shoulder to shoulder.

The Montgomerys' wagon was there before them and they hurried inside, where nearly thirty people were gathered in the large kitchen and living room. There was much joking and talk of the ungodly weather. The Perry Bains and their visitors were quickly absorbed into the hubbub. The children played games on the kitchen table. The men occupied the living room, centered mostly around Wilson. It seemed so festive that Wendy Salinger went out to the wagon with Della and brought in a box of hard candy, put it down on the table and distributed one fat stick to each child. Della had one too, and they all began sucking on them with great relish. Soon thereafter the men came wandering back in to settle the matter of exchanging food and money. They progressed halfway to the table and stopped to talk again about the tax structure and the special benefits people had who didn't really work for a living. Then Perry Bain broke away from the conversation and rushed across the room. Five-year-old Timmy Bain had just time to look up as his father jerked the candy from his hand, threw it back into the box and said, "Don't you *ever* take nothin' that don't belong to you!"

The room began to shudder. Bain's wife looked down at the floor. Timmy was trying not to cry. Everyone wished to heaven that they weren't there. Della had taken her sucker out of her mouth, then put it back in and sucked on it, trying to pretend she still enjoyed it. No one talked. The room seemed electrically charged.

But then the character of the silent tension changed and changed, until everyone was aware that it was coming from Wilson's eyes, which seemed to be seething with hate, and his face was completely white. He walked across the room and over to the box, took out the partially eaten piece of candy, threw it on the floor, busting it into many pieces, took out another and slid it across the table to Timmy, who was crying now. Then he looked over at Bain and the look in his eyes was so murderously hateful that no one there ever forgot it. "I'll pay for that one," he said. Bain walked back into the living room.

This was the first time Wilson ever outwardly displayed an intense or violent emotion. Many people talked to him about it later—hoping to find some glimmer of the hatred resounding behind his eyes—and he talked to them calmly and in his serious but shy fashion, explaining how suffering and injustice, although real, were wrong and were loathsome, and especially children, who everyone would admit had done nothing to deserve pain, should not have to endure it because of corruption and vanity, or even stupidity. Yes, everyone agreed to this. Jacob Amstide went one step further and maintained that not only children, but everyone was innocent and undeserving of suffering—which originated from mistakes and fears . . . and hell.

"But assuming that's true," said Wilson, "then it was wrong for me to interfere. Isn't that what you mean?"

"No," Jacob answered. "You're innocent too."

"I don't believe that," said Wilson, "about suffering coming from hell, or from mistakes, or from anywhere. It's merely here, and we must deal with it. There's right and there's wrong."

Naturally, everyone believed that. For instance, Merle Brown had compiled a mental list of atrocities that he felt proved the absurdity of the world, and after loosing these examples on his neighbors like a swarm of biting flies, asked how could God be just. That's not the issue, they told him. They were concerned with Wilson's character. Here was a man who everyone thought had no dark side. Then it was reported that he did—to the extent that he would shame another man before his family—challenging him physically almost . . . and then the next day have not the slightest trace of the emotion left in him. It was like a man possessed by something and then turned loose. It interested them.

But it was for the most part soon forgotten. After all, how odd is it really to have a momentary temper flare, where all the petty grievances of several months come together in a perfect pinnacle of outrage, actualize, exorcise, and afterward leave no trace? How odd is that? Not so very. Indeed, what would married life be without just such instantaneous outbursts, where a few spoken words become a symbol for absolute, incorrigible evil? It was Wilson's sameness that was of more interest. It seemed he had no alternative selves and was either completely open or completely closed (depending on how it seemed to you) toward everyone. Even the government, how it was conducted and the quality of the laws that managed to squirm out of it, didn't seem to alter his outlook. He had no interest in women other than his wife.

Della began teaching school jointly with old Mrs. Fitch, the two of them making a comic pair standing side by side in the schoolyard supervising games; small Della, pretty, and quick as a yellow warbler, looked as though she were about ready to run off and get in the circle, her hair and clothes buffeted around her by the wind, while old Mrs. Fitch, dressed in heavy gray cotton, her hair coarse, bound into tight curls, did not seem as if she could ever move.

All the children were taught in the same room, through the eighth grade. The only difference between the younger and the older ones was that they carried different books. So while talking out loud with the fifth-graders about history, it was necessary to have the others busy with something that did not demand the teacher's attention. It couldn't always be done, and Della, as a way of learning the profession, quietly (and sometimes, under Eleanor Fitch's disapproving frown, not so quietly) watched over those grades of students and answered their individual questions.

Some things could be communicated to all, like reading stories of pirates and buried treasure, animals that could talk and dark forests. These times they traded off, though mostly they belonged to Eleanor, who seemed to Della to be possessive of them and only let her read the books of little emotional consequence.

While Eleanor read, Della sat in the back of the room next to the doors, and once, as the old practiced voice told of the death of Brighty of the Grand Canyon, she began to cry, and hid her face in her hands. Eleanor looked up and saw her, then quickly looked down again to the book, thinking privately between the next sentences that there was nothing wrong with it in itself, but it was something to be kept from the children, who could not understand that some people never completely grow up but that that didn't make them less than grownups. Except Eleanor suspected that in some way it did—in some way there should be a drawn line between feeling like crying when the burro dies and outwardly doing it. Later, in her house, she pondered this question, and decided that feelings had a reality of their own and that actions had little to do with them. Remember, she was very old, and soon retired from teaching, leaving Della there by herself.

But Eleanor came back for visits, and would arrive at the schoolroom unannounced, usually in the morning, bursting in through the door as though she owned it, and begin talking right away. Sometimes she brought her two canaries, Ebeneezer and Melissa, and talked about their habits. These visits saddened Della, because she knew Mrs. Fitch was lonely and that she needed a place where there was life—where she could talk of dress, and manners, and the great scholars, nature, numbers and the romantic imagination—a place where things mattered and were of consequence—a place full of meaning.

Eleanor had tenacity, and her brittle old bones hung on to life and refused to give up; and her mind refused to be dissolved into spirit and fastened like a many-tentacled bloodsucker onto reason. Her thinking remained clear, her memories intact. She continued her visits to the school, even when all of the students who could remember her as a teacher were gone into high school and, bashing in through the front door with her canaries, they would look up and think, Here she is again, the old weird woman. And Della was saddened, and many evenings took Wilson with her over to Eleanor's house to visit. But Eleanor didn't care about that. She loved children.

One morning she arrived in her buggy while Della and her students were sitting in a corner of the schoolyard, picking along the ground as though searching for a lost ring. Eleanor tied her horse (named Perseus, and left her by her husband, who had bought him because he was afraid of him, and there was no faster or more high-strung horse in Sharon Township) and hurried over to take control, in case they were not aware of the proper way to hunt for lost things in the grass—everyone not to move, and to look carefully around him. Moving around causes the grass to be trampled and it is possible for the object to become pushed down into the dirt, where it will be impossible to find. What she found was that they were engaged in searching for four-leaf clovers, all of them down on their hands and knees, pushing their fingers through the green clover heads. They said hello to her, and Della began to get up, but Eleanor motioned for her not to bother—that she would simply watch for a while. It was a lovely day, and the warm, fall air felt good on her face, and she thought privately, Ah, only we old ones know what it is like to breathe this and feel fully alive. Then she was taken up with watching the hunt. One of the youngest girls had the classroom dictionary, and it was her job to press the lucky clovers in between the pages. The hunters fanned out and began covering more ground, finding very few, though searching with a solemn devotion. "We'll never find enough for all of us," moaned one child. "Here's one!" screamed another. "Look! There's a snake!" "A snake!" "Leave him alone and he won't hurt you." "He won't hurt anyway. I catch 'em all the time. Where is he?" "He's gone." "Here's one!" "Let's see." "That's not a real one. It's just busted."

"It is too." "I can't find any." "Here's one! Oh, never mind." "Go look in your own place." "Don't step there."

But as she watched, Eleanor became increasingly amazed at what was happening within the excited hunt, and could not move her eyes away. Della was carefully, quietly taking up four- and five-leaf clovers and passing them unnoticed over to be stuck in the dictionary. Everywhere she turned would be another, as though she did not have to look, but merely reach her hand down and one would crop up to be tugged out of the ground. Even in places where the children had already searched. But they were not noticing. Della was finding them and pushing down the clovers around them so that they stood out; then she would walk away, and later the children would find them and begin screaming, "I got one! I got one!"

Eleanor, inside her heavy dress beneath her old face, thought, I've never seen anything like this. It's uncommon. What can it mean? Does it mean anything? No one can be that lucky. She merely knows how to hunt for them and is practical—No! It's uncommon.

Della was finally forced to take hold of one first-grade child (the only student left who had not found a clover himself and was on the verge of tears) and lead him over to a place where she had several located and waiting; and even then he stepped on one and only found the other by Della suggesting he not stoop over, but get down on all fours—helping him in such a way that both hands were on either side of a five-leafed one as big around as a golf ball. He picked it and took it over to the dictionary. "Here's another one," he said in an unconcerned way, but watched the older girl press it into place and gave a little jump when she slammed the book shut.

Della said it was time to go in, and then hollered that it was time, because sounds travel poorly through children. It was only then that she noticed Eleanor's eyes bent upon her. She told the older ones to monitor a study time, and together she and Eleanor watched them clear the yard and disappear into the building. Della turned to her, smiled and began to speak, but was interrupted.

"Magic," said Eleanor. Then she paused, took off her hat, patted her hair and put it back on. Della looked away and wondered if she were going to finish, or begin, or if the word was at the tail end of a private thought and had escaped by mistake. Some old people she had known had been like that.

"Sometimes I've wondered if there's anything reasonable about magic," Eleanor continued. "I mean, if it's real." Then she bent her eyes down on Della again.

"Well, I don't know if it's real or not. . . . Maybe. . . . What do you mean by magic?"

"You know, magic. Not black magic or superstition. White magic. Is there such a thing as white magic?"

"I don't know."

"Anyway, I'm sure there is. Its study is not for evil purposes. It reveals luck. It's a kind of preparation that makes you lucky. Do you know anything about it?"

"What kind of study?"

"I don't know for sure. Yes, incantations and such."

"I guess I don't know anything about it."

"Forgive me," Eleanor said, and stepped several feet closer toward the schoolhouse, her shoes hidden in the clover. "I'm not being precise enough." Then she began again. "When I was young—much younger than you . . . How old are you?"

"Twenty-seven."

There was a pause. Eleanor began again. "Actually age means nothing to me. Understand that no one ever ceases being . . . expectant of life. Now tell me quite simply, how were you able to find those clovers so easily?"

Then Della understood the reason for Eleanor's concern with her. Her eyes lit up, she smiled and made a motion as if she were going to clap her hands. "Oh, that," she said. "That's just me and finding things. I've always been able to do that. Wilson always says that he can never—"

"Do you mean you knew, when you came out here with them, that you would be able to find them so easily?"

"Well, yes and no. First of all, I guess I never think about it. Then there have to be some to find. Once Wilson lost one of his nails he uses for putting tobacco in his pipe and was so sure it was in the store that he made me look for it there. It's a very special nail. But I knew it wasn't there. And it wasn't."

"How did you know? And aren't you saying that even before you came out with the children, you had a fairly good idea that there would be some of those four- and five-leafed clovers out here?"

"No, no," exclaimed Della. "I know what you're thinking now, and it's not true. I know it looks that way, but it isn't. I assure you, it isn't. It's only my way. I find things. It's the way I've always been. When I was a little girl, I found things. If you were me, everything would be common and very ordinary."

"This seems so odd, Mrs. Montgomery, to be talking like this, if you know what I mean, about such things. But, truly, you must sometimes feel that there are great forces. Yet what must it be to feel that and still know the way you do about, well, magic. It must be a mystery partially revealed."

"No, no, you didn't understand me."

"Yes. You were trying to tell me that life for you is dull, and that's not true, but I know why you're trying to say it. You think I'm foolish."

"No. I think there is only the feeling—the feeling of mystery about what you know nothing about. Those things you understand are no good to you for that feeling. I imagine, Eleanor, when I watch you drive up, what it must be to control such an animal, and how proud you must feel knowing you can do it without any help. And what it must be to be so tall and straight."

"It doesn't seem the same thing. Those things are . . . ordinary."

"Do you mean to say—" Smiling.

"No, life is not ordinary, Mrs. Montgomery, and I feel that I am making a spectacle of my own narrow nature. But before we stop—and I don't wish you to do anything but answer—tell me of other things that you know about, like finding things."

"That's all."

"I don't believe it. I've always felt that you were very special."

"No, no, please—"

"Stop. We will talk no more of it. There's no excuse for leaving the children alone so long. It makes demands on them that they aren't ready for. They can only be quiet so long—and they want to be good—but they are forced by their natures to become unruly, and the conflict isn't good for them."

She turned and began walking toward the schoolhouse, through the clover, which hid her thin ankles.

Wilson arrived at the schoolyard five minutes before four, and waited until the door was thrown open and students scattered across into the road like bats from the small mouth of a cave. Their noise followed them around the corner and they were hidden by the green-and-gold corn. Della fitted the key to its lock, turned it, tossed her shawl one final time onto her shoulder and came to the wagon. Wilson lifted her up and they set off toward home. The humidity, together with the afternoon heat, wrung beads of sweat out of their bodies and into their clothes. Wilson remarked that he felt "clammy" and that, breathe as he might, he could not seem to get enough air, because he was suffocating all over. White, soapy lather formed between their horse and her harness straps and breast plate. The sounds of her steel shoes on the dirt were perfect thuds—thud, thud, thud—accompanied by the creaks and shudders of the weather-swelled buckboard. Tiny chips of mud clung to the wheels and fell away.

"What we need, you know," said Wilson, "is one good gully-washer, and enough of this drizzling. It's almost like not rain at all—just the air becoming so sticky and wet that loud noises shake water out of it. Oh, by the way, did you know that the amount of water in the air and on the ground never changes? I read that the other day. Doesn't that seem amazing, that it's always the same? But of course when you think about it, then you see it's obvious."

"Obvious things are always the most amazing."

"Come on now, there you go again."

"Wilson, that's different. There's some truth in that. It's not one of my usual generalizations."

"Oh no," laughed Wilson. "Just because it's got *some* truth in it doesn't mean it's true. Besides, all generalizations contain *some* truth, or they'd be complete nonsense and you couldn't understand them."

"What makes you think, Wilson, you can be the judge of how much truth is enough? That seems pretty presumptuous. Why does it have to be so hot today?"

"That's what makes it so hot, because it doesn't have to be. There can't be any reason for it. And even if there was a reason, it couldn't be a good enough one."

"Poor Wilson," said Della and laughed.

"I don't see what's so funny," said Wilson, looking as though he were trying to be brave about his suffering. "You shouldn't belittle someone trying to find peace, and unable to because of the weather."

"Oh no," said Della, laughing much louder now. "What a terrible thing I've done. If I only could have known. Wilson, can you ever forgive me?"

"My own family, mocking me."

"I'm sorry, Wilson."

"My own wife yet. Oh, it's terrible."

"Wilson." Della was reaching over to him, shaking in laughter. "Please . . .

"No," he complained, "I'll be all right. In time. I'll forget someday." They were driving into town now. Women were raking grass cuttings out of their yards and piling them along the road, watching the Montgomerys pass and listening to them. Della waved, and continued trying to appease Wilson, who was hot and would not forgive. After the Montgomerys' voices were gone, still Della's laughing cut through the sound of the wishing rakes. Pulling a stuck stick from hers, Mrs. Miller resumed humming.

At home, Wilson opened up the store for Mrs. Wecksler and sold her some buttons and a spool of thread, though in her own sly way she complained of not having a better color selection to choose from, which Wilson accepted, but he got a little mad and indulged, after she left, in a prolonged moment of self-satisfying spite. He straightened a new display of pipes that he had bought from a salesman a week before—pipes that were made by a doctor and could be broken down into three parts. The doctor himself was pictured in the display, with a beard, and explaining that his pipe was a "remarkable scientific discovery—a modern, scientific adaptation of age-old principles, handed down from the aboriginal knowledge of good smoking enjoyment." Then Wilson locked the front door, turned the sign in the window around so that it read closed and went back into his house. Up from the basement with a bottle of homemade beer, he sat at the table and talked to Della as she worried over a slow-bubbling stew and ate soda crackers one at a time.

"Did that Byron Bernard come back and pay his bill yet?" she asked.

"No, but he'll come."

"I don't trust him much. He's supposed to owe money to a lot of people. Joan Taylor says Mark isn't going to sell seed to him any more."

"I'll bet he does."

"Why should he? Why should others have to pay for him."

"I'll still bet he does. Anyway, it hasn't been that long. Besides, he's forgetful."

"He wouldn't be forgetful if *you* owed *him* money. Those kind of people always expect to be paid themselves right away—those stupids."

"Whew," whistled Wilson, and ducked. "That one nearly hit me on the way out."

"Here, eat a cracker." She tossed him a square, and it landed intact beside his glass of beer. He picked it up and nibbled on it with his front teeth.

"Something very strange happened today."

"What?"

"I'd taken the children out to hunt four-leafed clovers, and we were in the corner next to the beans—just east of the schoolhouse. Eleanor drove up in her carriage and tied Perseus and came over. Then she stood there watching, and right away I forgot about her being there at all, because more and more she comes in now. She doesn't start right off talking, but sits in the back of the room just watching. Sometimes for hours. So I've gotten used to her. But today, after a while, I could tell by the funny way she was looking at me that something was troubling her. I could tell, but I didn't have the least idea what it could be. Not the least—"

"And she was amazed at your divinatory arts." This was how Wilson always referred to Della's talents.

"How did you know?"

"That's easy. Just about every time someone looks at you in a funny way and you don't have the least idea what's going on in their heads, it turns out to be your divinatory arts."

"That's not true. There *you* go again."

"Tell me any other time someone looked at you in a way you didn't understand in the least."

"OK. Wait a minute. Let me think."

Wilson drank from the bottom of his glass, and confirmed again the fact that he had out of blind, inexcusable ignorance put in too much beer malt. It had the same bad taste as a very cheap wine, improperly fermented.

"I know," she began again. "That time Mike Brown came in and bought cheese and I knew he was worried, but I didn't know he'd taken his wife to the hospital. And he didn't tell me either—you found out."

"That isn't the same thing. Sorry, you lose. He wasn't even looking at you, and it didn't have anything to do with you. Wait a minute," said Wilson. He got up, poured the rest of the beer into the sink and went into the pantry, returning with the coffee grinder. He carried it, with the bean canister, back to the table. Wilson liked to grind coffee. "OK," he said.

Della bit off the corner of her present cracker. "I could tell she resented me—though I think she would have denied it even if she put the question to herself. But she talked for a long time about what she referred to as magic forces. Doesn't that seem odd, Mrs. Fitch talking about magic forces? I didn't know what to say."

"Why did you have to say anything? You always think you have to say something."

"Well, I couldn't just stand there like a ninny. You can just say that because you weren't there. It wasn't as though she was talking to herself. Then it was that I seemed to feel the resentment."

"You just imagined that," said Wilson, and emptied the little drawer from the bottom of the coffee grinder onto a page of newspaper spread across the tabletop. He repeated: "You just imagined that. Those feelings never existed in Mrs. Fitch. You thought so because you felt nervous, and feeling nervous makes you vulnerable to suspicious thoughts."

"Do you really think so?"

"I'm sure of it." Wilson put the drawer back, fed in another handful of beans and resumed grinding.

Della put the cracker away and peeked in under the lid of the stew—then poked a fork into a potato and let the lid back down.

"That's enough coffee, Wilson."

"Just twenty-five more beans." He began putting them in one by one. "Then let's go sit outside."

"It'll be time to eat pretty soon."

"Well, then, let's go outside now."

"After dinner. Then we can sit till it gets dark."

"All right . . . but I'm going to get another dog."

A short silence ensued.

"No. No more dogs. One is enough. No more dogs. We decided on that."

"I know we decided on no more *normal* dogs. But this one isn't normal, Midget. This one's unnatural. He's a fishing dog. Lewis was in today and said that it's his neighbor's dog and that he sees it out with him all the time in the boat, sitting up in front quietly as can be—or along the bank. Not at all like our dogs. This one's a coon dog too. He'll put old Duke to shame."

"Then get rid of Duke."

"Get rid of Duke!"

"We're not going to have two dogs. The last time we had two dogs, they—"

"That was different. It was Jumbo's fault. She was never very moral or responsible—but that was because of her childhood. Anyway, you shouldn't hold grudges. It's unfair." Wilson began putting in more beans, and a kind of hostility came into his eyes as he began grinding, and a ripple of anger lined thinly across his forehead. I could have killed him, he thought. I could kill him now. He had no proof it was her.

"I'm sorry, Wilson. Don't think about it, please."

"When I think about it, it still makes me mad. He had no proof. It could have been a pack of other dogs. He didn't see it! He didn't see it and he couldn't know. He had no right to shoot her."

"Don't think about it."

"Damn it, I want to think about it, I tell you. I want to. I'm going to think about it until I can hate him into a little shriveled-up bean and grind him up."

"Stop it, you stupid. You don't hate anybody."

"I do."

"You don't."

"Leave me alone."

"You want a punch in the nose, or a pot of stew on your head?"

"Stop making jokes."

Della took out a cracker, broke it into an oblong, and put it between her teeth and lips, frowned, opened her mouth into a false smile and said, "Grrrr."

"Stupid," said Wilson, but the hostility passed out of his eyes, hid for several moments in his tightened jaw and then disappeared back into the dungeon of his feelings where he kept it nailed to the wall.

Della let the cracker dissolve, then swallowed it. She opened the lid, poked the fork in at the potato lumps and took the lid off. "All ready," she said. "Get that messy thing off the table."

Wilson took the grinder back into the pantry. He picked the paper up by two sides and let the coffee slide down into a container marked ground. Not quite all of it would fit in, and he sheepishly poured the rest into a jar lid and set it on the iron stove top above the heated water. He lifted the fire cover and stuffed the newspaper into the heart of the stove, where the flames danced around it for several moments as if wondering what kind of an object it was and if it was capable of burning, then savagely set upon it and reduced it in a matter of no time at all into a thin crust of ash, worthless and without weight. Wilson put the lid down.

"Fire is brutal," he said.

Della lifted giant spoons of stew out of the iron skillet and filled up the plates.

"Yes," said Della. "It seems so ruthless and terrible."

"I'm famished," said Wilson. "And besides that it's easy to see how they thought in mythologies that it was stolen from the gods."

They began to eat.

"I wouldn't think that. That doesn't make any sense to me."

"Of course it does. You're just not thinking about it right. See, it doesn't behave like anything else—anything. There's nothing so thoroughly, painfully destructive. It makes no sense in the scheme of nature—it serves no function."

"I agree with that," said Della. "But just for those reasons I would think it would seem all that more unnatural among gods, who were supposed to live in a more beautiful world. Don't eat so fast."

"Once it finally gets down to the right temperature it's driven your hunger within an inch of its life," he said, and continued, "but think how uncivilized it would be without fire. Everything we think of as being refined is in direct correspondence with our not having to live in the snow."

"I don't think there's anything wrong with being civilized. And you can't either," said Della.

"So it's gotten to that!" cried Wilson.

"Go ahead and eat as fast as you want."

Wilson went back into the store and returned with a honeydew melon, which they nearly devoured before the water on the stove began making sounds like tiny hammer blows on the sides of the pot. Wilson managed to talk her into carrying the coffee outside to the porch swing. Duke met them and tried to jump his 125 pounds up against Della's 95. Wilson wrestled him down the steps and ran off into the yard with him, looking for something he could put between them and pull. Della looked out at the pale blue sky, the thin stratus clouds in the distance, the flat bottom parts lit golden and the rounded tops shaded dusty gray from the invisible sun below the horizon. The trees in the distance were beginning to fade into each other. Duke growled as he tried to pull an old shirt spotted with paint away from Wilson. Then they gave it up and began fighting with each other, Duke growling and Wilson laughing. I love you, she thought and her feelings rushed inside her. She tried momentarily to keep them in, then felt herself dissolve outward, farther than the yard, farther than the horizon, and as far as she could see into the sky, but his net drew her back.

Wilson soon returned and they drank their coffee together, watching the darkening evening. There were too few clouds to keep the light herded around into view, and because the moon had not yet risen, stars quickly began to come, as though a pin were sticking tiny holes into the black cloth covering, letting small streams of light down from far above in a place where it was never dark. Soon they could see Boötes and Hercules with his four-star club, his right leg winding around in a circle. The Great Bear stalked across the horizon in all his sidereal glory. Above him, nearly at the zenith, the two milky streams of the Milky Way intersected.

"What do you suppose the constellations mean?" asked Wilson.

Della began, "My father used to think you could smell panthers."

"How so?" asked Wilson, finding it difficult to keep his thoughts from wandering.

"He said they smelled sweet and warm—that if you were walking at night—especially if you were afraid, because animals have a haunting sense of fear—and you smelled a sweet, warm smell which as it grew in strength made you forget your fear and drew you toward it—that was a panther. Also he said they sound just like a woman screaming, and they only scream at night, and sometimes scream from the tops of trees in order to drive you mad with fear. He told me panthers love blood, and in the moonlight they cast a shadow of a man on the ground, and that if they died a normal death then an evil child would be born, but if they were killed then their souls could rest. He said the smell was a mixture of sweet clover and animal warmth, with sometimes a little clove. He shot one once."

They remained long after they had set the empty cups away from them on the porch floor. Della got up once to begin the dishes, but Wilson drew her back and promised to do them himself, tomorrow. He suspected Della knew more about her father than she was willing to share with him; but as they grew older and their faces looked more alike, each time he asked her about him she would offer more. He already knew of the smell of panthers, though she had forgotten telling him, and was waiting, as she talked, for something he hadn't heard. He thought momentarily about life and its problems but his thoughts wandered, and before devoting himself completely to a new theme that he had come upon, he acknowledged that, no, he didn't care as much for the problems and questions of life as he had when he was younger, though he felt it was not that he was incapable (that his wits had slowed), but that it seemed increasingly of little consequence and a full life could be accomplished just as well without them. "If it's all right," he said, "I'm going to go fishing Saturday night with Sam and Dave."

"Where are you going?"

"Down to the English River, I guess . . . for catfish."

"Fine," she said. "Can you take me over to Clara's before you go?"

"We're going to be out almost all night. We've got Dave's boat and we're going to use bank lines."

"Good. Then I can ask Clara to come stay with me. I want to find out if something's wrong at their house. I get a feeling from Meg that things aren't going well. The poor girl seems to sulk all day and never talks to the other kids." She went inside. Wilson remained for another half-hour talking to Duke and thinking of flatheads lying in mud-bottom holes in the river. In the morning Della saw a tree covered with Monarchs bunched for migration, so thick that the tree, except for the trunk, did not exist at all, and was only butterflies.

Wilson left early in the evening, before Clara Hocksteader arrived, though Della had made her promise to come before dark. He wondered if he shouldn't go a mile and a half out of his way to the river to make sure she was on her way, so if she wasn't coming, he could return home and tell his wife, because sooner or later she would begin to worry. But he didn't. He took his team out of the cover of Sharon's trees, exposed them to the face of the twilight sky and watched the mouth of the road to the Hocksteaders' yawn open on his left, beckoning him to be sure first of all of Della's feelings, and he went past it, forgiving himself at the same moment because of his tearing desire to be in the boat. The night grew darker. He put on a jacket and felt to see if he had brought matches for his pipe. He breathed the heavy air, and lay imaginative plans for the crafty big fish. His team went at a slow trot, and felt Wilson tug back on them every now and then, though Sam and Dave were already there waiting. Purposely he was going slowly because he was putting himself ready to fish. Thinking slow, deliberate thoughts, moving with extreme caution and exacting precision, he was trying to think like a flathead. Sam and Dave, waiting for him at the water, were not talking, but were, like Wilson, fixing themselves to fish. It was late enough in the fall so that the mosquitoes and biting flies, gnats and chiggers were gone. In the timber, barred owls sounded like a dinner table of laughing, howling dwarfs.

At the bridge, Wilson got out and dropped the shaft away from the team and took them down into the ditch, where his first thought was to leave them in harness; then he decided there was no excuse for that and went back to the buggy for the halters and tethering rope. Returning the harness to behind the seat, he took out the leeches and one hand pole and was aware, while climbing down beneath the bridge, of the still unbroken reflection of the moon on the water, like an unblinking eye. Below the wooden planks in the shadows along the bank were Sam and Dave, their gray hats muting their faces, straight sharp gold hooks and spoons sunk farther than the barb into their blocked crowns. Around his neck Dave had lengths of line, some longer than others, and some weighted with shot, making a kind of mane falling down-below his waist. When he moved, the hooks rattled faintly together like frozen teeth. Sam had the gaff and a lantern, and he held it up above his head in order to help Wilson make his way along the bank through the brown stalks of weeds. The water seemed to be not moving at all.

But once in the boat and away from the hard mud, a strong, deep current caught ahold of the bottom of the boat and carried them downstream. And still the surface seemed unruffled. The moon's reflection stretched out into a thin yellow line in front of them, coming to one end of the johnboat and disappearing. They fought with the oars and rowed slowly upstream, no faster than a walking dog. Sam had put the lantern in the bow, lighting only the ends of the plants along one bank. Deep, silent strokes of the oars, making noise only from the creaking oarlocks. They passed up the river, around Four-Mile Corner. No talking or moving except for the oars. Here they could hear the shallows. Once in them, the water noise was deafening. Then they kept to the south bank, where it was deeper, and went on. One hundred yards upstream the river broadened and there was a gravel bank extending halfway across. Wrinkled circles of swirling water were lit by the lamp. The noise of the shallows was gone. Wilson, sitting in the stern, saw Dave light a cigar, and every time he inhaled Wilson could see his face.

At first Wilson had felt he would rather not have the lamp, because on the ride from home he'd had the pleasant sensation of slipping unobserved through the night, drawn by sounds which were not his own. At first he'd felt that the light was not fitting and, at the very point where it became of use, became too bright and destroyed the feeling of selflessness and unity. But by the time they had cleared the shallows he'd decided that the light was better—that it was more honest for three men on a river to carry a lantern, confessing their intrusion and adding something which, viewed from a distance, was impelling, mysterious and beautiful. It was a way of offering themselves for inspection, and though they were not, and could never be, part of the natural world of night, by doing it they could feel accepted. It is better to admit that, thought Wilson, and to stay away from fantasy. They heard several ducks get up from an unseen backwater, and a whippoorwill. Bats flying above the surface of the water passed through the wingspread of their yellow light, searching frantically for what remained of the summer's insects.

A creek willow stood out over the water, and onto several of its branches they tied weighted lines, baited with leeches which smaller fish could chew on without damaging them and without hooking themselves. They broke off three dozen branches of varying lengths, and as Dave rowed on farther upstream in the silent, quick water, Wilson and Sam tied on the lines and threaded the brown leeches. Then in places Dave would pull over close to the shore and Sam and Wilson would jab the thick end of one of the limber poles a half-foot into the bank so that the line fell into the water just at the edge. One quarter-mile upstream they were out of poles and lines. They pulled the bow of the johnboat up onto a sandbar and several minutes later had a fire burning next to the water. All of them smoked, sitting on logs. The wood was dry (shag-bark hickory) and it burned clear and bright, and the pockets of air exploding in the dead cells of the wood, sending sparks upward, was the only sound they could hear. The moon was below the trees on the opposite side of the river.

Then downstream a channel cat broke water, and its thrashing filled the silence. Wilson got into the boat and Sam pushed him away from the bank and he floated downstream. The lantern still burned resolutely in the front. He found the fish, anchored, and brought him in with the help of the gaff, unfastened the hook from his mouth and threw the undisturbed leech and line back into the water. Being careful to avoid the horns, he fastened the fish onto the stringer and tossed him into the water. Maybe three pounds, he thought, or maybe less. Then another began thrashing twenty yards upstream and he got that one too, rebaited the line, reset the pole in a new area of the bank and rowed back toward the fire, where he soon saw Sam and Dave, both of them nearly sixty, sitting and looking at the orange fire. The whippoorwill again, then a screech owl, then two. I should do this more often, thought Wilson, it's foolish not to when the experience is so satisfying.

Dave pulled him back up on shore, and they fastened the stringer to the bank. He had barely sat down when another, louder, thrashing began. Dave took this one, and Wilson watched him floating effortlessly down the dark water until he could no longer see him or the lantern, and Sam sat down and they began to talk about famous dogs, their courage and resourcefulness. Sam regretted the death of Jumbo, and they recalled several nights of running fox. The light of the fire enclosed them like a room.

TWO

Though for some reason Della had not had children until fairly late in life—late according to the usual age for becoming a mother (she was twenty-nine) and many of her close friends were worried about her welfare because of her bones being too old to stretch—it seemed that after she got started she never stopped, and she was either just getting ready to have one and people would comment, "She sure is round, have you noticed?" or she was carrying a new one and giving it to Wilson or Mrs. Miller to look after while she went off to teach school. Many people told her not to do it—that they could find someone else to fill in at the school until everything settled down—but she wouldn't agree and claimed that Mrs. Fitch would do what she could, but that she (Della) was the only one who knew exactly where each of the children was and what kind of progress they could be expected to make, emotionally and intellectually. And whatever sacrifice they imagined Della was making, to have her there instead of anyone else was what they really wanted anyway.

One of the boys was named John, after Wilson's great-grandfather. If Della could be said to have favorites—and of course she couldn't, and didn't, but still if someone were to *have* to say which one she liked the best, if she *were forced to* give an answer other than all of them—it would be him. There was a hidden fierceness in him, lacking in the others.

John Montgomery did not stand out as an unusual boy until he was almost ten—mostly because he had always been shy. Even in school where his own mother taught he would blush whenever he spoke. He looked pretty much like a direct cross between his older brother Alex and his sister Rebecca, though more withdrawn than either. At first, that was all there was to him. Then he began to stand out. It was noticed that at infrequent unpredictable times he would slip into moments of self-absorbing sensuality, as though he could not contain himself and was overpowered by pleasure, like being carried away by a joke—an image so dramatic it suggested a personality split. But then it was also noticed that the shyness returned immediately afterward and he would look very guilty. And this, though it explained in a minor way the shyness, presented a question of its own; because it was not natural that a boy of that young age would have learned what it is about emotions that he should be ashamed of. He would certainly not have learned it from Della and Wilson. It was just as though he had been born with the two coincidental characteristics: his tremendous capacity for feelings, and the accompanying guilt.

He was well liked, though not comfortable to be with during the few times when he would fall to enjoying his lunch to such an extent that everyone sitting across from him at the lunch table would be forced to admit that their own enjoyment of eating must be a very shallow thing in comparison. Also because of an icy chill in the room in which he greedily cut off contact with everything else but himself and his sandwiches—turning from the world of reason, communication and people to the world of his own swirling emotions and sensations. It was unpleasant to be so ruthlessly ignored; but the shyness, which he retained throughout his life, compensated and endeared him to people. It seemed he was always afraid someone would find out, and because those times were known to everyone, the knowledge was an intimacy, arising from knowing more of him than he might have wished.

As John grew up, automobiles began to replace horses, and the huckster wagon was abandoned after it became less time-consuming for families to get to the store themselves (the bigger stores in Iowa City as well). But cream still flowed through Wilson's grocery store like water. The road to Hills was widened, and the fences were set back several feet on each side. A hardtop was set down and became Highway 1, crossing the road to Hills in the middle of Sharon Center. A garage was made out of Barns' store, with two tall, thin pumps close to the highway. A high school was built across from the Masonic Lodge.

John's older brother Alex was old enough to be accepted into the Army at the same time the United States decided to enter its first war with Germany, without the approval of his mother. Wilson had no opinions, either on the war or his son's desire to be in it, and silently drove him to the recruiting station in Iowa City in the wagon. They shook hands, and as Wilson left he watched Alex being taken in by the other boys there, laughing nervously and talking about military weapons. At home Della told him, "I can feel that it was a mistake, Wilson." Of course this was not a judgment of the war—only the way she chose to tell him that, as far as she was concerned, their son would never come home.

"You can't know that," said Wilson.

"Yes I can."

John Montgomery had already decided that, and watching his brother ride away in the wagon with his bag of belongings, talking excitedly to his father, he said goodbye to him. He removed his brother from his active mind and put him into memory, where he remained forever. So the news of Alex's patriotic death (he had died by personally carrying a very sensitive bomb into a house with thick walls, taking with him into small fragments seven German officers, four flunkies, three long-nose machine guns and a naked whore) had little effect on him, because the fact and story of Alex's death had no connection with John's own memories of him, which he had already decided would be all there would ever be. His lack of emotion was not noticed in the house at that time because of all the others.

Wilson bought their brownstone house in the country three years after the war ended, and though he did not live in it full time until years later, he secretly kept two dogs there, fed by Remington Hodge, and visited them often with their other dog.

(Duke had taken a disease which caused him to go blind and be in such discomfort that Wilson killed him.) He explained to Della that the extra dogs were probably from neighboring farms. Sometimes they spent Sundays in their country home with the younger children, leaving John and Rebecca to open the store Monday morning and mind it until afternoon.

John, during those times when his naturally suppressed sensuality would erupt, could drink more, cause more destruction and be less decent, more depraved, make more noise, attract more secretly wanton women, keep going longer and be more penitently sorry afterward than seemed realistic, and while he was attending the small high school he was the never ending topic of conversation and amazement. It was said that he had on one occasion, on a bet, gone into Iowa City to a house of prostitution and in a state of intoxication and without a cent in his pocket had entered and remained for nearly two and a half hours before rejoining his friends seated impatiently across the street drinking from a bottle in a paper bag, where he resumed drinking and set off to find a place with more gaiety.

The speculations concerning the course of events beginning at the time he entered without any money and closed the door and ending two and a half hours later were as varied as an entire month of *The Arabian Nights*. Some (Merv Miller was one of them) believed he must have collapsed due to the effects of the improperly and dangerously prepared whiskey as soon as he shut the door, and out of the kindness of their hearts they had let him sleep until he woke up. But it was hard to believe in the kindness of a prostitute's or a prostitute's manager's heart, as they were all personally terrified by the mere idea of the place. "Perhaps they were afraid to throw him out for fear of drawing the attention of the police." But for the same reason that it was difficult to imagine Betty's Place housing generosity, it was impossible to imagine the hardened people inside being afraid of anything. So the line of thinking, naturally, continued from then on to the assumption that he was busy during that time, and exactly how many women one could assume to be in there, and how much they did what they did for money, and how much they would do for pleasure, and what kind of pleasure it was to take up two and a half hours. And then just as these problems were beginning to press less and less heavily on the imagination of the small town, two women somewhere in their twenties arrived in a worn, unsightly carriage—having driven themselves—and stopped at the gas station and asked with "rough, wild voices, and one had frizzy hair," the whereabouts of John Montgomery. They were directed across the street to the store, where they went, stayed not longer than ten minutes and headed back in the direction of Iowa City. Nothing conclusive could be drawn from the visit, but even to explain it coincidentally was exciting and problematic, and vicarious pleasure flowed like water long after the six men in the station had stepped out into the clear afternoon and watched until the bare heads sank side by side out of view over the hill.

It was not long after this, during the time when John was being condemned, floated and exalted as being bound up in whoredom, that there arose an unexpected concern for his mind, which was imagined to be in great danger of giving up the ghost and splitting clean in two—the two parts of him being so widely distant and hostile to each other. He was watched very carefully for signs of dissociation, or ordinary madness. These new, more serious thoughts never had the required idle time to be lifted off the ground. Wilson had a stroke. Everything else was forgotten. Della found herself surrounded by her thousands of friends, who seemed to be sure that if they never let her alone, they could keep her from slipping away until Wilson would return with his spiritual net. And by the time he was back from the University Hospital he seemed (from all the evidence) to be his old self.

The issue of John's breaching personality was forgotten, the two wild-voiced women had become thought of as a queer phenomenon of experience, and if he was imagined to be too full of life at times, it was also remembered that, for the most part, looking him in the eyes would make him blush. The serious thoughts about his father had pushed all the other, more trivial, mean thoughts back into perspective.

He was very popular with the girls at the high school, and it was said that a well-brought-up girl could share a happy evening with him and never once have her ideals compromised. There was some fear, of course, that while out with one of them he would all of a sudden change over, and no telling what would happen after that. The girls were supposed to be able to sense this frightful desire for lust beneath the surface of his gray eyes. His bashfulness made him nearly impossible to talk to, but the lurking suspicion that he might at any time get it into his mind to drag them off into a cement corner and rip away their clothes and not take no for an answer made him attractive for a long time. But, like an unfulfilled promise, it wasn't enough, and when the girls were older and foresaw their lives being taken out of the school and stranded in the barren, sun-bleached world of their parents, they were quick to give him up and settle for fulfillment of a more normal kind.

John Montgomery seemed to have no intention of marrying, and accepted it as quite normal that his friends and finally even his sister and younger brothers settled into homes of their own (Rebecca to Iowa City and Henry to Duluth) while he remained alone and unattached and showed no indication that he would ever plan to do otherwise, and even left off stopping in on Mrs. Saunders, a young widow nearing thirty.

Bachelors were not unheard of in the area—in fact, it was remembered that the two relatives who had been the reason for Della and Wilson coming to Sharon hadn't ever married. Nothing uncommon about it. Nothing bitter or morose, only personal choice. Because of his shyness, John had never been on close, intimate terms with anyone (except, perhaps, his older sister), though no one who had gone to school with him would deny that he was a friend. It was noted that bachelors were invariably of that same sort, so everything fitted into place—terribly sad, but natural.

In a magazine John saw an advertisement for a training school in Detroit for automobile mechanics. He talked the matter over with his father, and within a month arrived in Detroit and enrolled as an automotive-engineer trainee. He worked nights as a dishwasher in a night restaurant to pay the tuition. Once a week he wrote a full-page, small-margined letter home to his parents from his one-lamp room, and after the nine weeks Della had nine letters that had been read out loud before dinner, safely inside a cupboard drawer. "He's always been so conscientious," she told Wilson. Then he came back with a certificate, and a well-detailed plan to build a garage and fill it with steel six- and twelve-point sockets, breaker bars, drop-forged impact wrenches, lock washers, cotter pins, ring compressors, two- and three-claw bearing pullers, mill bastard files, feeler gauges, bench vises, taps and dies, drums of oil and flat-nose pliers. The bank in Hills loaned him the money, and a wild bunch of unemployed construction workers built him an enormous one-room building big enough for an airplane on top of a cement foundation, diagonally across from the grocery.

"They've made it big enough," remarked Joe Miller, "to contain him."

"What's that supposed to mean?" asked Della with the nasty implication that it better not mean anything.

As John grew older, he learned more about himself. From the very beginning he must have been aware of a frightening inconsistency in the way experiences came to him. He must have felt (especially in moments of remorse) that his life was insubstantial because he could have two completely unrelated ways of viewing it—two attitudes, neither of which could be said to be less valid or real. A feeling of disintegration—drowning, with nothing to grab hold of that could float. When he was young he must have wished to be rid of his self-consciousness while coveting the reckless abandonment. He must have thought he would gladly cast off his usual shy self and emerge from under a dead skin, an authentic, brightly colored, fully human testimony of feeling. Then later, after he had come back from Detroit and swung up the wide wooden door opening into his warehouse-size garage, rented the late Dr. Bokin's house across the street, joined a group called the Society for the Observation of Birds and begun reading the Bible at the rate of two chapters a day, interested, but not industrious enough to look up the word references along the middle of the page—he was convinced his life could become more wonderful if only there were not that uncontrollable center of emotional rampage. He began to resent it because of the feelings of shame it brought him later. And from that time on he was careful to live his life in such a way that when those times came—and they were less frequent as he grew older—he could keep it to himself without reaching out and including others. But he could not deceive, and everyone knew from his shyness and gray eyes that nothing was changed, and he was expected for years to be building up for a gigantic outburst.

But then everyone forgot. Because they didn't see any evidence of his sensuality. After five or six years *they forgot about it.*

Remington Hodge's father used to call on the name of the Lord to verify that John Montgomery could fix anything, and that it was common knowledge clear into Iowa City and through to Solon (which to him was tantamount to universal knowledge) that *there's a guy in Sharon who can really weld.* To those old farmers there were three things: family, food and machinery. So here it is, the family belongs to Della, and Wilson is there for food, and what happens then but John is the best welder on earth and as long as he's alive and either there's a light on in the house across the street or the garage door is open it's as good as a promise that everything will be all right. It's impossible to say what a good mechanic means to people who have nothing to depend on but what they can touch.

John was by no means the first in Sharon Center to get an automobile for himself. Actually there were already so many by then that there was no reason for any notice at all, except everyone knew how Wilson felt about them, and the concern was to see how he would take it.

"If he wants to, that's his business," was all that he said.

One afternoon five or six farmers were at John's, sitting on the machinery and talking and spitting, a little too far along into fall to be without jackets, when Sy Bontrager came up in his tractor and sat down with them. John had his hood and gloves on, and sparks flew like a roman candle. Corn-picking season had nearly arrived, and in the fields black scar marks showed on the tops of the plants where the skin had frozen. Naturally, they talked about weather and the approaching winter.

Sy had a piece of iron he wanted straightened, and when John tipped up his hood in order to see what he was working on in full light, Sy asked him where he kept the anvil. John told him in the back somewhere and closed down the hood and resumed welding. Sy went back to look, and because one man could spend all day looking back there, three or four of the others went to help. They found it behind two oil drums and a short block.

"Here, I'll get back in there and hand it out," said Brenneman.

"Just lift it on out," said Henry Yoder, "from there."

"No thanks." Brenneman got back between the drums and set it up on the block.

Marion took it out and set it on the floor. "I heard," he said, "that there was a fella in Clinton who could pick one of these up with one hand, by grabbin' ahold of it by the horn."

"I could do that," said Sy.

"Come on."

"I could. Bring it on out here where there's plenty of air."

Brenneman carried it out into a clearing beside the lane. "OK, go ahead."

"Wait a minute. Now, just exactly what did this fella in Clinton do?"

"He's hedging!"

"No. Just what did he do exactly?"

John had taken off his hood and come back. Marion told him that Sy was about to try to pick up the anvil by the horn.

". . . . so he just lifted it off the ground. No further. Just off the ground."

"Come on, Bontrager."

But for all the joking it was noticed that Sy was nearly a giant, and that his hands were bigger than a normal head. But still it seemed impossible. Then he bent down and wrapped his sausage fingers around the end of the horn, tilted it up so that it pointed straight in the air and lifted. At first nothing, but it didn't slip either; and then Marion, who had his face on the ground, shouted, "It's off. Drop it, Sy, it's off." And he dropped it.

They congratulated him and he went off to find a hand sledge to straighten his piece of metal. Marion grabbed ahold of the horn, gave a little tug and shook his head. No one else wanted to know exactly how hard it would be. "In all your life you'll never see that done again," said Brenneman. "It's incredible anyone could be that strong."

"He always was big," said Henry Yoder.

Then everything settled down. Brenneman got a set of leathers for his pump and left. Henry Yoder left with Marion in his car toward Marion's place. Sy straightened his hitch and put it up behind his tractor seat and drove away. John worked on a small one-cylinder motor, taking off the flywheel to get at the points. Marion and Henry Yoder came back, parked across the street and went into the store.

"I tell you, he did," they told Wilson. "He picked it right up off the ground, as easy as you please."

"It's impossible. Sy Bontrager?"

"Yes."

"Well, he's big . . . No, it's impossible. There's a fly in the soup somewhere."

"He did it."

"It's physically impossible," and Wilson went over to the window next to the street and looked out. No one over there but John, walking around and looking into the street. Wilson looked absently out at him, thinking privately to himself about all the things he had to do before winter, the windows, the rain gutters, some of the roof, get bales around the foundation, install . . . John walked across the garage again and looked out, oddly enough, Wilson thought, as though he wanted to be sure he was alone. Then he bent over, and from the store window and in a line clear down an aisle of tools and oil drums Wilson saw him lift his anvil with one hand by grasping the horn, straight up until it was several inches above the ground, behind which he could see the red Riley oil drum, then set it down and hurry back to the small engine.

Wilson's mind raced. For the first time in his life, he thought: What can possibly be inside him? What is he made of to be able to do that when he's no bigger than I am? There's never been any indication of that. Muscles are muscles, and bones are bones; what could make someone so different?

"He did it, I tell you. He said he could and then he did it," said Marion.

Yes, he probably did, thought Wilson. It's possible. It's not that strange if a big man can do it. But still he wondered; and after his store was empty, he closed the door and went over to the garage, thinking that he would have a better look at both the anvil and his son. He watched John putting tiny brass jets and springs into the carburetor of the Briggs and Stratton, and there was no indication there of anything. "Hello," he said when John looked up, and tried to look casual and uninterested as he went over to where the anvil sat on its back, pointed straight up into the air. When John turned around he grabbed ahold of it with both hands and lifted. And stopped. He felt sure he could, if he really wanted to, with both hands, but one hand! It seemed impossible.

"I was sorry to hear about your dog," said John, and blushed as he looked at his father.

"So was I," he answered. "It's been three days so far and I still can't keep from thinking about her running around in the front yard the way she did, and the sound of her digging under the porch."

"I think," John began, very shyly, "that you shouldn't get any more dogs. They're not worth it. Something always happens—"

"They're worth it! I've got a chance to get a wolf cub, anyway. A timber wolf. Marion said his brother shot the bitch in the middle of August and has three pups in the shed behind his house. I guess she was killing his sheep. But there's nothing hereditary about wildness. It's learned. They'll be just like dogs—only wouldn't it be fine to have a real wolf?"

"I don't think it's worth it. Mom almost had brain damage worrying the other night when you were out feeling sorry over that dog, wandering around along the river."

"My feelings are my own."

"Maybe so, but maybe—"

"Forget that. Listen, Marion said Sy Bontrager picked up that anvil with one hand—by grabbing ahold of the horn. That true?"

"I saw him do it."

"It seems impossible."

"I know."

"How could someone be that strong?" asked Wilson, and focused his eyes down into John's face.

John blushed. "I don't know . . . he's big."

He won't admit it, thought Wilson. He won't admit it. It's like he's ashamed. Very odd. If I could do that, everyone would know. I'd have the anvil put out by the road and once a week I'd lift it up; and if someone came into the store who had never seen me lift it, I'd pick it up again. And if I could do it with my right hand, then I'd learn to do it with my left, and then by holding it backhanded. (All of these thoughts he had while looking at the anvil.)

"Will you and Mom come to church this Sunday?"

"We already talked about that, John. If you want to, that's fine. But there's no reason to try to include me and your mother. Besides, I don't see anything to it. The whole thing is too . . . superficial. No, that's not quite right. Self-righteous is a better word. Vanity."

"That's not right, Dad."

"We don't go to church. Our lives are happy and full without it. Each worships in his own way . . . that's what I think. And besides, Della is dead set against it."

"I know. That's why you have to convince her."

"Foolishness. And anyway, Saturday night I'm going fishing."

"That's no excuse. Go some other time."

"What could be closer to God than being on the river? If there's anything in religion that belittles fishing or being outdoors in order to promote sitting in a building singing foolish songs and looking righteous—it can't be of any value."

"There's a difference between enjoying God's gifts and paying for them."

"Enjoying them *is* paying for them. It's neglect that falls in the red. And gifts are gifts."

"Despite how you feel, come anyway."

"I don't like your reverend."

"No excuses. You must come. I've decided it now. You must come."

"I don't want to."

"You must. Don't be childish; there's something to it, you'll see."

"Maybe. Where are those field glasses you bought? Della said she looked through them."

"Sure, they're in the house, and are really exciting, though I think I would have been better off to get seven-by-thirty-fives instead of eight-by-forties. It's too much magnification for using in the field. They're fine for sitting still or using on the porch looking at wind hoverers, harriers and kingbirds, though. They say the Germans made a better pair of eight-by-forties." They crossed over to John's house, leaving the pumps on and the doors to the garage wide open. "Now I remember what I was going to tell you," John almost shouted. "I saw an eagle the other day! An immature bald eagle. I couldn't believe it. I was walking along in back of Mortimers' pasture land and . . ."

Wilson thought, He can be more excited about seeing some old birds than anyone I ever knew. But he did have an interest in the glasses, and later, at the very moment he looked through them and focused them down, he decided he would get a pair of his own.

"Turn them around, Dad," said John, smiling, "if you really want to see something strange!" He had decided that subconsciously his father had given in, and would come to church, and would even talk his mother into coming once. The Bible and the experience of God were undeniably the biggest, most complete feeling he had ever had, and he wanted his parents to have it.

John Montgomery's religious knowledge was nothing more than a fundamental, very ordinary kind of experienced knowledge. There were two parts to it: the Bible and God, though the two were sometimes so closely related, for him, that studying one was comparable to learning more of the other. He thought the Bible taught him about God. He thought of it being the same kind of book (though of a much higher quality) as a bird book, which gave him information; and after he'd studied about each individual bird, his experience of seeing one was greater because he would know what to look for, and appreciate more the beauty of the bird as it related to how he knew they lived—in the brush, forest, grub-eaters, fly-catchers and foragers, their migratory habits and natural predators. So his secondhand knowledge (from the book) added directly to his personal experience, even though the two were very separate. Could anyone think a picture and a short paragraph describing a bird the same thing as seeing one? So the Bible presented an accurate description of God which, the more he knew of it, heightened his personal encounters.

The Bible was indispensable. The experience of someone seeing a lone bird without ever having heard of birds before and having nothing to relate it to, though powerful, would be a very shallow experience compared to that of a man who had seen millions, and who knew how each one lived and how particular and sacred each kind was in its own way. Naturally, that first experience would be a complete blow to the mind; at the same time, it would be recognized as superficial by those who have had not only *that* experience but many more after it, who clearly recognize the urgency and wonder with which the first comes but know it is not just the urgency that is important, but something else.

Then came the Depression, and Wilson was trapped by it. The farmers (though the price of seed had gone up so that they couldn't afford it, the machinery that they had bought on time from the bank was repossessed, no one could borrow money, roving bands of destitute people roamed through the cities) still counted on selling their eggs, butter, milk, cakes and dried beans to Wilson's grocery. And Wilson knew that if they could, if they possibly could, they would come in and buy meat and canned goods to keep up their half of the bargain. But they just couldn't. They didn't have enough money. Yet he felt responsible and when they brought in their cans of milk (being careful to bring no more than before, when they had been shopping there too, and usually less) he would smile and pay them from his cash register and joke with them. For several years he did this. Some of them bought enough to keep him from losing money.

He was almost forced to close. A stranger from Iowa City came once, then twice, and then regularly twice a week, buying more than one family could ever eat, or even two. This went on for several months until Wilson followed him back into the city to a big grocery store, where what he had sold the stranger was unloaded, brought inside, and sold to a man in a glassed-in box beside the checkout line. He talked to one of the two carry-out boys and learned that some fellow who ran a garage in Sharon Center hired it done in order to keep his old man in business.

Wilson put his store up for sale, and though Sy Bontrager was there at the auction trying to hold on to it so that it could stay in the community and maybe be opened again later, in better times, he couldn't outbid an old German named Sehr, who went over him on it and on the house on the corner across from it. Then Wilson and Della moved out to their country home and lived with their four-year-old wolf. At this time they began going to church and, after the Depression lifted, continued to go. They accepted an old automobile from John, because they were so far out, and in case one of them would be sick. Wilson began helping out farmers, working for them for nothing, and Remington Hodge's father says that "One morning when we were real little and were going out, wondering how we would ever be able to get in all the hay before it rained, Della and Wilson came driving down the lane and went out with us without a word, and they must have known they couldn't be given anything, not even a sack of corn. We did give them some bread, but it wasn't anything, not for what they did."

Wilson's fishing buddies, Sam and Dave, died, and Wilson waited a long time before he began going again, alone. Della continued to teach school, and in 1935 began being paid enough so that she and Wilson could live on the salary and save the rest of the money from the store, what little there was. Wilson's health wasn't good, and though his spirit remained unruffled, still he slept more, became weaker and lived under the continual din of a bad heart, which Della told John (who watched after them like a mother hen) sounded like it was trying to peck its way outside his chest.

Sharon Center eased out of the Depression. Loans became available. Everyone invested in freezers full of food and put them in their basements, which seemed better insurance than any other kind that they would never be caught wanting again. John had one put in his parents' house. People wished that the store would be reopened, and eventually, in '39, Sehr rented it out to some owl from Iowa City, who set it up more to sell ice cream than staples, and in the middle of winter disappeared completely, leaving the building locked and the shelves full. Men who worked for banks came in the spring and opened it up. Rats had eaten into the corners of the boxes, and the smell was unbearable. Sehr accepted no responsibility, because, as he said, the rent had been paid for an entire year. The windows of the store part were boarded up in house siding, and a family named Collins moved into it. They never mingled with anyone, and for the ten years they lived there were looked upon with suspicion.

John was now nearly forty, and up until the day he drove away, locking his garage and house, it was not remembered that he had ever left for more than several days in the entire eighteen or twenty years since he had come back from Detroit. He climbed into his car and drove away, heading west; and from that direction he could have been going anywhere. It was late spring, and clear into summer the garage doors remained closed, and there was wonder concerning where he had gone, and what might have been in his mind to go there, and what might have happened to him. He stayed away until the middle of July, when at night Hercules spun directly overhead and the edge of his mace touched the Milky Way's southern stream. Then all that had been forgotten about John was remembered. He came back married.

Her name was Sarah. John never said what her last name had been, or where he had found her, or what he had said when he first met her, how he had come to . . . anything. This frightening lack of information (it was regretfully acknowledged) was due to no one being on intimate terms with him—no one who could learn the details in confidence and spread them around. They thought she must be from the south, though no one had been any farther down than Missouri except Jack Sanders, and he thought she came from somewhere around Duluth, Minnesota, where his brother had worked with a road crew and had said there were women there that affected you like that.

Sarah was of normal height for a woman, and weighed in the area marked healthy in the penny-operated weight machines. Her hair was ordinary brown and not carefully kept, sprawling out in places. The dress she wore that first day in Sharon, walking around the yard and over to the garage and into the house and back again with laundry, was of coarse green cotton, covering even her arms down to the elbow. But none of these things were noticed.

Six or seven men were at the garage that first day when she came and talked to John about where the clothespins were. From twenty feet away they could smell her skin. Every movement from under the green dress sent warm, pulsing sensations down their spines. The soft muscles in her neck screamed to be touched. Her hands seemed obviously designed for caressing, and to look at the delicate inside of her forearms made them all blush. Noticing her ankles, they thought, My God, they're naked! as though the usual practice of women in July was to go about bound in mummy cloth. Her face, tanned by some foreign sun, glowed red in the cheeks. She talked to John and they understood only one or two words per sentence—because of that quality of half laughing and half sighing that danced through her voice. The faint outline of her naked body beneath the dress, the swell of her breasts and the roundness of her hips, made them continually swallow and rub their faces. Mike Calbraith said later, "I tell you, I couldn't move. My eyes watered. I couldn't hear. It was all I could do to keep from trying to touch her. My pecker was standing straight out like an iron poker, and she turned to leave and looked at us all and walked by. It was more than anyone could do not to watch, and, oh man, watching her walk! You could smell her, honest to God. She's the real thing if you ever wanted to see it. A few years ago I think I'd a done anything for something like that. I'd a murdered for it."

When John introduced her and her voice sang out, "How do you do?" no one could say anything. Harold M. made gurgling noises. Remington Hodge smiled. The art of using words to talk with didn't return until several minutes after she had crossed the street, entered the house and closed the door on herself. Naturally, one of the main questions in their minds was what John had ever said to her at first. What could anyone think of to say? Where did he find her? When you knew her as well as he must . . . wasn't it more than you could stand? Did the fear go away? All these questions loomed around them, and they composed themselves and looked over to John, in hopes of finding some of the answers. But he blushed in his usual way and hid himself in his work.

"You have a real pretty wife," said Brenneman. "I imagine she cooks well enough."

"I guess so," mumbled John, intent on loosening a nut.

Anything else was too hard to ask, and would have been futile anyway, because he had never been one to offer much of himself in the conversation. It was remembered then about his capacities.

A delegation formed and in three carloads went out to Della and Wilson's in order to make sure they knew. They drove in, unloaded and knocked on the door. Wilson came out and looked at them bewilderedly.

"Hello," he said.

"Hello," said Marion. "We just thought we'd stop over."

"All of you?"

"Oh. Well, I guess there is some number," he said, looking behind him. "But just a social call. How have you been?"

"Della!" Wilson called. "Della, come here!"

Della came out and rescued him, and let him wander off by himself back in the trees beyond the barn. It was becoming so that no one ever saw him, except on Sunday at church. When he did speak, it couldn't be depended on to make much sense. Della said sometimes he was like a child and had to be watched, because he was always leaving the refrigerator door open, and would get lost when he went fishing. Sometimes in his periods of obstinacy or when he would start throwing things she had to threaten to spank him in order to get him out of the rain or to go to bed. The doctor said it was arteries and the oxygen in his blood. Wilson said it was nothing and that he was the same as he'd ever been—as well as he could remember. But some things, he admitted, were easier to remember than others.

"Come in," said Della.

"No, no. We can't stay. We just dropped by to say hello. We were going for a ride and decided to pull in."

"Gracious me!"

"John's home," said Clara Hocksteader.

"I know. He came out last night. His sister will be glad to hear he's back. She's such a worrier. I must remember to write her a letter."

"Then you've seen her!"

"Who?"

"His wife—what's her name?"

"Sarah. No, we haven't seen her. She was busy with something at home. But they're both coming out tonight."

"Were you surprised that he got married after all these years?" asked J. Yoder.

"Well, yes and no. I'm glad he is, though. I'd always thought he would be so lonely by himself. Have you met her?"

"Yes."

"Are you sure you don't want to come inside? . . . Or, I know, I'll get some chairs and bring them out."

"No, please don't bother. We can't stay. . . . Then you didn't see her?"

"No. What do you think of her? Is she nice? How old is she, would you guess?"

"Not over twenty"—"Young thirties"—"Twenty-four"—"Twenty-seven"—"Forty," they answered together.

"It's hard to say," said Marion.

"Age isn't important," said Clara.

"Not really," said Mrs. Bontrager.

"That's so, of course," said Della. "What else do you know about her?"

"Nothing," said Marion. "We didn't really talk to her . . . just sort of saw her."

"Oh."

"She's . . . real pretty."

"Oh. John said she was pretty."

"What? He said what?" asked Lewis Neal from several people back.

"I said he said she was pretty."

"What else did he say?"

"Where did she come from?"

"Goodness, I don't know. I don't remember that he talked much about her at all. He was here for such a short time. He just came and checked the freezer and the car battery, said hello and went home. Why?"

"Nothing." Then there was a great discomfort as everyone began noticing how many had really come. It was also realized that if Della had not yet seen Sarah, she couldn't possibly understand. Later, *then* they would be curious to see what she thought. And because she hadn't, there was no reason to be there in such an overpowering number. They all left as quickly as they had come, giving excuses and promising recipes and so on. Della waved to them from the porch step as they drove away and went around back to find Wilson and get him in the house, though his odd behavior usually didn't begin until several hours after dinner, since she had to get him to take a nap.

John and Sarah came that night to visit, arriving before it was dark. A slow wind blew through the leftover afternoon air, and was laden with peach blossom, hyacinths, freshly cut grass, sweet clover, livestock dung, old fish from Wilson's cleaning shed, the compost heap, day lilies and a wide mixture of unidentifiable variables. So when Sarah walked up through the yard, Della thought it was only the wind and its pleasant mixture of wildflowers and earth. John introduced her. She put out her hand, and Sarah took it between both of hers. Della's feelings exploded. She knew then that the warm, sweet smell was Sarah's body. The touch of Sarah's hand sent shivers down Della's arm and she immediately jerked her own hand halfway out of her grasp, then put it back, realizing it would be rude, and snatched it back without a thought when Sarah gently pressed it. John took Sarah over to his father. Della watched as Wilson's eyes lit up, and she went over to him and got him to take his hand out of Sarah's by politely laughing and backing into his arm. They smiled at each other. Whenever Sarah looked away, Della's eyes darted all over her body. Once John put his arm around her waist, and Sarah wriggled just the slightest bit into it, so that it rested a half an inch lower than where he had first put it, in the beginning swell of her hip. Della's face flushed bright red, and she rushed off inside, returning with wicker porch chairs.

"Do you cook?" she asked, staring at Sarah's breasts, thinking in horror that such a natural shape could only mean she used no supports; but, forcing herself to be more composed, she realized it was only her imagination which saw the details, and the outline of the straps could be seen across Sarah's back, though there seemed a kind of indecency in that as well. No, it wasn't indecency. But *something* it was.

"Yes, I cook," said Sarah, and smiled.

"What do you cook?"

"A little of this and a little of that." She laughed.

They seated themselves, John and Sarah on the chairs and Wilson and Della in the swing. John's gaze wandered frequently to his father, who looked to have aged eight years since he had gone away, and who said no more than four words the whole evening. Della saw sadness creep into her son's eyes then, and thought to herself, *He doesn't understand that it's not so bad to be old.* Then she was drawn back to Sarah by her voice, and wondered why no one else had thought she was very strange. There had been a whole yard full of people talking about having seen her, and not one had said, "There's something a little odd about her, attractive and frightening." I must be mistaken about this, she thought. Feelings can be wrong. And to prove it she bombarded Sarah with countless questions to prove or disprove her normalcy, looking for her to either betray herself and confirm the suspicions or absolve them.

"How old are you?"

"Thirty-two."

"How old is your mother?"

"Sixty-three. How old is yours?"

"My mother's in heaven. Did you grow up in a city?"

"Well, yes and no. We lived in Mosstown when I was about twelve or thirteen."

"Is this the first time you've been married?"

"Mother! What a question. Believe me, Sarah, usually my mother's quite nice, keeps to herself. . . isn't nosy. . . ."

"I don't mind, John. I've been married before, Mrs. Montgomery."

"Has Mom been feeling all right lately, Dad?"

"Yes," said Wilson, smiling and looking at Sarah. "She has."

"Two times," said Sarah.

"Two times!" exclaimed Della, not wanting to show surprise, but unable to hide it. Two previous marriages seemed to pretty much confirm her suspicions, in some way not altogether clear.

"I know it seems like that," said Sarah. "It strikes me like that too sometimes. But, believe me, it all sneaks up on you so slowly that the numbers have nothing to do with it."

"Three husbands," said Della, this time more in personal wonder than in surprise.

"Mother! What's the matter with you?"

"No, John," said Sarah, touching his arm. "Listen, Mrs. Montgomery," and she looked intently into her eyes. Della tried to look away, but felt as though she couldn't. "I was married when I was sixteen. I had a baby. The doctor said I would probably have no more. My husband was a roofer and worked early in the mornings before the heat of the afternoon but when the surface would be more dangerous because of the dew. We lived together a year and a half. Then he fell and was dead. That's the way they told me: 'He fell and he's dead.' That was all. Naturally, I couldn't believe it at first. Even after I took everything out of the house that reminded me—his clothes, his guns—I sold his tools from the basement and cleaned up the piles of lumber he had taken off our old garage to make a boat with. Still it seemed he wouldn't go away, but was always just in the next room, walking around, fooling with his harmonica or thinking about buying an automobile."

Wilson began to fall asleep, and his rocking swing stopped.

"I thought it was more than I could bear. Then my baby died, and without reason. Just one morning when I went over to lift her from her crib, she was dead. We lived on the edge of town then and I ran in to our doctor and brought him, and he told me, 'She's dead.' It was a fact then. Dead. Now she could be buried. *Dead;* that meant she was no longer. That meant that something that had been wasn't any longer, come and gone. And I told myself that, and tried to keep eating, and tried to sleep, and found a job in a factory, and gave the house back to the bank and rented a room from an old lady, and lived for several years like I was dreaming. Several years, Mrs. Montgomery. One year, then two, then three. Month after month, never going out, having no friends, waiting quietly with Mrs. Wokey, and sitting in my room listening to her, peaceful until she went to bed and her footsteps carried by my door, because then it seemed like I would be alone. The sound of that old woman's footsteps was the most precious thing I had. So I always tried to be asleep before that. Many nights I would try to calm myself with self-imposed peaceful thoughts, then her terrible mounting of the staircase would begin and I would listen to the living, last sounds carrying by my door, wide awake. My light burned all night."

Della began to shake her head.

"No," Sarah continued. "The more despairingly I tell it, the more accurate. I lived for years like that. At first I tried to withstand the temptation of talking to myself, but gave in when my thoughts became much like talking themselves and the only way I could keep from saying little things endlessly to myself, like 'What are you going to do tonight?' was to say them out loud. So I conversed with myself about the daily routines of my life. Then two months after starting this the bus driver of the bus I took to work in the morning asked me while handing back my change if I wouldn't go to a movie with him that weekend. I looked at him and he smiled. I was frightened, but, looking into his face while he smiled, I felt like I had never seen what a smile was before, or what it meant. It meant simply, I am happy, and wish you to be.' It's a wonderful thing to smile—showing one's teeth. It's a guarantee that the world is what we make it, and not by definition ugly. He saw that I was frightened. . . . I'd never looked at him before. That will show you how I was those years. Three years of riding that bus and I'd never looked at the driver. He said I could tell him the next morning and his mustache twitched. So all that night I thought about nothing else. I talked it over with myself after Mrs. Wokey went to bed. I didn't go to work the rest of the week, so that I wouldn't have to answer.

"Sometime after my twenty-first birthday (birthdays have always been important to me) I did go out with him. He owned his own automobile, and after the movie (which made me laugh and picture myself as the heroine) we drove out into the country, and the wind came in the windows, and I could put my head out and watch the night reel by, my hair blowing back against the rear window. I was nearly delirious with private joy, and I was afraid he would see it on my face and would think it meant something. It seemed like we were flying. I know at one time he said we were going fifty miles an hour. That seems slow now, but nothing will ever be so fast. My mind was secretly racing. I imagined myself flying recklessly, casting all caution to the wind, putting my life on the line for a few moments of mad, frantic thrills. I had never felt like that before. I thought if Mrs. Wokey were to see me she would be shocked and scold me and tell me to get out of her house, though that would hurt her very much because she loved me and desperately wanted to keep me close to her old, quiet ways. I felt they were evil thoughts. Cecil drove me home and I rushed inside, ran upstairs to my room and watched him drive away. I sat by my little table until I was sure I had my pounding heart under control, and went downstairs. Mrs. Wokey was reading one of her magazines and I went out and got a bowl of ice cream and ate the whole thing. I thought what it would be for me to flip out a cigarette and light it—what she would think.

"'Thing's are mighty quiet around here tonight,' I said to Mrs. Wokey.

"'Well, yes they are,' she returned and looked at me from over her magazine.

"'Very quiet,' I said. 'Of course there's no reason for anything to be really jumping.' And I ran upstairs, feeling her eyes following me, went into my room and looked at my merry self in the mirror. But the next night, Sunday, I could not fall asleep before the footsteps came by the door, and the fear returned.

"Two years later—two years of falling back into my old fears and dreaming ways, and rising up above them for moments of happiness, only to fall back again, and finally leveling out—Cecil and I were married.

"The first several weeks of living with him, I remembered Bill and wondered if I shouldn't run away. But that was mostly when I was alone, and when Cecil came home I felt better, and then I didn't remember Bill any more.

"Cecil had a terrible temper, and though he was never violent around me, and tried to hide it, I could tell when he would bump his head or see something he didn't like that his true reactions, if he didn't keep them hidden and falsify them, would be abnormally brutal. Sometimes he would even look at me like an animal when I'd done something he didn't like. Yet those times were very rare. . . . It's just that he lived in sort of a set way. He always sat in the same chair, slept on the same side, approached any problems with the same attitude, wouldn't eat certain foods that he had decided long ago were distasteful regardless of the way they were fixed, listened to the same programs on the radio, went to bed within a half-hour of the same time every night and generally planned out every waking hour according to a long schedule.

"After a year they put him on night shift. He was very angry about that, and said there were plenty of other drivers with less seniority, and that there were only two night buses. So he had to work Saturday nights, which was his bowling night, and there was no end to the pain that caused him. I tried to get him to quit driving, and even offered to go back to the factory while he found another job, because after two months he still resented it as much as he had when he'd first been notified of his shift change. But he said he wouldn't let me work, and for some reason refused to look for another job in the afternoon after he had gotten up. It became frustrating, because he seemed so miserable, yet didn't seem to want to do anything about it. . . .

"Maybe I better stop."

"No, no," said Della, "go on. I can't tell you how interested I am."

"You're so kind. I knew she would be wonderful," she said to John, and put out her arm. He turned to her, away from watching his sleeping father, and smiled as though he'd been listening. On the horizon, an exhausted rim of pink was all that remained of the daylight, which stretched, yawned and finally slid unannounced below the dark line of the ground.

"Then after leaving home on a Saturday night at a little before eleven so that he could be at work at a quarter after and have a cup of coffee at the station before beginning the eleven-thirty run, he didn't come home. I waited clear through Sunday, Sunday night and Monday morning. Monday afternoon

I became frantic and telephoned Bart Lewis, a bowling friend of his. But he hadn't seen him, and sounded like he resented being called—as though my husband's business shouldn't concern him. At eleven thirty I called the station. The man from the bus company, in a voice like a radio announcer, told me that Cecil had not driven a bus since over six months ago. He elaborated to say, 'It was December and Cecil was upset about the shift change. We explained to him that it was only for a reorganizational period of two weeks while the new drivers and new routes were worked out. He got angry, demanded his money for the last week and quit, so soon that he never learned that because of so much protest the reorganization plan had been discontinued and the company agreed to have the training period of the new drivers be completed on the night buses. But he'd got his money and left, and never came back. Who did you say was calling?'

"I set the phone down into its cradle and looked at the floor. The green specks in the linoleum swirled around. I felt like I was drowning. December. For over three months Cecil'd been leaving home every night at ten minutes to eleven and coming home at seven thirty in the morning, sometimes as late as eight, but never as late as eight thirty. Every week he gave me money for the groceries, my own allowance, and paid the bills. Nearly every night he would complain about having to go to work just as the rest of the folks were beginning to have a good time.

"It was more than a betrayal or a lie. It had no explanation that I could discover. It was like someone saying to you, 'What you know isn't true.' And when, in indignation, you turn to your storehouse of undeniable facts to prove yourself, you find they've shifted just enough to make you out to be a fool.

"Then the shame: trying to find out what one's husband has been doing every night of the week, and Saturdays too, for three months. The bowling was a ruse as well, and alleged friendships . . . everything. His mother's address in St. Louis belonged to a trucking company. The high-school ring in his drawer turned out to be authentic, but the few years he'd spent there twenty-five years ago were gone from the memory of the teachers and only dimly remembered by others, who were able, however, to point out where he had lived with his parents. So I stood there and looked at the house, and realized how foolish I must have seemed to them, and to the people inside looking out the windows.

"I did everything in my power to discover the long circumstances that brought about the disappearance of my husband, and *everything* failed. Some mornings, on their way to work, neighbors reported to have seen him driving home, sometimes from the west, on Sutherland Drive, sometimes from the north from East Fourteenth Street and sometimes down the back alleys of Woodville. The matter was turned over to the police and they went about for several weeks with pictures in their shirt pockets, asking, 'Have you seen this man, this Cecil Baynard? He's disappeared from his wife.' And 'When did you last see him? Did he have any friends? Did he have a girlfriend that you might know of or have heard mentioned?' Simply nothing.

"By then I was twenty-three. I suppose many of my neighbors thought that I went into shock, because for a long time I didn't venture outside my house except for the barest necessities, and even then at the checkout lines I would ignore their eyes. But it wasn't that. I was simply making up my mind. I knew how much money I had, how long I could keep paying the bills, how long the creditors would take after I quit paying before they would refuse to absorb any more loss at the request of their conscience, turn off the electricity, snip off my heat supply and demand the three keys which allowed free, unobstructed coming and going from the house. I knew that when this time came I would have to be prepared to move and go on, but I didn't intend to be fooled into picking out a direction before I'd made up my mind how I was going to feel about what'd happened to me. I *refused,* in other words, to let the experience have any direct control over my life for the worse, and sat down to decide, practically speaking, just how things were with me.

"There were two things which struck me with particular force. First: the lunch pail. He never went to work without a packed lunch pail. I always filled it after the news and I couldn't remember a time when he'd forgotten to take it. And every time I'd arrive at an explanation for his disappearance and secret activities, I was reminded of the lunch pail." She stopped talking.

"Go on," said Della.

"He *never* forgot his lunch pail. The second thing was when after the police sounded the river—I believe that's the term—anyway, with hooks and such they brought up a body from the mud bottom, a man with pockets filled with sand and small rocks. He had no identification on him and they wanted me to see if he held any resemblance to my husband. So I went down to the morgue with them, but when we arrived and before we were inside, an inspector stepped out, helping a middle-aged woman by supporting her arm. She was in tears, and he quietly told the policeman who had brought me that they already had positive identification and that I could go home. It wasn't my husband. It was then, looking at that other woman, that I was reminded that I knew what it felt like to have someone dead: Cecil was not, and could not be, dead. Because I knew what that felt like. I knew that feeling too well, and if Cecil had been dead though outside my immediate knowledge, I would have known. That night he'd left his lunch pail. Something had been in his mind.

"So with these two things—the knowledge of his living, and the knowledge of him and lunch pails—I did the only thing to save my own pride. I quit caring and divorced him. I moved again, and lived by myself, working at a button factory. I expected to never have anything to do with marriage or men for as long as I lived."

John reached out and touched her, imposing silence. Wilson's breathing was heavy. Every once in a while he would jerk, moving in some faraway dream, keeping ahead of the foxes. Della looked at Sarah in the smoky night light and thought, There's still something not revealed—something that you've kept from me. You've not explained it all.

What happened in Della's mind was unusual. She took it upon herself to get to the bottom of Sarah's strangeness, and spent the next several years visiting her and watching her closely. She talked to her friends incessantly about how Sarah did this and Sarah did that, as though trying to prove by a lengthy induction that her son's wife was completely human. And they listened to her, half out of not wanting to be unkind and half out of interest in hearing some passing clue that would solve the mystery in everyone else's mind: What was she like when the shades were pulled and she turned her attention to her senses? It was many, many years before this idea even dawned upon Della—that the secret could be in the flesh, in Sarah's hips and thighs and arms and hands, and not inside. She looked for something beneath the skin, something in Sarah's personality to explain it, not thinking for a moment that there was personality *and* something else, different and completely made up of senses. Her discovery of this came much later. Her neighbors in town never took it upon themselves to invite her over to their houses on Saturday night, or any other night that it might start, to listen to the joyous moaning, screaming cat howls that came from John's house and went on for as long as several hours, each wavering note cutting through the stillness. Nor did they explain to her that they'd gotten to enjoy lying in bed, listening and wondering. On infrequent Sunday afternoons when the air would be full, their children would ask, "Mommy, why does she make those noises? They frighten me." "There's no reason to be frightened. It's all very natural." But the only thing they could *promise* was that it didn't *have* to be frightening, if you kept your wits about you when you heard it come ripping through the quick evening air.

They never talked about it to Della, and seldom among themselves, because the shrieking cat howls cut deep into them, like the voice of hidden, repressed desires, fantasies not actualized, abandoned but not forgotten. Hearing her was like listening to the screams of your own imprisoned passions.

Wilson had only one dog left—a fourteen-year-old beagle named Cindy, who still carried herself with dignity, though her legs were stiff and crooked and hardly held her up when she ate.

THREE

Eight men were in the garage. It was July, very hot, and cold sodas were pulled one after another out of the machine. It was no cooler in the garage except for the company and the absence of the pressing issues of field work. John moved at a snail's pace, but never completely stopped, taking apart a chain saw and welding together an auger cracked away from the shaft. It seemed the sweltry air grudgingly made room for them when they moved, swirling thick around their arms and faces, wringing out beads of dark sweat.

"You know, it's where we've forced them. They had nothing to do with it. Could've been us if the situation was reversed."

"But they seem to excel in some fields, naturally. It comes from them coming from Africa—the drums and dances and all."

"I don't recall ever hearing about basketball being played over there."

"Or football, or razor fighting."

"Or baseball."

"Wait a minute—they're not *better.*"

"Take the percentages. Take the percentages. What's the total population of—"

"It's like the Jews. It's being denied something, like they were denied complete freedom in business. So naturally they learned to be good."

"That's something different. They could learn that. But I could never learn how to be more coordinated."

"They don't seem to be too intelligent, and you could say they were denied good educations."

"Who?"

"The Negroes."

"Even when they're given a chance they don't really try. Talk to anyone who ever taught in a mixed school. They don't want to learn, and there's nothing you can do about it. What do you do, call their parents in?"

"Or parent. Usually the old man don't live at home."

"They don't respect authority."

"Jesus, how can you expect them to? Look at the—"

"We know it ain't their fault. But it's true. They don't respect authority. They live in the streets. They commit more crimes. They take drugs and all of 'em drink heavily. It's a matriarchal society—"

"A lot of 'em don't work."

"It's our fault."

"I know that. We all know that. Nobody's proud of it. But what do you do now? They don't respect the same things. If you let 'em in your school, the level of education'll go down. If you let them live next to you, they'll be trying to get at your wife. That's fact."

"Bah."

"Bah nothing. Marion's right. Why do you think people in cities hate them so much and keep them out of their neighborhood? Do you think they're mean or stupid, all of them? No, they know more about it than you do."

"I heard some fellas one day yellin', 'You're not human, you're animals,' at a bunch of school kids walking down the street in front of a Younkers store. It made me sick."

"There you go, see?"

"I'm not defending anything. All I say is that there's a reason. More rapes among coloreds."

"Look how tall they got by drinking orange soda and eating potato chips!"

"Here comes Morley."

"Hi, Morley."

"Wasting time again," said Morley, shaking his head from inside his car at the stop sign. Then on again.

"He's a good guy."

"Sure has tough luck, though, at least lately."

"It's mostly his wife's fault, though he won't let on so."

"What I think is that you have to keep them separate from us. There's no way either of us will get a real fair shake with them hating us the way they do."

"But they want what we got. They want all the things and money we got. They'd live right next door to you if you gave them a chance. There's no way to separate them."

"Sure there is. Give them their own schools. Let them educate themselves in whatever way they want. Let them own their own businesses. Let them take care of themselves."

"Their own prisons, too."

"And their own police force."

"And their own traffic court."

"And garbage collection."

"And welfare state."

"They'd never do it. They like being where they are—living on welfare—taking what they can get from us and laying back."

"If you think it's such a great life, why don't you try it? Sell the farm, move into town, go on welfare and start living the good life."

"I didn't say I'd want to live like that."

"Then it must not be so great, if you wouldn't want to. Right, John?"

"I don't know," said John, the first time he'd spoken. But he was listening to everything.

"I think they'd be happy to take care of themselves."

"How they going to get any food?"

"Well, there'd have to be some exchanges made between them and us."

"What are they going to give in return?"

"Probably something from the arts. Music, I guess."

"That'd be pretty hard to trade. I wouldn't give much for a song."

"You're just like that. If they could get any kind of advertising and exposure. When we went to Chicago last fall, Clara's cousin took us down to a colored bar and we heard a harmonica player who could bring tears to your eyes. His name was Little something. Little Walker . . . Little Wurther . . . something like that. His voice was beautiful."

"Music is natural to them."

"It comes from their coming from Afr—"

"No it doesn't. It has to do with feelings. They have more feelings than we do."

"That's true. They're not as smart, but they have more feelings, and are better at expressing them. It's something that we've done to them as well. But it's not all in our imagination."

"What?"

"It comes from our original puritanical upbringing. We've been taught by one way or another—by the work ethic and so forth—to be ashamed of our feelings—sex especially. So what we do is throw all of them off on the blacks."

"Wait a minute—"

"No," said Sy, interrupting. "He's right. That's exactly what we do. We think of them as being sexual giants. We think of them crying easier than we do, of being more compassionate, loving their wives more, feeling more anger."

"Right! And in consequence they've been allowed the full range of those feelings, whereas we've been denied them. We also imagine them to be free from feelings of guilt—and they are!"

"They live a more carefree emotional life."

"Just a minute," said John. "Are you saying that they are more *alive* than we are?"

"Of course they are," said Marion, and his tone of voice added, *Didn't you know that?* Everyone else agreed: John should have known that.

"And we hate them for it."

"Even before they were slaves they had more feelings, and then we pushed all those we couldn't use over onto them."

"But they know some of us don't hate them, don't they?" asked John.

"Come on, John," said Marion, "of course not. They hate us all, and think we all hate them. How could they think anything else?"

"But I didn't want any of what happened to have happened. And I don't hate them."

"They don't care about you. They'd kill you if they had the chance and wouldn't get caught."

"And feel no guilt."

"None at all."

"They'd be glad to do it."

"If you were lying helpless on a deserted street in their neighborhood without a penny on you, one of 'em would go out of his way to run over and kill you, just because of the chance to do it."

"Sure they would, John. *Didn't you know that?"*

John went back to welding, and didn't enter into the conversation again, though it changed course several times during the afternoon. As soon as everyone left, he closed the garage and went across the street and into his house. He was very troubled, and tried to get over it by immersing himself in his bird books. But even reading about the snowy owl, which he was sure he had seen several nights earlier, could not keep his troubles from spewing out. He felt as if he were drowning and had nothing to float up out of the water on except his worries. Finally, Sarah came home from shopping, and talking to her made him feel a little better. She was sympathetic, and even offered ways for him to forget about it; but it was a personal problem, and so had to be worked out by himself and in his own way. The difficulty wound itself around his religion and threatened to strangle it to death. How could the universe be as he imagined it if there were people in it who were fundamentally different from him?

Can they be more alive? Regardless of the reasons, can they really be more alive? Are their senses better? He did not talk to Sarah about this. *He did not expect ever to get an answer.*

Mrs. Pearson saw them first. Dusting off one of her seven-foot rubber plants by the window facing the street, looking out, she saw a green Ford moving at a walking pace in front of her house. She ran to the kitchen to keep its progress in view, saw it stop two houses away and three men get out. She ran out the back door and into her neighbor's house. "Lois!" she yelled, coming through to the living room. "Blacks! They're black!" Both of them went to the window and looked out.

The men were looking up and down Sharon Center nervously as though they were lost and looking for a signpost to tell them where they were, but not quite. They also looked as though they had decided nothing should move them from that spot of street.

"What are they doing?" asked Lois.

"I don't know."

"Look, they're coming over here."

"They've seen us!"

"What do they want?"

"They're coming over here!"

"Get away from that window!"

Emma Pearson jumped out of the view through the window to the safety of the wall.

"Settle down. This is stupid. This is my house. They aren't coming here. This is stupid." Lois watched them walk across the front lawn.

Emma Pearson went back to the window. "There's still one in the car!"

"Stop it, Emma."

Then the knocking started. Both women stopped breathing, and at each pound their hearts lurched. Then there was a pause.

"Don't answer it, Lois," whispered Emma emphatically.

"This is my house," announced Lois, but without quite the conviction she had planned. She took a step toward the door.

"Whatever you do," said Emma, *"don't open that door."*

"I will," said Lois, and crossed to the door. Just as she was about to touch the handle, the knocking began again and she jumped backward.

"No," said Emma, nearly inaudibly. "They'll go away."

Lois pulled the door open when the pounding stopped. Standing directly in the middle of the doorway as though preparing, if need be, to thrust them sprawling onto the lawn with a single body block if they tried to come in, she smiled and said hello very quickly.

"Could you tell us where John Montgomery lives?"

"Who?" she asked, not having comprehended enough of what they'd asked to say more. They looked at each other. Emma came over and stood behind Lois. One of the men handed a piece of torn newspaper to another one and he held it out. Lois stared at it momentarily as though it were a shrunken head, and then accepted it, and read it over seven or eight times (the part circled by a black pen) before she understood it. Then Emma snatched it from her. It was an advertisement in the confidential column of a newspaper in Burlington.

TO WHOM IT MAY CONCERN:
IT CANNOT BE POSSIBLE THAT YOUR FEELINGS
ARE MORE INTENSE THAN MY OWN.

John Montgomery
Sharon Center

"So what—what does that mean?" asked Emma.

"He lives in that house on the corner. Down there." Lois pointed, taking the piece of newspaper from Emma and giving it back to them.

"The white one?"

"Yes, that's it. The white one."

"Thank you." They turned to walk away.

"Thank you. No, I mean, you're welcome," said Lois.

"He works across the street," sang out Emma. "You may have to look for him there." They shut the door and went back to the window.

"Look how they walk!" said Emma. "It's indecent."

"It comes from their oppression," said Lois, as though she understood and had compassion for the world and all its people. "They're miserable people. It's such a crime the way they're treated—they are so frightened of us."

"You know what they say about them. The men, I mean—"

"Emma!"

John was alone when the three came into the garage.

"You John Montgomery?" said the tallest, pushing the newspaper clipping toward him.

John took it in his own hand and put it down. "Yes," he said.

Without talking, one of them left. The other two watched John and smiled when he looked directly at them and shuffled their feet with their hands in their pockets—making themselves out to be buffoons. John marveled at the subtlety with which they had learned to appear physically unthreatening, making themselves into clownish figures. But beneath that lay hate, maybe so far down that it would never come out, but, through John's eyes, undeniably, irrevocably there. He felt the impasse—the barriers. The men had told him that two weeks ago, but he hadn't believed them. *They'd kill you just for the chance.* He looked at them and wondered if it would be true. There was no way of telling. Too much hidden.

These thoughts filled his mind. Then into the open doorway stepped the fourth—the one who had not come in with the other three—and in the first instant of looking at him John knew why they'd come. They'd brought a champion—someone whose feelings, they thought, could outstrip even a dying saint's. John looked at him again and decided no, it had been his own idea to come. He was slightly bigger than a person needed to be and three inches blacker than any of his companions. John could see why they had wanted him to stay in the car. He was conspicuous—the kind of man a band of hooligans would love to tear apart and hang up in a tree—the kind of man who would never be safe outside his own neighborhood. As might be imagined, his hate was very close to the surface. Handsome and proud.

"That's him," said his friend, coming in behind him.

"I can see that," he said, staring at John.

He's presumptuous, thought John. I didn't really mean for them to come here. They should've written or something first.

"How do you want to hol' this here thing?"

"What?" asked John, knowing at the same time what he meant. But before the champion could answer, five Sharon Centerites from a bigger crowd across the street came in and sat down and began pulling out sodas from the machine.

" 'Lo, John," said Marion.

"Sure is hot," said Phil Jordan.

"You ought to get a fan put in here," said Sy.

"And a swimming pool."

"I didn't think you'd be working today, Marion," said Henry Yoder, walking in and over to the machine. " 'Lo, John."

All of this as if there were no one else for ten miles. Across the street was a group of men and women trying to look natural standing at the very edge of Mrs. Miller's lawn, next to the corner, nearest the garage door without being on the same side of the street.

Ernie came in the side door without knowing, and had to walk in among the black men to get over to the others. "Excuse me," he said. "Excuse me," and passed through them looking at his hands, as though he were walking around four rain barrels which, after he got out of their area, were rolled away by four invisible barrel-rollers.

"Afternoon, Ernie," said Marion.

"Afternoon," said Ernie. "I see you're not working today. That makes me feel better, because when a hard worker like you—"

"Listen to that! Listen to that!" said Marion.

John stuffed the advertisement into his back pocket, and blushed.

Somehow he managed to get rid of his neighbors and close his garage door, sealing the building in a cloak of mystery. The champion sent his friends out to the car to wait for him, as a returned courtesy. They closed the side door and faced each other.

"How you want to begin this here thing?"

"I can lift that anvil," said John. "I can pick it up by the horn."

"Come on, man, that kind of thing ain't it." Pause. "Sure, OK. I'll pick it up."

"Forget it," said John. "You're right. It doesn't have much to do with that."

"No you don't. You think I can't. You saying in your mind, 'He can't . . . he ain't the real thing.' " The black muscles tightened. The jaw fixed. The anvil came off the ground. He dropped it.

Then John picked it up.

"We've got some in the city," the black man said, "who could pick that up with their teeth."

"We got them too," said John. "What's your name?"

"Prentiss Hilton Brown," he said, with great dignity. "I already know yours, so let's get down to what's this all about." He took his pocket knife out of his pocket, opened it and went over to the workbench. He cleaned the tools away from an area so that only the dark grease- and oil-stained wood was exposed. Then he opened the front of his pants, took out his penis and laid it out on the table, standing up close to do it. He pushed the knife into the wood as a marker for the length of his soft organ, resealed it back inside his pants and looked at John. The polished knife blade stood poised straight down into the wood, a respectable length from the edge.

My God, thought John, and was so embarrassed and shocked it took him a minute to move or speak—staring as though hypnotized at the knife, wondering if it had really happened.

"That's ridiculous," he said. "That's got nothing to do with it."

"No, no. That's it. That's the whole matter."

"It's stupider than the anvil business."

"Maybe." He considered. Just from his face John could tell that the man before him was no fool and had every ounce of reasoning ability that John did. "Maybe. OK, forget it. That's not it."

"Oh no," said John. "I know what you're thinking," and in one tremendous rush of willpower he took out his own penknife (a smaller, less decorative knife with a rounded end and a screwdriver), exposed himself upon the workbench, pushed in the knife and recomposed himself.

Prentiss Hilton Brown quickly pulled the knife out of the table, shut it and put it into his pocket, even though it had stood farther from the edge by almost three quarters of an inch . . . longer, but definitely lacking in breadth. "You're right. That ain't quite the right thing."

These first two stages of their encounter happened very slowly. Mostly they looked at each other in deadly seriousness. At this point they both still believed, as surely as they had the day before, in the undeniable truth of their own convictions: John, that no one could ever be more alive than himself, and Prentiss, that he was. John was attracted by his belligerence. He feared and pitied it. What would it be like, he wondered, to be able to assume that the world at large was hostile to you and would wish for your personal demise as a simple matter of course? And to assume that not out of naive egotism (like someone who believes he is of a different kind) but out of an accumulation of experienced facts. It would be like an animal, he thought for one terrible minute, hiding and smelling for wolves. It would be tragic, because the whole purpose of the developed intellect, so far as he could see, was in allowing one to be free from that criminal hypothesis—in being able to say, "Nothing out there wishes me harm intentionally, and when I think it does, the very thought betrays my own shallowness and malfunction." But him. What does fairness mean to him? When happiness for me seems to be a feeling of harmony with the world, what is his happiness? Is it protected isolation? But that would lead to introversion. No, it would be either complete neglect of the other side or the pride of being a noble, even superior adversary. Then a tin bell rang in his head and he realized, in depth, something he had known before in a trite way: So long as any one person is oppressed, he will bind me to his outlook; he will declare himself an adversary, and in so doing the line will be drawn and I will find myself on one side or another. So goes the harmony. So goes any chance of prolonged happiness. His mind reeled. He rejected ideas as fast as he thought them.

They stood looking at each other in absolute silence. Then a knock came from the side door, followed by one from the front, both quick, sharp raps. Then another from the front, at a different place. A long silence. Two more knocks from the side, accompanied by the hesitant voice of one of the blacks: "Hey, Prentiss, let's get going." Then Marvin's voice from the front: "Hey, John . . . John, hey, open up."

Prentiss and John took a step closer together, as though they were both about to say something and wanted to be heard over the noise outside, coming to within ten feet of each other.

Outside, one of the blacks rattled the door handle impatiently and spoke again, somewhat pointedly now. "Prentiss, let's go. We don't want to stand around out here in this cruddy little town all day." At the same time Sy called from the front, "John, open here. I've got some work that needs to be done. Open up." And Clara Hocksteader shouted then, "John, say something. Are you all right?" and they started trying to raise the heavy overhead door which was swung down barring their entrance. Someone had got a board and was prying with it.

The side door opened six inches, one of the blacks pushed his head in and reissued the earlier request to leave, hesitated, nearly reclosed it as they finally got the door started up in front, opened it wide and presented his physical self as an urgent demand to get moving. The overhead door was swung halfway up and John's neighbors were coming in like a drove of sheep through a narrow opening. He looked at Prentiss again and together they started forward once more, just ready to say something. But in the same instant, as though at an agreed signal, they gave up and joined ranks. John watched as the half-sneer crept again into Prentiss' face, and felt himself bristle at it. Prentiss Hilton Brown turned and walked out the door, got into the car and was driven back to Burlington.

John resumed welding.

FOUR

"OK, bring it along, but hurry up," said John through the screen door. Then he returned to walking impatiently up and down in the yard. This grass needs to be cut again, he thought. I've never seen such a summer, an inch a day. An inch a day! A person ought to be able to watch it move.

"Should we bring some paper for starting a fire?" sang out Sarah from inside.

"No . . . yes . . . I don't care. Hurry up."

"Don't shout," said Sarah, bumping the door open with the picnic basket. "Oh, I forgot the blanket."

"We don't need a blanket."

"Yes we do. Here, hold this." She hung the basket on his arm and ran back inside. He began pacing again. Sarah returned with a heavy wool blanket, dropped it on the ground and went back for the small canister of cream. John began counting to himself, but at twenty-seven a dragonfly settled on the rim of the basket. It was solid blue, nearly iridescent, and its double wings were tinted the same color, like thinly colored glass, with lines of silver and sun dust. John stood very still. He'd seen many dragonflies, especially when he was little, fishing with his father, stacked up two and three at a time on the end of his pole, but *never,* so far as he could remember, one this color. It seemed so beautiful to him that even while looking at it he couldn't believe it. When it flew away he felt as if he just had to have another look at it, dropped the basket and carefully pursued it, bringing the glasses up to his eyes whenever he had a chance to look at it sitting still.

Sarah came out with the cream, saw the abandoned basket of food, a cat within three feet of it, and her husband walking quickly down the road, crossing over a fence, off into a field, looking every once in a while into space with his binoculars.

"Get out of here," she yelled, rescuing the basket and sending the cat off down below the fence. Sarah secretly didn't like cats and felt they were much too sneaky, and where some people thought they were independent and cunning, she thought they were stupid, vile, insensitive and cowardly. She threw a stick at it and it went across the road; then she looked around quickly for fear Mrs. Miller might have seen her. Satisfied, she went over to John's Ford, put the basket and blanket in the rumble seat and got into the passenger's side, easing herself down onto the soft leather. Wearing blue jeans was fun. She tied her scarf more tightly under her chin and just sat. No thoughts came to her, or pictures. She could see her husband coming back down the road, feel the warm sun, smell fall, hear noises and find small prism colors in the windshield; but vacantly, taking a mild pleasure in through all her senses, passively enjoying being alive—taking a vacation from motivation, interest and control.

John got in and started the motor. "What's up, fat-face?" he asked, easing out of the driveway, smiling inwardly at the sound of his mellow-toned muffler.

"Just sitting," said Sarah, putting her feet up on the glove compartment and accepting her whole self back. They almost never rode in the old Ford and when they did it was a pleasant novelty. It was a convertible with running boards, mechanical brakes and red paint. It made her feel important to ride in it, and waving at people from it was especially nice.

Still, she couldn't bring herself to wave at Ronny McClean, who stood in the ditch in front of his parents' house at the edge of Sharon. John would. She looked into her faded denim knees and put her feet down.

"I wonder what it's like to be like that," asked John.

"Don't talk about it. I'll get upset."

"One day he rode his bicycle over to Frytown and they finally found him in Lloyd Brenneman's fruit cellar, eating a little banquet he had spread out on the floor. That's the farthest he's been from home in forty years. That was . . . let's see . . . thirty or thirty-two years ago."

"Don't talk about it, John. It's awful."

"No it isn't. At least, if you grew up with him. He's never been any different."

"That makes it worse."

"It doesn't. I kind of like him. He's all right."

"You don't like him. You just say that because you think that'd be good to feel that way—I'm sure you have a secret ambition to be a saint."

"Sarah, that's unfair. I only—"

"I know," she said, and moved over closer to him. "It's just, you know, how you are. Being bad isn't so serious."

"Yes it is."

"You worry too much."

"Besides, I do like him."

"Why can't you just accept that a madman gives you the creeps? You never learned to accept things and forget them."

John's voice rose to nearly an argumentative level. "It'd make more sense for you to learn to accept that there're people like Ronny, and accept that it's not so bad if there are. It's possible to like someone for—"

"John, let's don't talk about it."

"Not talking about it doesn't solve anything."

"There isn't anything to be solved." Both sat in a gloomy silence. John felt the beginning of what could materialize into a roaring headache. The air seemed too wet, too hot, and his most cherished car seemed made of wood and corrugated fasteners. He drove faster. They turned off the blacktop onto gravel, and the dust flew.

Two hundred feet in the air a large bird looked down on them. At that height the wind covered all the noise from the ground, and he could not hear the muffler or the popping of the gravel against the tires. Only the motion, and the dust stretching out behind the red car like so many giant balloons. He was too high to be hunting, cruising in long circles. He veered slightly to intersect with a lesser angel, the sensation passing through him in all its colors, and quite out of his own control he let out a joyful *krreeeee.* Below, the car slowed down and stopped, the dust catching up with it and blowing on ahead. Lights flashing: two tiny glass reflections. He swung off toward the west, the hayfields and long-grass pasture.

"It's a broad-wing! I'm sure of it. Look at him—just look at him! Oh man, can you imagine him up there, the wind and— There he goes. Just look at him."

Sarah was turned, unhurriedly going through the basket, looking for her own pair of field glasses, wondering if she hadn't forgotten them.

"Here, take these, quick, look at him!"

Sarah adjusted the left eyepiece one half a digit to the plus side.

"Hurry up!"

She put them to her eyes, couldn't find the bird, took them down, relocated it and brought the glasses back up.

"That's nice," she said.

"He's too far gone now," said John.

"I saw him," she complained.

John put the car in gear and they were off again. Sarah waved at the Brogans sitting in their yard on steel-rung chairs. It seemed the motor was running smoother and he drove more slowly; soon he didn't think about the rattles, and by the time they arrived at McDuffs pasture both of them were enjoying themselves immensely. They left the convertible in the road and crossed the woven-wire fence at the place it was nailed to a maple tree which not only supported the old wire but had engulfed it and held it toward its center with a hand's breadth of wood. They walked back into the timber.

"Look," said John. "There's a kinglet. Look."

"Don't stop walking," said Sarah.

"No, wait. Look. Right over there."

Sarah stopped, and was immediately bitten by a vicious mosquito.

"Over there," said John. Then, "This place is full of mosquitoes!"

"I told you."

They continued on to the picnic table Marion McDuff's father had built. The pasture had been his wife's joy, and as a symbol of devotion he had built a table and a fireplace recessed against a sharply inclined bluff, in a partial opening of elms (the cursed tree), her name written in the fireplace cement. John and Sarah loved the little wild park. They fought off the bugs by cupping their hands and swinging them by the sides of their heads, and built a fire with the paper Sarah had brought. The gnats tenaciously hung on through the smoke, but retreated with the rising heat.

Then they sat on the picnic table and drank iced tea with lemon and honey. Out of the basket they took the warm turtle meat and ate it with salt, brown bread and butter. They talked about what animals it would be preferable to be, if you had to be born one.

"I wouldn't want to be domestic," said Sarah. "I'd rather be wild."

"It'd be nice not to have to be afraid of people, though."

"Domestic animals are afraid of people too."

"I'd like to be a dog," said John, "if I could be one of my father's."

"I wouldn't. I'd be a wild horse—a mustang!"

"Anything wild has to spend all its time scrounging for food, or being afraid of bears."

"Bears wouldn't bother a mustang," said Sarah.

"Of course they would. A horse wouldn't have a chance against a bear."

"It'd trample it to death with its sharp hooves. Jab! Jab!" Sarah made pummeling gestures, her fists representing hooves.

"That wouldn't be much of a threat. Bears have claws, you know, and have enough strength in their arms to whing a horse, especially a mustang—a very small horse—several feet in the air."

"Bears aren't that strong. Nothing's *that* strong. A fierce fighting mustang *stallion* could smash the biggest bear in the face." And her fist came down on the table.

"Many times bullets don't even penetrate a bear's head. It'd just pounce on a horse's back and it'd be all over."

"A mustang stallion," said Sarah, "would grab him off and fling him up into the air." And with her clenched teeth she imitated the action.

"I'd rather be a fish," said John. "A mud cat."

"And get caught on a hook," said Sarah, pouring out only one third a glass more of the iced tea, so that there would be two glasses left for later.

"Not just an ordinary fish. A smart one."

"I see what you mean, I think," said Sarah. That would be nice, she thought, lying in the deep holes during the day, sleeping on the bottom and watching the watery things . . . in a kind of liquid dream, the sunlight shimmering on the rocks, greenish yellow, all sounds soft and low—cows in the distance. Then going out at night into the shallows, hunting for smaller fish like a cunning, silent submarine, feeling the faster water carry you downstream, in among the roots of the shore . . . seeing the moon from underneath and hearing the oars of the Dark Lords in their long black boats, their footsteps on the bank, their fires winking across the tops of the ripples, deer drinking. Woodchucks eating green shoots. Leaves and water insects on the surface.

Their clothing inundated with smoke, an insect deterrent, they set off in search of birds, taking with them both binoculars, the thermos and the wildlife book. Sarah carried the blanket around her shoulders. She frequently let her thoughts be carried away by merely walking, or by the embroidery of the grasses. They waded in the stream, and she found smooth stones with color veins and put them in her pocket as remembrances. John saw a bobolink. They tried to catch crayfish until he became obsessed with finding an owl's nest, and they tramped over what seemed to her several miles. But the reward so outweighted the walk she could hardly contain herself and broke into laughter when she raised the glasses and saw as though directly above her two huge, round, dusty white horned owls frowning at her. "Who," she said. "Who. Who." That made her laugh more. John was so excited he could do nothing but talk about how owls' eyes were made and how, per square inch of flying surface, they were lighter than all other birds, their feathers softer, and how they had asymmetrical, adjustable ears nearly as long as their whole head. He read out loud from their book every scrap of information about them, and remarked that because there were two, it was a good year for owls and was an indication that the land would support them even through the winter. They seemed so comical because of their size, helplessness, dumb interest and aloofness—their unshakable faith in their own invulnerability at that height. They were also going to sleep.

Reading and thinking about owls made John want to find a place they could sit until it was dark in hope of seeing the parents hunting, gliding over with wild, burning eyes. They drank the last of the iced tea. They found a tall hayfield and lay down in it so that they would be invisible except from directly overhead. But despite the spectacle of the cloud formations, as subtle as frozen breath, with the darkening air came the bugs, and they were forced to give up the vigil and return to the fireplace. Several broken logs placed on top of the coals soon revived John's defeated spirit and they sat against the nearest elm and watched the flames. Darkness descended around them with the cooler air. Sarah went over to the fire and put on more wood and let the warmth saturate her clothing until just that point where it was too hot, and moved back, turned and began on the front side.

John looked at her silhouetted against the leaping colors, then at the colors themselves, and began to daydream. The daydream tapered back to the fire and he found himself looking at Sarah again. He went back to daydreaming but returned again to the seat of the denim pants; and when she gave a little jump back from the heat, her face glowing red, the air full of her smell, he felt his desire rise. Unsuspecting, she came back to the tree, stretched and sat down. He put his arm around her, and she moved closer, still unknowing. He sat with his desire for a few minutes to see if it would stand the test of time, then unbuttoned her pants. "Oh, John!" she said. "Not here."

"Why not?"

Sarah's senses (already inflamed by fear and embarrassment) nearly exploded, like a barrel of fish dumped into a river, when she felt her pants being drawn off and her bare skin exposed to the open air. She began to loosen John's buckle and pull his shirt down his arms. In his search for something to put under her buttocks, to protect her from the hard ground and to get her a little way up in the air, he found the blanket. "Oh, John," she cried. "Love me. Love me," closed her eyes on tentacled Hercules, and let her passion carry her to the other side of the doors of death, primeval darkness, and back again. Afterward, sweat rolling from where their bodies had touched, they dressed and made coffee, boiling water in a tin pail. They sweetened it and poured in cream from the little canister. Contented, and at the table, they sipped it.

I knew we'd want the cream, thought Sarah.

In 1941 there was a war. John was troubled, though he did not talk about it. The next year, in February, he told Sarah that he was going to enlist. It was supposed that he wouldn't be accepted because of his age; but he was gone within weeks. He was a faithful letter writer, though the neighbors were disappointed because the letters contained no war news. That year he came home for Christmas and stayed twenty days, then was home again a year later for a shorter visit.

The idea of Sarah Montgomery being alone was at first thought to be an imminent danger. It was even suggested to Della that she should insist her daughter-in-law move in with her and Wilson in the country. Della was excited at the idea, and asked her right away. Sarah declined, and would accept no sympathy, denying as she did that there was even the slightest gloom in her life, and maintaining that she was perfectly safe—or as perfectly safe as anyone else. Remington Hodge's father said: "I used to think at night sometimes, walking out to the barn maybe, or listening to the radio—of the image of that woman alone in her own house, sitting and reading, sewing, cooking for herself. I'd think about that and wonder, picturing myself there, see, standing knocking at the door, her opening it and . . . then I would force my thoughts away from it." On September 18, 1943, Sarah gave birth to a boy, July Montgomery.

The adult congregation of the Sharon Center Baptist Church was spread out on the front lawn and steps. Wilson stood with some men on the landing before the opened door and their voices rang with short, tenorous bursts of laughter. They were dressed in suits and sports jackets, white shirts and ties, and their manner of talking seemed to be influenced gently by wearing them, as though they were children in front of a great dollhouse, pretending to be grownup. Many of their faces were nut brown from working exposed to the summer sun. Sarah was virtually surrounded by the other women on the grass, protecting her, it appeared, from the unwanted looks of the men. They talked about gardens. The lawn sloped away from them toward a pair of soft maples and an overhead wind rattled and turned the silver underside of their leaves so that the foliage of the two shimmered in the late morning light. Their trunks, despite great breadth, looked as though they had at one time partially melted and the flat pieces of bark undulated over them in waves. Underneath these giants, in the cool shade, sat the children on thick little wooden chairs, the seats of which were no more than a foot off the ground and on the backs were decals of red bears, giraffes and smiling rabbits. They all sat in a cluster facing a slightly larger but by no means full-size chair, on which Della Montgomery perched like a goldfinch with a Bible opened in her lap. Their eyes were glued to her as though she and not what she was teaching them was a marvel of unexpected creation, and perhaps in their inchoate minds they half suspected that in an exuberant expression she would fly away in a flash of color, huge blue-and-white wings sprout from her polka-dotted dress and disappear behind a cloud.

July Montgomery sat in the very front, wearing his new pair of cowboy boots and a shirt with snaps instead of buttons. He was three and his dark eyes burned in intense concentration, growing slowly into a frown of bitter hatred, his small hands knotted together in fists. Della, interrupting her story, asked a question:

"And do you know what happened then?"

July answered as though there were no one else there, only he and his grandmother, as though the question were only for him. "They hung a sign up," he said darkly.

"And what did it say?"

"It said, 'Here's the king of Jews.' "

"Then what happened?"

"He died—because no water and they pushed a spear in Him." July could hardly talk now, and began to stutter when he tried to go on.

Della continued. "That's right, the soldiers killed Jesus with a spear and they took Him down from the cross and put Him in a tomb like a cave, and in front of the cave they rolled a great big rock that took all the soldiers to push, and they left Jesus there. Then three days passed."

Tears were forming in July's eyes, but his frown had eased. His fists uncurled. She continued:

"Three days passed while His friends felt so sad that He was gone, but Jesus had made them a promise. Do you remember the promise?"

"Yes!" shouted July, jumping from his chair. *"He rolled the rock away!"*

The eyes of the adults turned toward him from the church.

"No, July, that wasn't the promise. What was the promise?" she asked gently.

"He rolled the rock away!" hollered July again, his face now filled with uncontainable joy and good feeling. Della tried once more to settle him down and get him to remember the promise, but the image was so rooted in his mind that he was unable to let go of it and once more shouted that the stone had been rolled away, the angels of the Lord had pushed it aside and Jesus wasn't dead after all. The fact that He had promised anything didn't interest July, and he was so emotionally wrought up that he wouldn't stay in his chair and went running around pushing the other children and generally starting a fracas. Sarah came over and admonished him, but because it was so near time for Sunday School to be over, Della dismissed them and they exploded in all directions. The circle of women fanned out to keep them in view.

December 1946

Wilson's only dog, Cindy, was as broken and old as himself. They walked outside together in carefully measured steps, never going much farther than the barn and outer sheds, leaving paths in the snow. Wilson would think to himself, I can remember when she was young. She could run like the wind. What a dog she was! There're no dogs any more like she was. He thought of her as an old warrior who had fought many of his battles for him. It was Della's secret, terrible wish, hidden by seven seals of silence, that Cindy would not pass from the living world until after her husband had quit it. She did not want to watch that kind of pain kill him. She didn't want to see his worn-out heart hurt him again.

One day Wilson began to notice that he was feeling stronger. His arthritis began to slip away. He felt good enough to do some snow-clearing from the steps and sidewalk. He got the shovel and went outside. Della came out immediately and took it away from him and locked it up in the kitchen closet, despite his protests. OK, he thought after lunch, I will go for a walk this afternoon. He dressed warmly and walked farther than the sheds, out among the trees, close down to the bottom of the hill. Cindy, he noticed, seemed to be getting younger. She was running in the snow. I could walk on further, he thought. But I'll go back, because Della would worry.

He went back and said nothing. That night he had to tell Cindy several times to stop chewing up the furniture, but quietly so his wife wouldn't find out and blow up. Later Della took the flashlight away from him just as he was about to go out and hunt coon in the valley.

The next day he had the same walk. Cindy was running like a two-year-old and barking. He felt as if he could run himself. There was no pain in his chest. He felt strong. The crisp air was invigorating. Then Cindy let out a growl and the hairs covering her nervous spine stood on end. Wilson looked out into the timber and saw a wolf coming toward them. Cindy stepped forward to attack, but the wolf stopped running and began wagging its tail. No, thought Wilson. "Josh? Is that you, Josh?" The tail went furiously, whining and barking, but he stayed back. "Cindy," Wilson said, putting his hand on the old dog's back, "take it easy. It's Josh. It's only Josh. Come on, Josh." The wolfish dog came and Cindy smelled him and was soon friendly. He jumped up on Wilson, then ran off with Cindy, both playing like puppies. Wilson was so happy he could hardly contain himself, but, not wanting Della to worry, he went back up the hill.

Between the barn and the house he began to think: Now there's going to be a problem with Della. She won't easily accept another dog after I promised no more than one. But she humors me. Always has. I can remember when I brought home those mules. Boy, was that something! Two black mules with . . . His mind wandered, and he forgot about Josh, and went inside with both of them, kicked his boots off on the porch and let them into the house. They ran into the living room, growling and snapping at each other, knocking into furniture. Oh no, he thought, I should've left him outside. But it was too late and he waited in the kitchen for Della to begin yelling. After he had listened what seemed to him a long time to the ruckus and the curtains being pulled down from the windows, Della came out. "Take off those wet pants," she said, and went upstairs. He crossed the kitchen and looked into the living room, expecting it to look as if a drunken army had spent the night. But it was all right. Quickly he got hold of Josh and took him out onto the back porch. He could hear the sewing machine running upstairs. She must be getting very slow, he thought. He had everything under control before she came down.

"I thought I told you to get out of those pants," she said. "Put on your coveralls."

That evening Wilson listened to a talk show on the radio and ground coffee. He managed to smuggle Josh into the basement where it was warmer and set water and food down for him. Just before going to bed he let Cindy down for company. Sleep came quickly and he yielded up to it.

In the middle of the night, Wilson heard them both barking and howling and carrying on to no end. The ticking clock said it was 2:30. Della remained asleep next to the window. He got out of bed and went downstairs. Burglars, he thought. There must be burglars. He took the flashlight from off the top of the refrigerator and let both dogs upstairs. Immediately they squared off against the back door. Wilson went over and listened. "Keep quiet," he said to Cindy and Josh. "I can't hear anything with you carrying on so." They were quiet and he could hear scraping noises against the wood. Very strange, he thought, and opened the door. On the porch was a large yellow-and-black dog. "Hey, you," he said, "you get away from here now, you—" Then he saw the torn ear and scarred left side. The dog was lying down, trying to crawl into the warmth of the kitchen. "Duke," he said. "Duke! My God, get in here, you look like you've been buried in a snowbank. Get back there, Cindy, Josh; let Duke get in here." Josh was jumping on him and knocked him back against the table. Upstairs he heard Della's relentless footsteps coming down the hallway, heading for the stairs. "Quick now," he whispered. "All of you in the basement. Get *going* now. Get! There's food and water down there. Get."

He had them down and the door shut in time. The upstairs door opened and Della came into the kitchen. "What are you doing?" she asked.

"I thought I heard something. I got up to check."

"Did you find anything?"

"No," he said. "No, just the usual."

"Well, come back to bed. Your feet will freeze."

They went up together.

In the morning Wilson could remember hardly anything about the day before. Something unusual . . . yes, something unusual. Now, what was it? Halfway through his poached egg he remembered it and could hardly wait until Della took the car into town to pick up Sarah and go to the grocery store.

Then he let them up and took them out to run rabbits. They went off into the trees and down the hill. Wilson followed them. When he came up he had Jumbo with him too, running and jumping in the prime of her age. What fine dogs, he thought, looking at them. What fine dogs. Look at Cindy run! He felt very strong and even ran several steps uphill.

Two nights later, lying awake in his bed, watching the stars out the window, he had all of his fourteen dogs safely locked in the basement. New-fallen snow covered everything. He felt too good, he decided, to go right off to sleep, so he just lay and watched the stars, saying little prayers for the well-being of his wife, his children, some neighbors, and daydreaming.

"Wilson."

It's my imagination, he thought. Everyone knows I'm asleep now. Then he heard it again, more clearly.

I should know that voice, he thought, got up, put on his pants and shoes and went downstairs. In the kitchen it was deathly silent, only the faraway tick of the clock above. He went over to the cellar door and opened it. More silence welled up and around him—but no sounds of any kind from below. He went back to the table and sat down, then got up and recrossed to the door. "Hey," he said softly. "You all still down there?"

Nothing. He had a feeling that strange things were astir.

"Cindy, Spark, Jumbo, hey," he began a little louder, though hardly above a whisper. "Get up here, you dogs." Without his hearing a sound, as though they had materialized out of the darkness, all at once they were at the foot of the steps, ascending and clamoring. "Good," he whispered, "but don't be so noisy." The kitchen filled with them. They're being pretty quiet, he thought, considering how they could be. He let them outside.

If there's something out there, some burglars, he thought, they'll wish they weren't. At the kitchen door he watched them leave the porch and hit the snow without a sound and flash off into the dark of the barn and yard trees, as quickly and quietly as a cloud's shadow. No barking. Strange, thought Wilson, but then no one ever knows exactly why dogs do anything. Then he heard his name again: "Wilson."

"Who said that?" he said and switched on the outside light, holding the door ajar. He saw his dogs running silently at the edge of the light, moving slowly toward him, running in a large circle, dipping to and fro out of the darkness. Then two gray figures stepped into the light. Both of them wore hats and their faces were dark and without definition. They carried what looked like long, thin reeds bending at the tops, with winking spots of silver. They came up to the door and stopped. There was no light in the house. "Wilson," one said.

"Step up closer," he answered. "I can't see you clearly. I know that voice. Step closer, I can't see you." He went through the door onto the porch. They came up the steps and just inside.

"Step closer," said Wilson. "There, now I can see you. Dave . . . Sam . . . What are you doing here?"

"We thought you might want to go fishing," said Sam.

"We came to see," said Dave.

"The river's frozen over," said Wilson.

"We've got a hole chopped in the ice. Sam made it, clear down to the water."

"Why are you whispering?" said Wilson. "It's too cold out there."

"It's not so cold," said Sam.

"You're right, it's not too cold," said Wilson almost to himself, looking down at his pajama tops and bare ankles, not feeling the slightest discomfort.

"They'll be biting tonight," said Sam. "The big ones." The dogs were sitting silently outside. Frequently one would jump up and dance around in anticipation of going for a walk, but noiseless in the snow.

"I can't go, really," said Wilson. "I don't have my poles any more. Della locked them up."

"We brought one for you," said Dave, and held it out to him, the light from outside glistening off the silver eyes.

He looked at it. "It's sure a nice one," he said. "Feels like you could really bring them in with this one . . . I don't know, though. I better not. Della would worry."

"No she won't," said Sam. "She'll be asleep."

"No . . . I better tell her. I'll be right back."

"No, Wilson. Come on, let's go. She'd never let you." They stepped off the porch.

"Wait," said Wilson.

"No, come on," said Dave, his voice almost inaudible.

"OK, I'm coming," called Wilson, and followed them outside. The three walked down below the barn into the trees, Wilson's dogs running around them. "You know, I think you're right, Sam," he said, shaking his rod and looking at it. "I think they'll be biting—I've just got that feeling."

Della woke up at three and saw the empty bed. She threw on her bathrobe, stuffed her tiny feet into slippers and went down the hall, downstairs and into the kitchen. A blast of cold air met her. Holding her robe closely about her neck, she went to the door and closed it. She stood there looking out into the lit barnyard, shadows roundly filling the two tracks out into the darkness of the barn. The awful snow, thought Della, and the words came running back again and again like shaking someone falling between consciousness and unconsciousness, calling his name over and over—the awful snow, the awful snow—until she regained herself.

She went to the closet where Wilson's winter coat still hung, and put on her own. Then the fur-lined boots and scarf. She took down Wilson's coat and hurried to the door—then stopped again, looking outside. Dropping the coat, she ran into the dining room, and with a key from behind the teacups she opened their utility closet. From a little case between Wilson's tackle boxes she took the pistol and put it in her pocket. She took up the coat again on her way out, and the flashlight for the porch. She called his name and followed the tracks, noticing how closely Cindy had kept to Wilson, never wandering as much as several feet away. Though she did not think it now, she did later. Those tracks . . . they were much like soldiers'.

She followed them below the barn, halfway down the hill toward the river, to a place where there were rocks jutting up from the snow, crowned with ice. Her flashlight caught Cindy's green eyes. She went over. Leaning against the rock was Wilson, his eyes nearly closed. She took her hand out of her mitten and touched his face. It was cold and hard.

Della dropped the mitten. She stood back and closed her eyes, opened them wide, lifted her head up above the white, howling wilderness, watched the stars of Orion reel over her, his belt like a dagger in her heart. Then she felt the gentle pressure, Wilson's gentle pressure—his comforting net settle over her soul and bring it back around her.

"Come on," said Della to Cindy. "There's nothing here." The old dog whined and lay down at Wilson's feet, watching for his eyes to open, for him to get up and go back to the warmth of the house. Della took out the pistol and shot her, then went back home, the sharp, tearing, inhuman blast running a needle through her sorrow, bleeding into the insatiable pores of her body.

John was out of the Army in 1947.

From the dawning of his conscious thought July had been told that Daddy was coming home, though he had no idea of who this was or what he would be like. He did know that this Daddy, however, was likely to be an object of his mother's attentions, which all his life had belonged almost entirely to himself, and which he felt were vital to his very existence. She told him he would have to try hard not to be jealous, because Daddy loved him too, and Daddy's attentions were going to be just as good as, or better than, her own. And not knowing anything else, July could do nothing but wait and see. Then later she came to talk about the exact date he would be coming, and every day after that she exclaimed how, praise be to God, it was one day less. The closer it got, the more she neglected July and abandoned herself to her own expectations, filling him with dread.

John rode on a bus jammed with servicemen from New York City to Toledo. Many got off along the way, and there was a layover of six hours. On the bus to Chicago there were only eight men in uniform besides himself, trained from their duties to live with boredom and motion. Another layover in Chicago, a dinner of fried chicken and coleslaw in a diner on the Loop, and he was the only GI on the bus for Iowa City and Cedar Rapids, a seven- or eight-hour ride.

He tried to sleep and couldn't. For the rest of his life he would remember this ride. Outside the tinted windows everything smelled of the disgust and nightmare of war. January thaw, he thought. My father's dead, he remembered again. My mother: they might not have wanted to tell me about my mother. He resolved then, passing over the Mississippi and into Iowa, that if he could salvage his broken and splintered religion, if he could become a part, in a small way—any way—of those things he had so many nights feared were never true, if he could lie against Sarah's body and be only a little happy—he would never breathe a word of the last five years. He would deny them. The bus went on farther into his state and he began seeing familiar landmarks, familiar towns. His sleeplessness since getting into the States had honed his nerves to an edge, and by the time they pulled into Iowa City, fear was soaking him in cold sweat. Beyond the window Sarah stood against the brick wall. Tears wanted to be let out of his eyes. Men were staring at her. Her face looked anxious. His desire to touch her frightened him. Maybe, he thought, she won't want to. Maybe she'll say when we get home, "John, I've got to tell you something, while you've been gone away—" God help me, please help me, I am a wreck of a man.

It was in this condition July would have first seen his father, had John come out of the bus at that time. But a large woman getting baggage from the overhead rack forced him back into his seat. Angry and frantic, he looked out the window again. This time he saw his son standing behind her against the wall, and it was as though he had not known before and had just been told: Did you know, you have a boy, old enough to talk and understand, with a complete personality of his own. Here he is. He's yours.

He's a pretty good-looking boy, he thought, staring out of the besmudged window. He stands well, making no trouble . . . no idea what a man would think in a bunker—what he would do to save his own miserable life, the extent to which he would go . . . The woman with her bags bumped on down the aisle, and John slid out of his seat. At the door he stopped and gathered as well as he could all the loose ends and stepped down, reminding himself over and over: Be careful. Nothing can be taken for granted. Make no assumptions.

July felt his mother's hand tighten and tremble as the uniformed man stepped down from the huge metal bus onto the ground. "John," she called, and he came slowly over, carrying a cloth bag, holding his hat in his hand. Dark moons like blue wounds under his eyes, ugly hairs on his face, smelling clothes.

The man held out his hand and at first July was afraid to touch it, even though pressed to by his mother. The knuckles and joints and veins were so awful. July touched it and wanted to cry: it was so hard. Then the hand squeezed and he felt the power, the child-crushing strength that lay dormant like a crouching panther, controlled only by the sallow face's intention. Red lines in his eyes.

They went over to the car, and his mother wanted "Daddy" to drive. No, he said, he didn't want to. He sat next to July's window, July next to his mother behind the wheel. They left the station and headed home. The stranger looked suspiciously at the telephone poles and houses, at the dashboard and at July's mother's feet. His smell overpowered July's mother's. He spoke once on the ride home, asking about Grandma, only he called her Mom. The rest of the time he was silent.

Once home, he remained standing in the driveway, looking suspiciously at everything outside as though it might grow wings and flap away into outer space. The bird feeder (which his mother had carefully filled before they drove to the bus station) seemed to hold him mesmerized. His mother waited silently for him inside the opened door to the house. Finally, he came toward them with his cloth bag. July rushed to the door, slammed it and locked him outside so that he could never come in. He looked back to his mother, whose face was a betrayal of her erupting emotions: fear, hatred, sorrow and despair. She sank to the sofa.

The doorbell rang. "Go away," July shouted.

"Please," came from outside, and the word cut through the door and into July's throat. There was sadness and loneliness unimaginable in an older person. "Please," he repeated, and July opened the door. "Thanks, July," he said and put out his hand again. July took it and squeezed as hard as he was able.

"Ouch," said John.

Tears ran down Sarah's cheeks as she tried to stand up from the sofa. "Go outside and play now," she said.

July left, glad to be out of the oddly electric house. He knew "Daddy" had been joking, but still felt as though he could smash rocks with his fists. He closed the door and stood outside it.

"Would it be all right . . ." John was saying inside.

"I hope you're never satisfied," said his mother.

July left to play in the empty garage across the street.

FIVE

In 1948, Della Montgomery was prevailed upon by John to quit her country home, where she had lived alone since the death of her husband, and move into John's house in town, where (as she suspected) she could be watched more closely.

Coming up that first day, carrying her personal belongings in a shopping bag (a truckload would come later), she stopped on the porch with her son and his family, looked at them all, put her hand on the wooden railing and jumped over it, landing three feet away on the ground, walked up the step, picked up her bag again and went inside the house.

"How old is Grandma?" asked July.

"Seventy-three," said Sarah. "I think she's telling us she doesn't need help."

"She's still seventy-three," said John, and went in with a chair.

Della took for her place the little downstairs bedroom off the living room, flat against the back yard, with three rather large windows, done in a delicate broad-petaled flower print on a yellow-and-blue background. In it she had her two chairs, single iron bed, round rag rug, bureau and mirror, fish tank full of tiger barbs and silver neons, eight hung-up dresses, a pole lamp and a night table filled with odds and ends, from toothbrushes to things that meant a great deal to her. Settling into bed that first night, many thoughts came into her head. There were unfamiliar house noises, but there were other people in it. John and Sarah were upstairs. July too. She closed her eyes and pictured lying in the bedroom in her own house. *This is better,* she thought, and went soundly to sleep.

On the third night she was thinking quite happily to herself about the many things she had to do tomorrow when she heard a noise that frightened her and she got up, put on her robe and went out into the living room. It was almost like a cry. She went over to the stairway leading upstairs and carefully opened the door. Yes, it was clearer now, but less frightening, though strange and eerie. The crying rose and fell, then rose to an unearthly wail; then it fell away to moaning and stopped. The house became silent again and filled with her thoughts. She closed the door and went over to the couch and sat there in the darkness, listening. Perhaps a half-hour later she heard a door open, then feet descending the staircase. It was July, and she watched him open the door and cross over into the kitchen, walking with the blind determination of someone not completely awake. He put on the light, took a bottle of milk from the refrigerator, poured out a glass and sat at the table, drinking it with both hands. Della got up and went into the kitchen. July gave a little start, then relaxed.

"Hi, Grandma," he said.

"Do you think I could have a glass of that milk?" she asked.

"Sure. Here, I'll get it," and he got another glass from the dish drain and began filling it.

"Only half, now," said Della. "Or there won't be enough for cereal in the morning."

July handed it to her and they both drank.

"July," she said cautiously, "do you ever hear things at night?"

"Sure."

"What kind of things?"

"I don't know what they all are."

"Do you ever hear crying?"

"I don't know . . . I don't think so, Grandma. One time I heard voices, though, but Dad said it was the wind. Once I heard thumping whirring, but that was the antenna wire."

"Did you hear anything tonight?"

"No, I don't think so."

"You must have, think hard."

"No, I don't think so."

They put their glasses away and separated. Three nights later they met again. This time the noise began while they were together in the kitchen. "That. There, that. Do you hear it?" asked Della.

"That? That's Mom," said July, and put the milk back. "She always sounds like that, sometimes."

"Go on to bed now, July," said Della, and went back to her room and sat in the chair next to the window. She stared and thought for a long time, about Sarah and about the sound—about how all the neighbors could not have helped but know, everyone but herself. How in their minds there had never been a mystery; it all had been too obvious. Sensualist. She thought and stared, and finally decided: I could have been like that—Wilson and I—if only I'd cared to open my mouth. The sound is the only difference. Then she went away from the window and fell into an ancient, uninvaded sleep which carried her past breakfast.

It must be remembered that July grew up in a house like this one. His father worked across the street, and if July needed him, was always there, even in the daytime. Sometimes the two of them would go into Iowa City together and walk through the wide-aisled stores, where July would be looking quickly at everyone, thinking that all of them were seeing his father the way he saw him—strong, wise and very funny. And when they went with Grandma, he thought everyone thought she was Grandma. He very simply thought that there was nothing his father couldn't do, or know how to do, and nothing his mother couldn't eventually forgive and forget. His father could protect him from anything that could walk or crawl, anything that was physical and might come to get him, and his mother could protect him from his own terrifying thoughts, and the darkness in the hall closet and disease.

They knew him in school then as a friendly yet quiet boy, someone whom all enjoyed being with, and who could play baseball very well, but who wasn't particularly wanted on your team in a spelling contest. He was better in math. He'd inherited his father's strength, but it seemed to work more through his determined ruthless will than through his shoulders and arms—an enduring runner, but lacking the speed in short sprints.

One thing everyone remembers about him was the difficulty in getting him to change his mind. If he decided, as he once did in second grade, that yes, it was possible to see air, there wasn't any moving him. No, the teacher told him, air is clear. You can see everything clearly through it. *You can see it on radiators, and coming up from a pavement.* That's heat, they told him. That's heat waves. *No, it's hot air.* And for all the reasoning, he wouldn't budge, no matter how wrong he was. Most of the teachers would simply tell him that he was just being stubborn, and keep him quiet in that way. Sometimes it would turn out that his ideas were sound; but, good or bad, he would hang on to them with the same tenacity, and weeks later when you would try to bring up an incident in a light way, giving him a chance to take back what he'd said—like eating fish eyes can be a cure for blindness—he would jump into the argument as though he had spent the whole time thinking up more reasons to hurl at you.

Simply, he was one of us, and like us all, in his own way. Only a little more confident, perhaps, because of the great faith he had in his parents and their ability to manage all parts of his life that were out of his own control, allowing him to be very open and personable and radiate good humor and be obstinate.

He'd never known his grandfather except from what his parents told him, and Della (who, though she did not talk about him constantly, always said *we; we* did this or went over there, or *we* thought that was funny. This *we,* his mother explained to him later, was completed by the no-longer-present figure of his grandfather, a living, breathing person who was dead. The bodies of the dead went back to the ground. The living got old, and when they were finished, they were dead. His grandmother, he was told, was getting old).

July's favorite story of Wilson was a fishing story. He had supposedly gone up north once, into Minnesota, after walleyes and northerns, and fished in a two-hundred-acre lake on the outskirts of a small town. The water was hot, and the fish had simply not been biting. Nearly everyone else was off the lake, or swimming, or waiting for the cooler air of evening to go for bullheads. The walleyes, it was thought, were in too deep water, down deep with the bottom feeders, sleeping. It had been like that all week. Once in a while someone would get a small northern out of the arrowheads and water lilies, a couple of pan fish, but nothing of any size. Men were drinking beer in the shade along the lake though it was several hours before noon. Wilson was out by himself, sitting in the bow of a twelve-foot rented rowboat, fishing off a rock point. Maybe twenty-five yards out.

Two men sat at a picnic table on the other side of the lake, Jim and Moss Terry. They had been trying not to drink heavily, but had bought too much to begin with, had it cold in the cooler, and it was just a little too easy to drain off the bitter beer in the bottom of the can, chuck it into a nearby trash barrel, open another and kill the memory of the taste with an ice-cold stiff swig from the top. Moss Terry was ahead of his friend, but excused it due to having recently given up smoking, and every time his entrail desires would form visions of gray, curling, sweet smoke, he would reach again for a can.

"We should go easier on this stuff," remarked Jim. "It's a poor idea in the morning."

"It's a poor morning," said Moss Terry. "Too blasted hot. Try to keep from blowing that smoke in my face."

"Sorry. This is sure some vacation, I'd say. Been just as well to stay home."

"Relax. When else do you get to drink beer in the morning, safely?"

"I'd give it all—all the beer in the world—to feel one four-pounder bump on the end of my line. Hell, a two-pounder—even one!"

"Fish don't like it when it's this hot. Slows 'em down too much. We'll get some bullheads tonight."

"Bullheads! Drive four hundred miles to catch nigger fish."

"Don't blow smoke in my face."

"Sorry, Moss. Say, look at that poor motherfucker over there, snagged off those rocks."

Across the lake, Wilson, still in the bow of his boat, was standing up, every once in a while heaving backward, bending his rod in a violent arch.

"Only one thing to do with a snag," said Moss, punching triangles into the top of a new can, lefthandedly enjoying the sound. "Bust it off right away. It's never worth the effort of trying to save a couple of stinking five-cent hooks—and can ruin a whole day."

Wilson kept heaving backward every once in a while.

"Must be on the rocks," said Jim.

"Give me a cigarette," said Moss.

"No. Remember what you said—"

"Forget that. Give me a cigarette."

"Nope. You said no matter—"

"Come on, give me a cigarette. What kind of a guy are you, anyhow?"

"One who'd be scared to death to come over to your place for the next month after Cathy found out."

"Look. He sat down." Pointing.

"Probably worn out."

"Pole's still bent over. You'd think he'd let up on it."

"Maybe the sun's got to him. Must be awfully hot out there. Least he could do'd be move his boat around a little."

"I think it has moved, at least from where it was," said Moss.

"Probably straightened up a little toward where he's fastened. He's moving a little bit now. Must be pulling himself over above the snag."

"It's not worth it. As soon as you get hung up, snap it off," said Moss, yanking back in a gesture that snapped an imaginary line.

They were watching Wilson more closely now, noticing without comment the slow progression of his boat past the end of the point, out into the darker water.

"He's not reeling in," said Jim.

"No. It doesn't seem so."

Wilson moved silently out farther into the lake, his pole bent nearly over into the water directly in front of his boat. He trolled in this manner for a distance of several boat lengths, then stopped; here, out in the middle of the lake, he remained motionless for some time, his pole still violently arched over. Then he began moving again, this time clear over to the other side of the lake, where he stopped again.

"Get the glasses," said Moss, and Jim ran over to their car, returning with the binoculars, focusing them as he came.

"His pole's still bent."

"Let me see."

"He's not moving now at all, just sitting there."

"Let me see." Moss snatched the glasses and put them up to his eyes, just at the time when Wilson and his boat began to move again.

"He's off again," said Moss.

By noon Wilson had progressed halfway back around the lake and was headed toward them, stopping every once in a while for undetermined periods of time. A car pulled up alongside their picnic table. "Stay in the car," the driver barked through his opened door as he got out. The faces of six young girls pressed against the glass. A back door flew open. "Stay in, I said," he shouted, and the door reclosed. He came over to Jim and Moss Terry, approaching them with a caution known only to family men. "That fellow out there," he said, "I saw him across the lake. Is that a fish hauling him around?"

"We don't know," said Jim.

"I thought maybe you knew him. He's not from our resort. No one over there knows him." Car doors were opening silently and girls ran in all directions to the lake front.

"Get back in—Oh hell," he grumbled, and began to shuffle back to the car. Moss opened the cooler and held out a cold can of beer to him. He hesitated. "Take it," Moss said. The man looked back to his car and the tired eyes of his wife, sitting alone in the front seat, waiting for him to begin yelling at the children. "Bring her over," said Moss. "Hell, women like beer too." Jim was looking down at the grass. The family man took in one deep breath, wishing in it the drowning death of his whole family, blew it out and called, "Ann, these men here have kindly invited us to have a drink with them." Ann came out of the car and over to the table. "Bring the cheese," he said, and she returned again with a tinfoil-wrapped piece of yellow cheese. He took it from her, put it directly in the middle of the table, unwrapped it and laid an opened pocket knife beside it. Only then did he accept the can of beer, and clearly intended that they would share, he and Ann, instead of each having one. Because of the heat, though, and his overwhelming desire to drink long, satisfying, cold and even slightly manly draughts, they soon accepted another, even though the cheese stayed untouched. The scene was not nearly so terrible, Jim thought, as he had imagined when he had at first seen the girls getting out. They were within shouting distance, playing along the shore, but no problem. Wilson had stopped again during this.

"Go tell them to stay away from the water," Larry Cokeman said quietly to his wife. She got up from the bench and started toward the children. Wilson was moving again toward them, less than fifty yards away, staying in the deeper water away from the shore.

"It beats me," said Jim, looking through the glasses. "He sure doesn't seem too excited."

"Very odd," said Moss.

"You fellows been catching any?" asked Cokeman.

"Not really," said Jim. "It's been awfully slow."

"Same with me," said Cokeman. "Not enough wind to catch fish. You got to have some wind to catch fish."

"Water's too hot," said Moss.

Ann and the six girls were headed toward them.

"If I was a kid," said Jim quickly, "I'd be down there swimming in the water and get away from this heat."

"Wouldn't that be illegal," said Cokeman, "just jumping in any old place along here—without a lifeguard or anything? Somebody'd come along and arrest you."

"Why? It's public property, these lakes. Kids is public too. There ain't no signs anywhere."

Ann returned with the six girls.

"Why don't you girls go put on your suits and get in the water?"

Jumping with excitement, they returned to the car with their mother, made a U turn on the road and headed back toward Wild Pines Resort.

"Only five of them are mine," said Cokeman. "The other one's a neighbor's. Jesus, he sure doesn't seem much excited."

Wilson was coming past them, maybe twenty yards from the shore.

"Hey, do you have a fish?" yelled Cokeman. "Is that a fish pulling you around?"

"Yes," said Wilson. "I got him over by the rock point and he's pulled me clear around the lake."

Jim, Moss Terry and Larry Cokeman ran down to the water, following him along the shore, hollering out to him. Then the giant fish stopped again and lay still on the bottom until after the girls had returned and were splashing in the water near their mother, who lay on her rubber mattress and floated serenely out to the edge of the deep water, gazing up at the clouds, and telling by the voices nearer the shore that all was safe with the girls.

"Drop the anchor, quick!" shouted Moss. "Drop the anchor! Dragging that around'll slow 'em down."

"I'll bust my line that way," said Wilson. "Eight-pound test."

"How deep is he?"

"About a hundred feet."

"A hundred feet!" exclaimed Cokeman. "A northern, huh?"

Moss and Jim tried to look like they weren't standing next to him.

"Catfish," said Wilson, and began moving off.

"It can't be a catfish," whispered Moss. "Too far north. It's got to be a muskie."

"A muskie!" exclaimed Cokeman.

"No, a catfish," called back Wilson. "A mud cat."

"How long?" called Cokeman. "What do you think it weighs?"

"Hard to say," said Wilson.

The three men went back to their bench. Each was trying to picture how big—how it would look—this giant fish down on the bottom, moving when it wanted to, pulling a boat from an eight-pound test line. As they finished the beer, they discussed how it might not be possible to land him at all, given that he could just lie on the bottom and be like a hundred-pound piece of rock. But the vision of what he must look like down on the bottom, the size, and how it might be to see him surface first, filled them with excitement, and they went off into town to buy more beer and get sandwiches for Wilson in case he came by again, and to spread the news. Two carloads of men returned with them from the bar. Other cars were on their way. By the time Wilson's erratic, slow movements had taken him around the lake and back along the southwest shore, there were over twenty people in the water and forty-five along the bank. A plastic bag of sandwiches and two cans of beer, with an opener, were ferried out to him by a young girl on a big, patched inner tube. He answered questions from shore and continued on. Middle afternoon was hotter than noon had been.

Before long, several boats full of fishermen came out to meet him and until 5:30 went around the lake with him, talking of how it might be possible to land the fish, telling fishing stories and taking turns holding on to the pole when the fish was moving, to feel the power. None of the men really wanted to ask to do this—almost an unwritten rule that whoever gets the big one (unless he's a child) is the sole recipient of the fun of landing him. But

Wilson could see how much they wanted to feel the power of the fish, and insisted that they all try it, so long as they were in the bow of the boat and did not pull on the line—just feel the strength as he swam. Moss Terry was the only one who refused to take a turn. "I've felt 'em before," he said and wouldn't go up to the bow. All of them tried to figure how the monster could be landed: perhaps they might feed a light chain and grappling hook down the line and try to snag him under the mouth, or they might get a net and, judging from where Wilson thought he was (according to the amount of line out), settle it down on him from another boat moving at the same speed. But by 5:30 the fun was gone for most of them, and they became as straight-faced about it as Wilson himself. One boat went back in. The other knot of fishermen waited forty-five minutes and followed, leaving Wilson a Thermos of coffee, a steak sandwich, apples and chocolate.

Except for Wilson and one other, evening found the lake deserted, the water ruffled slightly by a ground breeze. The sun crossed a mystical line above the horizon and the air immediately began to cool. The smell of the pines became noticeable. The water became darker and looked wetter . . . loons on the surface and whippoorwills in the timber.

Darkness fell. Wilson was coming around again toward the southwest shore. His fish had been stopping more often, and for longer intervals. But now he was running again. Alone, Moss Terry sat at the picnic table, a pale fire burning beside him to keep off the bugs, smoking cigars without inhaling them. No one else on or beside the lake. Then Wilson felt his pole go limp. He's turned, he thought, and pulled and reeled. Nothing. The weightless line fed into the spool. He reeled until the hook came up out of the water and caught in the end eye. Putting the pole down, he took up the oars and rowed to shore, where Moss Terry helped him out of the boat. They wedged the anchor among the shore rocks and went up to the table. Wilson paced to loosen his stiff muscles.

"Line bust?" asked Terry.

"No. He just shook it loose."

"Must have been something to feel him hit. What was it like when you first knew you had 'im?"

"It wasn't like you might think. See, as soon as I knew it was a fish and not a rock or log, I knew I'd never be able to land him. He was just too big."

"But you have to try."

"But you have to try."

"I know," said Moss. "I had one like that several years ago—just knew it was too big. . . . You don't really think it was a catfish, do you?"

"Couldn't have been anything else."

"It could've been a muskie."

"I don't know much about muskies," said Wilson. "But I'd think it wouldn't act like that."

"More of a fighting fish."

"Exactly. . . . You live around here?"

"No. I live in Ottumwa."

"Oh, really? I'm from Iowa, too. Say, you know where we might find some bullheads?"

"Not for sure, but they say there's a bridge down a ways on the creek where they get 'em."

"The creek off this lake?"

"Yep."

"Do you feel like going down there?"

"Sure. Want to take the car?"

"I don't care. But I shouldn't leave the boat here on the rocks."

"OK, let's take the boat."

Moss went to get his tackle and they set off across the lake, slicing through the cool air and water and night sounds, dangerously, without a front light, propelled by a three-and-a-half-horsepower motor.

Unlike his parents, July was not a sound sleeper. He accepted it as nothing unnatural to be woken in the middle of the night by the smallest sliver of noise, or an internal twitch that would hurl him from unconsciousness and into his room. Whatever fear he might have felt at those times—at the very edge of awakening—was quickly dissolved merely by mentally locating his parents, who like silent fighters would come galloping into the room of his emotions, driving the Dark Powers back beyond the walls. He would lie there and listen, and sometimes fall back asleep. Frequently he would get up, go out into the hall, past his parents' room and downstairs—sometimes to eat, and sometimes to sit in the living room, from where he could look outside at the illuminated crossroads, hoping to see an automobile with its red taillights come up, stop and disappear, wondering what mysterious purpose could be inside—what kind of face would belong to the driver—what sad, doomed circumstances awaited his arrival.

Many of these times he shared with his grandmother, and in the summer they would carefully go out onto the porch and sit without talking, drinking glasses of milk or Kool-Aid, until he'd be told to return to bed. With great reluctance, he would leave her and go up and lie hardly breathing, wanting to hear when she came back inside. He didn't talk of these times, not because they were in themselves particularly private, but because everything is private to a child.

So he knew (without really knowing), long before either of his parents, of Della's insomnia. Naturally, he didn't think to himself, Grandma has insomnia; in fact, he probably didn't think anything at all; he just came to take it for granted that whenever he might come downstairs at night she would be sitting in the living room and he would wonder what she was doing in there by herself.

"Why doesn't Grandma ever turn the lights on?" he asked his parents one night.

John's face turned ashen. "What do you mean?" he demanded, and July was afraid to answer, and guilt swept over him for saying something he shouldn't have. He stammered, but didn't have to answer because his father went outside, closing the door with a slam. Quickly, Sarah came over and sat beside him on the floor with his truck, and in her silent-fighter voice talked to him, and explained quite clearly and exactly how oldness, old age—that time at the end of a person's long, happy life—that time just before they became dead—made them act in ways different from people who were not at the end of their lives—and that the whole thing, most importantly, the complete overall picture, was good and rejoiceful.

So from this he learned two things: first, everything that he noticed about his grandmother, everything hard to understand, was good; and second, don't talk about her.

That first night when he was introduced to Wilson, he didn't know what to say. He'd come downstairs and was sitting in the living room, waiting for red taillights. Della had come in from the porch, whispering and talking as though she were not alone. Noticing him, she had come over and said that Wilson was tired and couldn't stay up much longer. July's imagination ran wild, but still he could find nothing to fasten it to. For a moment he was frightened, because he didn't know how to act with this dead person in the room. But he learned that the presence of Wilson was no threat to him; in fact, he was much like July's own *imaginary* persons: he was not expected to talk, or have a mind worthy of attention, but sometimes it could be assumed that he had opinions; yet mostly he was just there. The difference between Wilson and July's imaginary friends was not to be completely overlooked, though, he felt. Imaginary friends had no true substance, even when they were having opinions. *They* simply weren't there. Anyone would admit that. But Wilson, on the other hand, was of the natural order, and so couldn't be said to be without substance. There were the living, and there were the dead, who might be gone, but who were nevertheless existent.

Della closed the door to her room so that Wilson could sleep.

"Where will *you* sleep?" he asked his grandmother.

"I can sleep here on the couch," she answered. "But, mercy me, with the house so full of people, we better make sure we've got a place, or all the beds will be taken up."

"We could always sleep on the floor, Grandma," he said, wishing they would have to. It reminded him of stories of people fighting for their lives.

"We may have to," said Della.

"Let's do."

"Not until we have to."

The next time he had come down, there was no mention of Wilson—only the ever present reference to him in *we* did this, *we* thought that was funny, *we* were never so frightened.

But there was also a sadness, a deep, impenetrable sadness which filled her that night—a loneliness that his own companionship could not relieve or even dent. He felt helpless, worthless and of no good at all. Della talked strangely of people and things that would blend into each other. "My whole life," she said, "has been three Sharon Centers: the Sharon Center when we lived at the store, the Sharon Center when we lived in the country and the Sharon Center here. All three of them."

Once, standing out by the bird feeder, looking at the little town, she had said, "This town is me." July had heard her. Whenever he could, he went with her about the house and yard. Some days her visitors would fill the house to its seams—people who to July looked like ancient, withered figures of wood, smelling of age and inching along imperceptibly, talking, talking, talking. He would never forget that. *This town is me.* Sometimes an old gent would come over, held together by the cracks in his face and his unflinching interest in the past, and three days later there'd be his funeral to go to. (July didn't go to funerals, because his father said it wouldn't be good for him and would even drive him home after church, if the funeral was afterward, and return without him—just so he would miss it.) "It's not good to know much about death," he heard him say to his mother, "before it makes sense."

"I agree, John," she said. "I agree. Take him home."

"Good God, it doesn't make sense, Sarah. It never makes sense. I can remember when Dad and Mom—"

"Yes it does, don't think about it now. You're tired."

That was all July heard then.

The front door gave the slightest bang, and July sat up in bed. Nearly a full moon outside, the ground silver with frost. He got up and went quickly downstairs. The door to his grandmother's room stood wide open, the bed empty and flat. He went through the porch and looked outside. Della was crossing the road. He ran barefoot after her, careful not to let her hear him. The cold was not noticeable in his excitement.

Della walked across the intersection, her feet leaving dark prints on the road. She went into the Collins's yard and up to the house. She stood for a moment in front, then went around to the side and let herself in. July caught up to her halfway through the cluttered, foul-smelling living room and, all his life having been afraid of the people who lived there, took hold of her arm and whispered, "Grandma, Grandma, come back home." She turned and looked at him as if he weren't there, moving her mouth imperceptibly, knocking over a straight-backed chair. They were locked fast where they stood, she in a spell of her own and he in fear. There was a noise. Then another. Old man Collins, wearing a pair of pants, came out of a door. "What the hell!" he said in a deep, menacing voice. July pulled on his grandmother's arm, but she was like a half-driven nail.

"You shouldn't be in here." Della spoke in her own, unhurried voice. July let go of her. "This room is too cold. The wind comes through the wall."

Old man Collins had come over to them; July started to come between him and his grandmother, but stopped. Collins's voice, as he recognized them, was no longer menacing but unbelievably tender—more unexpected to July than if he had taken out a gun and shot them both.

"Ma'am," he said. "It must have slipped your mind, but you don't live here any more. You ain't lived here for years—way back since this was a store. The front room's been torn down. Years ago."

"You shouldn't be in here," said Della, looking from him to July. "This room's too cold to sleep in. The wind comes through the wall. Despite the tape, you can't keep the wind out." She looked at the space the door would have occupied if it had been closed, not seeing through to outside.

"Ma'am," he began again, "you don't live here now. I'm old man Collins. Your house is across the street. You better be gettin' on back now or somebody's going to be gettin' worried about you."

Then it slowly happened that Della became aware of her error, her momentary jog in time. She realized it, but not like waking up from a dream—more like realizing within a dream that she was dreaming.

"I'm sorry," she said, and stood staring at the walls.

"Hell," said old man Collins, "it doesn't make no difference to me. Any time you want to come over, just come on over. But why don't you let this boy here take you on back now—or maybe I better call up Mr. Montgomery. Do your parents know your grandma's out of the house, boy?"

July was trying to speak, but all of a sudden Della turned directly around, as fast as an insulted soldier in uniform, her thin body sticking out of her nightgown in legs no bigger around than arms, and marched out the door. "Come on, Wilson," she called to July.

Later, back in the house, she said to him, "I know you're not Wilson. I know who you are and that you think Wilson isn't here. But don't you see it matters to me?" Again the loneliness and the deep, layered sadness.

"Milk, Grandma," said July. "Let's get some milk."

July looked upon the memory of this night with some hostility, and for several weeks running he waited out his waking hours upstairs and did not venture down for fear he would again find her going out across the yard. He excused this behavior because of not hearing any noises. But when one night he clearly heard the front door *bang,* he knew he'd have to get up. Once out beyond his room he felt the grip of helplessness, and knocked on his parents' door. His father came immediately out into the hall in his pajama trousers, his bare arms powerful and the muscles in his shoulders standing out like hammered iron. "Grandma," said July, and his father ran downstairs, waiting neither for more information nor for him to follow. One look at her opened door and the unruffled bed and John was out into the yard, just in time to see her go into the house across the street.

By the time July got there his father was carrying her as weightlessly as if she were a large, realistic doll, her head moving from time, to time, staring. When she looked at July, he felt as though he were standing in someone else's body, so completely did the gaze un-know him. Old man Collins, again with his sympathetic voice, was saying to John, "No, it ain't any bother. We was just talkin' the other night 'bout how hard it'd be on—"

"If she ever comes over again," his father brutally cut him off, "call me. Daytime, nighttime, call me. Don't talk to her. Call me." Then he left. Old man Collins looked hurt, and closed the door. It seemed to July that his father must have hated Collins; it seemed as though that was the only explanation, so from that moment on, July hated him too, and hated his children, Everett and Loren, and hated his cats and the heap of junk of a car he drove.

This was when Della's arteries began to harden. John took her to doctors in Iowa City. He slept on the sofa at night, and chased her back into her room whenever she came out. He refused to let her talk to him as if he were Wilson (something everyone else tolerated, even Mrs. Miller, of whom they said she wouldn't let her own father use the name of anyone dead while in her presence). "You're confused, Mom," he would tell her. "Get hold of yourself"—as though all she needed to do was shake herself and the layers of years would fall off like the skin of a lizard.

Remington Hodge's father explained: "That was John's undoing. All of us have our undoing—some more than others, some less, but that's not the point. What's important is that everyone has things which they can't deal with reasonably. A more reasonable man than John would be hard to find—so reasonable that he seldom was able to choose sides. But the business with his mother reduced him to having no sense. He chose sides then, it might be said, but unreasonably, putting himself at odds with nature itself. See, he acted like he had no intention whatsoever of granting that everything must have an end. His reason simply failed him there, and he would chase off to Iowa City and lead doctors back to his mother by the throat, demanding that they put an end to her ailment, and they would tell him, sometimes right in front of her, 'There's nothing wrong but age. You're getting along in your years, Mrs. Montgomery.' And she would smile as though having received a compliment on a new hat. But John would shake in rage. 'What do you mean!' he would demand. 'No one dies of old age. It's *something wrong* that takes them, some malfunction. Fix it.'

"But, like I say, that shouldn't be held against anyone, because we all have our undoings—where reason'll be cast to the wind. And don't misunderstand me, I'm not saying here that I admire that or that it impresses me; for instance, in the case of my Aunt Winifred, who let the business with Jack and that girl from Plainsville poison her whole life. In fact, if there's any principle to live by, it would be reason—live reasonably; a hundred times a day one should stop and ask, 'Is this reasonable, what I'm doing?' There simply can't be enough reasonableness in someone's life."

Despite John's unceasing refusal to let it happen, his mother slid away one night in her sleep, and he found her curled up, the quilt tucked under her chin, the next morning. At first he didn't react to it at all, closed the door and sat down on the twisted sheets and blankets covering the sofa. Then, when his true feelings began to clear in him, he had a terrific urge to drink, and went to the kitchen in search of a bottle. Underneath the sink, he thought. But there was none. He thought when he'd last seen it—the bottle of 86-proof bourbon. Then he remembered that he'd given it away. How long? Yes, that would have been to Myra's boy—fourteen years ago. The realization let another increment of his true feelings loose, and he started back toward the couch. But the full impact came sooner than he expected, and he didn't make it. As he looked at the door to his mother's room, the thunderhead inside him ripped open. The downpour temporarily blinded him in deep purple, tears flowed like water on his face, and holding his shaking hand out toward the wall to support him, he cried like an animal shot through the stomach.

Sarah and July came downstairs and it was hours before the shaking subsided.

Later, after the funeral, July heard him say, "When I was a little boy, I used to lie in bed and imagine that my parents were dead. That very thought terrified me. They told me, 'It's just a make-believe worry. We'll always be here,' and that comforted me. But now it's just like it happened then. It could be no worse. . . . Who will take care of me now?"

July's only real interest in his grandmother's death was in the mechanics of it. He had wanted to (though he didn't) go into her room and look at her—if, indeed, she was still there—to see if she looked any different. Sarah told him that "Grandma's body—her dead body—is all that's left. Grandma herself is gone." So he knew that behind the door lay something, but that something wasn't his grandma. Then at the funeral he got to see into the casket, and he wasn't nearly as horrified as he had thought he might be, looking at a personless body. The unrealness of death—the chalk color and closed eyes—was so completely uninteresting. He realized Della couldn't possibly be lying on the pink pillow, which had been his only fear—that somehow everyone was wrong and she hadn't been able to get away and was imprisoned inside her dead self. But he could see that wasn't true, and he could see everyone else at the funeral knew that (except maybe his father). The minister talked of heaven and Della being with Wilson, herald angels and the mansion in the sky. Naturally, July accepted it all.

For several weeks, maybe as long as several months, he was troubled by his father, who didn't at all seem to be acting in accordance with the way things were. He acted oddly, as though he hadn't even known Della was just an old lady and was ready to die soon, and now she had and that was good. July could see no reason to be very upset—not nearly so upset as when their cat had been run over. Old people die and that's that. But his father acted as though he didn't know that.

Then slowly the depression lifted, and the face shadow, which had at one time been dark gray, turned ashen, but never went away. From that time on, the past had hold of John, and though he could still be "reasonable," he no longer desired to go forward. He wanted to go back. Instead of creating, he wanted to recapture. Instead of dreaming, he wanted to remember.

Many times during those first several months John took time off from work to be with his family—even afternoons when he refused to return to the garage after lunch, though his lot was filled with people waiting for him. He gave up working Saturdays altogether. He told July, then seven and a half, of a man named Kingfisher. They'd gone for a ride and stopped just before dark in a small diner in Liberty. John ordered a cup of coffee and the tired waitress brought that and a strawberry malted milk to their square, mean table next to the window. The blue star of lights above the diner reflected onto them from a silent pool of rainwater next to their car in the gravel parking lot. A young couple by the jukebox hollered at each other and played records. The waitress smoked cigarettes down to her fingers at the counter.

The cook, her broad forehead covered with sweat, took the stone to the grill.

"I can remember my father telling me about a man his father had told him about," John said, in the same quiet voice he'd been using all afternoon. July sat, taking it all in, the voice, the words, the reflection, the music, the smoke and the cold, wonderful taste of the malt up through two paper straws which he held in his mouth like fangs.

". . . named Kingfisher. I guess he was born somewhere in the East, Connecticut or Rhode Island, and it was suspected that his mother had been part, if not all, Indian. The first time someone tried to kill him he was ten years old. His dad was a foreman of a crew of indentured lumberjacks—prisoners, that is they were, men who were brought over to this country to work. America was so wild then that the only thing that lay between them and freedom was a matter of several miles of forest. One morning some of these fellows got a chance to overcome a guard and get rid of their irons. Another guard came out of the underbrush unexpectedly and three of them were shot before they overpowered him. They wanted food more than guns, and they figured to make it to the foreman's cabin near the settlement, get the stuff and hightail it west. They didn't plan on Kingfisher's father being there, and he got more of them before they came in, and the sight of the blood and their desperate hope of escaping filled them with reckless, unreasonable ferocity. One of them saw the small boy running out toward the settlement through the trees. 'Get him,' said the leader, and two of the escapees took after him with a double-edged ax, two knives and a muzzle-loaded hand gun.

"Hearing them behind him (and knowing he could be outrun), he left the well-worn path. He went for the settlement by relying on his size and ability to scramble through the brush and briers and fallen trees. He went on wildly, thorns cutting into his face and hands without his noticing. He could hear them crashing behind him but falling behind farther. He ran on, feeling he'd make it. The ground grew rockier, rising sharply. He went up, and then discovered that he'd trapped himself. Ahead, directly down from him, was a sheer drop of more than thirty feet. There was no way to turn back without running toward the noise of the men. He looked around, wanting more than anything to begin crying, his heart pounding like a warring drum. The crashing came closer. He found a large rock, as big around as a muskmelon, pried it loose from the ground and began climbing up a maple tree, placing the rock up before him on each succeeding branch. He climbed as far as he could before he saw the men, then stopped and tried to hug close to the trunk.

" 'Look, he must be around here,' shouted one of them, between panting. 'No one could get down there,' and he motioned to the drop-off.

"Kingfisher watched them walk beneath his tree, going over to the edge.

" 'He's around here,' said the other. 'Go back and make sure we didn't miss him and he isn't sneaking back down.'

" 'No, he's around here close by. Has to be. We'd hear him—'

" 'Go on down and check, you idiot. If he gets—'

" 'OK, OK.' The one with the ax went back down. The other walked along the rim of the ledge, making sure there was no way down and hoping to find him tucked away behind a stump or log. After the time it took to fully regain his breath, going on a hunch, he went back and started, methodically, to check the ground for signs, thinking, If the little fool was running, we'd hear 'im. He wasn't that far ahead. The idea came to him, just at the moment he saw the matted underbrush around the tree, that he might be up there . . . and he looked up maybe one full second before the muskmelon-sized rock, dropped from twenty feet in the air, smashed his head. Kingfisher scrambled down the tree and peeled the pistol from the man's hand, stepping on and off his wrist to make death release its hold. Already he could hear the other man coming back.

"He ran to the edge of the ledge and hid behind an obvious rock, and—he couldn't help it—began to cry.

"The sight of more blood brought the urgency of the situation back to the remaining escapee. The fear of capture and inevitable doom. These things and the ever louder sound of the boy's hysterical crying unfortunately made him forget about the gun, and he went over. With his eyes watery and his nose running, sitting down, Kingfisher shot him. . . ."

John went on talking in detail, leaving his coffee untouched. But July wasn't listening closely any more. His attention had been rerouted into the image of Kingfisher behind the rock, crying uncontrollably, holding a gun with a hole in the barrel as big around as an eye. And though he continued drinking the malt up into both sides of his mouth, staring straight forward, his head was completely taken over by the scene. Behind the rock, a character half himself and half a wild, dark-skinned ten-year-old, holding that gun and crying and then letting him have it. His interest wandered back again just as John was saying, ". . . so the mayor was explaining to his marshal that Kingfisher, then eighteen years old, had been seen sleeping in the canyon and that he was to go get him and, if he was alive, take him over to Carson City, when the marshal took off his gun belt and badge and put them on the desk. 'I quit.' " Then July's head refilled with the image of behind the rock—only this time it was totally himself that crouched there crying.

". . . they sent twenty men on horses out into the hills after him, hoping to recover the money and collect the state's reward. They had no intention of bringing him back alive, and had food and ambition enough to be gone several months. They assumed Kingfisher would not expect so many, and that they would have a chance to get a couple of slugs into the gray before he could begin his run. The excitement was like a fever. After several days they located him and he began to run. Two days later they had him trapped somewhere in Plum Valley, his horse dead. The twenty riders formed a line, not more than thirty yards between each man, like for driving deer, and started into the valley. Four hours later, two of them rode out, one with a bullet in his chest. The other one, just as they were leaving the valley, looked back and for the first time in his life saw the great Kingfisher, on foot, leading one of their horses, going up into the hills, a rifle on his shoulder and a dagger which reflected the sunlight in his hand.

"He was a killer," his father explained. "In his life he killed more than a hundred men. You shouldn't get the wrong image of him: he was nothing to admire. He was an outlaw, and so the least of all kinds of persons to admire, but it's interesting how even in such a low, low person—how his life can be kind of an inspiration—but only in idea—only in idea. Killing is the ugliest thing in the world. But if you don't think about that—if you just think of the strength—the unyielding cunning to stay alive at all costs, against all odds. He was in prison once where he went a week without water, and when they took him out and let him walk along the wall—this was in New York—he saw ten thousand people, all of them come to see him die. They gave him some water and led him back to the cell (he wasn't going to be hanged until that afternoon) and he got away. He got away! It's unbelievable! Maybe it's because we all have a private fantasy of doing something unbelievable—at just the moment when everyone else has given us up, when the odds are ten thousand to one, to snap out and unbelievably get away. How sweet life must seem after that! And a legend like Kingfisher is only an attempt to capture that sweetness. Oh, they had him there, right there in the prison—can't you imagine it?—this fellow who's nearly sixty—who's never been caught before—and he gets away!"

John got up and went over to the cash register. The tired waitress squashed out the last quarter-inch of her cigarette and came over. Behind the counter, she lit another. He put a fifty-cent piece on the rubber mat. Thirty-five cents came up at the top of the register.

"Say, mister," she said, blowing smoke through her words, "that was some story, about that Kingfisher." She handed him back fifteen cents in yellow fingers. "Come again."

The cook turned. "Stop flirting," she said, and swatted her on the rump. They looked at each other and laughed and looked at John.

"Thank you," he said, blushed and quickly left.

SIX

The Funeral—1953

July was sitting on the porch looking through the screen, and then at it, wondering how he was able to see the square wire holes so clearly and at the same time see through to the lawn as though there were nothing there. The memory of the last four days was a blur. The square holes. The lawn. He was becoming afraid again. He rocked the swing harder, and made himself do two things: look at the wire holes and review what he had done that morning, from the moment he'd gotten out of bed for the last time. *I went over to the window. No, first I put on a shirt—the red one—no, it was green, corduroy—my favorite—can hide in trees with it and no one can see me. Dad always said . . . Dad always said—I went over to the window and looked out. Swallows and flies. I went back and sat on the bed. Put on my socks. Red. Saw the drawer and took out my junk box. I looked at the beebees, chrome buttons, keys, padlock . . . padlock . . . padlock . . . yellow dog chain, broken knife, beer opener.* He felt the fear subside and allowed his vision to wander from the screen, outside, inside, around the porch. Red. The shirt was red. The green one was in a lump on the floor. *I'd forgotten that,* he thought. *I'd forgotten that because*—Then he was afraid again and went back to the screen. *I went over to the window. Swallows and flies. I breathed against the window and drew a circle with my finger. I put a dot in the middle. I sat down on my bed. My socks are red. My shirt is red, the green one on the floor. Hiding in trees. Then I put on the other sock and the drawer was open. I took out my junk box—*

"Here, July," spoke his Aunt Becky, her fleshy arms big all the way to the shoulders, "you must have something to eat. A person can't go without food. You must eat something." She carried out a tray and set it next to him on the swing, after stopping its motion with the side of her hip. July stared at the sandwiches and Jell-O and looked back to the screen. "Now, I want some of that eaten by the time I get back," she continued, kindly, but as though she would take no monkey business either. Then she stayed for a silent moment longer and went back inside, leaving the door open. He was glad when she was gone. She made him feel small. Until four days ago he'd never seen her—or didn't remember. It wasn't that he didn't like her, or that he was incapable of recognizing the kindness . . . only that he felt he was being watched naked. In fact, he'd liked her from the first moment, but it was irrelevant: his understanding went deeper.

Four days ago. He got off the schoolbus. There was a car in the driveway. He didn't know who it belonged to. Inside were Mr. and Mrs. Binford, whom he'd never seen outside Sunday mornings at the church. They stood up when he came in and looked as though they'd been interrupted while stealing silverware. He thought they must owe his father money and were waiting for his mother to come out of the bathroom. He took the square-folded lunch sack out of his back pocket and put it on the kitchen table. He wondered if the Binfords would be like his friends at school—would think it was the mark of poverty to have to save your sack and not squash it up in a ball with the waxpaper and half a sandwich inside and throw it in the trash. (Actually, no one had ever said it, but he knew what they thought. He'd told it to his mother and she had said, "Foolishness," and that had been the end of it.) Usually he would try to fold it up when no one was looking, but out of pride would not do this if it took much effort. The Binfords were talking nervously together and they came into the kitchen. He had the feeling that his mother wasn't in the bathroom. Like suspected thieves, they talked to him about school. He opened the refrigerator and looked for last night's dessert—black-bottom pie. But even the plate was gone. So were the potato chips from under the counter. July was beside himself with how to be rid of the Binfords. Finally, he could stand it no longer and in the living room called "Mom" at the top of his lungs, both as a statement that it wasn't his responsibility to entertain them, and in the hope that she was upstairs somewhere and would come down. But she didn't, and they came rushing back into the living room. "Your mother isn't here," said Mr. Binford, and seated himself nervously, absurdly, on the couch. "She won't be coming back," said Mrs. Binford. *"She's dead,"* they said together. "They're both dead," said Mr. Binford alone. Then Mrs. Binford sat down beside her husband and they folded their hands and looked as they did in church. The telephone rang, and they both jumped. July sat looking out the window, and heard the receiver taken up—then murmured talking from Della's old bedroom—as far away as the cord would reach. *The first time anyone tried to kill him he was ten years old.* Then the receiver was put back.

Whenever he turned and looked at them, they were sitting in church, hands folded. Four hours passed. It became dark outside. Mrs. Binford turned on a light, on low beam, and went back to looking without direction. Finally, a car came into the driveway. The lights were shut off. Walking sounds. A knock on the door. The Binfords opened it together. Mumbled talking. Then his Aunt Becky burst into the room wearing a light green dress, her voice loud. "All right," she said. "Are you July?"

He nodded his head.

"Good. I'm pleased to meet you. I'm Becky, your Aunt Becky. I came as quickly as I heard. God, it's like a dungeon in here." She ran around snapping on lights. The Binfords were watching her from next to the opened door. "Go on now," she said to them. "July and I will manage just fine. Get on out of here." They inched their way out and Aunt Becky gently slammed the door as soon as they were in the yard. "Now!" She sat down fatly on the sofa. "We must get things straight. First, as I guess you know, your parents have both been killed—in an automobile accident. Second, it was nobody's fault, but that doesn't matter. He was my brother. My name's Becky Frunt. My husband Perry will be here for the funeral. At that time we'll decide whether or not to live here. But don't think about that now. You'll live with us whatever, and get along fine. We have one girl, but she's ten years older than you and will be going away to college in the fall. You'll stay home from school until after the funeral, then you'll be going back. Until then there are many things to be done. First, where's your room? . . . No, later. Have you eaten?" July shook his head. "Then we'll have to make dinner, won't we?" He nodded, and they went into the kitchen.

After dinner, though July didn't eat because he couldn't swallow, they went up to his room with a white ball of string. Together they strung the string from the corner of his bed, across the hall into the guest room, up to the ceiling and to a small brass bell above the guest bed. "There," said Aunt Becky when they were finished. July had looked several times at her enormous rear end. "Now, if you need anything you can just pull the string. OK. Fine. Do you have any games?" They went downstairs and July got out a Clue set and they played until far after midnight. She won nearly every game.

He was eternally grateful for her, and during those four days as he came out of shock and into the horror of understanding, she was always there with this and this and this that had to be done. "Now we must clean the living room." "Now we must do the dishes." "Now we must go to the store, bring the bottles." "Now we must go for a walk." "Now we must play Canasta." "Now we must write letters—you too."

But today she seemed tired. July picked up one of the sandwiches and opened it. Chicken salad. He put it back together and took a bite, but couldn't swallow. Then the longer it stayed, half chewed, in his mouth, the more the nausea grew. He looked behind him for fear Aunt Becky was watching. She wasn't. With his fingers he took out the mutilated piece and threw it to the other side of the porch. Then he began ripping the sandwich and putting it into his pants pocket. Even doing this, he was watchful for her. Later she came back out and took the tray inside, looking at it with suspicion. He could tell she was worried today. But he didn't care. She was irrelevant.

A blue car pulled up front. Three people got out. The man and the woman he recognized. They were his Aunt and Uncle Montgomery. The other man he'd never seen before. He wore a straw hat with a band around the bottom of the crown, and chewed an unlit cigar. His Uncle Sid talked intently to Aunt Franny as they came up the walk. The stranger lagged behind, looking at the house and lawn as though someone were trying to sell it to him and he didn't want to look either impressed or completely disenchanted . . . skeptical. All three showed signs of having ridden a long way.

Uncle Sid and Aunt Franny introduced themselves with great solemnity and deliberation. Once again he felt the nagging question: How are you making it?—searching his face for signs of how he wasn't making it at all, of how the horror had ruined him. *The first time anyone tried to kill him* . . . Everyone, it seemed, wanted to be able to be looking right at him just when he exploded. Then the stranger was introduced. Uncle Perry, Becky's husband. He tipped his hat and took the unlit cigar out of his mouth for an instant as a gesture of his good will. Then went quickly back to surveying the house for structural flaws and other indications of its retail value. July said nothing to any of them. He was learning, among many other things, that he had an excuse to ignore people—an excuse that they accepted as well as he needed.

They went into the house and left him alone. From inside he could hear his Aunt Becky's voice raised to an insidious, loud whisper. "You miserable wretch. The *least* you could have done would be to put on a coat. Get rid of that cigar. . . ." He let the words pass through his hearing like the sounds of nature—meaningless and irrelevant. They had no more importance to him than the stupid birds on the birdbath: he cared nothing for them—nothing. He began rocking again, and pretended that a place in the screen where several strands of wire had been torn was a gunsight, and every time he came forward and the sight lined up in his vision with the bird-bath he would squeeze a soft, terrible trigger inside his stomach and blow them apart with tumbling lead slugs. By moving his head a little to one side, just at the time when the sight was lined up, he could get them all. Feathers and blood all over the yard. Then they flew away and the fear returned. *I got out of bed. I put on my shirt. My red shirt. I went over to the window. I drew a hole with a dot in it. The hole disappeared first. Then the dot. I went over to my bed and sat down. I did not pull the string. I could hear . . .*

An hour before the funeral Aunt Becky came and told him to get dressed. He went upstairs and found his suit laid out on the bed, clean socks, a white shirt, clean underwear, and even his shoes polished. The floor had been dusted with a dry mop. His box of junk was neatly put back in the drawer. He went over to his window and looked out. Footsteps in the hall. Someone came into his room and stood there. He did not turn around. At first he felt the presence staring at the back of his head, pushing his face against the window. Then he decided that there wouldn't be anyone there—that as far as he was concerned he would be alone in his room—he would not only refuse to answer, he would not even hear the question. He felt a pleasant, restful sensation of this solitude filling him. He stood inside his bone sanctuary until he'd completely forgotten about no one else being in the room, and when he turned there was no one. As he put on his clothes he thought for an instant: *Now, wait a minute—someone was in here,* but he stopped. They were irrelevant. They had no importance. Then for the first time (though for only a fleeting second) he thought of his parents in such a way that he wasn't frightened. He thought of them as being still alive somewhere, like just in the next room reading or talking inaudibly, thinking about him. But soon came the image of them riding in the car on some white road slick with frogs, black oil blood in the steaming radiator wreckage . . . and he wished he were dead. *The first time anyone tried to kill him he was ten years old.*

They all went together in one car to the funeral. No one talked. His new Uncle Perry had been drinking. It was hot. July made himself become part of the moving landscape.

The parking lot of the church was filled. Cars were stopped on the road and people in dark clothes walked along the ditch. Two long black cars with gray curtains on steel rails pointed outward, opened in the rear, less than a heavy stone's throw from the iron railing of the front step. The naked sun nailed July's eyes.

The lush smell of bought, manicured flowers filled the church. He was squeezed in between his two aunts, the third row back from the altar. Beyond the first row were two caskets, lids down. The room (though he had been in it every Sunday since he could remember) seemed twice or three times as large, the people larger, the stained-glass windows as big as a house, the altar like a mausoleum. An undertaker unclipped the little chain at the end of their pew, let himself in and refastened it, causing the small plaque suspended in the middle to swing. re- served for family. He inched over to Uncle Sid. They talked in short, breathless whispers. Once his uncle gestured to the cas- kets. The undertaker held his hand down several feet from the floor, as though indicating water level. His uncle smiled. They shook hands and the undertaker went outside the aisle, walked around the front, surveying the crowd like a large, unruly family, then went back toward the entrance hallway, where he met an- other undertaker and disappeared. Finally, as the silence became deafening, the minister came out and, with a white fleshy hand gesture, brought the group to a standing position. The organist hit a sinking chord and hymn number 107 tonelessly filled the air. July could feel Aunt Becky singing, her great sides heaving, but he could not find her voice in the sound. He felt very small. Then the minister let them down with his hands.

July began to reason. He realized that ever since he'd come home from school four days ago he hadn't had a reasonable thought about anything. Now he was beginning to put things together. It was the tone of the minister's voice that first presented a clue. It was deep and sincere, emotional and slow—but many of the phrases jolted July. He'd heard them before—sitting with his parents, he'd heard them before—shutting his eyes and leaning his head against his father's hard arm, *he'd heard them before.* The realization was like a slap in the face. He listened to the voice more closely: it was the same voice, a little slower maybe, and more deliberate, but that was pretense . . . the voice was the same! He quickly looked to his Aunt Becky. Her eyes were lowered to the floor as though wrapped in prehistoric thought. But he could see—he could tell that the full importance of the caskets and who was in them had not even bruised her and never would. Snapped thoughts yammered through him. He stole a quick, furtive look behind him and sat for long afterward with the vivid impression of the faces. Sad faces. But he could see . . . he could tell. There was only one person there who thought something was *wrong,* and that was him. One lady next to the organist stood up and began a song, then had to sit back down when her voice choked her. But no one besides himself felt there was anything wrong—terribly unfortunate, *but not wrong.* The old world was still clicking away. Waves of understanding passed through him.

I was deceived, he thought. *Somehow, though the blame is mostly mine, I was deceived into believing nothing terrible would ever happen to me. Everyone else knew . . . that all it takes is one bit of bad luck—the tiniest quirk of fate, and zip, bring in two caskets,* if the little fool was running, we'd hear 'im. He believed he understood why everyone seemed to be staring at him—it wasn't that they wanted him to explode before their eyes—it was just a casual interest in if he was a fool or if he wasn't. Just curiosity. *Look in his eyes and see if he's one of the fools, the halfwits, who believe nothing bad is ever going to happen to them—who believe their parents will live forever.*

Then the minister called for a moment of silence, broken shortly by the sinking sounds of the organ. The feet began shuffling. The church filed out with low, murmured talking.

Soon the long, black-headed snake line was curling its way over to the cemetery, where from just over the top of the hill you could make out the imported angel. An opened book at her feet contained a short quotation from a letter John had sent to Becky several years ago: *No one could be happier than we are. Today, the twenty-first of April, there are over two hundred birds in our yard, each one singing and eating from our three feeders like there was no tomorrow.*

"That's some stone," said Uncle Perry, and Sid smiled as though he'd made it himself. Clearly, there was nothing anywhere near its size—a giant among tombstones.

July was glad he was able to leave before they began filling in the dirt.

That night, at the table with Becky, Perry, Aunt Franny and Uncle Sid, he ate something.

"Tomorrow you must go back to school," he was told. He spent the rest of the evening in his room reading comic books. Most of them he'd read before, but some were new, presents from the parents of his school friends. He read both the new and the old with the same enjoyment. He let the words run slowly into sentences and understood them with little interest. He let the pictures flash onto an opaque screen just in front of his mind—an area where there was almost no thought—looked at them one at a time, then let them disappear. He realized that he was reading only at the beginning and end of each book. He read a *Bible Stories* comic (something which he normally could hardly stand) three times, and even then realized that once again he'd missed the plot. Who was the rightful king? And whose fault really was it that Saul was the way he was? And what could possibly be wrong in letting your enemy live and in not slaughtering his animals but giving them to your own men to feed their hungry families?

Then he undressed and went to bed. He listened to the talking downstairs, but couldn't understand it. He knew they were being especially quiet so that he wouldn't hear. His parents used to talk down there and he could hear every word. He lay awake until after Sid and Franny Montgomery's car had left and Becky and Perry turned out all the lights and shut the door of the guest room. He wondered if the string would still pull the bell, or if the top of the door would squeeze it tight.

Then he began to think again of what a fool he'd been, and imagined what going back to school would be like. He pictured himself coming home from school, his friends on the bus, old man Collins's cats and the front yard. He went on picturing these things until an arc of electrical understanding flashed across his mind: they were trying to fool him again. All of them. Everyone he knew was trying to make him into a fool again. They were trying to make everything easy for him so that he could forget, and within a year maybe—the time didn't matter—he would have forgotten. He would be so happy that he'd be set up again . . . believing again nothing bad will ever happen to me. No! he decided. I'll never forget. *Just at that point when they think they've got you, when the odds are ten thousand to one, to get away!* He slipped out of bed, dressed, took all the money he had in his bank, $12.43, his jacket, his father's pocket knife, a small automatic pistol he'd taken a month ago from among his mother's things in the attic and kept hidden in the bottom of his drawer to take out to look at when he was alone and wonder how she'd ever come upon it, eight shells, the ring of keys for good luck, a dark blue stocking hat, a billfold full of pictures, and was gone from the house.

Not wanting to be seen close to home—for fear the drivers of the cars would know him—he kept to the ditch all the way to new Highway 1. Twice he had to lie down among the weeds so that the headlights of the pickups would miss him.

Once at the highway he began hitchhiking immediately, and within several cars was given a ride. A middle-aged fat man leaned over with much effort and swung open the door for him. "Kind of late to be out, isn't it?" he asked, and did not start the car rolling.

"I guess so," said July.

"What seems to be the trouble?"

It was an odd moment for July, one in which it seemed things could go one way or another—either end or begin. On one hand there was a true desire to be back, unsuspected, in his room. On the other hand, the very idea of such comfort made him feel sick.

"I've run away from home," he finally blurted out.

The man smiled. "OK, now we're down to the truth. Where do you live?"

"In Iowa City, and I want to go back home."

"Sure you do. Let's go."

The automobile pulled out onto the pavement and sped through the night. In town, July told him that he lived near the depot, and they turned off Riverside Drive.

"That's it," said July. "Let me off here." He pointed to a yellow house uphill from the railway station. After he was out of the car he walked around to the back of the house as though to use the back door, slipped down a walkway and came out on the street.

Although the railway station was closed for the evening, the first train to come by stopped and let off three people. Several cars down, on the other side, away from the boarding ramp, July climbed on. After he was out into the open air of the country, the wheels banging on the rails under him like demons pounding rock with cold hammers, he swung open the door and went inside. Some people looked up from their seats, but looked away, disinterested. Though it was before eleven, most everyone was asleep. He found two empty seats and sat down next to the window. A conductor came in from the front and July felt him linger for a moment next to his seat and pass on.

Before the sun came up they stopped four times, then kept rolling clear up until noon. By overhearing conversation he learned that there was a diner ahead somewhere, and at the next stop he went to find out. There was. He took a table to himself and a black waiter dressed in white came over to get his order. "Hamburger," he said, without looking at the menu.

"And what has we to drink?" asked the waiter in a fast, clean voice.

"Water."

The waiter went over to a window, spoke through it and sat down.

The train lurched ahead. July took out his money and disentangled a dollar bill, and put it on the table, feeling, as he did it, grown-up. The waiter returned with a plate from the window ledge—put there by unseen hands—and a glass of water, set them down and snapped up the dollar quickly and as though it had no value, punched out the change from the machine at his belt and went back to where he'd been sitting. July counted the change . . . fifty cents. Then he secretly looked at the menu, hamburger . . . *45¢*. Cheated out of a nickel! He looked over at the black man and wondered how he could look so innocent, but knew he hadn't nerve enough to go over and demand his nickel back. He accepted the loss—deciding at the same time never to let it happen again. As he lifted the sandwich sideways, grease dripped onto the plate from between the halves of the bun. He bit into it, tasted the gristle and began to put it down. No, he thought, that's little-kid's stuff. This here is the real thing. He opened up the sandwich and put salt on it, the way he'd seen his father do many times, and ate it, drinking the water in one lift to his mouth. Then he went back a car and sat down. Later the same conductor came up to his seat and told him to "stop moving around."

"OK," said July, realizing, as he should have before, that his age was his disguise—he was taken for belonging to one of the little clusters of family in the car behind him. The thought made him smile, and he mused pleasantly, looking out the window after the conductor had gone, dark shapes like flying witches flashing past outside: If that joker'd given me any more static, I'd've blown off his head. He felt quite dangerous. A blue fug of smoke enveloped the car. A boy about his age walked past toward the diner and looked at him without stopping. July saw him in the window reflection. *Better watch out, little kid,* he thought almost kindly, *or you'll have the trouble of your life.* He felt in his pocket and the gun was warm to the touch. Then he went to sleep.

At the next stop everybody got off, so he did too, judging it expedient. There was also the chance that the train was going no farther. In the station he bought two candy bars from a vendor, twenty cents, and thought for the first time about where he might be going. He went over to the opposite wall and looked at the schedule in order to find out where he was. Cleveland. Then he found a map with railroad lines drawn on it and looked at Cleveland in relationship to Iowa City (Sharon Center wasn't marked) and smiled. It made him feel important to be out in the world for the first time. He followed the railroad lines out of Cleveland and decided where he was going to. Philadelphia. Yes, he decided, thinking very clearly and without emotion—completely detached from any reason—Philadelphia. Then he checked the schedule again and planned out to his own satisfaction when the train he wanted would be leaving. He tossed the last candy wrapper into the trash and went into the bathroom. As he was standing with his back to the room, someone came out of what he'd taken to be an empty stall, stood several feet behind him and said, "Hey, buddy, you want to blow me? Fifty cents."

The voice was hostile and his urine immediately stopped flowing. He tucked himself back inside his pants, managed to say, "What?" and turned around.

"A blow job, punk," said the young man, his pink shirt opened halfway down his stomach, his black hair slicked back against his head, curling at the neck, "Where you been, born yesterday? Suck my dick for fifty cents. Come on, hurry up."

July couldn't talk, and the youth was advancing. In horror, July could see what was expected of him.

"No," he said. "I don't want to."

"Come on, punk—" Then the door opened and his assailant went quickly over to a urinal beside him, where he appeared to be relieving himself. Two older men, coming in, caught enough of the abnormally hurried movement, and intuiting from July's expression, they immediately separated. One of them went outside to guard the door. The other took off his jacket.

"You lousy fairy," he said, talking to the back of the pink shirt. "You gonna wish you never tried anything like this on a young boy. I'm gonna beat you within an inch of your life." Violence seemed to ooze out of every word. The young man in the pink shirt looked over his shoulder and terror filled his face. His eyes were wild and for a second he looked at July with such pleading, hopeless fear that July completely forgot his own previous dread of him. Compared to the man waiting for him to turn around, he might as well have been an invalid, so terribly bad were his chances. The man kicked him in the small of the back and he screamed, his head striking the chrome pipes. Half falling, he turned to run, but was hit back up against the urinal. His legs began to fold and he screamed again. The man held him up with his left hand and beat his face. Blood ran down into his opened shirt. Then he was kicked and he doubled over with an agonizing groan, falling to the tiled floor. Then the man stomped him, a look of impersonal disgust on his face such as July had seen on the face of Bob Sloan as he beat a garden snake in the schoolyard with a stick. Finally, he was unconscious, though July thought dead. Then he saw the breathing.

The man turned to July. "Are you all right?" the man asked, in a gentle, fatherly voice. July nodded. "Come on, let's get out of here," and he picked up his jacket, led July carefully around so he wouldn't step in the blood, with his arm on his shoulder. Out in the terminal the men asked him if he wouldn't like to have an ice cream. July shook his head. They shook hands and the men left when they saw someone walk toward the restroom.

July went outside to wait for his train and sat down. Two hours passed without his noticing. A shroud of violence covered everything. He was stranded in the gap between what he imagined he was and what he was. He felt a sickening fear threaten to take him over—the stranger in him rise up very far. But before the train to Philadelphia arrived, he had escaped. I'm sorry for what happened, he thought. I'd have stopped it if I could have. I didn't want it to happen. I . . . I don't care. He's of no importance to me. And to prove it to himself, he went back into the men's room. The victim was gone. The floor and walls had been cleaned. He was vaguely disappointed, but very relieved.

The train came and he nestled in among a large family as they boarded, and sat among them until the conductor had passed, making sure not to look at any of them. (Children at that time rode free when accompanied by their parents.) Then he separated himself and got a seat of his own. In the middle of Pennsylvania the family got off and he thought it best to find another seat. He chose one next to an old lady, who let him sit by the window. Right away she began to talk to him about arthritis and sewing kits and he felt safe.

He got off in Philadelphia at an underground terminal, 30th Street Station, and walked up to Walnut Street. He felt a mixture of excitement and agitation at being at his destination. He listened to the noises and watched people walk by him. It seemed like a good place. The river was not too far away. He walked for a long time.

He went into a diner opening on to the street and bought a sausage sandwich for forty cents. A large sign above the grill said no tipping. He didn't know what that meant and decided he'd have a lot to learn. But it certainly seemed good. The sense of being on his own filled the sausage and he ate it as he walked along the street, looking into the shops and offices. He saw a couple sitting on the steps of a town house, judged from that that it was legal and two blocks later sat down himself. Several people passed by who smiled at him. As it began to get dark he found himself in a park sitting on a bench. He went up to a pleasant-enough-looking man sitting across from him to ask where he might find a place to spend the night, but only was able to get out, "Say, mister, I wonder if you couldn't—" before he was cut off.

"Beat it, kid. Write to your Congressman for money." The man got up and walked briskly away.

July watched him sit down again in a different part of the park. Then later, as it grew darker, he watched him walk away and enter a very tall building. Because of nothing better to do, he followed, but was stopped from entering by a doorman in a blue, brass-buttoned suit and hard-billed hat. "Go on, now," he said. "Only people who live here can go in." He seemed kind, however, and was old, as though held together by the very uniform itself because it was so tight and stiff.

"I need a place to sleep," said July.

"Holy cow!" said the doorman humorously, and July smiled. "Get on home quick as you can while they'll still take you. Parents may be terrible, but they've always got spare beds to sleep in."

"My parents are dead."

"I'm sorry," said the old man. July could see a change come over him, a look of sinking back into his tough, wrinkled face. "Get on away from here now. I can't have you standing around, the people don't like it. Get on, now. Go down to the YMCA. Over there—" He pointed. All of the kindness had drained from his voice, and July realized he'd been shut out. He'd seen the look before. In fact, his father had worn it once or twice while listening to the news and reports of accidents and calamities, and July had realized that the announcer could say anything and his father'd think nothing whatsoever about it.

He walked in the direction the man had pointed out, repeating over and over again the letters YMCA, having no idea what they stood for. Naturally, he didn't find it right away and, it being after dark by then and few people about, he went into a bar and asked the bartender.

"Why, a young fellow like you should be after the YWCA!" There was great laughter. July didn't understand and his look conveyed that. "OK, I'm sorry. Just go out and turn right. Go two blocks and make a left. It's right there." July followed the instructions and, to his surprise, found just that—a building with the letters YMCA running down the side. He went in.

There was a little bell on the counter to ring and he touched it gently. Three boys, older than himself, came in and went by him, up the stairs. One of them had his shirt opened halfway down his front, revealing a dirty T-shirt. He wondered if that boy would know what had happened in the men's room in Cleveland, or know the person who was almost killed. Right away July wanted to leave, and was just beginning to when a heavyset middle-aged man came in-from somewhere and, in a voice sounding as if he had a hole in his windpipe, asked what he wanted. July told him. The charge for a room was $1.50 per day; provided he would stay on the second floor (the other rooms were more expensive), which gave him the use of the common bathroom and access to the Ping-Pong table, magazine room, television room and cafeteria. Before he could take out his money to pay, the man began reading from a list of new regulations, explaining as he did that these new inexpensive rates, facilities and advantages were only available to those who were making a considerable and conscious effort to better themselves: no drinking, lights out after ten thirty, no smoking, no fighting, meals were served at regular times in the basement for money, going to school was an absolute, income from after-school jobs had to be reported, no girls allowed upstairs or in the television room, chapel service on Sundays required, a choice of Catholic or Protestant services, linen to be turned in Monday morning and checked out the same evening, no spitting or swearing, and any breach of these requirements would necessitate going into a probationary period of two weeks, at the end of which time it would be decided—given that no more rules had been broken—if the desire for self-betterment was strong enough. The ward he was to be on was an experimental one, just being tried. The doors were not to be locked and counselors were always on the floor.

July could see no way out of it. He had his money in his hand and got out $1.50 and put it on the counter. "Your room will be number twelve," he was told. July looked again at the man's neck, thinking that surely he must have a hole someplace where air was escaping and robbing him. Then the man started to cough and July went upstairs, and drank from a drinking fountain before locating his room.

There was no lock on the door and that disturbed him. He could hear talking, but not well enough to know how far away it was coming from. He shut the door and surveyed his room: a bed, a dresser, green walls and a window. He looked out and felt a surge of confidence—thinking of himself as a part of the human immensity outside. He stood and let this feeling saturate him, then he turned and sat on the bed. An unspecified number of people walked by his room, talking and joking. He could distinguish some swearing.

As quietly as possible, he moved the dresser over against the door. It was surprisingly light. He checked the drawers and found them empty except for a Bible, which he took out and put on top of the bed, seating himself beside it. Then with slow, nearly sensual motions, one at a time he drew out every object in his pockets and arranged them carefully on the bed, all of the pennies in a long line, quarters together, dimes and nickels. The paper money refused to lie neatly and he pressed the bills several times in the Bible and set them down stacked a quarter-inch apart. He opened both blades of his knife and put it down, pulled out the pistol and sat for a long time holding it, then took out the clip, unloaded it and laid the bullets side by side in a row, their yellow jackets beautiful. He polished the chrome of the gun and the pearl handle with his shirt and put it down too, at right angles to the bullets. He took each key from the ring and laid them out. Then most slowly, and with the most ceremony of all, he took out his billfold, opened it and one after another laid out the pictures, not in a row, but in the pockets left between the other things in his personal inventory. His father and mother smiled up at him from the bed. One picture showed him with them, standing next to the garage eating a piece of cheese. He felt their approval: they wanted him to run away. They were proud of how brave he was. They were pushing him on—on to what he wasn't sure, but he felt right.

He sat looking, and several times changed one picture's place with another for a better balance. He counted his money. Less than ten dollars. He put the money in piles. Then he had a new idea and laid it out again. He counted everything, all of his personal inventory. Every piece that could be called something of itself, he counted. Seventy-three. He had seventy-three things counting the Bible, which he decided was his as well, or would be. He looked around the room for something else that could be his, but there was nothing. Then he pulled off a button from his shirt and put it on the bed. Immediately he felt it was a stupid thing to do, and wished he hadn't done it and began to be afraid. But the smiling pictures looked up at him and his parents' voices told him, no, it was OK. They wanted him to have seventy-four things.

He began to count them again. He heard a bell sound somewhere. Then many quick footsteps, but little talking. He put his money into one pile and was putting it into his pocket when a knock came on his door; the doorknob turned. "Lights out," said an older man's voice as the door bumped into the bureau. "Let me in," the man demanded angrily. "These doors are to be left *open*." The bureau was noisily pushed aside and from the dark hallway into his lit room stepped a man of about fifty, wearing a dark lightweight suit tattered around the sleeve cuffs. July sat still, not knowing what to do. The man came several feet into the room and stopped dead still, as though struck in the face. July could see that he was looking at the gun on the bed. Still he didn't know what to do. The man seemed paralyzed for what seemed like hours, but finally he moved and shut the door so that none of the boys who were hurrying down the hall to see what was up could look into the room. July began quickly stuffing the keys, knife and pictures back into his pockets.

"Give me that gun," said the man, advancing toward him, his voice shaking slightly from his outstretched hand. July was pushing the bullets as fast as he could into his pants pocket. One fell to the floor and clattered. The noise seemed to make the man more shaky, but move more quickly. "Give me that gun," he repeated.

July picked up the empty clip, shoved it up into the handle of the pistol and sat there with it, tears beginning to form in his eyes. "It's mine," he said.

"Give it to me," the man repeated, coming up all the way and touching him on the shoulder.

July, having decided what to do at the split second he began doing it, ran past the man and made it to the door, where, trying to get it open, he felt hands grab him from behind.

"Stop. Give me that gun."

July turned and with all of his force pushed. To his astonishment, the man went backward almost to the bed, giving him time to get the door open, get the empty pistol into his pocket and begin running down the hall.

"Stop him!" yelled the voice, and three boys at the end of the hall, two older than himself, stepped out of their rooms, barring his way to the staircase. July fixed his eyes straight on the biggest one, the one on the right, and ran at him; then just before making contact he changed course and ran through the middle, taking the smaller boy halfway down the stairs with him.

"Stop him!" came the shouting again, but the man with the hole in his windpipe couldn't get around the counter before July was through the lobby, through the door and into the city night. Down the staircase tumbled counselor Tracy and thirteen or fourteen boys, one of them yelling, "Get the fucker, he broke my arm! My arm's broke!"

"Terry, stop that kind of language! The rest of you get back up to your rooms or you'll all be put on probation."

They reluctantly left. Bill Jensen and counselor Tracy looked at Terry's arm, found it to be not broken and sent him upstairs, reprimanding him again for his bad language.

"What'd he do?" asked Terry.

"Never mind. Get on upstairs."

He went. Together, the older men went outside onto the sidewalk and looked down the street as far as they could see. Bob Tracy lit a cigarette. His hands were still shaking. He threw the match beyond the curb. "I'm going to quit," he said sadly.

"What happened?"

"The kid had a gun. I panicked. I guess I wasn't expecting anything like that on the second floor with the younger kids. I've handled things like that before. But this time I panicked. I didn't know we had a new kid—just saw the light under the door and stopped in to get him to douse it. Then the gun on the bed . . . I panicked, and scared him. Now God knows the damage. The last thing in his mind was to point that gun at me, but I went at him like a hardened criminal—'Give me that gun, give me that gun,' like some kind of cop."

"It happens to everybody."

"Well, everybody it happens to shouldn't have a job working with kids. Who knows what the damage—"

"Come on, let's get some coffee. We've got to put together that requisition for film equipment."

"They'll never give it to us. If it costs one red cent . . . That poor kid." They went inside.

July was running. Every shadow, every moving car, every doorway he thought concealed a policeman whose only goal that evening was to kill the kid with the gun from the YMCA. One old woman sitting on the step of her house yelled at him, calling him a thief. Four blocks later he stopped running. Run when you have to, he thought, otherwise it attracts too much attention. Far away he heard a siren and the adrenaline froze his blood. Then he heard another siren in another direction. Surrounded. He saw a stone wall across the street from him, and with the help of an iron fence, he got over it to the other side. He found himself in a small courtyard of an apartment complex. He stood back against the wall in the shadows and waited. He stayed there until after all the lights in the apartments had been turned out and he'd heard enough sirens to know that if they were all after him, they didn't have a very good idea where to look. Then he decided to move. The door from the courtyard into a back alley could be opened from the inside, and he used it. He was hungry.

After an hour of walking, he managed to find his way back to the diner, which was still open. One of the movie palaces was spilling its patrons back onto the street, and in the commotion July felt safer. He bought another sausage sandwich, this time of a different color. There were no places to sit down and he ate it standing, being thankful for the well-lit room and the people impervious to him. He bought a bag of potato chips. A police car pulled up in front. There was a moment while it sat there like a white-and-blue toad. Then both doors flew open and two policemen came rushing into the diner crouched low like two halfbacks. July dropped his potato chips. One of the policemen threw him back away from the counter with a quick brush of his arm. A girl at the end of the counter next to the rainbow punch machine made an effort to run, but was quickly caught. She screamed, kicked and swore, and one of the policemen cuffed her on the side of the head. Then they bodily lifted her away from the edge of the counter she was holding on to and carried her out, arms and legs flailing, cursing, and stuffed her into the back seat of the car and drove away.

"You better pick them up," the man behind the counter said to July, motioning down to the potato chips. "Someone's likely to step on them."

Having someone's attention, July mustered all the courage he had and asked, "Why . . . why did they do that?"

"I don't know, probably just some hooker on junk. Maybe she's in the rackets." He went away to wait on someone.

July picked up his potato chips and went outside. He was beginning to be very tired. Just as he had felt the lights of the diner bring him comfort, now he felt the comfort of the darkness enfold him. He crossed Broad Street and went over to City Hall, creasing the bag across the top and putting it gently in his jacket. In the open walkway through the building he stopped and looked at the walls, which seemed to be made in order to resemble millions of fat worms wiggling over each other—one big seething mass of living stone worms without faces. He walked through the square, over the metal marker—the historical center of Philadelphia.

Following the only two people he saw, he went down some steps to a trolley landing beneath City Hall. Then, out of curiosity, he went down another flight of stairs to where turnstiles like robots stood in a long row, a fat man behind a heavy wire screen made change and beyond him lay the loading platform of the L. One more flight down, he came to the waiting platform of the Crosstown Express. Huge cement walls as thick as refrigerators with torn posters and writing from some prehistoric age. More turnstiles.

He stood in the darkness. Then the earth itself began to shudder and a light appeared like a frightened beacon and the Express came flashing and banging, metal screeching and doors clattering, up out of the black cavernous hole, stopped still like a giant metal insect and crawled off again into the darkness. July was filled with wonder. He imagined those cars could take him anywhere in the world, China even, if he got on the right one, without ever coming up out of the ground, unknown by the millions of people above, the driver's eyes gleaming wild like a madman's—two holes bored in the walls of a furnace.

To his astonishment, there was still a level lower, and he descended sleepily to the wooden landing platform of the Frankford Elevated. This was empty except for three long benches and a large green wastepaper basket. July went to the edge and looked up and down the tunnels. He let himself down the five-foot drop from the platform to the track level, went back underneath the landing and lay down on the dirt, his consciousness hanging from him by a thread. The inhuman thunder of the cars began to lull him. The maze of wires, discernible here and there by cracks of light from the wooden planks above him, hummed like tuning forks. He took out his gun and loaded it, leaving the chamber empty, however, wrapped his hand securely around it and fell asleep, dreaming of women with large savage hooks who flayed people alive and ate trash from garbage pails. Twice he woke cold and shivering, and pulled his jacket tighter around him. Especially his back was cold.

The following day July left his gun and extra bullets under the landing. He ate pancakes in a grease shop on Broad Street. Then he went to a dime store and bought a flashlight to study his new home. He noticed a change in the way people looked at him this day as compared to the rest of his life, and within a short time accepted it as a normal response without realizing that it was because of the dirt which had soiled his clothes. He wasn't able to get back unobserved to where his gun lay concealed because there was always somebody there on the platform, or across the tracks on the opposite side. He realized fewer cars ran at night, and fewer people were on them. He would have to wait always until dark—or later, maybe on a Sunday, find another way to get down.

He went off to buy some blankets. He entered the first large department store, and when the salesgirl saw the look on his face when she told him the prices, she promptly and courteously gave him directions to the Army surplus store, where he purchased two—leaving him with only one dollar of his paper money.

He bought a large bag of popcorn and ate it sitting on his blankets in the park. He wanted to take out his pictures, but he didn't want to do it there in front of everyone and without the gun. He stayed until just before dark and returned to beneath City Hall.

Around seven o'clock he slipped down under the platform and put his gun back in his jacket. Using the flashlight with great caution (in order to avoid being seen from across the tracks on the other side and, because it was new, not to wear down the batteries), he found a small dirt-floored alcove tucked back into the solid concrete behind and beyond the wood roof of the platform. Originally it had been built to accommodate a set of control switches and relay boxes; but because it wasn't needed, except for wires shrouded in conduit pipes running in every direction across the top, it was empty. It was long enough for him to lie down twice lengthwise, once and a half the other way, and stand up, excepting in two places where a low conduit pipe was directly above. Because it was not just beneath the platform and had a cement roof, he felt more protected from the footsteps above—they were less audible. He could also shine his light directly into the back of his room without being afraid of anyone seeing it from across the way. There was no wind. The rushing clatter of the L, though less overbearing, was still close enough to be reassuring in its monstrousness, like a drunken night watchman who would come stumbling up the dark tunnels with a torch, stop, look around and be gone.

He decided he would have to get a tarp from the Army surplus store. He took one blanket, folded it into a two-foot square and sat on it, crossing his legs and feeling the concrete of his wall against his back. The other he folded in the same way and put in front of him. Then out came the pictures, and in the darkness—for he could barely see in there except when a train was coming—he symmetrically spread them out. Then he took the flashlight and one at a time let the intense circle of yellow light spill onto them. Then he closed his eyes (in order to build the suspense) and reorganized them so that each of the eight pictures had a new place. He sat and concentrated—which card is in the middle? which card is at the bottom left?—and tried to let the feeling of each picture reveal itself. Then with the flashlight he'd check, and see the faces come looking up at him.

Next he laid out all of his things, the three favorite pictures in the middle. And counted them. Forty-seven, counting the two flashlight batteries, the lens and the bulb. There was shouting outside and the sound of a bottle breaking and he ran out to the front of his room to look, fearing he was in danger. But after the sound of fast-running footsteps and a single long wail, everything was back to normal. The train pulled away, and he went in again.

When he was ready for bed, he reloaded the gun and, like the night before, closed his hand tightly around it, pulled the blankets up around his shoulder and shut his eyes. Only then did he begin to worry about money. He remembered the potato chips, ate them and fell asleep.

The following day was a Thursday. He got a chance after the morning rush to get out unseen and climb up onto the platform. He had a glass of milk and a hamburger for breakfast, and ate slowly. It was sprinkling needles of rain outside. He went to the Army surplus store to see about getting a tarp. They were too expensive.

Walking back out of the store, he realized the deadly implications of his situation: the things he wanted—and he did want them—he couldn't buy. In order to get them he'd have to steal them. His whole sense of himself reeled at the thought. A thief! He began walking aimlessly, thinking the matter out. He saw other children not much older than himself, most of them black, on the streets away from school and he wondered if they were thieves as well as shoeshiners. He already knew that some of them were beggars. In fact, he'd given one a dime the day before, but had resolved never to do it again because of the coldness with which it had been accepted—so cold that July had wondered for a second if he'd been asked at all, or if he'd simply taken out a dime and tried to force it on this little kid.

Then he began picturing himself as a thief, and everything he looked at he thought of carting away and taking back to below City Hall. It exhilarated him to a certain extent. He imagined that the eyes of the people he passed were looking at him and thinking in awe, There he goes, the thief. How brave he looks. Will the police catch him today? But whenever he thought of his parents he could not keep his mother from going to the kitchen to get the flyswatter, dragging him behind her, and as these thoughts kept returning, he found himself mentally giving back all the things he'd stolen and put in his cement room. So, finally, everything was back where it belonged and the eyes said, There's that wild kid, the one who could have been a thief but wasn't, who stole cars and diamonds but took them back. He went into the library off Rittenhouse Square to use the bathroom.

He looked in the daily newspaper for a job. He knew about doing this because his father had told him stories of the Depression when maybe twenty men would gather at another man's house to look in the want ads—there being only one paper among them all—and then, defeated, would go outside and play horseshoes all day—anything to be away from home for a while. He found nothing that sounded as if he could qualify for it. Most of the kinds of people advertised for he'd never heard of: trainees, lab techs, production-line operators. But he thought he could order books, so he asked the librarian if they needed help, but they didn't.

That afternoon he got a job selling newspapers. A man in a drugstore said he'd give him all the papers he wanted for seven cents each and that he could sell them for ten. He bought twelve papers, withholding seven cents of his money for fear thirteen would be unlucky. He took them into the park and quickly began to learn how to say, "Hey, mister, want a paper?" both loud enough to be heard very clearly and at the same time so impersonally that it took no courage at all. It seemed as though he sold five right away, but couldn't get rid of any more. Then two policemen told him to get out of the park, and made him follow them to the edge of it and look at a sign and listen to it read to him in the tone of a threat, where he learned that no soliciting meant you couldn't sell newspapers there. The policeman who hadn't said anything up until that time bought a paper.

The wire wastepaper baskets along the street made July nervous. He was trying to sell something that had already been thrown away hundreds of times. He went down to City Hall and sold three outside the landing of the L.

Someone grabbed him by the collar and turned him around, nearly lifting him off his feet. "Listen, kid, get the hell out a my area or I'll kick the livin' shit clean out a ya." It was the fat, swollen-faced man he'd seen behind the stand a flight up. The man turned him around again and shoved him toward the exit. July dropped the remaining three papers and went back to pick them up, but the man dashed at him, surprisingly quick for his size, and swung a leg up to kick him like a dog. "Beat it," he yelled. July dodged him and fled up the stairs and outside. But on the way by the stand, abandoned as soon as the fat man had heard from a friend coming up that there was someone down on the docks peddling papers, he took a handful and sped across Broad Street and past the movie theaters. Two blocks later, after he'd stopped running, he counted them. Only five. He sold them all outside a delicatessen and produce market, bought a bag of caramel corn and some french fries and went exploring for the rest of the afternoon and evening, until he could safely return to his room. That night, just before he went to bed, when he'd come out to take a leak beside the tracks, he saw a wolf that looked like a man walk down into the tunnel across on the other side, on two legs.

The following day he learned that he could get newspapers off the company truck—whole bundles at a time—for four cents a copy, and that he wouldn't have to pay for them until the end of the week, and if he got up early enough in the morning to catch several stands of seven-to-seven-thirty bus riders, or stood in front of the big offices at eight, he could easily sell seventy-five or a hundred. If he had a good day, he could sell the rest of his bundles by noon and be finished for the day. On a slow day—when it was raining and the pages were soggy and there was nothing but gossip in the headlines—he could work for all he was worth and not sell half a bundle. After a while, when he could see one of those days unfolding before him, he would throw it in, let the company share the loss (they never charged him for papers he couldn't sell, but didn't pay him for *trying* to sell them either) and go to a movie on 14th Street, where in the dark of the theater he would plan how he could manage to sell beneath City Hall without getting caught by the oaf who'd paid $5000 for the territory.

He saw many of the other paper boys getting their own corners from older boys who'd finally get out of the business, buying them, which in the paper company's mind, and most certainly in their own, gave them exclusive right to a whole block, where it was possible to try for every paper man's dream: steady customers who know you and always buy from you—enough to keep you afloat even in lean times and still give you a crack at the good days when you might sell four hundred papers. These corners cost usually between $100 and $200. July didn't buy one for two reasons: first, he liked the feeling of being able to go anywhere to sell, the thrill of hitting it rich in a new neighborhood; and secondly, if he was going to have his own place, it was somehow going to be beneath City Hall.

He worked each day and, except for very unfortunate ones, could depend on making $6.00. Two of the six, no matter what, he put into a glass jar, for a savings fund. It cost him between $1.50 and $3.00 to eat, depending on what he felt like, and the rest he spent on furnishings for his room, and clothes as he needed them. The days grew colder and he was forced to save for a pair of warm socks, a secondhand coat with a fur collar, two more blankets, and gloves.

In some of the places he frequented to eat, the help got to know him, and one old woman who lived in Germantown told him about how he could use the restrooms and showers in the basement of the civic center. Most of the panhandlers and streetwalkers knew him by sight because of his wide area of circulation. Every once in a while he'd get a free meal at the mission and one of the men would secretly give him a snort from a bottle of wine. He began keeping cats, but it was difficult and a little heart-rending because every so often one would disappear without a trace, leaving only gloomy fantasies of what might have happened and frightening him into imagining someone had found his room and was coming in while he was away selling papers to steal cats and look for money and guns. But luckily July came upon a cat one night climbing roofs, a big black-and-orange tom with long hair and half of its left ear missing, that never disappeared after he'd taken it home.

What a difference it made to have that cat! He couldn't believe how lonely he must have been before. He looked back on himself before the cat as a different person altogether, morose and a little stupid. Sometimes he would go to a movie after dinner, just because he wanted to get back to Butch so badly—in order to draw it out and make himself feel more important, so that he would come back full of excuses as to why Butch, sitting disdainfully in his cardboard-and-blanket house, had to wait so long to be fed. They slept together, and if it wasn't snowing Butch would occasionally accompany him on his paper rounds. Naturally, no one at first believed a cat would follow anyone around—not purposely; but, nevertheless, *There goes July Montgomery, the paper kid, who lives nobody knows where with his cat* was what even Boz Green clear over by Fairmount Park thought when he'd look out from his crackerbox studio and see them, and sometimes (though he was nearly broke himself) would leave his painting, go out on the street and call him over and get a paper.

"What's up?" asked Boz.

"That depends what you're after to be up, Mr. Boz," said July.

"And how's Butch, your indignant cat?"

"Oh, Butch is a little put out today. It seems I've tricked him once again into going out and getting his feet wet."

Butch was sitting down on a dry step, frowning.

"You haven't been around lately, July."

"No . . . *Paper, mister?* . . . No, I've been in Old Town a lot as of late, mixing it up you might say with high society."

"Is that so? I hadn't heard."

"Yes, it's true. We get along just fine. They want me and Butch to join, but Butch feels he isn't quite up to it yet."

"Why's that, Butch?" asked Boz, bending his voice down to the cat, who looked away from him down the street.

"You'll have to ignore Butch's manners," said July. "He's not quite himself until afternoon."

"You want to come in for a cup of chocolate, July?" asked the painter cautiously, for this was the first time he'd invited him up.

"No, don't think we can make it. We're running short today, and Butch is afraid of stairs. But thanks for the offer. Sunday paper, mister?" And they were off again.

"That Boz," said July to his cat, once they were a good block away, "you be careful of him. He'd like nothing better than to fuck you in the ass."

That night, after getting a couple of triangles of hot pizza and eating it walking, they went back to City Hall. July looked at the fat man's newspaper stand, locked tighter than a drum, and thought to himself, Something's going to be done. Soon.

The first-shift night man was in the change booth on the second floor. He was the only one of them that July liked, except for Charlie, who wasn't often there. No one at all was on the landing and the Crosstown Express swooped through without stopping. So empty that the echoes were more pronounced.

"Hi, Wade," said July, lifting Butch up against his coat where he could see into the window. Benton (Bent) Wade was a midget, July knew, because he'd seen him one time outside the change booth. When you could only see his head and shoulders you couldn't really tell for sure. The small hands were not conclusive evidence.

"Hello, my friend," said Wade, stacking new rolls of quarters in the quarter cylinder. "Hello there, Butch. As ornery as ever, I see. Wait, I believe I have something for you." He reached into his lunch bag, took out a waxpaper-wrapped sandwich and opened it up to pinch off a small corner of cheese. Then he held it out through the cup-shaped dispensing hole. July held Butch over closer and he took the cheese off Bent Wade's finger.

"Thanks," said July.

"Have you sold any of those films?" asked Wade.

"I sold three."

"Which ones?"

"Two of *Prison Women,* one of *Peter's Revenge.*"

"What about *Fanny Flappers?*"

"No good. I think it's an old one. Everybody's seen it."

"Well, bring the rest back and I'll try to get some more. That joker told me that was a new one. How about *Sweet Regret*? What's the matter there?"

"Too much. Nobody wants to pay over five dollars, not if they can't see part of 'em first."

"OK, well, bring the rest back. Did you try down by the museum? I heard there's guys down there—"

"I went there. Wrong day, I guess. Nothing but old ladies and winos."

"Well, bring the rest back some time this week and I'll give you the money on 'em. I know someone who wants a *Sweet Regret* and I'm all out."

"Sure, Wade. Can I get two dollar bills?" He put down the same amount in dimes on the wooden dish; Bent scooped it up in one motion and gave him two bills. "Thanks. See you later."

"Take it easy, kid."

They left.

The Woodland II car came up out of the north tunnel and July stepped back to signal it on, then recognized Bobby Barns, who knew him, and waved. Bobby tipped his hat comically. The car rattled by without stopping. July appreciated these Sunday nights more than any time of the week. The desertedness of the vast concrete cavities, the absence of voices and the sweet feeling of complete isolation that it gave him made it seem like being in an ancient cathedral, a place where a person might go to be alone.

Inside their cement cubicle July reclosed the cardboard door, struck a match to light the lamp and carried it back into the main living room, where he had his pallet, a chair across from Butch's box and a small, low table just big enough for the cat to sit on and watch him turn over cards for seven-row solitaire. The faces from inside the pictures stared at him from the wall where they were displayed, glued to a piece of black construction paper. The gun was taped beneath the table, handle pointing toward his chair, but it'd been almost three months since he'd taken it out to look at. He took off his yellow paper carrier, and brought the films Benton wanted out of another and stacked them on a miscellaneous box next to the door, where he'd remember to carry them up some time later that evening. No, he decided, he'd take them back some other day. He didn't feel like going out.

Then he got the cat food, mixed it with a little water from the gallon jar and set it down. Butch scowled at it and went into his box as though a statement of his independence was more important than independence itself. *You dumb cat,* thought July, took up the book he'd begun last night and resumed reading. Another trolley went by outside without stopping. Then he remembered that he'd forgotten to put away the $2.00. The jar was buried underneath his bed; he dug away the two inches of dirt covering the top and pulled it up, and scraped off the clinging brown earth so he could see all the money without blemish. He rolled the two dollar bills from his pocket tightly into a thin, cigarette-sized cylinder and poked them down into the round center of the other bills already in the jar. They unraveled partway and expanded. Again, almost as badly as a week ago, he wanted to take all the money out and count it, but he held himself back and quickly resealed and reburied the jar for fear he might lose control. He didn't want to know for sure how much was there. He'd barely had enough time to forget since the last time he counted, and that was, let's see . . . He fixed his mind away from figuring and relaid the tarp and blankets. He really didn't have any idea what the money would be used for—if it would be used at all—but felt sure it would buy something—something big—something that, once he had it, would completely change his life. He went back to reading and daydreaming.

SEVEN

In the world of selling newspapers, a roamer is not universally well liked. Many times each day he will—by virtue of necessity sometimes—step on a part of the city which belongs to another paper barker, thus automatically drawing down that person's economic potential by one half. Even if his intentions are to do nothing more than walk across the block in order to get to another, he'll attract the malicious suspicions of the person who paid money for the sole privilege of working that part of the street. In most cases, it's not even necessary to step on it. It is usually enough for most paper boys with stands, or spots on corners, just to *see* a roamer in order to flush up immediate thoughts of murder. After all, they figure, I've paid good money for this spot and it isn't fair that someone like that should be allowed to go just anywhere he has a mind to. Though basically individualistic and tough-minded by nature, in this matter they were as uniform as a row of clean soldiers: they didn't like roamers.

Because July Montgomery was aware such feelings existed, he went out of his way to keep from making his presence felt, though in complete honesty it was also true that he was guilty—on one or two occasions—of going out of his way to catch an opulent group of bus riders before a certain particularly unpleasant fellow would be able to get to his stand, thus completely gutting his early-morning market and leaving him stranded in his barren zone, his customers reading the sports page and munching doughnuts.

Earl Schmidt had a corner on 21st and Market, having bought it from Gary Snider who'd had it before him and paid $200 for it. It was a good corner, on several bus routes, near a quick order restaurant, and had a lot of traffic down both sides, and on Sundays he could make $20 shoving papers into the windows of the cars. He was a year older than July, but short for his age, his hair chopped off in a fashion that his father, a labor leader, called a crew. He wasn't allowed to have it any other way.

Earl didn't like July. When July'd come that first day, his face as pale as a sheet, looking frightenedly, stupidly, around at all of them, wondering if there was work—from the first moment Earl'd thought, Now there's a farmer if I ever saw one. Farthead. How'd you like somebody to kick your ass?

His first impressions of most people were not too good, but in July's case they never improved. They actually got worse. And after July began working 21st and Market and once sold out a half-bundle there before Earl arrived, the mere sight of him made Earl seethe with rage. Twice, in front of the other boys who picked up their papers at the 24th Street pickup, he'd called him out, threatening and ridiculing him, but both times July'd backed down so graciously and with such humor that for the sake of his own good name Earl couldn't press him further. This salted his private anger.

I'll grind him up. Earl thought things like that to himself when he was alone. His hatred was so perfect, so single-minded, so completely pure hot, that it was almost a pleasure, and sometimes he would sip at it all morning. *I'll eat him alive and tear out his heart.* Then after the cat began following July wherever he went, and even the others who didn't like him because he was a roamer thought it was *so cute,* Earl could hardly keep from fainting at the sweetness of his loathing. Those days he couldn't work, when his father had him enrolled in a once-a-week course offered by the Army called Command Tactics, most of all he missed that first glimpse of July when they all came together to get their papers off the truck.

He decided on an ambush. Every day for a month he thought to himself: Now, how is this going to be? What will I do? What will I say just before I flatten his face? Who do I want to be with me to watch? He set the stage for it many times, in many different places and would think it through, sweet, all the way up until his friends were dragging him away from the bloody mass of jelly, saying, *OK, Earl, the little fucker got what he deserved, better not kill him. Jesus, your fists are like lightning.* Then he'd begin it again, this time in a warehouse full of coffins, rain on the metal roof, July hearing his name called and freezing in fear.

"What I'm thinking is an ambush. We'll get him just as he comes by that alley in back of Jack's Place, and take him off down in there and . . ."

Al Decker and Marty Spinner looked at each other without any obvious expression, keeping away from Earl's livid eyes. "Come on," Al began, very cautiously, "just tell him to keep off your corner. Get as tough as you want to, but, Christ, jumping him—three of us."

"If that's what you want," Earl said, nearly shouting in excitement, "then I'll take him myself. We'll get him back in there and you two can just stand back and I'll take him myself."

"Come on—" said Marty, but was cut off before he could continue.

"All I want you guys for is to drag me off him. When I fight, something snaps out in me and I can't control myself. I nearly killed a kid several weeks ago over in Fairmount. I just snap out."

Al and Marty looked away from the eyes again and back to each other. Naturally, they weren't about to say anything about the only time they had seen Earl in a fight, which had been maybe a year ago and it had been more like him being snapped instead of snapping out—though clearly the other guy *had* been bigger. The hatred was a little frightening to them, and they were hesitant about saying something to draw it toward themselves.

"Well, I don't know," said Al.

"You're both chicken," said Earl. "You're yellow."

This taunt, which by itself has probably been responsible for more misdeeds among young people than any other, cut them to the quick. It's a wicked threat, one which almost anyone can wield with the same weight, one which is secretly used against oneself with terrible consequences. Its seriousness can never be overlooked—the weapon of self-destruction, yet the foundation of noble action.

"He *should* have to go out and get his own corner," said Marty.

"We won't hurt his cat," said Al, as though complimenting their higher motives.

The next morning at the pickup place, July in his usual morning grogginess didn't have any reason to expect that it would be different from any other Tuesday. There was a heavy overcast, and with melted snow on the street, his cat had gone back down beneath the platform. The sun was just beginning to come up and the streets and buildings were either gray or blue. He carried his bundles off a little way from the rest, cut one open with his knife and stuffed the papers into his carrier bag. Then, picking up the other by the strings, he set off for Pine Street, every once in a while taking a paper in to a shop owner just opening up.

It was a good morning. The paper he carried made it seem like any minute the secret Communists in the country would make their play. "Commies arrested," shouted July, and stood back, making change as fast as he could with both hands while they grabbed papers from the stack on the sidewalk and talked quietly, seriously among themselves—not wanting to jolt the lull of the morning. He went two blocks more, over to 14th Street, and sold all the papers from the first bundle. Then he hurried up to Broad Street in case Billy Casey wouldn't have come out today. He hadn't, and July rushed over and stood where Billy would have stood if he hadn't been drinking and sleeping through the alarm clock, on a corner where he could go out into the street if need be and hit everyone for four blocks west of City Hall who was heading over there to get on the L or the Crosstown or the Frankford.

When, about nine thirty, he'd sold all but a dozen papers he went to breakfast. In the diner he sold two more to Mac Shempt and Morris Walter, the two policemen who had long ago carried the angry girl from the open diner on 15th Street. As he chewed his toast he saw Earl Schmidt across the street, but thought nothing of it.

"Hello, July," said a voice beside him and he turned back to the counter just as a man he recognized sat down. He wore a suit, and clean, pressed white cuffs reached out over his thick wrists. The wedding ring on his left hand was studded with jewels. His smart overcoat hung next to the door. With a quick second-thought movement as natural as blinking, he reached down with a paper napkin from the dispenser and rubbed away a spot of soiled water on his pants leg and tossed it on the floor just as the waiter arrived. The slight fragrance of the cologne added just that final touch to the almost too pure smell of cleanliness. It was in this man's character to be completely at home in a diner of the kind July frequented to save money, without compromising either his opinion of himself or his mannerisms. His hair was thin and beginning to gray, yet his face was clearly too heavy and firm to be very far into its fifties. His eyes were solemn, but his large hands, which seemed always to be moving and gesturing as he talked, could only be remembered as jovial.

"Scrambled eggs," he said. "Three of them, mixed with cream, four pieces of toast, sausage, a large glass of orange juice, tea with lemon, and while I wait I'll have a roll—that one there, in fact," and he pointed inside the display case to a jam-filled pastry which made July's mouth water though he'd already finished eating his full meal. "Oh, yes, and get this fellow anything he wants."

Behind the counter, Dwane Burt was pulling out a roll and at the same time trying to gather up the old plates, napkins, water glasses and ketchup bottles that the big man kept shoving over to clear everything away from the counter in front of him.

"Nothing for me, Dwane," said July.

The man frowned and looked petulantly at the roll, then at July. "Give that one to July," he said. "It looks a little pale outside the case. I'll have the one in the corner. No—the other one."

"Thanks," said July.

"People have to eat," he said, and in an aside to the waiter added a half-portion of hash browns and ketchup to be set beside the scrambled eggs.

"OK, Mr. Carroll," said Dwane, and went away into the kitchen.

"Your cat . . . Where's your cat? Bring him in here and we'll get him some cream. What's his name, anyway?"

"Bu-u-tch," said July, his mouth full.

"An appropriate name, if I do say so. Where is he, did you say? Outside? Bring him in by all means. Wait—Dwane will bring him in. That was certainly a good roll—how about another?" July's was not yet half finished. "Of course, mouth too dry. Dwane! Hey, Dwane!" Dwane stuck his head out of the kitchen. "Something to drink here. What will it be? Chocolate milk by all means. A glass of chocolate milk . . . two glasses! And another roll if you please—the same kind." Everyone else in the diner was looking at them, but he seemed not to notice and went on waving his fork and talking.

"It was too wet for him," said July when he got a chance. "He doesn't like to get wet, so he stayed home."

"Home," said Carroll. "And where's home? That is, where do you live? Perhaps I know some people in your neighborhood. I know thousands of people, or at least they know me. It's a pity your cat isn't here. I like animals, and would have a hundred myself if Rose wasn't allergic to them. They make her sneeze, don't you know. Very curious. So where do you live?"

"Oh, clear over on the south side," said July, as he'd learned to say whenever he was asked, unless, that is, he *was* on the south side (which he rarely was), when he'd answer something different. Carroll's food arrived and was set before him steaming up from the plate. With the fork he'd been holding ever since it was put in front of him, he dove into the eggs and potatoes, taking two bites of toast for every one of anything else, complaining, "Toast must be eaten quickly. Darn stuff gets cold too fast." Between mouthfuls, when his fork was empty, he would wave it around in small circles. He continued: "The south side. I know that neighborhood. What street do you live on? Parnassus, perhaps. Say, we need some more food here. Dwane! What'll it be? Oh, never mind, waffles then. Waffles, Dwane, two plates. Hurry! So I was saying, what street was that you said?"

"Parnassus."

"Here, have some of this toast. It's beginning to get cold. Take the jelly too. I detest these little packages. Who wants to take the time to open them?" He shoved two pieces of toast over at July, and six packages of grape jelly. "Parnassus, huh? What block?"

"Sixteenth."

"Parnassus doesn't have a sixteenth block," he said, swinging the fork. "Therefore, you're lying. Take my advice, never lie unless you know it can't be found out. Otherwise, tell 'em the truth or clam up. Where're the waffles anyway? Don't use a spoon to spread jelly. My God! Here, Dwane, bring a clean knife. Heavens. And tea. Do you like tea?"

"No," said July.

"You'll grow into it. Excuse me, these sausages are getting cold." He forked them in separately, chewing each about four times before swallowing. July couldn't help but feel a little smug sitting there next to him, thinking everyone's eyes were on them, and that he must be quite a fellow to have such an opulent friend. The waffles arrived. Mr. Carroll deftly flopped two of them over onto the second plate and set it before July. The syrup arrived in a glass pitcher with a flat metal finger which kept it closed when not in use. More milk arrived in Dixie cups. July began pouring the syrup.

"No, wait!" exclaimed Mr. Carroll. "Butter first. Always butter first—tastes too dry without it. Here, take these." He slid over a handful of butter pats. "Dwane, bring some more butter, please. It's a shame your cat isn't here. Anything interesting in the paper?"

"Commies arrested," said July.

"In other words, you don't know."

"I never read them," said July. Then shoved his mouth full again. He wasn't really hungry, yet the idea of something free, the tiny hunger that he did have, the taste of the syrup and a desire to be able to keep up with Mr. Carroll kept him at it.

"I never read them either when I sold papers: just look at the headlines and get an idea of what the first-page features are about. That's all you need. Then I got a job digging ditches. Here, look." He put down his fork, wiped off his hands with two napkins, pushed his sleeve back several inches and held out his hands and wrists for July to inspect. "See, the left arm is bigger, hand and everything. Comes from digging ditches. Everyone told me then, 'Hey, Frank, don't dig ditches. Let's go to the tavern. Let's go get some girls. Working's for clods. Let's go down to Atlantic City.' But they did and I didn't, and sometimes when they'd see me down in some ditch they'd holler, 'Keep it up, chump.' But after I had earned the money I wanted, I quit and went into business. The first years were hard and nobody knew me 'cause I had my nose to the grindstone all the time and hardly ever came out of the store. But I stuck it out. Everyone said, 'There's no money to be made in selling furniture—like yesterday's newspaper.' But now they look at me and what do they see?"

July looked at him with his mouth full, and lifted his eyebrows a little.

"They see this suit, worth over three hundred dollars. They see my house and my wife—Miss New Jersey, 1936. They see, in short, what they wanted to be but didn't have the stamina to work for. Dwane, cream for this tea, please."

July glanced outside and saw Earl Schmidt still standing across the street. He didn't think anything of it.

"What does your father do?"

July had learned to avoid telling anyone about his parents being dead, because every time he did the person he was talking to would retreat as if in revulsion. But he had a strong desire to tell Carroll, and also a slight fear that if he said his father was a worker in the General Electric factory, Carroll would twirl his fork, looking up to the ceiling, and say, "Montgomery, Montgomery in the factory, let me see. Montgomery—no, I don't believe so. You must be lying again. There's no Montgomery there. In fact, no one whose name even begins with an mo. You're lying again. Very stupid."

"My father was a mechanic and welder," said July. "He had his own garage bigger than four of these rooms. My mother was so beautiful that men used to sit all afternoon outside the garage just hoping they might be able to see her." Tears had formed in his eyes, and he blushed. Carroll's hands stopped moving and he turned and stared at him, almost frowning. At first July couldn't look back.

"Look," said Carroll softly, but very firmly, "some things you have to learn to keep to yourself after you get older—things that are better left unsaid. But just between the two of us, everything I have—all of it—I'd turn over at the drop of a hat for a chance to see my folks again, just to see them setting the table in our kitchen and have Mom scolding him for not wanting to use the matched silverware unless we had company. *Any of us would.* But it can't be done—not in this life at least; so the only thing we can do is make the most of it we can, without them. Let's get out of here." He took out his billfold, and without hesitating over the bills—as though he'd decided the day before yesterday what he was going to take out—he plucked up a five and laid it on the counter.

They walked down to the corner together and then parted ways. Just before he got into his car Franklin Carroll said, "Say, that kid over there across the street isn't following you, is he?"

"No," said July. "At least, I don't think so—or if he is I have no idea why."

"Ugly-looking kid just the same. Say, next week. What do you say about eating here again? Same time. And bring your cat . . . Butch. Yes, bring Butch."

"We'll see," said July. "But thanks."

"Phooey." The door slammed and the Cadillac pulled out into the traffic lane and bullied its way down the street by means of its two chrome bullet-shaped bumper extensions.

July went toward Rittenhouse Square, as good a place as any to come upon late risers—people who didn't have to work and at about ten thirty would come wandering out of their apartment buildings slightly inebriated and hoping the day would get over with quickly. These people, if you could get close to them and talk softly, would usually buy a paper if for no other reason than to have the human experience of placing a dime in a warm hand and getting something in return. July sold out there, and began walking on Spruce toward a neighborhood grocery store where cat food was cheap. He was thinking about Mr. Carroll.

Passing Jack's Place, he was thrown bodily into a small alleyway by unseen hands which had grabbed him from the back. Without turning around, he ran, hearing two or three pairs of feet behind him. "Get him! Get him!" Directly ahead was a wooden wall eight feet tall. It occurred to him that he was trapped, but he was too afraid to accept it and only slowed down enough to bring his movements more under his control, as though he intended running on through the oak boards. Using his speed as a lever, he jumped against the surface of the wall as though there were a ledge to support him, grabbed hold of the top and scrambled over, never seeing who it was behind him, and lit out for home.

"Did you see that!" exclaimed Al, looking up at the wall. "He just went right over it. How'd he do it?"

"Easy," said Earl, walking back and forth, smacking his fists together. "He used his momentum for a lift up." He kept pacing back and forth, muttering loudly. "He's had military training. That's an old Marine trick. We simply didn't realize what we were up against. Don't worry, we'll get him—now that we know what kind of intelligence we have to cope with. We may be forced to carry weapons."

"Do you really think he's had *military* training?" asked Marty.

"No doubt about it. Marines. He'll be tough to take. Most likely he's had 'touch kill' training as well."

"Touch kill!"

"That's a special hands-and-feet combat fighting. Very deadly. Worse than karate."

"Really?"

"Sure, much worse. But don't worry, I know the technique of it, and though very deadly, it's useless against a front-on upward thrust attack—like a fast uppercut or knee. But it might be good to carry weapons, just in case. Maybe he's got a shiv and knows how to use it. Anyway, I've got a plan."

"Beat it, boys, that's a private yard," came a man's voice from above, and they ran back out onto the street.

By the time July got back to City Hall he'd calmed down pretty much, and was maybe even a little exhilarated at having gotten away so easily. But he was frightened as well. Once on the landing of the L he'd seen a mugging, in which two younger men had put a strangle hold on someone and taken his money. In Fairmount he'd seen two guys fighting with chains and automobile aerials. And once right in front of the pizza shop on Market a man had pulled a black taxi driver out of his car and beat him with a piece of pipe. But despite this, he'd convinced himself that nothing was liable to happen to him because he was only twelve. Now he knew that wasn't true. He wasn't safe. Someone—more than one—had tried to mug him. It was the only explanation he could imagine. He thought of the voice: "Get him! Get him!" and shuddered.

"Somebody tried to mug me," he told Charlie in the change booth. But he noticed, sadly, that Charlie was drunk.

"What'd ya expect?" came yamming out of the cage. "Just what the hell'd ya expect? Who said you'd be safe—walking around like some street urchin? The police, now, tell the police. Ha! You know what they do when someone calls in to complain of being robbed or for murder? Someone like you or me? They tell ya to stuff it."

"I've got to hurry," said July. "Thanks for the dollars."

"It's people like us who haven't got a chance. They make it so whatever we do there's always . . ."

July walked away. It took him nearly a half-hour of waiting around before he got the chance to get back underneath the platform to his cement room. As soon as he was out of the light and into the darkness he felt a peacefulness overtake him. He knew he was safe.

He closed the door carefully and lit his lamp. Butch's eyes were green inside his box. He carried the light back and sat down. "Someone tried to mug me today as I was going after cat food," he said. Butch came out and jumped up on him. "How would you like to be mugged, huh? Answer me that. 'Pull over there, cat. Your money or your life.' How would you like it?" Butch sat on his leg and looked at him as though he would neither like nor dislike it—just that it would be beneath him.

Later that night July went out and bought a hamburger and french fries to go, with an extra helping of ketchup to dip the ends of the fries in, and a small cup of milk with a lid, which was put into the white paper sack along with the rest so that it would lose its chill before he got back. He went to the bathroom in City Hall for what he hoped would be the last time that night and went down to his room and ate dinner with his cat, who patiently lapped up the warm milk with his small sandpaper tongue.

The following morning, upon waking up, he felt sure that the experience of the day before was behind him. The memory of the voice—"Get him! Get him!"—was like something out of a dream and had no more right to his conscious attention than did any other blurb from a nightmare. He gave Butch the last ten swallows of milk, wound his alarm clock and mentally said good morning to all of his pictures while he dressed. No matter how cold it was up on the street, it was never less than about forty-five degrees in his room. Butch was reluctant, but with coaxing was talked into joining him. They were a little late in getting to the pickup. Most of the boys had already left. It was mid-March and the days were becoming noticeably longer and less mean. On a clear morning like this one the sun seemed to be up a whole hour earlier than just a month ago. Earl Schmidt, Al and another boy were the only ones still there and were talking quietly together. July had an urge to go up and tell them of how he'd almost been mugged the day before, but they obviously were talking privately and looked as though they wouldn't like being disturbed. He picked up his two bundles, carried them aside and cut one open.

"He's got a shiv," said Earl. "Don't look now, you fool! My guess is he's on to us, and is trying to draw us into making a mistake and challenging him here in the open where he'll have a chance to use his gun."

"Come on, he doesn't have a gun," said Marty.

"Don't kid yourself, buster. I wouldn't be surprised if he had his cat's claws dipped in poison either, and trained to hand command. We've already underestimated him once, let's not make the same mistake twice—it might be our last."

"He wouldn't kill us."

"Not if we outfigure him. Did either of you guys bring guns?" They shook their heads. "OK, good. Too many guns is a mistake. Besides, it's better you don't have any. An amateur with a gun is a danger to himself."

"Look, Earl, I could start to resent—" began Al, who, though a year younger, had a good physical sense of himself.

"Skip it. No offense. Look." He pulled out a .38—the kind usually worn by policemen—from under his coat where he'd had it stuck in his pants. The sight of it held the other two in a spell. July left for Pine Street, hoping to have the same luck there that he'd had the day before.

"Is it loaded?"

"Of course it is. It's a danger to ever leave a gun unloaded. If you know it's always ready to fire, then you'll never make a mistake—thinking the chamber's empty."

A little after nine July saw the pretzel man across the street and went over to get one, carrying Butch because the traffic was heavy. Waiting for his turn, he sold a paper, then two and then three. He set Butch down on the sidewalk and began making change. He sold another. His turn for a pretzel came up and he stepped forward: "Just one," put on mustard, hesitated, then decided against a hot chestnut and paid a nickel. When he walked back out of the small knot of people he didn't see Butch anywhere. He called and looked around the corner, and up and down the curb. Then he checked the ledges and basement window casings. He began to panic. "Hey, mister. You seen a cat—a black-and-orange one?"

"No, sorry."

He looked wildly out into the street. Nothing . . . just a wet paper bag which deceived him for a second. He crossed in the traffic to get to the other side. A car honked furiously and someone shouted at him.

"Hey, mister, you seen a black-and-orange cat?"

"No, sorry. How about a paper?"

"Sure."

"Here, keep the change. What color did you say?"

But July was gone, running to look around another corner. Then he crossed the street again and began knocking on doors. "Have you seen a black-and-orange cat? It disappeared just a couple of minutes ago, right out in front of your building."

"No, sorry."

He looked for over an hour, and stopped a patrol car—despite his fear of being arrested for something—and both men got out and helped him look, and let him listen while they called in Butch's description to the department. They said they'd look for him from their car. A half-hour later they returned, driving at a snail's pace, and told him he might wait until the afternoon and go down to the city pound and see if Butch was brought in—and why wasn't he in school? July thanked them and made up a lie about his parents having permission for him to be out until after the noon hour and went away as quickly as he could without running.

At one o'clock he was given directions to the city pound, got on a bus and went down. The sight of all the animals howling and looking through their wire cages in hopeless, doleful despair made him begin crying. But he stopped soon after, and resolved never to again. The manager talked to him and informed him that there were no more cats to be seen there today, and no, it was impossible that they might already have disposed of Butch—and wouldn't. He could come back every day for the next year, if he wanted to, and check. Their policy was to keep any animal they brought in off the street for at least a week before they put it to sleep.

July went back to Pine again and resumed looking, having no real hope of finding him, but afraid to return to his room alone. A young boy stood in the middle of the block. July approached him; but before he could ask if maybe he hadn't seen a black-and-orange cat, the boy said menacingly: "Hey, white boy, I've got somethin' for ya." And he pushed a folded sheet of paper, quite soiled and rumpled, into July's hand and ran off down the street, twice throwing back the finger. The letter was put together the way magazines always showed threatening letters—words from a newspaper pasted together—the effect being quite impersonal and sinister:

If you want your cat back. Alive.
Come to locust parking lot, 23rd. St.
At 12 midnight unarmed and alone.
We know all about you

He read it over to himself several times. It didn't seem to make any sense. It was as if bad luck or fate had written him a letter threatening him even further; that is, there was a knowledge somewhere that couldn't reasonably exist. He almost wouldn't believe what it meant. He put it in his pocket and went home. For over an hour he sat on the bench above his room and watched the trolleys. He thought he heard his name called from down in the tunnels, but it was just the groan of the tracks and the howling of the wind. Then he slipped down under and into his room. Sitting in total darkness, holding his mother's pistol, he thought: *We know all about you.*

His terror began to rise. He lit his lamp and set it in front of the door, letting the flames flicker in his mind. He became more afraid and the terror rose again. He became incapable of thought. Words refused to form, or when they did their meaning would be drained from them like madmen's talking. Then the stranger inside him came very far up and he began watching himself from the inside being afraid, whipping the terror still further, looking at it like a spot of bright flickering light, getting brighter and brighter, flaring up and going down. And then ten minutes after he was sure he could take no more the specter came in.

July knew he was a specter because to enter he didn't have to use the door; he came through it. His hair was as black as a raven. His hands and arms were like brass. His fathomless eyes glowed with compassion.

July's terror subsided. The stranger inside him sank back down. A peacefulness overtook him. "I was so afraid," he said. "They have my cat."

He took the note out of his pocket and handed it to the specter, who took it and read it, then let it fall between his fingers as if it were of no importance at all.

"There's nothing we can do about it now," he said, and his voice was strong and gentle. "I wonder if you couldn't put that gun down, or at least stop pointing it at me."

July taped it under the table. "What am I going to do?" he asked.

"When the time comes you'll simply do it," said the visitor. "Have you put away your two dollars today?"

"No."

"Well, why don't you do that? Maybe even count your money?"

"OK," said July. "But I don't have any bills—no, wait, yes I do." He uncovered the jar and added two dollars to it. Then carefully took out the whole wad, squared it up evenly and began counting it with pleasant, lingering deliberation.

"How much do you have there?"

"Wait, I'm not finished yet . . . one hundred . . . and twenty . . . four dollars. Wow! I didn't think I had that much. I thought maybe a hundred fifteen, but *one twenty-five,* that's almost one fifty!"

"Better put it back now," said the specter.

July agreed and buried it, smoothed out the bed and sat back on his chair.

"What'll we do now?" asked the specter.

"We could play cards. Do you know crazy eights?"

"Not really. But I don't care to play. Why don't you play and I'll watch? I'd enjoy that."

"I'll play solitaire, three-at-a-time turn up."

"Fine."

July played three games. "Bad luck," the comforting specter said each time. Sometimes he pointed out plays July'd overlooked, or commented on things like, "You've got to get that eight out of the hole." Finally, July won. Then the specter said, "Why don't you lie down and go to sleep for a while? What time is it?"

"Seven fifteen," said July.

"Well, I'll set the alarm for ten thirty. That'll give you plenty of time. But if you're going to be able to do anything you'll need to be rested, or your nerves will collapse just when you need them."

July got under his blankets fully dressed and closed his eyes, then reopened them. "Say," he said. "If you're who you are, how can I be who I am?"

"What a question," laughed the specter and his face glowed even brighter and July looked away for fear the radiance of it would lull him to sleep and he'd miss the answer. "And since you put it that way, I guess all I can say is you're not." July closed his eyes. "That is, if one of us were in question, I'm afraid it would have to be you." July fell asleep.

When he awoke he was alone. He reached behind the clock and unset the alarm, though it had not yet gone off. With the lamp lit, he discovered it to be just several minutes after ten. He went out and passed water on the ground; then he came back in, shut the door and began to contemplate what he was going to do.

Earl, Al and Marty arrived at the parking lot a quarter of an hour before midnight. Marty carried the cardboard box with the cat in it. The lot was asphalt, and large enough for fifty cars. A ticket booth sat at the entrance, closed from nine to six thirty. There were twenty-odd cars parked haphazardly. The corner they chose was empty for two stalls each way and was at the back of the lot. Between them and the alley was a chain-link fence. Earl took the box from Marty and set it down against the brick side of the building and fence.

"Now, let's run over again what we're going to do."

"He'll never come. Let's wait awhile, then let the cat out and go home."

"Don't worry, he'll come. Now, with the cat in the corner he'll have to come into the clear, here away from the cars. We'll see him as soon as he comes in anyway and I'll have plenty of time to get ready."

"I don't know," said Al. "We could get in a lot of trouble for this."

"Naw."

"As soon as we see him you two should get behind that Buick. I'll get behind this car over here and call to him and tell him to come into the corner where he can see his cat. Then, after he's beside the box I'll call out and tell 'im I've got a gun and to throw all weapons down."

"What if he doesn't?" asked Al.

"He will: I'll tell him that if he doesn't I'll fill the box with lead."

"Holy Jesus, we could get in trouble for this. What if we kill him?"

"They'd get us for sure."

"No they wouldn't," said Earl. "They'd never join us with a motive. There's no way they can find you if they don't have a motive to go on."

"But we've got a motive—why else would we be here?" Al said.

"That's the way I see it too, Earl. Let's turn the cat loose and go home. This whole thing's gotten out of hand. Fuck, if you want to fight him, just go up and bust him in the mouth. What are we doing here anyway? Really, what are we doing here?" He tried to laugh then, to offset the whine that had crept into his voice, but he couldn't pull it through and lost Al, who for his own pride's sake couldn't condone such an obvious display of shameful emotions.

"A grudge isn't a motive," said Earl. "Besides, what's to worry about?"

"Say, if you aren't going to use your gloves, Earl, could I put 'em on? It's freezing out here."

Earl gave them to him. "Then while I've got him covered, you two make sure he's clean—he'll be helpless with the flashlight in his face—and I'll come in and take 'im."

Then they went over it again, and crossed to the entrance to look down the street. Earl took his gloves back and they returned to their cover and talked through the plan again. Changing it a little, he decided Al should hold the flashlight and stay back away from July when they searched him, thereby making sure of a good shot. When July's silhouetted figure stepped into the lot they all froze.

July was as afraid as he could ever remember being, and nothing within the realm of complete and utter destruction would have surprised him. He half expected all of the car headlights to flick on and come moving toward him, or hear his cat's final cry.

"I've got a gun!" Earl sang out. "Come over here into the corner. I've got a gun, remember." July went over, beyond the cars obstructing his view of the box. Why can't I be braver? he asked himself. Why do I have to be so frightened? Please be all right, Butch. He walked faster. "All right, hold up," came the voice. "The cat's in the box. Throw down your weapons, Marine boy, or I'll fill the box with thirty-eight slugs." Pause. July was too afraid to talk or move. "OK. Go search him." A flashlight came on and aimed at his face. He could barely make out two figures coming toward him. "Remember, I've got a gun," came the menacing voice again. He controlled himself no longer. The urge to run overcame him. He grabbed up the box, put it under his left arm, threw the handful of gravel rocks from his right hand at the light and ran.

"That son of a bitch hit me with a rock!"

"Get him!" shouted Earl, too excited to begin running himself. "Get him! He's afraid! He's scared to death! Get him! Get him!"

"He hit me with a rock—shoot him!"

"Get him!" They began running after him.

"Shoot him!" cried Marty and Al together.

"Never mind that. I don't have any bullets. God, was he scared! Get him!"

Running with the box under his arm slowed July down considerably. He lost more of his lead when four or five teenagers tried to stop him, figuring him to be a thief. Down an alley, back onto the street. He could hear their footsteps gaining on him, but there was nothing he could do. He heard them gasping for breath right behind him, then felt them grabbing hold of his shoulders. He dodged to the right, freeing himself for a moment, and continued running. But he couldn't get away and they forced him down into a basement staircase. Frantically, he tried the door at the bottom, but it was locked. His three assailants were coming down, one of them saying, "Stay back, stay back, he's mine. I'll take 'im. Boy, is he scared!"

The realization that July was frightened—terrified of them—brought Earl such joy that he wanted to laugh out loud. His desire to beat July to a pulp so completely overcame him that his whole body seemed to be shaking and throbbing as he came down the steps. But he didn't comprehend the extent to which July was afraid, or how badly he wanted to get up the stairs and out onto the street again. July was so afraid of being beaten to death at the bottom of the steps and left there by the locked door that, without a thought, he opened the box, picked up the only thing he could find and with a broken brick in each hand ran up the stairs.

Earl was hit three times in the face and once in the chest. He sank down and felt feet clambering over him, and, shaking with the ecstatic memory of July's fear, feeling the trapped laughter swinging around him, he passed out. Al was hit once, ripping his nose open, and came out of the stairwell with Marty breathing down his neck, running. July, with his cat beside him, came up onto the street, let the bricks fall, turned and ran with Butch in the opposite direction as though the Lords of Death were after them, Butch running with his tail flat out behind him, right down the middle of the deserted street.

Once back in their room, July sat for a long time in his chair staring at the table in front of him, where lay the remains of his successful game of solitaire.

Even after he'd caught his breath and the adrenaline had melted back down the sides of its pot, he remained wrapped in thought. How could he accept his own cowardliness? The memory of the uncontrollable fear—if there had been a cliff there instead of a locked door, he would've gone over, like a herd of stupid sheep—made him utterly ashamed of himself, and in his own eyes he was the lowest of the low. All honor cast to the winds. Coward, coward, coward! he silently screamed at himself. What would his visitor of earlier that night have thought of him if he had known that there was such an emotion in him? Clearly, if he had known, he never would have come. July wished for a second chance. He pictured what he would do. Standing up against the fence with the flashlight in his face, he pulled out his gun and coolly, gloriously, let the bullets fly in all directions, was hit once in the arm, then the leg, sank down on his knees, let loose another two shots, killing them, and was taken away in an ambulance with police sirens.

No, it hadn't been like that. It could never be like that. He'd had his one chance and had muffed it. Coward, coward, coward. Weak, weak, weak.

Butch jumped up on his lap and raised him partially out of his thoughts. "Ho, ho," he said, pointing his finger into Butch's fur. "There you have it—mugged. How'd ja like that, huh?" Butch looked at his finger in contempt. "Ho, ho, I saw how scared you were—'After that cat, boys. After him!'" Butch looked as if it were all beneath him. That's fine for you, thought July—being afraid doesn't mean anything to you; you're just a cat.

He fed him the last of the food in the can, and tossed it out the door because it was beginning to smell.

The next morning found him frightened again. He'd not stopped to think before going to sleep that he'd have to either return to the same place to pick up his papers, where he couldn't avoid meeting with the very people who had threatened him—the reasons for which he partially understood and partially didn't—or give up his job. He lay under the blankets and didn't want to get up. But after he'd thought about it and seen that those were the only alternatives he had, he went off to the pickup, leaving Butch behind in his box.

Al and Marty, who had run off down the street leaving Earl momentarily to die from loss of blood maybe, had come back just as he was regaining consciousness. Marty, to explain how he happened to be without a mark on him, ventured, "As soon as I could hear the bullets whizzing by my head, I knew it was no healthy place."

"He got me with a glass-studded blackjack," added Al, at the same time calling attention to his nose. They came up onto the street, Earl carefully feeling his face for swelling and stinging cuts. "That kid's nothing to fool with," said Al, but tentatively, unsure what the drift of the following conversation would be.

Within the myriad images going through Earl's memory of the evening, one became clearer than all the rest—the face of July with the flashlight on it, filled with fear. The full power of the image almost caused him to lose consciousness again because it made him feel so good. And as he was walking down the street back to their neighborhood he heard them saying not only that July'd had a loaded gun that he was shooting with a silencer, a blackjack, cleats on the heels of his shoes which he could easily and with accuracy kick above his head, years of military training, but that in some miraculous way he'd managed to get himself thrown down into the cellar stairwell so that he'd have the chance to kill all of them. Earl realized what they were saying and accepted it as easily as a breath of fresh air; and within the privacy of his mind he would take July down, notch by notch, until he'd reduced him from a figure of awesome respect to the face in the flashlight. The sensation was even better than before, and he actually sank swooning to his knees when the first wave of it hit him. Al and Marty took hold of him to lift him up, but he yelled at them, "Leave me alone, please leave me alone."

So the following morning didn't turn out to be a second chance for July after all. Clearly, Al and Marty had no wish to begin any trouble with him, and communicated this by way of exchanging quick glances.

He felt Earl was different, and for several weeks afterward July found occasion to test himself, gathering all his courage to go over near 21st and Market, giving Earl a chance to start something—which he didn't. But he also didn't stop looking at July with a contemptuous expression, even if only when he thought himself unobserved. Several weeks more and Earl was gone. It was said he'd been accepted into a private school of some sort in upper Michigan. Al and Marty grew a little friendlier after that and the three of them often talked several minutes before they set out in the morning, though July never felt very comfortable with them, especially with Marty, who seemed to be able to pick up the bundles of newspapers with no effort at all.

That spring July talked to the fat man in the newspaper booth beside City Hall. At first he hadn't been friendly, but as July stayed with him he loosened up; and after stopping by every day for two weeks, always pleasant but always about the same thing, July won him over and they formed a kind of partnership—an agreement for mutual gain. In the beginning the agreement was enforced by the fat man, Ed Shavoneck. When he arrived at the stand with the key, he'd open up and take out a small hand truck and give it to July, who would be there waiting. July would make two trips from the pickup—seven bundles—and bring them back to the green plywood stand. Then every paper he took to sell himself would cost him five cents instead of three cents, but he would also be purchasing the privilege of being able to sell them down under City Hall amid the streams of people going to work or shopping.

He could still roam when he felt like it, but as the weeks and months went on he felt less and less like doing so. It was simply too easy to stand in one place; he sold more papers; he saw more girls in bright dresses, an interest he was beginning to acquire at a distance. Butch could spend every day with him. All in all, it was undeniably better. He missed the feeling of autonomy that being in a new area gave him, but it was replaced by a sense of belonging in some mysterious way to that organ of the city beneath City Hall, and being in a way a part of everyone passing through it—even the girls. More people came to know him than ever before. He could tell by their expressions that they recognized him and even the ones who never bought a paper accepted him. He was a part of their lives. It came to be said of him that he actually lived somewhere down in the tunnels.

When Ed Shavoneck began to trust him, their partnership unfolded. He gave July a key to the stand so that he could get the hand truck, bring the papers back, set up the display racks, candy, cigars, magazines and key rings, and have three jelly rolls and a cup of coffee with one and a half packages of sugar there waiting for him when he arrived, forty-five minutes later than if he'd had to do all this himself. In the afternoon he could go home just that much earlier. Then he taught July how to keep the kind of records he wanted and let him run the stand by himself on Saturdays and Sundays on a fifty-percent basis. Then Shavoneck began taking every other Wednesday off. His life seemed much better because of the extra free time. For several months, every time he returned after leaving the stand to July he counted everything and tried again to figure out how he could be being cheated unawares. Then later he didn't bother, and his life was pleasanter still.

This might well have been the end of the story of July Montgomery. He'd raised himself from having seventy-four things to having a job bringing in a steady income. He took comfort in being well known. He learned it was important to keep your clothes clean and bought enough pants, shirts, socks and underwear for a change every three or four days and washed them in the laundromat at two-week intervals. He learned about leaving tips for waiters and the good feeling he could generate by dropping his street voice when he talked privately to someone. He found that his personality was not fenced in by being a newsboy, even when he was in the green stand. He was taken for being the kind of person he acted. He had responsibility and a small Coleman heater, the kind used for ice fishing, to keep his room an even seventy-two degrees. He got another upholstered chair, and had a print of a brook scene hung beside the photographs. He'd read every paperback in the stand, and it wasn't uncommon that someone would ask his opinion or advice about them. He did the ordering. He got his own Social Security number, and filled out a tax statement every year. He had a post-office box which gave him great pleasure to go to and unlock, taking out free things he'd sent away for from ads in the back of magazines. Some afternoons he'd get drunk on whiskey and beer Shavoneck would buy for him, eat huge quantities of greasy food and go to a movie in one of the better theaters. He neither loved or hated anyone except his cat.

It never occurred to him then that more could be demanded from living. Years went by in the same relatively comfortable way: minor ups and downs during the week, leveling off when viewed from the perspective of months. He and Ed Shavoneck became friends, of a sort. They had a narrow band of experiences and thoughts which they offered each other as common ground. On either side of this band, say the red frequency, lay the greater part of their selves, but nevertheless within it they had many perfectly enjoyable and safe discussions.

Through the mornings July would imagine this or that girl had a secret crush on him and thought his shoulders looked powerful and that he must be wild and a man of the world, dealing so effortlessly with all kinds of people, old ladies and hoodlums, and knowing everyone of importance and everything that was going on in the underworld and was very well read too and nobody's fool, and had an extremely fierce cat. He began smoking cigarettes and wearing shoes with hard plastic heels that made sharp snapping noises when he walked.

He grew quickly during these two years and at fourteen and a half was only three inches shy of six feet, but thin as a rail. He prided himself on being able to say he was sixteen.

His savings had grown into such an enormous wad (he'd been adding to it $3.00, and sometimes $4.00, a day ever since his partnership) that he was sure he could never spend it on one thing. The bills took up three jars instead of one, and to count them all took too much time, especially when he knew there was an even $1400 contained in two of the jars together, so he'd only count the third. It seemed to him childish, too, to want to count the bills out one by one—something he was ashamed of ever having done.

He had a Bible now that he'd picked up from the Goodwill store—a fat one two inches thick, five inches high and four inches wide, tightly bound and almost impossible to read next to the inner margin. He kept his pictures inside it to keep them from curling and yellowing on the wall. His desire to read it was not religious and came upon him only once a month, or less, when he felt lonely and had nothing else to do. It was a way of bringing his parents closer to him. His father had read it; his mother had read it; now he read it, and when he did, time flashed, the voice of his mother and the expression of his father became clear, and it was a very real thing not being alone.

As time went on he began to think this business of reading the Bible was cowardly; needing to have your parents with you was kid stuff, and he gave up doing it. Butch, he reasoned, didn't have such things, and got along without them; so would he. And the book remained unopened for a long time, even to take out the pictures.

Though it was not a regular practice, he and Franklin Carroll still occasionally ate breakfast together. But lately Carroll had been pushing him around and making him feel uncomfortable.

"So, what did you say you were going to do with your future?" asked Carroll, spreading the butter over his pancakes with a knife, stacking one on top of another.

"I didn't," answered July, watching Butch under the table lapping cream.

"That's what I thought. No consideration of the future. Blind as a bat. Opportunities flying by you," and one of his hands made a fluttering motion across the tabletop. "Look, what have you got now? Imagine yourself at my age, carrying around newspapers. No, you're doing all right, don't get me wrong—here, have some of these sausages. You're way ahead of where I was at your age—how old are you?"

"Fourteen." He felt the mounting pride of looking older than he was flare up from his pancakes.

"Oh, you're well ahead of where I was at fourteen. But you have to always be thinking *what you could have.* Never let that thought slip away. It keeps you going forward—what I could have. Pardon me, miss, I wonder if we couldn't have some more tea here, and fried eggs and toast."

"How would you like them done, sir?"

"Easy over for me, and hard for the boy."

She went away into the kitchen. July watched a man come into the restaurant, looking very tired, as if he'd just woken up. He came past their table and sat down. Franklin Carroll looked quickly at him, then resumed talking. When the waitress arrived with the eggs, he effortlessly drew out his pen, wrote a couple of words across the corner of the place mat, tore it off, folded it and handed it to her, whispering something which July couldn't hear. Then he resumed talking as though never interrupted.

"Your cat, for instance, even she—"

"He," corrected July, watching the waitress carry the paper into a small room behind the counter. A man came out behind her and went back into the kitchen, then returned with the cook, a big man, heavy and bald, wearing a wide white apron. The cook came over toward them and continued to the table of the man who had just come in and was waiting for someone to take his order.

"I'm sorry," the cook said. "I'm afraid you'll have to leave." The man rose halfway out of his booth, but sat back down. Then he looked over at Carroll and let his gaze pinch together in some of the deepest hatred July had ever seen, got up and left. Throughout all of this Carroll had never looked over, or quit talking or eating.

"Tell me, what plans do you have—I mean, what would you like to be?"

July took time to think, not daring to say what he really wanted was to be the kind of guy who had a girlfriend. "I'd like to be a card dealer or a pool hustler."

"Those guys are nothing. Believe me, they're nothing. They look good, I know, lying back and being smooth and betting bluffs and running forty balls. But next week they come shining up to you for two bits. I tell you, they're nothing. Most of them are hooked on drugs, they drink Thunderbird wine for breakfast and are in terrible health—which reminds me, though I don't suppose you care, those cigarettes of yours will stunt your growth. You'd better give them up."

"I might be a writer," said July.

"Forget it, they don't make any money—one in a thousand, and then it gets eaten up by lawyers and agents who cheat them. I had a cousin who wrote a book once and it ruined his life. Do you want something more?"

"No, I'm fine," said July.

"How about the cat?"

"He's fine too, thanks." Butch had jumped up and was sitting next to July, preening himself.

"I'll tell you what—you come to work for me. You're a little young, but I think I could use you. It won't be easy. The—"

"No, I don't think I better do that."

"Well, I'm certainly not going to push you. But you owe it to yourself to think it over. So think it over. It might turn out to be an experience you could use later, even if you decide to have no part of the furniture business."

"No. I don't think I'll want to."

"Like I said," said Carroll, getting up from the booth, "think it over. Remember, you won't want to be as old as I am selling papers. And without an education—face it, July, you're sunk." On this note, he left, leaving his usual $5.00 on the table. July watched his blue Cadillac move off into the traffic. He hurried to pick up Butch and went outside, knowing that without Carroll there with him it was only a matter of moments before someone would come over and tell him to get the cat out.

He went to a movie that afternoon and sat through it twice. When he stood up to leave he realized that he'd not really seen it at all, but had been sitting there in a daze, occupied with thoughts and visions of being an old man selling newspapers and having a girl down in his room.

Walking out of the theater, he decided never to eat breakfast ever again with Franklin Carroll, and denied that he admired him or liked him or even thought he was worth knowing. *He wants, me to be ashamed of what I have . . . and he wants me to be ashamed because it will be obvious then that he's better. He's a slob. Besides, what does he care about me?*

That night he bought a dime bag of ice and drank a glass of orange-flavored vodka. Staggering carefully about the streets, he felt himself to have the world by a shoestring. He went into a second-story pool hall and played pool until he'd lost all the money he had with him, then he stopped over at the penny arcade and talked with some boys he knew there and played pinball. A group of Negroes came in and a fight started. He and Willie O. got one of them and were hitting him when the police arrived. Everybody ran. Tables were turned over in an effort to keep away from the nightsticks. July and some of his friends got away and ran down the street. The police cornered and put handcuffs on all of the blacks but one who'd gone through a window to get away, and threw them into the wagon along with Willie O. and one other white boy July didn't know.

That night he felt lonely and fell asleep with his radio playing into his ear through a little wire.

EIGHT

One morning July found himself in a situation he couldn't believe—one of those circumstances that prove to be, by virtue of the great luck involved, both exhilarating and perturbing (for fear that what appears to be true cannot possibly be). He'd gone into a small restaurant and been fortunate enough to find a place to sit down. This establishment was immensely popular because of its low cost and reasonably fair meals. He ordered coffee and two sweet rolls, and put a newspaper on the counter—a gift to the management. The room was jammed with people. The tables were doubled up, with strangers sitting together, though in most cases neither talking nor looking at each other. The two waitresses were nearly running under the nervous, austere gaze of the man behind the cash register. Then it happened. The man sitting on the stool beside July got up abruptly, threw down a quarter and left. With vague interest, through the mirror behind the glass racks, July watched the man's reversed image navigating toward the door. He moved aside and allowed to enter what July was sure was the best-looking girl he'd ever seen. His heart got excited, and he looked wildly about the room. Could it be true that the only place to sit was beside him? He didn't believe it. He watched her looking around, then, after apparently making up her mind, come straight toward him. His heart leaped, and he looked absently at the fingernails on the fingers of the hands in front of him holding a round-topped salt shaker as though he were trying to strangle it. The sound of the plastic giving beneath her on the stool, the smell and the pure *sense* of her being there crawled up the back of his neck. His heart pounded so fast that it caused a vacuum in his stomach. His hand shook as he moved the newspaper on the counter several inches out of her way, a kind of gesture, he felt. Dropping her shouldered handbag to the floor and hooking her shoe toes into the stool made his vision blur. Everything about her seemed so polite, so proper. She must be older than me, he thought; but she'll think I'm sixteen.

His coffee and rolls arrived. "This is for you," he said casually and pushed the paper forward. "My regards to the management." The waitress took it away and gave it to the man behind the cash register, who immediately began to read it. But she didn't return to take the girl's order.

She might even be seventeen, thought July, stealing furtive glances through the mirror. She looks like she's been around, all right. She had a tough, no-funny-business look about her, and sat staring coldly at the countertop. No one seemed to be noticing her, including the waitress, who rocketed by carrying food and dishes. He decided, This is it, and turned toward her smiling frantically.

"Why don't you tell me what you want," he said a little too loudly, "and maybe I can attract some attention." He laughed as though what he'd said was partially a good-natured joke about the restaurant, and drank from his black coffee, though he didn't like it except almost white with cream. She smiled back and his heart just stopped altogether, like the racing wheels of a buggy locked tight with a brake.

"That's sweet of you," she said. "Why don't you just see if you can get me what you have—the same kind of rolls. They look so good." Her eyes flashed like black, wet stones.

"Over here," said July in his selling voice. "We'll have two more rolls here—the same kind, and a cup of coffee." He tossed a dollar bill on the counter in the manner of Franklin Carroll. His change was returned with the order, but both were laid down unpleasantly, the coffee spilling a little over the top and down into the saucer.

"Must be early in the morning," he said to her, proud of how much control he was having over his voice.

"Must be," she said coldly, then softened the wrinkles in her forehead, smiled politely at July and began drinking her coffee black.

Wow! thought July. Wow!

"It was a nice sunrise this morning," he said, measuring his bites to coincide with hers so they would be leaving together.

"I didn't see it," she said. Again the coldness—almost hostility—but she realized it and looked at him to make up for it, adding apologetically, "I don't usually get up that early. Just naturally lazy, I guess."

They laughed.

"Of course," he continued the thought, "I mean, aren't we all? I mean, what I usually think is if I watch it come up I should be asleep before it gets dark—sort of to pay myself back." He laughed and she smiled, then turned away and resumed eating her remaining roll, each bite a delight to July because he'd paid for it. He gulped his own down whenever he noticed he was getting behind.

"How about something else?" he asked, as she was finishing her coffee.

"No, really, thank you. I must be going." She picked up her bag and walked out. July hurried behind her and got to the door first and opened it for her. Everyone seemed to be watching them.

"Say, don't run away. I mean, I haven't come upon anything like you in a long time—and it'd be a shame to lose you so early in the morning."

"You'll get over it," she said—the coldness beginning to rise again. But again she apologized for it. "Say, I really did appreciate the breakfast, and you're sweet, but I must be going or I'll be late for school, and I've already missed too many days this semester."

"Oh. School," said July and fell to walking silently beside her.

"We could go to a movie," he said, after several blocks.

"No. Look, maybe some other time. I really have to go, and you better not walk me any further or you could cause trouble for me—really, I mean it."

"OK, sure. Some other time . . ."

"That's right."

"When?"

"Sometime if we happen to meet—"

"Oh no . . . when?" He was trying to laugh, but there was a sickening feeling in his stomach which was making it harder. He thought he could see the beginning of the end. He wondered what kind of trouble she could be talking about.

"All right. You don't give up, do you? Just once. We'll go out just once—and don't get any ideas. I've got a feeling I'm way too old for you . . . but you are nice, so tonight—"

"What time? Tell me where you live—tell me your name—give me your phone number—I'm about seventeen."

"Come on, that can't be true. I'm not even that old. Really, I've got to go. I'll meet you right here at seven thirty tonight. My name's Charlotte. You don't need to know anything else. I wouldn't ever want you calling me or coming over to my house. Now I have to go." July couldn't help but look very sad. She touched his arm. "Really, I'll come. And thank you for breakfast." Then she left.

The rest of that morning and afternoon was composed of the longest minutes July had ever been through. Each one was so stretched out that whole dreams could fit into them. How many times had he resolved to himself that she would never come? The cut about him not being almost seventeen dried up his soul. He wanted her more than he'd ever wanted anything. He refused even to talk to Butch about it, and his little cement room, which just the day before had been perfectly fine, felt like a slum and shamed him. Worries of personal inadequacy beset him.

At a quarter to seven he began to wait, although across the street. What had been tempered with better emotions was now pure fear. At seven thirty (according to the clock in the drugstore) he crossed the street. She hadn't come. Of course, he thought. All along I knew she wouldn't show. As he stood in the appointed place, his pride dangling from him by a string, several boys he knew yelled at him from out of a car and he waved, hoping they wouldn't stop. They didn't, but tossed out a half-empty can of beer at him. He jumped back to avoid getting wet and flipped the bird at them, laughing. They returned it, and raced on down the street.

When he saw her round the corner a block away, he couldn't believe it. From that far away her long legs and small waist were evident. Wow, he thought. Someone yelled an obscenity at her from a moving car, but she didn't turn her head, walking as if she hadn't heard it.

"Hi, Charlotte," he said, when she was up to him.

"Hi," she returned, but he couldn't help thinking her voice expressed more—a desire to have never come. The hostility was still there. "Let's go."

They began walking.

"Where are we going?" he asked hesitantly.

"We're going to a movie, remember?"

"Oh yes, so we are, so we are. Which one?"

"That's up to you, you're the boss."

He smiled and blushed.

They went to the theaters on 14th across the street from City Hall. Eating pizza, they chose a movie about reincarnation and radiation, where insects were born with human minds, paid and went in.

After some time he put his arm around her in the dark obscurity and she leaned her head back on his arm; but he couldn't force himself to go further, and she took no initiative to encourage him.

When the movie was over he said, "Let's watch it again."

She said, "It wasn't that good. Too much fake."

"Everything gets better, second time around. Most books, for instance, never really make sense until the second time through. *The Case of the Thread,* for example—" he began, wanting to show his literary knowledge, but was interrupted by a man behind them leaning forward and saying: "Shut up or get out."

"Stuff it, shithead," mumbled July.

Walking with her out of the theater and into the street, experiencing that sensation of passing out of looming fantasy and into realness, July wished his parents could see him—without any fears, self-doubts or apprehensions, a beautiful, mysterious girl on his arm, her eyes wild and dark. They went to Baker's Drug Store and drank cherry sodas and July told a slightly altered account of when three toughs had kidnapped his cat.

When they were back on the street again he wanted to get her to walk in the park, but she didn't want to. The hostility had not returned, but a kind of obstinacy was beginning to rise. They wandered from store window to store window, agreeing and disagreeing on the worth of the items on display. At a certain point he realized that she had begun a slow navigation toward home and that he wouldn't be able to turn her back. Each step was a step into the closing of the night. He fought against it, but there was nothing he could do. And then:

"I've got to leave you here. It's been fun. I've had a great time."

"I'll walk you home."

"No. I wouldn't like that."

"It's not safe for you out alone. There's too many monsters loose. This is the weekend they let them roam—once a month. Keeps down on the state's food budget."

"Well, they wouldn't go for me. I'd be a bitter pill to chew."

July wished desperately to say something here about how he'd like to chew on her, and the very idea of biting her made him fill up with heat. Instead, he said quite seriously, "You aren't *afraid* of me, are you?" and looked away.

Charlotte burst into a fit of laughter. "How sweet you are!" she exclaimed, moved quickly to him and kissed him firmly, tenderly, but quickly on the mouth. "But I must go."

"Again," said July. "When will we see each other again?" The sensation of the kiss almost knocked him down. "Give me your phone number."

"Stop it. I told you I couldn't do that. I said, 'Only once. Just once.'" July looked at her. His face was as though he'd been publicly whipped. "Damn you," she said. "I told you not to go thinking anything about me. We could never be together. Damn you—I told you that."

All July could do was stand there and nod his head. After she said, "I'm sorry," and turned to go, he said, "Just once more . . . one more time."

A terrible moment ensued. At the end of it, she agreed. He feared it was only because she thought he might cry. She promised to meet him for a matinee movie on Saturday—but nothing more . . . and that was to be the end of it. Then she left. July felt naked, alone, and watched every inch of her disappear around the corner.

He followed her from a safe distance. She went a few blocks, then turned west and began walking in the shadows close to the buildings. At one corner in the middle of a very ominous-looking neighborhood, where the houses were three-story stone and the lights inside made them seem like rows of tremendous horses' skulls with candles ritualistically set inside that gleamed from the eyes and nostrils, Charlotte stopped and stood for several moments as though trying to decide where she wanted to go. Evidently making up her mind, she set off again and soon entered one of those horse skulls with only one nostril glowing. Broken windows on the third floor. July stopped across the street and tucked himself into a shadow beneath an awning, as dark as the inside of a pocket. Whenever a figure crossed the lighted window his heart would flare up, thinking it was she. But it was always unclear, moving aimlessly, a kind of phantom shape. He waited until he was thoroughly dissatisfied with himself and began walking back home, keeping on the edge of his senses, looking for signs of that trouble she'd said would find him if he walked her home. Underneath the platform with Butch he let his memories open and felt himself dissolve into the concrete.

The following day was Friday, and he worked through the morning in a daze, selling papers and making cheap talk like a madman who decides to have nothing to do with his exterior self and lets it function without him.

She'll never come, he thought. She never wants to see me again—that's simple. But then the memory of her kiss would come back, and because of the depth of feeling it produced in him, it seemed to say to him, *One event, one emotion*—the same feeling would *have* to be in her.

He quit work early in the afternoon and went down and talked to Butch for an hour, sounded all his thoughts and counted all his money out onto the pallet—even the jars that he knew contained $700 each. He began to fill one jar up again, reconsidered and stuffed it all, down to the $7.00 from that morning, into a brown paper sack: $2073. Butch overlooked all this activity with measured disapproval. Carrying the bag as though it were lunch, accompanied by his cat, July went up onto the street and headed for the several jewelry stores that he knew uptown.

Barney Snells owned and operated the Snells Jewelry Store by himself. In the past he'd tried to employ other people, but it had never worked out. He had no friends and few enjoyments. He disliked eating, and whenever he and his wife would attend a back-yard party of one of her acquaintances in the suburbs, he would ask for his steak very well done, just to watch his hosts wince and shake their heads in pity for his bad taste. He would go out of his way to buy a tie or suit that would make him look older and more drab than he was. He read nothing but science fiction, and one of the reasons none of his help had lasted was that he resented the extra companionship and noise. He played chess by mail with someone in Alaska he'd never met; and had his playing board set up in the back room of the store, and each day he would confront it as a way of waking himself up. Both of his children had run away from home when they were sixteen and he'd never heard from them again; he imagined his wife corresponded with them in secret and sent them money from his account, but he didn't hold it against her. He prided himself on having no opinions except about jewelry.

His greatest love was diamonds. He appreciated them beyond anything—the way they held the light, their purity, their rarity and strength. Breaking down a crudely cut diamond into smaller stones, eliminating pores and feathers, polishing each facet (especially on a King Cut) and making the set was an adventure in which each fiber of him participated, and he spent days at a time with his eyepiece held in his eye, turning a diamond this way and that, letting the light spray out of the facets into spectrums, his mind lost to all thought. He could recall dreams—long, complicated dreams—which were composed of diamonds turning in light, other diamonds coming in, clashing, breaking, splintering, and more diamonds growing up. One dream that he remembered with particular pleasure had begun with only the color blue and out of it had come the nine large stones of the Cullinan, and later starred the Florentine yellow.

He was an authority on diamonds. His chess set had a diamond (Magna Cut) set into the top of both the white and the black king. At the end of the game the winner held the matched pair.

He carried a small diamond replica of the Koh-i-noor (New Cut) in his watch pocket.

He was a wealthy jeweler because the experience of buying from him always proved satisfactory—he never seemed to want to let anything he had go, whatever the price.

When July came in he had the eyepiece to his eye and was painstakingly tearing apart a setting on a wedding ring that he'd come upon in trade during a trip to New York the weekend before—a wedding set which had been made to resemble the famous set made for Henry VII by Leopold with the main stone offset by four smaller ones around it—the purpose being to focus essentially red light from the facets of the larger and through the smaller, accentuated by the gold, producing small red light veins at thirty-two places along the circumference. But the job had been sloppy and many of the facets were ground at the wrong angle to catch the red spectrum band. He put the eyepiece down and stood up, looking with wary circumspection at July, his cat and the soiled brown sack which he set on the glass case.

"Watch that cat there," he said, "and mind he doesn't jump up on anything."

"Here, maybe you better wait outside," said July, and opened the silent door for Butch, who indignantly stepped back onto the sidewalk and sat down.

"Now, what can I do for you?"

"I want to buy something for someone," said July, and abruptly stopped talking, as though to offer any more information would in some way compromise his feelings. Barney Snells looked him over closely and thought he looked barbaric—his hair shaggy and long, his ears dirty, his clothes unpressed, shoes dry-splattered with mud, and a quite ruffianlike way of standing, looking down into the cabinet, his dirty bag (which looked to be full of greasy potato chips) and his abrupt, harsh voice, like a street hawker's.

"See here, now. Just what is it that you're wanting? All the things in here are extremely expensive—more than I would think you might at this stage of life be considering."

"This here," said July, pointing his finger against the glass, leaving a smudge. "Let me see this one."

Barney came quickly over. "Don't touch the glass," he said, "and take this bag off here."

July took his sack and stepped back a few inches, but remained pointing. "That one there."

Barney hesitated with "Go on, get out of here" just on the tip of his tongue. He was aware that he was being just a bit of a grouch. This didn't bother him, but he felt a vague interest in what July'd picked out. So much could be told about people from their taste in jewelry. Often some completely intelligent -appearing couples would reveal their underlying stupidity by choosing huge, gaudy designs, brooches lacking all subtlety, and rings with setting flaws, stones little more pure than industrial grade. One's taste in diamonds, Snells believed, was a mirror reflection of the soul. He opened the case.

"This one?"

"No. Over to the right."

"This one?"

"No, further . . . now down a little . . . too far."

"This one?"

"Yes, that's it. Let me look at that one."

Barney lifted it out. He felt an admiration for the boy beginning in him. From the whole case, he'd picked out the only piece of real value—a small necklace with three diamonds in the pendant, brown, yellow and white tinged with blue, very small, but set with breathtaking sensitivity. Thin wires of gold held the stones together. Barney had had it for a long time. He had $300 on it and no one had even asked him to take it out before.

"This is a really nice one," he said. "Look here how these tiny wires seem to lead your eye from one stone to another, emphasizing just a little the white one—don't touch it! And notice, only a twenty-one-inch chain would be right for it—it needs a wide angle coming down to it. Any higher would be out of the question, and any longer would be base. The person who wore it would have to be thin, of course, and pale hair wouldn't be good either."

"She's dark," said July.

"Black hair?"

"Yes."

"Oh. Then this wouldn't be quite right. It would be good, mind you, but you'd be dissatisfied, I'm afraid, in the long run."

What had happened was that Barney had become interested in talking about jewelry, and the fact that he didn't expect July to have enough money to buy even one of his poorest pieces made no difference. He put the necklace back carefully and began a slow browse from case to case, in search of the perfect thing—it was a necklace that July said he wanted, not a ring (though that would be his second choice) or a bracelet or pin. He talked as he went and asked July questions, each time surprised at his natural knowledge—his inchoate sensitivity to beauty. This boy is worth a thousand, he thought—truly remarkable to have such feelings so young.

"Where are you from?" he asked.

"Hawaii."

They talked and disagreed, but finally reached a mutual decision with a single-diamond pendant, 108 facets, on a white-gold chain. Barney felt it was the best (of a certain type) that he had in his store, and believed it fully worth the $1600 he had paid for it and even the $2000 he asked for it. But he'd been talking for a long time and his congeniality was beginning to waver. He wanted to get back to the ring he was taking apart, and visual memories of a small fissure in one of the stones became recurrent and pleaded with him to come back and find a solution for hiding it. Also he particularly disliked the situation of people finding just what they want—just what they think will change their lives (and in most cases, he believed, would)—standing, looking and knowing it can never belong to them. Much better that they should never come in at all. So, just at the moment he was ready to ask July to leave, the paper sack was upended above the counter, opened, shaken, and a tremendous pile of dollar bills fell out. The boy counted out $73 and separated it from the pile.

"There's two thousand dollars," he said. "Put the necklace in a box, please."

Snells put it in a box, a little shocked at the ugly sight of the bills on the counter, soiled and wadded up. Checks were the only real way to do business. "There'll be tax," he said, handing July the small wooden container, and disdainfully began to count the bills.

July didn't have enough to pay the tax, but Barney accepted the $73 and a pledge for the remainder when he could get it. It never occurred to him to think that he had no right selling such an expensive piece of jewelry to a fifteen-year-old boy—that he could be morally reprehended for it. Not at all; he simply was glad for him to be able to have it, and thought that if at his age he himself had had a diamond of such quality, his whole life would have been much better. All things should work out as well, he thought.

July, young as he was, didn't have the adult experience of being immediately dissatisfied with his purchase. In fact, from the moment he was out on the sidewalk with Butch he forgot about the transaction and thought only of the diamond in his pocket . . . as though it were alive. Possessing it was exciting. What it promised to do for him was even more exciting.

They took a couple of cheeseburgers, milk and fries home with them, and spent the rest of the evening taking the precious necklace out and putting it back again, reading several pages, and taking it out again and looking at it with the light, putting it on Butch and putting it back. Sleep didn't come quickly because tomorrow was Saturday. The future happiness of the rest of July's life would be decided then, one way or another.

Of course she won't come, thought July the following afternoon. I never really expected her to. She doesn't love me. Four o'clock went by. He imagined everyone in the park, in their light colorful clothes, talking about him: *See that kid over there . . . he's waiting for somebody. There's one born every day.*

How long do you think he'll stick it out'?

Some————s will never give up.

Sad, isn't it?

There's one born every minute.

At four thirty, a half-hour late, she did come. As soon as she came up to him she began talking.

"I wasn't going to come at all. Then the idea of you hanging around waiting . . ."

He felt happy, like anyone who believes that one of the old virtues has paid off.

Without saying anything of the diamond, he took her to the matinee. In the darkness of the theater, with the backs of their heads lit from the projector hole, he rejected putting his arm around her. Even through his elation he could tell that she'd made herself very sour for this afternoon and he was afraid she'd say something like *Watch it, Jack,* out loud. So he sat there in silence and tried to get through to her with his intense feelings. He wondered what to say when he gave her the necklace—what would be appropriate yet nonchalant?

After the movie was over, it seemed events were rushing by him so quickly that he might not have time to give it to her at all; it was all he could do to keep up with what was happening. As soon as they were out on the street she wanted to go home.

"OK. We better say goodbye now." Her white teeth flashed. "No use in dragging this thing out any more than we have to . . . I should never have come."

"But you promised," said July, laughing.

"But I promised."

"It's because you're honest. I'm like that too. You know, every time I strike a match without closing the cover, I always think for a second—remember that line, 'Close Cover Before Striking'—that I've broken the law and that I might be arrested. When I don't think of it that way, I think I'm devil-may-care. Sometimes I close the cover and feel safe."

"It's not honesty," she said. "It was laziness."

"Laziness?"

"I don't know. Quit asking me questions. It's just sort of laziness. That's all."

"Let's go get some grinders."

"I'm not hungry."

July could feel his hold on himself slipping. She was walking faster. He knew that inevitable corner was just ahead where she would not allow him to come any farther. This would be the last time. There would be no more. He hadn't wanted it to be like this. But it was now or never. Stopping to pry out the box from his pocket, he fell behind. Running, in a very emotional voice, he called out, "Wait, wait. I have something for you." Several young men in suits were walking up the street toward them.

Charlotte stopped, wheeled around and snapped the box out of his hand. "What's this here? What is it? You bought this for me? Let's see." She opened it and grabbed the diamond. "Oh, a necklace," she said. "Very nice." It dangled from her outstretched hand. "Yes, it's very nice, but I'm afraid I can't accept it, I told you—"

"I want you to have it," said July. "It's *for* you."

"That's very nice, but really, you must go now. These are friends of mine coming here."

The two young men were nearly within hearing distance, walking casually but determinedly, both nineteen or twenty.

"Another time. We'll see each other another time," he said quickly.

"No, no more times, I told you that. Oh, I should never have come. Here, take this back."

"Hey, Charlotte," called one of them. "We were just coming to get you. We must hurry if we're to get there by six. Aunt Alice will be simply mortified." They had come up to them now.

"Who's this here, a friend of yours?" the other asked, almost pleasantly.

"Yes," said Charlotte quickly. "Yes, here." She held out the diamond to July, who stood there stunned, motioning with his hands and backing shyly away.

"You keep it," he whispered.

"We've interrupted a love scene!" called the one young man to the other. "Charlotte, really!"

"Shut up," she said.

But the one, obviously irritated in being late, pressed on. "What have you there—a necklace?" He held out his hand for Charlotte to show it to him. "Let's see," and snapped his fingers. July took another confused step backward.

"Wait." She followed him. "Take this back. Don't mind them."

"You keep it," he whispered inaudibly, turned and ran. The young men howled with laughter.

Even as he ran, he felt himself filling with anger, and after running down the first side street, he stopped. Then, shaking with rage, he peered cautiously around the corner to where the three stood. The young men had the necklace held in front of them and soon they were all laughing. One of them said, "A paper boy. Really, Charlotte, a paper boy!" Then they began to walk toward him and he pulled his head back. When he rechecked, they had stopped again and were hanging the diamond around her neck, then admiring her as she pretended to be a model, laughing. As they came closer their bright chatter grew louder. July held on to the wall with his left hand, as though he were in a faint, while his right hand, tightened unconsciously into a fist, had splintered the little wooden jewelry box and pieces of red felt showed between two of his fingers. Dry tears ran down his throat.

When they stepped into view, she was in between the two young men. July rushed forward, hurling the one closest to him out of the way, and in one quick motion caught the delicate chain in his hand and ripped the necklace from around her neck. She screamed. The two young men were stunned with surprise and looked at him bewil-deredly, as though he were some phantom of the night. July gave them a quick defiant look, turned and ran, disappearing in several long bounds into the darkness of an alleyway.

That night he sat by himself on a bench and watched cars moving on silent rubber tires.

The following day he didn't leave his cement room at all, even to eat. He lay, or sat, and stared at the walls. His estimation of himself was low, stupid and shameless. He took the diamond to a pawnbroker, who eyed him with suspicion as he noticed the broken chain, and offered him $100 for it. "Give it back," July demanded, and it was given back. He refused to take it back where he'd bought it, and resolved to keep it; and later he fixed the broken chain with a pair of tweezers and kept it in one of his glass jars.

The experience hung over him like a cloud and, whatever he tried to do, he couldn't seem to manage without reflecting upon it, and finally, once again, the laughter would loom up just as it had in the empty street, and he'd hear the voice. "A paper boy. Really, Charlotte, a paper boy!"

While working with Ed Shavoneck, he'd think, Newspaper boy. Lousy newspaper boy. Once more he tried to pawn the diamond, but was once again insulted. So he added it to his collection of most valuable possessions: his cat, his gun, his bullets, his pictures, his Bible and now his diamond. Many times he carried it with him in his pocket and took it out and admired it.

Days passed. He worked behind the green counter as if in a trance.

In a phone booth.

"Hello—this is July . . . July *Montgomery*. If you still want me, when can I go to work?"

"Oh yes, July." Pause. "How's your cat?"

"Fine."

"Good, good. Excuse me, but do you remember that job I was talking about to you? I mean, did I really offer you a job?"

"Yes, we were talking about it a few months ago, at Shapiro's."

"Oh, yes, Shapiro's. Just a minute, will you—" Then he must have cupped his hand over the receiver, because July couldn't hear clearly enough to know anything about the conversation he was having at the other end. It wasn't very long before he was back on the line.

"Here we go—you still there?"

"Yes—about the job."

"Oh yes, the job. Well, why don't you come on over and we'll talk about it. You know where the store is?"

"No."

"Well, it's . . . Sure you do. It's in the phone book. You must have used a phone book."

"Oh, I guess I did at that."

"You should learn to use your head. When are you coming?"

"Right away."

"Fine, fine. Look forward to seeing you. Goodbye."

"Goodbye," said July, but the connection had already been broken. I'll have to remember that, he thought: *Keep your finger on the receiver button and press it just as the other person starts to say goodbye—leaving the impression that you're only half interested.*

Carroll's Furniture was not nearly as large as July thought it would be. He'd pictured himself going to work in a store with large glass doors, in a place where if you didn't wear a $400 Fifth Avenue suit, you'd look out of place. No, this was a crouching toad of a building, surrounded by a railway storage yard, a warehouse and an immense parking lot. Little, frame windows and a door hardly big enough to get a comfortable chair out. (Foolish, he thought; all that goes on through a back door.) He went in.

The inside looked bigger than the outside and was very clean and the ceiling was high, with good lighting, but not a place where being without a Fifth Avenue suit would be noticed. For such a large store, July thought, it seemed funny for it to be so empty. But it was Wednesday morning—possibly a poor time for selling furniture. Carroll seemed to materialize out of nowhere and took him back into the shop.

The job, he learned, was not quite as glamorous as he'd imagined. But then Carroll didn't see anything wrong or degrading about it. "You won't make much at first," he explained, "but after you learn your way around I can use you in more places. In essence, you have to start somewhere, and so that's the bottom."

What it consisted of was sweeping, dusting, helping to unload furniture trucks, refinishing and reupholstery work in the shop, and sales work in the evening (but very little of that because he was too young and unknowledgeable). The pay was less than he had made as a newsboy, but he could live on the second floor with his cat, furnish it as he pleased, and Carroll would put in a bathtub. He could use the toilet behind the cash register (which meant, though he didn't say it out loud, that he could roam at will throughout the whole building). Twenty dollars a week.

July accepted, and they shook hands. In a moment of unexpected outwardness, he showed his new boss his diamond. Carroll showed him a larger one on his ring, took him upstairs and showed him the little apartment quarters in a room that had been an office when the building belonged to a textile merchant. It had been equipped with a kitchen when the upstairs had been rented by a square-dance club, and was now out of use. The rest of the floor was storage space for furniture, as was the third floor. Carroll reiterated that he would have a tub installed and showed July that he would have his own private entrance and exit—a small fire escape leading to the ground from a door beside the refrigerator.

"It's an awfully big room," said July.

"Well, it's good you think so at least. Any complications about leaving where you are now?"

Pause.

"None."

"Fine. It'll be good to have someone here at night. We had two break-ins last year. Yes, I'm sure we'll get along just fine. Now you'll have to excuse me, I've things to do. Why don't you go get your stuff? I'll see if I can't have a lock put on this door here opening into the storage area, and sometime next week we'll get a fellow to put in a bathtub. Where do you want it?"

"Well, I don't know," began July.

"Well, think about it and let me know." He gave the room a quick last look. "Oh yes, might not be too bad a little room, fixed up. Is there anything else? Now I must run. I'll see you later."

July was left alone in his new room. He couldn't believe he was so lucky.

It wasn't entirely true that leaving his cement room underneath City Hall was without complications. He knew there would be some as soon as he was down on the first landing, and by the time he could hear the trolleys running, he felt like an insect—the kind of person who could abandon a place that had seen him through all his trials, that had sheltered him and belonged only to him—had known no one before and would know no one after. To give it up in exchange for a room owned by someone else, whose location could be known to anyone . . . Refrigerator, hot and cold running water, a bathtub, electricity, toilet, winter heat and windows—all these seemed like the earmarks of misplaced priorities—luxuries owned by people who cared nothing for the real things in life—the old things, the safe things and the sacred things—by people who forsook their pasts and lived without feelings.

He slipped underneath the landing and went back to his room. Butch was there. July closed the cardboard door, lit his lamp, set it on the table, lay down on his pallet looking up at the conduit pipes and decided to go back to being a newsboy and let Franklin Carroll get in his bathtub and sail down the river. He fell asleep. Terrifying thoughts filled his dreams, causing his body to sweat and jerk.

When he woke up there was a specter in his chair. He could see the orange-and-yellow light flickering through her bones. She was quite old and dressed in a fashion common to a much earlier age. Butch was walking back and forth in front of her on the table, blocking the lamplight, then letting it through, her face darkening, then growing brighter. There was something about her that was very comical, and though he couldn't put his finger on just what it was, he knew it had something to do with her eyes; for that reason he was careful not to look into them for fear of laughing.

"So it's back to the newspaper business," she said, picking up his deck of cards and trying to get them to fan out in the way of cardsharps, but having a hard time of it.

"I guess so," said July.

"It's not a bad business. I mean, it's pretty good money. You should get yourself a new deck of cards; these stick together something fierce." She put them down and frowned at them. Butch walked around them because they were in his path.

"Would you like something to drink?" asked July, sitting up. "I've got a little whiskey here."

"You know I can't eat or drink anything—testing me, no doubt. Now see here, young man, don't think you shall impress me with this drinking business. What seems to be the matter with this cat here—walking back and forth like some prowling monkey?"

"He's sort of suspicious by nature. He was kidnapped once."

"Well, *I'd* never take him, you can depend on that, and I wouldn't think you'd worry about his being stolen in the future. That one time must have been a fluke. After all, who'd want such a suspicious, prowling cat? It'd make me nervous."

July, trying as hard as he could, was unable to keep from snorting out a little laugh.

"And what seems to be so funny?"

"Nothing."

"I'll have you know this is the first time in maybe one or two thousand years that anyone's laughed at me. A little too sure of yourself, I'd say, for such a young snip . . . or impudent. Hey now, what's this taped under here?"

"That's my pistol. It used to belong to my mother. Take it out and look at it if you want to."

"Heaven forbid that I'd ever touch such a thing. What ghastliness! Whatever use would you have for such a thing? It has a white handle, of all things—utterly ghastly."

"It's a belly gun."

"What!"

July simply couldn't help it and began laughing again. It was like having the most perfectly naïve person imaginable right there before him, reacting in just the way you'd imagine; but at the same time (and this is where the humor came in) her unworldliness was so invulnerable that nothing could ever penetrate it very far.

"It's a gun for close shots—right in the gut."

"Someone should have taken a stick to your mother when she was your age. But come now, what is it about this room that makes you think it's so special? It doesn't look so hot to me. In fact, I don't think I'd want a son of mine living in it for even one night . . . and the noise of those trolleys is awful."

"Ever since I came to the city I've lived here. It's my home. Butch and I, we like it just fine."

"Probably why he's so suspicious. It's too damp for a cat."

"He doesn't mind."

"He tolerates it, is what you mean. Face the facts: it's not ideal. And anyway, what was it that fellow said about you and being a paper—"

"He said, 'Paper boy. Charlotte, really, a paper boy!' "

"I thought it was something of that order. So if he feels like that, isn't it a pretty good sign other people do too?"

"Who cares what other people think?"

"Well, in a *moral sense*"—the way she so seriously emphasized these two words made July want to laugh again—"of course nobody should care what anyone thinks. But there's hardly right or wrong at stake here."

"Sure there is—what's right or wrong for me."

"There's nothing *moral* about that. Things moral always include other people, and, really, being a paper boy isn't much." July felt a little angry at this, and was just ready to say so, but she spoke first. "Don't go flying off the handle. Look at it this way: it's not the job, is it? I mean, selling papers isn't exactly the issue, it's this room. You'd think you'd be an insect if you left it, as if it were an old friend."

"Yes . . . and I *would* be too."

"Perhaps. Anyway, why not keep it and your new one as well, and take the new job?—which you know you'd like better. . . . I mean, I doubt if you could rent it out."

"I couldn't justify even being gone for one night."

"I have it! Why not leave some of your special things here?" She became so exuberant, with gestures flashing every which way, that July had difficulty understanding. "Keep your diamond, and your cat too (so much the shame), but leave everything else.

Wrap your lamp in an oiled bag so it will light when you come back for visits, leave your Bible, leave your pictures and cards and blankets—everything. That way you can have both. And think of the fun of exploring that tremendous building at night."

A faint scratching sounded on the cardboard door, from the outside. "Gracious," said the old specter. "I hardly thought they'd find me so soon. I must be going. It's been fun talking to you." What happened then so thoroughly astonished July that for the rest of his life his memory tried to eject the event. The woman rose and at the same time stayed sitting, went to the door and passed through it and at the same time moved not at all. So there was a continuous band of image all the way from the chair to the cardboard door, perfectly vivid and clear at each place he'd care to look at it. Then it began to blur, and the repeated image of her face became only a pale band of color, rising at the chair and going to the door. Below it was a bright white line from what had been her collar, black from the fringe around her shoulders. And like a light echo the whole phenomenon began to vanish, as though being rinsed away by ripples of clear water, leaving only two deep blue lines from her eyes, then taking them as well. July went quickly to the door and opened it. Nothing.

Without bothering to straighten up, or taking any precautions against water condensing inside his nearly empty lamp, he took Butch, extinguished the light and went out, closing the door carefully and fondly behind him. They waited a long time for the platforms above them and across from them to clear, and climbed up, ascended past the Crosstown and the L and climbed onto the street. Carroll's Furniture was a long way away and it took them nearly forty-five minutes to walk it.

They established their new living quarters to their immense satisfaction. True to his promise, Franklin Carroll had a bathtub put in one afternoon while July was sanding scratches, mars and old polish off a rocking chair. That first night he ran it full to the top, sitting on the rolled edge looking down into the clear water.

"It's so clear," he said to Butch, "if it wasn't for the waves and the sparkling, you couldn't see it. It's heavy air." He had to let a little of the precious liquid down the drain before he took off his clothes and climbed in. The pleasure filled him. He felt light and brilliant. He wished for the little boats and ducks that he'd had in Sharon Center and remembered his shameless childhood in which he'd played with them without appreciation or regard.

But even with the water he couldn't overcome his late-night terrors and, despite the long distance, he was forced, for the first months, to return to his cement room four and five times a week to sleep. He would begin to swell with foreboding, the sounds throughout the warehouse would magnify, his stomach would wrinkle up like a raisin, he would hear his heart beating in his ears and he'd know it was time to return. The damp, chilly room and the pictures would revive him.

Then the visits were cut back to three a week, then regular weekends, then only once, more out of duty than need.

There were times when Franklin came to the store during the night and met with men in the basement. These meetings never lasted longer than a couple of minutes, their voices were always low and July never saw who it was that mysteriously appeared there for him to talk to. Afterward Carroll would sometimes come up to his room and knock politely.

"Hello, I saw your light on and I thought I might stop in. Not bothering anything, I hope."

"Oh no. Come on in."

"You sure have fixed this up nice. Hello there, Butch. Anything else you need?"

"No, we're just fine."

At first, this was about all their talks would consist of, and Franklin Carroll'd leave. He respected a person's privacy, as he wanted his own to be respected.

As the year continued, July's presence in the building came to be taken for granted. One might encounter him sweeping here, then up on the third floor looking for unusual pieces of furniture, then in the shop laying down layers of shellac, then outside polishing the windows, then down in the basement cleaning out the furnace, like a spirit from the building's walls, his cat dark against the stone foundation. Carroll began to feel more comfortable with him. Coming upon him unexpectedly, he'd give a little start and then say, "Oh, July, it's only you." He began to drop in on July and sit in the large chair they'd dragged in from the storeroom and talk until after midnight, drinking Kool-Aid and telling him stories of his life when he was a boy living on the streets of Philadelphia, and always managing to find a way to leave four, five or six dollars behind when he left, as though keeping a strict moral solvency between the money and the time July spent listening to him.

But these meetings were rare. Carroll was too busy for them except after those infrequent times when he'd arrive unexpectedly at night, talk to men in the basement and come up. He and his wife entertained and had many social engagements. They were interested in horse racing and owned a boat that they kept at Atlantic City. July saw Mrs. Carroll come into the store from time to time and talk to Franklin in the closed office. He was never introduced and was known to the onetime holder of the Miss New Jersey title only as the cleaning boy who lived in the room on the second floor. Frequently they were gone for weeks at a time, and once they went to Japan, leaving Bob Reed, Franklin's most highly paid salesman, in charge of the store.

Carroll thought July should have an education, and against his will persuaded him to attend night classes at Temple University. After two years of these classes it would be possible to take a test qualifying him, if he passed, for a high-school equivalency certificate. The classes weren't difficult because he'd already learned to read quickly. But he resented the actual class *time* spent listening to the dry, underpaid voices of the student teachers from the university, especially one, whose pale face betrayed a life that had dried up at twenty-five—a deal had been made with his soul: "Listen, keep quiet and we'll survive vicariously in the back rooms of the world." His gray laughter was frightening. Yet, despite this, July was learning and whole highways of interest opened up around him. If nothing else, those sad teachers could hurl ideas at him thought by men and women who lived forever outdoors and on the summit of experience.

July was growing in a physical sense as well, and although he continued to picture himself still as a small boy, in the eyes of strangers he was clearly six feet tall, rawboned and potentially dangerous. Lugging bulky furniture in and out of trucks and up and down flights of stairs had hardened his muscles, yet he retained the quickness and agility of his age.

Those evenings when he wasn't at night school he spent reading and studying the planets and the moon from a telescope Carroll had bought for him at an auction. Sometimes when Carroll would come up from the basement the two of them would carry the forty-power apparatus up to the roof and July would focus something in and Carroll would peer through the eyepiece and exclaim, "Magnificent." But that would be the end of his interest and he'd settle down into one of the two chairs they had up there and, gesturing continually to the night, begin talking. July would try to talk to him about some of the things he was learning that excited him, in a way proving to him that he was actually getting all that could be expected, but Carroll would wave his hands and say, "Yes, yes, that's all very good. Someday you'll need that information. For every grain of knowledge you absorb the world will pay you back a thousand times."

From his interest in astronomy July acquired a fondness for being on the roof, and many times when his purpose would be academic, such as finally seeing the great double star in Perseus, he'd be lulled away from the telescope by the noise from the street, which seemed muted and distant from that height, and the rest of the night would find him walking pleasantly and aimlessly along the perimeter of the roof, sitting and letting the lights and noises and chilly air fill him to the very brink of contentment. But he'd hold these nights against himself: he was in an intense training period, at the end of which he intended to be rich, cultivated and thoroughly attractive to women. A hibernation of work. The time it would take was not definite—certainly longer than it would take to secure the high-school diploma, but how much longer he didn't know. The only thing he could be sure of was that each day he spent studying and absorbing information and looking into the lives of men like Benjamin Franklin and Immanuel Kant was one day closer.

At the age of seventeen, having ended his classes at the night school, he revisited his old room below City Hall (it was so low that he could no longer stand straight up in it) and when he left he took with him the small, thick Bible and the pictures of his parents. Doing this, he felt as though he were robbing his own tomb. The photographs were showing signs of age. This grieved him. He took them back to his apartment and with Carroll's help laid them out and rephotographed them and had five-by-eight enlargements made of two; framed them in the shop and hung them in the master position on his walls. He made up his mind to read the Bible from cover to cover as a scholarly endeavor, as he was led to believe it was not only an account of an historical race, preserved from cracked parchment paper, but the symbolic source for all Western poetry and the basis of the Christian religion. He took up the task one evening after coming down from the roof and was immediately filled with a kind of horror which he could neither express nor understand. He put the book away and returned to the roof, thinking that his dinner might have had some influence over his emotions. After an hour he took it up again and the same ineffable feeling descended upon him, this time more intensely. I won't be bullied in this manner, he told himself, and forced page after page into his memory. Before the end of the second book of Moses he was filled with such an inexorable dread that he had to put it down and flee to his room beneath City Hall. It was as though something else was trying to speak through the broken language, and it was something he couldn't fathom. Later he put the book into his bookshelf and pushed the experience behind him.

He took the equivalency examination and passed.

He got a chauffeur's license so he could pilot Carroll about the city, on occasion into New York, and run errands to the bank. He was responsible for keeping delivery records and handling all written correspondence.

Late one night Carroll came upstairs and rapped anxiously on his door. July was reading and stood up with a start, wondering why there should be so much excitement.

Franklin came in with a rush. "Quick, quick," he exclaimed. "You must do me a favor, just this once. Hurry, get your coat. Think you can handle a truck? Hurry up, hurry—of course you can, you're an excellent driver."

On the way down the stairs to the basement Carroll shoved a piece of paper into July's pocket, explaining that there was an address on it, somewhere in Chelsea, Mass. He opened the door for him and escorted him onto the loading ramp in the basement. A cold blast of air met them. The doors were open and an enormous trailer truck stretched out into the back lot, alley lights reflecting through the windshield and side wings of the cab, looking like a gray twenty-ton silverfish.

"I can't drive that," July complained. As he spoke he noticed they were not alone. Two men were crouching on the ground alongside the truck, one of them leaning against a black tire. All the lights were out. The back end of the trailer was locked with a padlock, the motor was idling and diesel fumes filled the air. From what he could make out, the two men were young, early twenties, dressed in heavy, dark pea jackets. One of them—the one on the ground against the tire—looked as though something might be wrong with him. His chest heaved as if he were breathing hard. The other walked about nervously, up to the door, back to his companion, talking in low, unintelligible words.

"Sure you can," said Carroll. "There can't be anything to it. Drivers don't know anything. Don't you see, you *have* to." There was a frantic note in Carroll's voice—a sound July had never heard there before.

"What's this all about? Why aren't the lights on? What's in this truck?"

"Don't ask questions. Quick, you have to get this thing out of here. Hey, you—you, Sonny!" he shouted to the pacing man, who came back to them. "There's nothing to driving this, is there?"

"We got to get Murf out of here," he complained.

"Shut up. Murf can freeze in hell for all I care now. We've got to get this *truck* out of here. Is there anything to it?"

"Naw, anybody can drive one."

"There, you see, now get going."

"Those things have a thousand gears," protested July.

"Hurry, *please* get out of here. Take this." Carroll shoved some bills into his coat pocket and practically dragged him up past the heaving young man to the cab. "Come back as quick as you can. Don't talk to anyone. You've got to! Christ, get this thing out of here. Hey, you idiot"—to Sonny—"get him out, take 'im to a hospital if you want." The man turned to help his companion up. "Wait! What about these gears?"

"There's a plate on the dashboard shows where they are. Careful going through the city. Be easy on the brakes till you get the feel. Be careful going through New York."

"OK, that's enough, now get him out of here."

It wasn't difficult for July to tell that at the present moment Carroll and the young man had no high regard for each other. And as a testimony to the kind of loyalty he had, he climbed into the truck and closed the door, eager to help out in the best way he could.

"If you're stopped," said Carroll through the window, "say nothing and we'll get you out—but don't call here." That was all.

July depressed the clutch, put the shift lever in the first position, as nearly as he could figure, and rolled out of the loading dock and into the lot. The motor screamed and the tires inched ahead. Boy, is that a low gear, he thought and shifted into second, double-clutching in neutral as he'd once heard you should do. He got onto the Schuylkill Expressway and headed toward New York City.

Once on the open road, his anxiety over handling the big, roaring monster settled back, and bits of conversation, like phantoms, formed dream pictures in his imagination, moved about by his own fearful expectations: *If they stop you—If they get you—Don't call . . . Be careful going through the city.* How could one be careful in a semi? Careful of what? Every car he saw, he was suspicious of. He prayed there would be enough gasoline in the tank to last the whole way, because he was afraid of any encounters. His headlights on the road seemed miles underneath him.

Because it was so late at night a certain comradeship seemed to exist between him and the other truck drivers on the facing lanes, and they winked their overhead lights at him. He imagined them making long hauls across the country against a strict deadline, and driving long into the morning because of stopping off in some wayside town and being taken for a ride by a long-legged hooker from a crosstown bar, their money gone but left with pictures to turn in their heads through New York, Pennsylvania, Ohio, Indiana, Illinois, Iowa, Nebraska, Wyoming, Colorado and into Salt Lake City. He thought of how these red and orange winking lights brought him such comfort and were such a jolly expression of good will, yet how awesome and terrible were the gigantic trucks themselves, and he was filled momentarily with warmth for the American people.

Then came the outskirts of New York, the Tappan Zee Bridge, and he forgot everything but his worries. He had no idea what he was carrying, but his imagination contained everything from kidnapped children to plastic explosives. Whoever was after him, he was sure, would stop at nothing to put a bullet through his head. He became afraid, and felt very foolish for being coerced into it in the first place. If it was so important, why didn't Carroll himself drive? Why should *he* be taking any risks? What was this all about?

He thought he might just pull the truck over to the side of the road and leave it . . . perhaps all criminals actually involved with danger were young and very foolish and didn't know enough not to have anything to do with it. But all these thoughts went up the stack as soon as July saw the toll booths and the flashing lights, STOP AHEAD, PAY TOLL, ALL TRUCKS TO THE RIGHT. This is it, he thought, and touched the brakes. They locked the wheels tight and nearly put him through the windshield, the tires screaming hideously. He eased up on them and shifted down into a gear much too low and the motor and transmission sounded as if they'd given up. No one else was on the road, nothing for the people in the booths to look at but him. *Be careful going through the city!* He was a hundred yards from the booths and was already doing six or seven miles an hour.

The huge truck limped all the way up to the flashing red light and stopped.

July rolled down the window, reached into his pocket, pulled out one of the bills Franklin had put there and handed it to the attendant, his eyes half closed in expectation of the worst.

"Say, you better pull over," said the man, taking the bill inside, "and take a nap. Looks like you were about asleep back there."

July tried to breathe, but continued holding his breath.

"Jesus, this the smallest bill you got?" The attendant was back at his window, holding out a $100 bill.

July silently cursed Carroll.

"Yes," he said. "Sorry. It's out of that secret little compartment in back of my wallet, you know?"

"OK. Say, what you carrying?"

"Pig iron: turnbuckles and transmission carcasses."

"Just a second." The attendant went three booths down with the $100 bill. July almost gave himself up for gone and was sitting over on the seat, ready to get out the opposite door if need be and run for all he was worth, when the attendant returned with the change and a stamped receipt.

"Really, buddy, I'd pull over if I were you."

"Think I will," said July, carelessly cramming the bills (most of them ones and fives) down into his pocket. "Thanks." Other cars were coming now and he pulled away, heading for the New England Thruway.

For the next hundred miles, past weigh stations and highway-patrol stations, he thought, Why'd he want to know what I was carrying? What interest could he have? It was impossible for him to accept that it was just one of those unexplainable examples of someone, to no end and for no gain to himself, making a friendly gesture. No, more likely it was a government man hoping to catch him in a lie.

Into Boston and through to Chelsea.

"Say, sorry to bother you, but could you tell me where Bettle Street is?"

"Three blocks ahead. It's a one-way."

"Thanks."

The number Franklin had given him was the address of a large, low-lying building that offered only two doors, one very large and obviously a truck entrance and one small, for people. There were no windows anywhere. He pulled into the drive, up to the door, feeling quite inebriated with having succeeded in his ordeal and expected to be greeted with excitement. The small door opened far enough for a face to be thrust through it, then closed. The big overhead door swung back in two pieces. A man's arm came into the opening and waved him forward. July drove in, the headlights of the truck illuminating thousands of boxes, both wooden and cardboard, stacked to the ceiling. When he could see through the mirrors that he'd cleared the door, he stopped.

"Keep going," said a voice.

He went on several feet, then several yards.

"Far enough," came the voice again and he stopped, cut the motor and lights and sat in a penumbra of exhaustion.

The door was pushed open. "OK. Let's go," said a harsh voice.

He climbed down onto a concrete floor.

"Here you are." A bill was handed him by a large man with a shrunken face, with skin like white-and-pink scales. "Now run along."

Once he was outside, the door was closed behind him and he heard it lock. He noticed that the sun was just coming up and looked down at his hand as he walked along the street, having forgotten that he was carrying the money. Fifty dollars. A lousy fifty bucks! he thought. Guys do what I just did all the time for a lousy fifty bucks! Those two guys back in Philly were going to make this run together—like they'd probably done how many times before—for twenty-five bucks apiece. July felt cheapened. He managed to flag down a cab and told the driver to take him to the nearest hotel, where he rented a room, had a six-pack of beer brought up to him and fell asleep before he could finish more than four. It was nearly dark again when he woke up and began looking into transportation back to Philadelphia.

Arriving by train at two a.m., he was reminded of how he'd come there years ago, small and lonely, an experience in a washroom in Cleveland hanging over him. He felt ashamed for himself. A hazy noise filled the station. Marginal people sat on the benches, neither looking at him nor away. He felt an urge to go home—back to Sharon Center, to stand in his father's garage and let the feel of men come into him from the tools, watch the telephone wires cross the street to his house and the barn swallows line up as though waiting for a parade and old Mr. Stanton, blind as a toad, come picking his way from his yellow house a quarter-mile down the road, tap the elm tree at the edge of Millers' yard, abruptly turn and walk into the open garage door to spend an hour talking to his father about the old days when his grandfather Wilson tracked a chicken thief with his dog clear over to Frytown and up to the house of an old, bitter woman who lived in it with six cats and could hardly have lifted a chicken, let alone carried three of them out of the house, through the briers and back through the woods. No, he thought, I won't allow myself to feel this way.

When July arrived at his room and turned on the light, a brand-new television set stared at him from the middle of the room. A red ribbon was tied around it and *Happy Birthday* written on a card in Carroll's handwriting, though his birthday was not for four months. Upon opening his refrigerator he found it crammed with food and expensive cat dinners. He took out a can of beer and sank into his favorite chair, underneath the pictures of his parents. Butch came over and sat on his lap, but jumped down when a drop of the cold liquid fell on his head. A copy of Freud's *Interpretation of Dreams* lay half opened on the floor and July picked it up and found the faint pencil mark where he'd left off reading. In his exhaustion he let a couple of sentences flash across his retina, but had no power to decipher them. He thought of himself impersonally, and tried to assess how far he'd come. For a moment, because of the weakness of his mind and body, and the sensation of having finally returned home after an ordeal, he wondered, What is all this worth? What good is learning this? Doesn't a dog or a baboon live just as well without it? Isn't it all pretension and snobbish amusement? In the final end result, wouldn't it be better just to be a libertine, or work as a geek in the circus?

He dragged himself off to bed, and under the pillow found a scrap of paper money. But in the darkness he couldn't tell its value, and hadn't enough ambition to get up and turn on the light. Butch jumped up and fell to purring in the hollow of his leg.

He gave Carroll every opportunity to explain the circumstances leading up to the previous evening, and even asked him once. He declined to say anything.

But July's curiosity was aflame, and though he continued his arduous studies (aside from his job he spent six or seven hours reading, and weekends found him in the museum and library), he still found time to wonder about the mysterious truck. Sometimes late in the evening he'd go into the basement and check the many locked doors, hoping to find one left open by mistake. He scavenged through the offices upstairs in search of keys to open them and papers that might help to explain what he didn't know.

One afternoon on a trip to New Jersey to look at some kitchen tables whose tops were supposed to withstand setting down a hot frying pan, Franklin said, "You've got to stop poking around."

July drove on without speaking. Carroll was quiet for several miles and the silence between them was disturbed only by the thumping of the tires in the cracks of the concrete highway.

"What do you know?"

"That you have four thieves who work more or less full time for you, and maybe one more in Pittsburgh."

"What else?"

"The truck I drove to Boston three months ago belongs to you, indirectly."

"Mmmm." Franklin turned on the radio, dialed in three separate advertisements and turned it off.

"This country's run by a set of laws," he began, his hands beginning to gesture. "A set of laws put together by men of Congress, each and every one of them out for his own interests. A law gets passed when a majority of them can get together in a block and vote legislation in over the opposition of a minority, whom the law will *not* help. Their interest is money. The President's interest is money. No President ever leaves office before he's at least a millionaire. This whole country's interest, *down to nearly every waking moment,* is money. People kill themselves and each other because of it. Work ethic, social ethic, business ethic—nothing. Only a money ethic. Wars are fought for it. It's the only *really* sacred thing in the world, but the least talked about. A normal man, during the normal course of each day, thinks about it between three and four hours—that's an average—and that's thinking about it *directly.*" July began to interrupt, but Franklin cut him off. "But there's very little talking done about it. To live in my neighborhood you'd have to be making—" July was frowning. Carroll's voice level rose. "Wait a minute. Look, if you think this is all crass, or beneath your comprehension, then you better grow up and look around. Just what do you think ambition means? Or incentive, or security, or well-being, or power, or self-betterment? Name me one smart man who is broke. If money's of comparatively no importance to you, then you're comparatively low in the brains department, because it is *the* most important!"

"There's religion," said July stubbornly.

"Pooh! Too many marriages break up because of money problems, or are formed out of greed. Priests ask for money to cancel sins. Christianity spread because the church was wealthier than any other institution. Try to get the guy in that car there to do something for you with a promise of everlasting reward, then try flashing a hundred in his face.

"To live in my neighborhood, you'd have to be making fifty thousand a year. Now nobody—*nobody*—who's making that kind of money is secure about his income. There're no unions to protect that figure. He's constantly thinking, Maybe I can make more, maybe I'll fold. The anxiety level is staggering. But do you think you ever hear anyone talk about it? Never. It's 'Nice weather, how's boating on the lake this year? Seen any bluebirds? Ford's got quite a little car this year. Let me tell you about our trip to the Smokies.'

"Now, I'm not trying to say that everyone's a crook, or that everyone would break the law if the odds looked right, so long as they could afford a good lawyer or a judge. No, there's a sucker born every minute, and some people, it's true, never grow up.

"The last thing you'd ever ask a man about is how much money he has, or what he does to get it—because *having* it is respectability.

So it's like this—want a chocolate bar?" July shook his head. Carroll ripped open the wrapper and, breaking the candy into its small squares, popped them into his mouth. "It's win or lose. Everything's a gamble. Start a gas station and maybe you'll make it and maybe you won't. It depends on a million and one things, none of them liable to come up twice in a lifetime. It's knowing when to get out, when to get in, when to split up and when to come together. The government puts a tariff on certain imports that we could normally buy very cheaply from a country that does a better job of putting them out; hence, certain manufacturers are protected and make more money, but that also opens up an illegal trade—smuggling. The cost of losing is greater, of course, maybe three or four years of your life, but then the profits are greater and *guaranteed* so long as you don't get caught. No worries about rising costs of materials or labor, and the officers of the law can be bought as well, if need be. Same way with anything illegal. The demand is always there, the market never closes.

"Look at it this way. Some fellow breaks into a building and steals ten thousand dollars' worth of office equipment: typewriters, duplicating machines and such. Now, the owner of that office, he goes first, if he's *smart,* to his insurance company and collects the ten thousand that he insured it for, after some kicking and groaning; then he goes out into the black market and buys the equipment he needs (maybe even his own stuff, who knows?) for two thousand, giving the middleman a nice fifteen-hundred-dollar profit (five hundred of which goes into protection), fills up his office and that's the end of it. If he's robbed again, the whole chain can start over: otherwise just the insurance company wins (and they win, by the way, because of other people getting knocked over)."

That same week, without explaining why, Carroll took July to New York and onto the floor of the Stock Exchange, where old men took notes on small white pads.

It was Carroll and not July who felt that they had to leave. On the street outside he looked tired and a little frightened.

They walked half a block. Then he wanted to turn around and go back; but just as they reached the entrance to the main room, where the electricity from inside seemed to crack and spark around the frame of the huge doors, he stopped, turned again and led July away. An ashen color had come over his face. Back at the car he said, "Drive home," and was silent nearly all the way to Philadelphia.

"I went broke there once," he said. "I was young. I thought I knew what had to happen. I was sure wheat had to keep going up. When they dumped it, a hush came over the whole building. There were some there who weren't watching it, of course, and they searched the boards like madmen to find out what had happened, then cared no more than if it were a fluctuation in the temperature. You can't imagine it. Whole lives ruined in a matter of seconds. My wish is that someday you'll make it there. Someday you'll beat them."

"Beat who?" asked July.

"The ones who never lose."

July's studies became more difficult. His ability to concentrate was coming apart at the seams—as if there were differences trying to get worked out inside him. Partially it was the $50,000. He knew Franklin didn't make that much, but he also knew that he needed to, that he couldn't live anywhere but where he lived, or on any different terms, and it was that red margin that made July wonder. Still, if he could choose, he'd be Franklin just as surely as when they'd first eaten breakfast together and July had noticed his clean shoes and the way people jumped when he called their names.

One night that week Franklin came up to his room with a round paper sack under his arm. It was only eight o'clock and he'd never come so early before. Also, his Cadillac wasn't parked across the street. He looked as though he'd been walking all night in the streets. July thought it very strange.

"I've brought a cold bottle of wine to share," he stated as he came in. "You wouldn't have a corkscrew around here, would you?"

"I don't think I do have."

"Well, get a knife, and some glasses. We'll cut it open." He set to work with the knife, paring away at the cork, and finally pushed it down into the bottle. "To your health," he said, when the glasses were poured. They drank. "What's this book here?" He picked up a copy of Plato's *Phaedrus* from the floor.

"That's a book by Plato."

"Terrific, keep to it. You've got the right idea—learn a few of the old ones, then when someone tries to make a fool of you, you can cut them down with a couple of lines from the ancients." He put the book down. Then, later, he said, "Well, anyway, you just keep on with what you're doing."

From where July sat he could see outside. Franklin's Cadillac pulled up across the street, stopping so abruptly that the tires gave a quick little squeal. In the frosted light he saw Mrs. Carroll jump from the car and walk fast over to "the building," as July had come to think of it. The door downstairs opened and slammed.

"Franklin!" she screamed at the top of her lungs. "Franklin! I know you're here somewhere." Her voice seemed frightening to July, even coming up through the floor. It was so emotional. Franklin put his finger to his lips and whispered, "Sshhh," turning off the overhead light while he did so.

They sat in the darkness and listened to her walking and yelling downstairs, listened while she went into the basement and for several minutes was panting and screaming right outside his room. July tried to keep hold of his memory of Carroll, without the least concern, putting his finger to his lips as though to say: *Nevermind, there's nothing to it. Just a little game she plays.* And he told himself over again that Franklin knew more about the situation than he did. It was all he could do not to run out and call to her. It made him feel that *he* was partly to blame, sitting there hiding in the dark. The first feelings of resentment toward Franklin that he'd ever had began to show themselves, but the utter shame he felt in having them rolled them back up like a scroll.

They listened to her throwing things in the office, breaking windows and sobbing. Finally, she left, and July watched the Cadillac lunge away from the curb and roar out of his vision.

"Phew. She gone?" asked Carroll, half laughing.

July wanted to answer, but couldn't. Franklin flipped on the light, and in amazement July noticed that he'd been drinking out of his glass during the whole time the light was out. It was nearly empty. He felt relief. Franklin was obviously right: there was nothing to be upset about, otherwise he wouldn't be able to sit there and lazily sip his wine—it would be impossible. So July was convinced that he'd been mistaken—it had all been for show, and they went downstairs to see what was broken.

Much of the furniture was toppled over. Window glass was everywhere. The heavy desk in the office was overturned, and one wooden chair had all four of its legs busted off. July began cleaning up, but Franklin, finding the spectacle very amusing, told him not to bother—they'd get to it in the morning—called a cab to come take them to a good place to drink, and they left. As they rode he asked if July wouldn't be interested in taking the truck, just once more, up to Boston. July told him no.

After saying good night to Carroll and abandoning him to his friends at the private club, July walked back, and cleaned up as best he could, so that, except for there being no glass in the window frames, everything looked much as it had before. Only after he'd finished did he feel like going to bed.

The memory of the evening upset him, and he tried to think his way out of it, but with no success. Two days later he saw Mrs. Carroll and searched her face from across the room for signs of an explanation. But none appeared. Only a falling grimness that seemed to deny any ability on her part to pretend anything. She stayed five minutes and left without waiting for Franklin to come back from lunch. Franklin remained away from the store until almost five; when he came in, he opened the safe in his office, took something out and left.

When the police came a day later, July and Carroll were filling out an order form. They knocked on the door frame of the office. The door was wide open.

"Come in," Carroll said, stretching out his hand. "Sit down. What can we do for you? My name's Franklin Carroll. This is July Montgomery. If there's—"

"We've got a warrant to search here," said the one in uniform, very coldly, and produced a document to that effect. The cloth of his shirt rasped like starched canvas.

"Well, look wherever you like," said Carroll, without the slightest trace of fear in his voice, but no longer trying to be pleasant.

"Do you know a man by the name of Bobby Thompson?"

"No."

"From New York."

"I've never been there. Look where you will. There are three floors here, and all of them are open. Help yourself."

"We need the keys to the rooms in the basement," said the plainclothesman. "That's all we really care about."

Franklin turned to face the wall. July watched as pale, thin waves of color washed across his face, one after another. He looked at his watch for a moment as though he were thinking about something.

"Sure, here," said Franklin, and tossed them a ring of keys. "Go with them," he told July. The words cut him. "I'll be right down."

July knew that the keys he'd given them didn't fit the locks in the basement, but he went with them anyway and showed them downstairs. They made no attempt to talk to him. *Go with them.* The tone in which Carroll had said that had been the same tone he used with the policeman, as though he, July, were no closer to him than they were—as if he were a stranger. At the first lock they went through each key on the ring twice to make sure, then hurried on to another door. Before they were even halfway through the number of possibilities for this one, it began to dawn on them that something might be wrong.

"Better go check," ordered the plainclothesman, and his partner turned and ran up the stairs. In the confusion of leaving, the keys were dropped, and, losing his place, he had to go through the whole ring before confirming his maddening suspicion. Just as he finished, "He's gone, Murphy," came from upstairs, and he kicked the door. Then, noticing July was still there, he said, "He'll pay for this," and directed him to lead the way upstairs.

"Get on the phone," he shouted as soon as they reached the first floor. "Have his car's description sent out."

But the other was across the room in the middle of a lamp display. "There's no hurry," he said. "A guy like that can't get very far away. Look at these things here—these 'lava lights.' I've never seen anything like it. What'll they think of next?" In anger, the plainclothesman charged out of the building and over to his car radio.

"How do these things work?"

"I think it's heat," said July.

Bob Reed was standing with a small family who were looking at sofas. He excused himself politely and went over to the policeman. "Say," he said, "what's the trouble here?"

"It doesn't concern you. Boy, these are really something. How much are they?"

"Seventeen fifty."

"That much?"

"Is Mr. Carroll in some kind of trouble?"

"For all I know, you are too, so you better get yourself a lawyer and stop asking questions. This smaller one here, how much is it?"

"Fifteen fifty."

"That much?"

July went into the office and sat down on the desk. The plainclothesman came back from outside and with the uniformed policeman came into the small room that still had no windows and shut the door. The latter carried a lava light and searched around for a plug. "Wait till you see this thing. This guy said it was heat that did it." He found an outlet, unplugged the desk lamp and plugged in the light. The heavier orange liquid in the bottom refused to rise.

"It has to warm up," said July.

"What were you doing when we came in?"

"Filling out an order form."

"What kind of order form?"

"Here." July handed him the paper.

He looked at it and put it down. "Where did Carroll go?"

"I have no idea."

"Do you know a man by the name of Bobby Thompson?"

"No."

"You want to take a ride down to the station?"

"Ask me something I can answer."

"You know that your boss was involved with a company that exported stolen goods overseas and sold them through discount houses?"

"No."

"What did you think?" asked the uniformed man. "That all the truckloads of stolen property taken during a single week in the city were sold through secondhand shops? No, there's no market of that size anywhere. If there was, it'd be discovered. There had to be a mechanism for getting rid of it—an export business. Hell, in an underdeveloped country most secondhand stuff would look like new."

"A neat little business," put in the other. "And I suppose you didn't know anything about it."

"No."

"Look, it's beginning to work! Isn't that amazing. They cost seventeen fifty, though."

"That much?"

July was glad for their questions. He didn't want to be left alone. The companionship of his own thoughts was not welcome.

"Where do you live?"

"Upstairs."

"Upstairs here?"

"Yes."

"Hmmm. How long has this been going on?"

"What?"

"Living in the store."

"Five years."

"Hmmm. Did you know—Say, Bailey, why don't you go up and check his room—just to make sure?"

"The salesman said he drove away in his car."

"Go ahead and look anyway."

The uniformed policeman left.

"It's funny," the remaining one said, settling down into a chair with a cigar and putting his hat next to July on the desk. "We've been looking for an outlet for these 'dentist office' burglaries ever since the mid-fifties. We broke up a couple of smaller gangs who actually had delivery trucks and you could call in your order and have the stuff brought over. But they handled musical equipment almost exclusively. Then we turned over this stone in Chelsea—outside of Boston—and who do you suppose was underneath it? Right, Mr. Carroll. And the damnedest thing is—after all these years he'd decided for some reason to get out, and ever since week before last he's been closing down his contacts and turning his hired thieves back on their own. None of them will testify, of course—criminal morality—and with the trouble we had in getting anything to base a warrant on, we thought he'd surely have his own place cleaned out. I'm surprised. But I suppose you knew all of this."

"It's a surprise to me."

Bailey returned. "Nothing but a bunch of books, Murphy, and a cat. Cruddy little place to live. You'd think the kid was a monk. Are you a monk, kid? Probably not. Ask him where he got the TV. It looks new."

"Where'd you get the television?"

"Honestly. If you don't think so, check the serial numbers."

"I already got them, Murphy. Boy, do I get a kick out of those lights."

"Now, where do you suppose Carroll went off to?"

"I don't know. Maybe he went home."

"No. They'd've brought him back already. Oh well, he won't be hard to find. He's too used to being obvious. He's been rich too long. I wonder what a guy like that must be thinking now—knowing he's going to prison. There's a basic stupidity in all criminals—at least in criminals who commit passionless crimes. Jesus, if there's anything important in life, it must be health first, then not being in prison."

"What's with all those books?"

"Nothing."

"You going to some school?"

"No, why? Make you suspicious?"

"Don't be smart or we'll take you down to the station. As a matter of fact, I like books myself. Just very odd is all."

"I liked books when I was a kid," said Bailey, "until I grew out of'em. Records too. How long do these lava lights keep working?"

"Nobody knows. They just came out."

"Do you have a crowbar or something we can get into those rooms in the basement with?"

"I don't think so. Why don't you just shoot through the locks?"

"You've been watching too many late shows. That'd be dangerous. Anyway, go find a screwdriver and we'll take off the hinges."

The three of them went back down into the basement, pulled the pins out of a set of hinges, and with amazing difficulty pulled away the door, flipped on the light inside and went in. There was nothing but cardboard boxes. Bailey immediately began looking through them, but they turned out to be all empty. The next room they got into had boxes containing everything imaginable, except a lava light, much to the disappointment of Bailey, who was hoping to be able to confiscate one as evidence and put it on the main desk in the station.

"Here, look at this," said Murphy, and roughly shoved one of the boxes into July's hands. July looked down into it, resentfully wondering why he was supposed to be looking into it at all: old watches with some of the gold worn off, pieces of jewelry, an electric sander, a radio, fishing tackle, an ornate keepsake box—things taken out of homes, not offices. He set it down and pushed it away.

"So what?" he said.

"You remember taking any of that stuff yourself?"

"No."

"Ever been arrested?"

"No."

"Ever been in trouble?"

"No."

"Ever been to Boston?"

"No . . . I mean yes."

"Slipped up, didn't you? It was Chelsea, wasn't it?"

"No."

"We can check, you know."

"Go ahead."

"I think he's clean, Murphy," said Bailey. "He doesn't look like a bad kid. Where are your parents?"

"They're dead."

"Too bad. How long?"

"Over ten years."

"Traffic accident?"

"Yes. How'd you know?"

"Happens all the time. Both parents dead, young kid, almost always a traffic accident. Really, I'm sorry."

"Thanks."

"Now, level with us, what do you know about all this?"

"Nothing."

"OK. Murphy, let's take 'im down to the station." And they went upstairs. But as it happened, after another police car arrived, and then a van to take away the stolen goods in the basement, they decided against it and told him not to leave the city and that they'd come to check on him from time to time, and after Carroll was picked up he'd be notified and probably there'd be some things to talk over by then. But in the meantime the store would be closed and he was advised to look for another job, as was the salesman. Both of them, they were told, were eligible for unemployment benefits. The salesman followed them out to their car asking questions. July heard the heavy wooden door in the basement shut and the van pull out of the lot. He went to the front door and locked it, put out the closed sign and felt the silence envelop him. He went to the office, opened the desk drawer and took two green tranquillizers from a bottle with *Mrs. Franklin Carroll* written across the prescription label.

These were the first pills, other than aspirin, that he'd ever taken, and he had no idea what to expect. Trying to anticipate their effect kept his thoughts closely centered on himself and away from the reasons he'd taken them. Upstairs, he ran a bath, watching the tub fill up with the clear water. He undressed and got in. The light drained from the room as the afternoon wore out, and he remained immersed in the dark, thinking about why it might be that Freud never really addressed himself to the *reason* why there should be such a distortion between the dream, dream material and dream thoughts. First he thought it would've been too difficult and mere speculation. Then he thought perhaps it was for that very reason that the book was extraordinarily profound—because he refused to say anything he couldn't justify. Then he changed his mind and decided there were a lot of things Freud said that couldn't be reasonably justified; he began thinking half of Wittgenstein and half of getting married to someone he'd never seen before, as part of a bet, and began to fall pleasantly asleep. Only then, just as he was letting some of the lukewarm water out and was running in a fresh supply of hot, did it occur to him that he was under the influence of the tranquillizers, and that his serenity of mood was entirely attributable to tiny dust particles of green chemicals in his brain.

July was not the kind of person to greet new things with perfect ease, and this was no exception. What could life mean if the grains of a common chemical, manufactured crudely and with almost no effort, could have such an effect on one's mind? With horror, he saw this had awful implications. Good feelings—happiness, compassion, even well-being and reverence—had no more solidarity than a whiff of menthol, and were no more worthy of praise than drunkenness. It seemed like a rotten, insensitive world in which that was true; but because of the tranquillizer, he couldn't get very worked up about it. They've got you coming or going, he thought: it leaves you wanting to say, *I won't take any pills because that's false emotion,* to which they can parry, *Don't then, who cares? Go ahead and worry.* One of those endless situations where a fool can be made to look like a fool. He got out of the tub, turned on the light, dressed and set about fixing himself something to eat.

About this time a knock came from the door to the fire escape, and guessing who it might be, he opened it to Carroll, who immediately rushed into the room, bringing in a blanket of cold air from outside. One elbow of his jacket was ripped out.

"You took a chance coming back here," said July.

"They have somebody downstairs?" His voice was nearly inaudible.

"I don't think so, but maybe on the street."

"That's OK. I came down from the roof."

July turned off the overhead light and lit a small table lamp next to the fire-exit door. Carroll collapsed into a chair. "Quite a day," he said. His face and hands were gray, his eyes wild with blood lines. "You got anything I might eat?"

"Sure. I was just making something. Your car—you didn't leave it outside?"

"No, no, it's nowhere around here." Pause.

"Jesus," exclaimed July, trying to keep himself from breaking into tears. "I didn't know—When you asked me if I'd—"

"Forget it. It wouldn't have mattered. I should've had a couple of the boys take it up."

July looked at Franklin's hands, folded deadly in his lap. "I didn't tell them anything."

There was a silence then, and July stirred the soup and cut pieces of cheese with the bread knife, and took down some crackers and bowls. "Milk?"

Franklin nodded, looking at the floor as though it were a great hole in the ground. Suddenly he stood up, but then seemed for a moment not to know why he had, and rubbed his hands on his face. "I've got to go downstairs," he said finally.

"Wait. It's almost ready, then I'll go down first and look around."

They sat at the small table. Franklin ate quickly, spooning up the soup as though it were hot water. The crackers and cheese seemed dry and hard to swallow. Taking a drink of milk, he commented matter-of-factly, "A little sour. You ought to go out tonight and get a quart, it'll be completely gone by morning."

"I don't drink much milk," said July. "It always seems like it'd be too much bother to pour it out, except for the cat."

"Slovenliness. Say, what did they talk about today? What'd they ask you?"

"I guess they found that place in Chelsea. They know about the thieves. They didn't say anything about the truck. They said you were trying to quit. Is that true? Want something else to eat?"

"No, no, this was fine, just fine . . . . Well, I was thinking I'd better take it kind of easy. I told the kids to lay off the household stuff—but, see, the thing was, they could break into a house and get a clean sweep of any change around and stuff like that, and sometimes they could make a nice bit that way, with less risk, and then stick me with the appliances—which wasn't so bad except hitting homes is a poor idea because it makes everybody mad at the police. So I told them to lay off and keep to the stores and equipment, and even paid them a higher percentage on those. But it was still too easy to get a house now and then, and I had a couple of boys who were real cocky—had never done any time or had any real close calls, you know—and I figured I was going to get into trouble there. So, anyway, I decided I better get out. Not only that, insurance companies aren't paying out the way they used to and it's costing too much for coverage, so security's getting better. And I had a good offer on the building in Chelsea, and the truck. Did they go through the safe?"

"No."

"Good. But no doubt about it, they've got somebody outside. Must be an old trick. They'd never leave an unopened safe unguarded."

"Probably not."

"Well, I've got to get some checks down there from a bank in Germantown, and I'll make one out to you and you can cash it in the morning. And we'll have some money to leave on—not much, but the account's in another name, so we won't have any trouble getting it. They've got everything else all tied up. At least, that's what Rose says."

"I hope she's not too upset," said July, feeling stupid.

"No, I don't think so. But, anyway, we'll have almost a thousand dollars to start on, after we get an old car in your name, and that's more than most people ever have to start out." He stood up and went to the door.

"Let me go first," protested July.

"No, no, there's nobody down there. I just got to get those checks from the safe"—as though he were talking to himself. "I'll be right back." But he stopped at the door. July forced himself to look him in the eyes, but when he did he found Franklin's were staring at the door, as though he were looking into the grain. "I was wondering," he said, "if you wanted to go out to Wyoming with me . . . or if we didn't like the climate we could go to Colorado. I've got a lot of friends there."

"Sure," said July. "Sure. But wait—let me go down first."

"We'll get on just fine. Start out slow, of course, so as not to attract any attention. Maybe a restaurant or something. Before long we'll be right back on top. It's the fun of the game. Fifty-fifty.

I've got a lot of friends in Colorado. . . . I'll be right back." Then he left, closing the door behind him. July could hear him walking across the bare wooden floor and begin descending the stairs, stepping heavily and slowly. Then he must have stopped and stood for almost a minute before continuing down. As soon as he reached the carpet below, all traces of his progress ended.

The silence was oppressive, and sucked at the very edges of July's nerves. Across the room Butch yawned inaudibly and continued staring at the legs of the table. A blanket of dark softness filled the windows. From nervous habit, July took out his diamond and turned it quietly before him. At a certain angle it acted like a mirror and he could direct a small spot of orange light onto the table from the lamp behind him. He heard the hinges on the heavy iron door make one thin, horrible *screech.*

He tried to picture himself and Carroll driving together out to Wyoming in an old Buick, smoking cigarettes, sleeping on the seats in parking lots and rest areas, drying their hands on the fronts of their shirts and eating grocery-store cold food—but the vision languished. There seemed too much to think at once.

He thought of Franklin and the dark softness seemed to come in farther at him from outside. Perhaps there'd been somebody downstairs all along, hiding in the corners, waiting. They'd get Franklin and they'd get him too. They'd know. He shuddered. Franklin. They'd said he couldn't stay hidden long. It was ghastly, how they could say something like that with such authority, as if it were a common, easily observable phenomenon—a man being unable to change even though his life was at stake. It's not like that, thought July. It's not like that. A person's pushed to his limit and he'll go to it. There's no other choice. Franklin, without family now, without position and respectability, would simply learn to live all over again, and at nearly fifty would light out for the unexplored West. This had to be—otherwise there'd be nothing more to life than those two things, family and respectability. Great as these things were, there had to be something greater, a reason—

At this point the discharge of a gun downstairs filled the building. July ran to his door. Crossing to the stairs, he heard glass shatter and the banging of the door. He took the flight of stairs in three long bounds, hit the first floor and arrived at the office at just the time he saw Bailey, still in uniform, crossing the showroom from the front. Inside, Carroll lay across the top of the desk, dark blood running from beneath his ear, the safe behind him opened and a pistol in his hand. July glanced once at the policeman and without a thought leaped for the gun.

"Wait!" yelled Bailey, jumping behind a sofa and pulling out his revolver, aiming it directly at the middle of the office doorway. July, waving the pistol, looking wildly about for him, filled the space.

"Wait!" yelled Bailey again, having July's heart in his sights knowing that it was to be decided in the next tenth of a second, before he could say another word. The couch that partially hid him would be like holding up a piece of paper in front of the .38. After July's first shot he'd have to kill him. He was scared. He saw July's eyes find him, burning with uncontrollable passion: the gun came over.

"Wait," Bailey yelled, "I didn't do it! For God's sake, kid, I didn't do it! Feel the gun! Feel the gun!" He watched the struggle go on in July's eyes, like the smaller child on a seesaw, kicking his legs and rocking back and forth to get the heavier end up in the air. At first it looked as though he couldn't do it and Bailey tightened down on the trigger. Then he saw him begin to think. All of this in a period of about a second, as it began to come to July what it meant. What a fool, thought Bailey, I should've said it more clearly. "He shot *himself!*" he yelled. There was not the slightest hint of fear in July's expression. He felt the barrel with his left hand, and stood there holding it in this awkward fashion. He turned back to look at Carroll and at the same time he lowered the weapon. Bailey stood up and came quickly forward, sensing this to be a critical time to get hold of the gun, before he changed his mind again. He gently took it away.

"I'm sorry," he said, left July and went over to the desk. He took up the phone and dialed a number. "This is Bailey. Better send some people over here. Carroll just shot himself. . . . No, nobody was hurt. . . . He's dead."

He replaced the receiver. July came farther into the room. Bailey picked up the checkbook on the desk, opened it up, refolded it and put it in his shirt pocket.

"Sorry," he said again. "You'd be surprised how often it'd happen this way . . . or how many times they'll try to outshoot you, which is all the same. Seems odd, doesn't it?"

July turned and went upstairs.

"We'll want to ask you some questions," said Bailey, but July didn't stop and walked all the way to his room and shut the door. He sat and waited for them to come and get him. Cars arrived and more men came in. Talking. More cars. More talking. An hour went by. Then two. Finally he heard someone coming up, but it was just a policeman to take down his full name.

Then everything was quiet for a long time; then the sun filled the windows with light and then Murphy, this time in uniform, knocked on the door and let himself in. The clock above the television set said eleven fifteen.

"I was wondering what you were doing up here," he said, and sat down. "Thinking, I suppose. Say, you're the kid who used to sell papers down near City Hall, aren't you? Mrs. Carroll said that and we sort of remembered then."

July nodded.

"It's funny," Murphy continued. "In some ways that seems like a long time ago—I mean, that was before I was even on the city's payroll, and worked over at Westinghouse. Boy, that seems like a *long* time ago. I can remember going to work on the trolley at night—I worked the eleven-to-seven shift, and coming home Sunday mornings if I worked Saturday, when there'd be nobody on the streets, and I'd feel especially smug about being up and around then, like it was just me and the pigeons. But in some ways it wasn't so long ago. I mean, what was that—five years? Must be.

At the same time you'd think five years'd be longer than that. I was twenty-nine then—almost thirty. What do you think of that?"

"Nothing."

"No, I don't suppose. Look, we don't have anything on you, and as far as we can tell, you've never been in any trouble before, right?"

"Right."

"So you're free, white and twenty-one, as the old saying goes. Jesus, you *do* have a lot of books here." He stood up and went to the door. "And, personally, I think you'd be an idiot to let something like this ruin even another day of your life." He left, and closed the door behind him.

Franklin's death confronted July in many ways. It seemed factually final on one hand; yet there was also an unresolved character to it as if it were still happening—as though something was *expected* from him. At the same time it tried to make him *infer* certain larger things he didn't want to. *It's a cold, hard world,* it dictated to him, *it's a terrible place where something like this can happen. It's a hateful place that would cause him to do that.* But July didn't want to think that. It could just as easily be, he would try to argue, that the world is what you make it and there are those who will make theirs wrongly.

Life is worth nothing if Franklin could so easily reject it in favor of whatever else might come.

No, he argued, there are some who choose foolishly; mistakes are made every day.

No one could make a mistake of such magnitude.

Someone has.

The police killed Franklin. Society's laws killed him.

No, he did it himself.

He was forced into it. Things get so bad, then you break. You can't be responsible for what you do. Finally you snap out.

Then it's weakness.

We're all weak. Accept it. Sooner or later—

It doesn't have to be so.

Pain and time are the same. You'll never escape from them. Madness is here too. Go ahead, pretend you're sane. All is vanity.

Obscure things don't impress me or frighten me.

God as a loving being doesn't exist. It's only chaos.

Then Franklin killing himself obviously has no meaning, so why should it concern me?

Everything he believed in was taken from him. Have pity!

He believed in nothing. That was his trouble. Pity I have, but at the same time I kind of resent his killing himself.

You heartless ingrate. It was your fault!

No it wasn't. No it wasn't.

Here he broke into tears and, sobbing shamefully, fell asleep. Six hours later he woke up, washed his hands and face in cold water from the sink and resolved never to cry again as long as he lived or feel any emotion whatsoever. He looked at himself through the mirror in a very determined manner and admired the strong, angular lines of his face. I simply didn't care about him that much anyway, he told himself, and packing all of his belongings in a suitcase, and, walking with his cat, he went down the stairs and out the front door, never to return.

The doorbell rang and Rose Carroll answered it, letting the door swing back until the heavy chain held it fast.

"Hello," said July.

"Hello," she said. "What do you want?"

"Well, I came to see about something that was sort of worked out between Franklin and me."

Butch had stuck his paw through the opening of the door at the bottom, and reached around.

"Here, now," shouted Mrs. Carroll. "Get back there. Go on, get back." And she shook the door back and forth, being careful though not to catch his paw in a pinch. "What's this about?"

"Well, for quite a while now he'd been putting twenty dollars a week away for me—because I wanted to save it. I mean . . . and so I was wondering—"

"No. I don't know anything about it, if that's what you mean."

"I thought he might have said something at one time or another about—"

"No, he never mentioned it. Sorry."

"Then I was wondering if maybe in his will, if he—"

"Nothing. I'm sorry." She saw July's face fall. "Look," she said. "Look, what did you expect? You think someone who'd do something like that cares about anyone else? You think before he did it he thought, 'Now, that boy, I promised that boy—'? If he was that kind of man, you think he'd do something like that? He gave this house to his brother, whom he hasn't seen for fifteen years, and the store to a neighbor who moved to Miami, a Jew."

"That's a pretty hard attitude," said July.

"Well, you think about it, sonny. Now, about how much did you add up that he owed you?"

"Eighteen hundred dollars."

"Well, you just think about that, and how all these years he didn't get around to making sure you'd get what was coming to you, and believe me, there's a hundred five-minute ways he could've chosen, if only he would have thought, *once,* 'Say, I better make sure nothing happens to the money July's got coming—that I'm saving for him.' You just think about that. Hey, get back there!" She shook the door again and nudged Butch's two paws out with her foot. "Now, go away with your cat, I've got to take a shower now."

July and his angry cat walked toward downtown and caught a train to 30th Street Station with Butch in the suitcase. From there they walked all the way to City Hall and were very tired.

Things had changed since he'd last been there. Now instead of token booths on just the first and second landings, there was one on all three. The drivers didn't collect money anywhere at 14th Street. This presented a problem, but none too serious. It would simply cost him fifteen cents to get down to his room.

He bought a token, went through a turnstile, seized the right moment and slipped down.

But as soon as he was in his old room, he knew that this one night would be all he'd want to spend there. It seemed like such a dismal little hole in the ground, damp and smelly with fumes and grease from the trolleys. And for the first several hours, every time one would rattle by he'd wake up.

At eight thirty he crawled stiffly out of the pallet, surprised that the alarm clock still worked, and lit the kerosene lamp. Again he marveled at how dismal and small the room seemed. How miserable I must have been then, he judged, to have lived here and actually liked it, even if I thought I was happy. Butch, he noticed, was out of place as well. July put his old ring of keys and the automatic from under the tiny table into his jacket pocket, though some of the keys had melted together with rust.

That day he rented a room in a boardinghouse, leaving him only $5.46, and took a civil-service examination at the post office. Later that week he got a job sorting mail.

NINE

July had renounced, or had tried to renounce, everything in his life that he associated with being in the furniture store. He despised all learning. He renounced all ambition to do anything other than be alive. He receded into himself so far that his own thoughts became an objective entertainment to him and he spent whole evenings sitting and accompanying himself with substanceless daydreams. He made no attempt to fix up his room. He took it as it'd come—bare walls, one overhead light, a dresser and a small table with two mismatched chairs. An iron bed sat in the corner next to a white refrigerator that ran continuously. Butch and the green walls were his friends. He'd given up all hope of ever having a human companion, and all desire to try. If people were meant to be together, he thought, they'd be born in bunches. He used the kitchen in the house only late at night, when the others weren't likely to come upon him there, carrying his utensils down with him and judiciously cleaning up when he left. With a small heating coil which he kept on the windowsill next to his bed he heated water for coffee in the morning before leaving for work. He drank it in his underwear without cream or sugar, sometimes two cups. He shaved only when the whiskers under his chin began to irritate him, and was careful not to make any noise in the halls. At work he sorted letters and talked to nobody. When he would come close to one of his fellow employees, he'd look away. The supervisor said hello to him every morning, told him anything that he had to know, and was always forgetting his name and covering up by introducing himself with, "Hey there, we have a tracer here on a . . ." instead of beginning, "Say, July, we have . . ." July never noticed.

But in spite of himself and all his intentions to live in the most miserable of ways, he found that he truly missed (or needed) several pleasures that he'd acquired a taste for while in the furniture store, and after denying them to himself for many months they began to gnaw at him, so that each day he would crave them more. It's only a habit I acquired, he thought. A stupid habit I was fool enough to fall into. A bottle of beer is better than any habit. "Three weeks," he told Butch (because twenty-one days was a magical time for changes). "In three weeks, if the desire isn't gone yet, I'm going to give in to it . . . in a small way."

After twenty-one days he still had the craving, so he went to the library and asked to be given another borrower's card. The librarian, an old woman whose cold gray hair looked as though it hadn't moved a smidgin since he'd last seen it and remained packed tightly to her head in little furrows, recognized him. They exchanged a silent greeting. He allowed himself only a book a week, but chose with great deliberation.

His second concession was to permit himself a visit to the art museum once a month. And because most of the exhibits lasted that long anyway, he was able to see a variety of work. He loved paintings. The good ones he could live in. A single picture could easily take up ten or fifteen minutes of his interest, and he only let go of it because there were so many others, like the trees and the forest. He tried to come when no one else would be there and he could roam undisturbed, letting his imagination run wild, usually on Tuesday night. Often his taste would not concur with that of the museum, and there were even some paintings in the permanent collection he didn't care for. But those were usually easy to overlook. Each visit he would choose several to memorize in the greatest detail and many times during the following month—especially while at work—he would think about them; and the more he did it, the easier it got. They were better than daydreams because they had no motion, and better than sleep because he could control which picture he chose. They were a little like death in the way that he would use them.

With working Wednesday afternoon, Thursday and Friday at a dress shop, the occasional visits from her parents on weekends and classes at the Philadelphia School of Art on Monday and Wednesday mornings, Mal Rourke's only real chance to get to the museum was Tuesday night. She usually went after dinner, leaving her roommate, Carol, to fall asleep on the apartment sofa watching television.

The first time she saw him she thought he must be the janitor, with his hair and eyes as fierce and dark as chimney soot. His face was whiskered and bristling like an old broom. The pocket of his gray shirt (a match for the pants, which together made a kind of uniform) was ripped away and hung down in a triangle with a ragged edge. He was looking at a painting of two ladies snapping beans in an orange field, and as soon as he noticed her he went into another room, looking for a mop, perhaps, she thought.

It was a month before she saw him again, and except for the absence of any other people, the palatial stillness of the high-ceilinged rooms and the same torn shirt, she would not've remembered him. And like the first time, as soon as he noticed he wasn't alone he dropped his gaze to the floor and disappeared around a partition, into a small alcove. He walked without making a sound, on rubber-soled shoes. This time she knew he wasn't a janitor because as she was leaving she heard the whispered voice of the old night watchman who came to close up telling someone that it was only five minutes until closing time; and when she looked over to see whom he was speaking to, she saw the gray uniform from the back, the shoulders wide and shaggy black hair curling over the collar. Waiting for the bus outside, she watched him come down the white steps and cross the street, never once looking up from the pavement.

July had no thoughts of her at all. He'd *noticed* her, but thought of her as no more than a brightly colored obstacle that he'd had to walk around twice. There were some things a person couldn't dismiss: food, shelter, work, routine patterns for getting through the next day; but other people could be overlooked and viewed as dangerous and troublesome. He had plenty of things to occupy himself with. His life was running smoothly, and if it never changed an iota, that would be all right.

This attitude worked very well for him, and he had no reason to be dissatisfied with it until that girl came up to him one Tuesday night, stood so close he could smell her clothes and her hair and said in an unbelievably soft voice, as though she lived in a song, "Hello, I see you like this painting too. It's always been one of my favorites. He has such an eye for detail and stress. Those trees are really well done. Every time I look at them I feel like I'm dreaming."

After that, July felt an emptiness come into his life. There was something missing from everything. He turned to look at her in bewilderment, his eyes blazing. She looked back and smiled a quick smile. Immediately he dropped his gaze, blushed and said quite abruptly, "Well, I guess if you like it, that's fine." Then he walked quickly away like a child underfoot.

That night his room was a chamber of horrors. He knew his voice had sounded abrupt: it would have been just as well to slap her across the face. At least, it would be the same degree of insult.

All week these thoughts tormented him without respite. What could she think of him but that he was crass, rude and ugly?

"There!" he exclaimed to himself. "See there what trouble comes from. The slightest engagement!" He redoubled his vow to have no other people in his life.

Perhaps if she just understood that it wasn't in him to be nice.

Ridiculous! What would a girl like that ever want with a stupid mail boy? A mail boy who insulted her?

But if she knew it wasn't meant to be an insult.

She wouldn't care. The fantasy itself made him a little sick . . . and what he decided to do was forget about her completely and the very next Tuesday night just explain to her how what he'd said wasn't meant as an insult—just as a way of saying he thought he was worthless. This, he thought, would clear him of any loose ends, and he could get back to his old way of life. It was the lingering sense of guilt he wanted to get rid of, and this would do it.

The first Tuesday he didn't see her. Though he came early and stayed until closing.

The next week, after making one careful sweep of the building, he stood hour after hour just behind the glass door, waiting to see her coming. Closing time came and the night watchman turned off all the inside lights and stood silently beside him for several minutes looking out with him before opening the door and telling him it was time to go, letting him out into the still, wet night.

The next week he returned to the museum, but this time he sat on a bench in one of the little rooms in which the china was kept in glass cases. He was looking at the designs in a cup when the front door gave a little metallic snap as it closed, announcing her presence.

That sound went through July like a red bullet, and despite all his plans and intentions of having no involvement, his heart began to throb with almost audible ferocity. The design in front of him dissolved into a blue blur and his face was hot. His hands were cold. This is terrible, he thought. I should never have come here. I'll go home and everything will be all right then. He pictured his room, and Butch, and sitting on the bed and looking out the window and turning on the radio and reading the book for that week and felt his heart subside.

She stepped inside and took off her gloves and rubbed the bottoms of her shoes on the mat, threw her long brown hair back with a quick, shaking toss of her head and opened her coat, revealing a swath of yellow and white. She stepped off the mat and stopped, as though adjusting to the inside, put her gloves in her pockets and went into the first partitioned area where the current exhibits began. He watched her disappear, stood up and walked quickly to the front doors. But when he reached them he didn't go out. The touch of the door bar seemed to keep him in. He went silently up to the partition behind which she had disappeared. By the time he reached it he was trembling, and he put out his hand to support himself against the wall. He looked in and saw her standing on the far side, her back to him, looking at a huge painting of a herd of cattle and a group of picnickers lying sprawled in the grass talking and eating. She had taken off her coat and draped it over a bench. Her brightly colored dress seemed to fit her well, and when she shifted her weight from one leg to the other, it seemed that the whole room crackled with adjustment and everything echoed for several moments afterward. July felt as if he were dying of thirst.

Without knowing what he was going to do, he left the protection of his wall and moved imperceptibly, slowly and silently into the room. Then as soon as he was in he thought he'd better leave; then became afraid she would see him running out like a slinking rabbit, thought he'd better go forward, took another step and wondered if he was too far already and if she would turn around and be startled by having obviously been snuck up on, and he thought if he were to introduce himself from there it would frighten her. He took a step backward. He didn't know what to say. She turned around and saw him, and it *did* startle her a little; he'd been right about that. But what he hadn't expected was what happened in the next millionth of a second. The expression of her face changed from being startled to recognizing him. This in itself gave him an unmistakable thrill and his voice started shaking though he wasn't talking. But what followed was almost enough to knock him over and he took a step back toward the wall. Her expression went—immediately—from recognition to a smile. "Oh, hello," she said. "You gave me a start."

"I'm sorry," said July. "I didn't mean to . . . I just thought that . . . I thought that I didn't want you to think I was insulting you." He smiled self-consciously.

"For sneaking up on me?"

"Oh no," he laughed. "No. I didn't mean that. I meant, you know, the other day. . . . Maybe you don't remember, I mean that's OK, but it doesn't matter, I mean nothing really does. I have no feelings." But as though she weren't hearing what he was saying at all, she was being attracted by the openness of his face, which betrayed everything he might have wished to hide, and she took several steps closer to him and her size seemed to triple.

"What?" she asked.

"I mean the other day when I said 'I guess if you like it that's all right.' Do you remember that?"

"Yes."

"Well, I'm sorry." He turned a quarter of the way around as though he might leave, then he turned back, blushed and said, "I love paintings."

"So do I," sang out Mal. July judged her to be about nineteen or twenty. "I'm a painter," she added proudly.

"I know. I mean I thought you might be . . . or a model. I thought you probably were. You seemed to know so much about it. But, see, you probably thought I was too, or maybe a scientist or something, but I'm just nobody. Really, I only come here once a month. See, all I really meant was that if you like something then I think that's a good thing. I didn't mean anything else."

"What," she said, "did you mean about not having feelings?"

"Oh yes," he said, stammering and looking at the floor. "That's right."

"What's right?"

"I don't have any feelings."

Mal's initial forwardness was gone, and now she spoke more softly. "That's preposterous."

"I mean that's the way I think about myself. Most of my life's like that. I really should be getting back home."

"Say, you're really nervous, aren't you?"

"No."

"Why don't you relax?"

"I am." Pause. "I have to be going now . . . but thank you."

"What for?"

"Oh, nothing, I guess . . . Goodbye. I have to be going now. Do you think maybe you'll be here next week?"

"I think so."

"Well . . . good, maybe I'll see you then." And he left.

Mal Rourke returned to her apartment that night just as her roommate, Carol, was waking up from watching television, her face heavy with sleep. "Hi, Mal," she said and went into the bathroom. Mal took off her coat and hung it up. She went into the little kitchen and took a Coke from the refrigerator. Carol came back into the living room and changed the channel of the television, looking for movies.

"Gladys called tonight," Carol said.

Mal walked into the living room. "What did she want?"

"To tell you her brother Earl was coming home next week, on leave from the Army."

"Hurray," said Mal sarcastically.

"Do you want me to tell her to buzz off next time she calls?"

"No. I'll call her back tomorrow."

"I don't like her," said Carol.

"Oh, she's all right."

"A little intense, I'd say."

Mal wandered across the living room to the open doorway of their bedroom and looked at one of her paintings hanging on the wall—some bright red crabs fighting with their pincers on a sand beach among broken sticks. It didn't look very good to her, and she turned back to the living room.

"You know," she said. "I met a guy tonight—"

Immediately Carol's interest quickened. "Where?" she asked.

"At the museum. At first I thought he was the janitor," and she gave a little laugh.

"Is he black?"

"No."

"Why did you think he was a janitor?"

"Sort of his clothes, I guess. But I talked to him tonight and he's nice." She laughed again. "He said that he didn't have any feelings."

"He what? Why did he say that?"

"Well, I don't really know."

"Did he say anything else?"

"He said he loved paintings."

"Well, he's not very consistent. Doesn't sound like someone I'd care for too much."

"Probably not."

"Why don't you go to the museum some other time? There's no telling what kind of weirdos are liable to turn up down there on Tuesday night. . . . Or take somebody with you."

"He scared me at first. He walks so quietly, he was nearly up to me when I first saw him today."

"He was probably going to jump on you from behind. I'm not kidding, you better stay away from there if you keep running into guys like that."

"Oh, you," said Mal, and went into the bedroom and took out her drawing pad.

Despite what July thought was his better judgment—because all the facts, so to say, added up against it—he decided for the last time during lunch hour at the post office that he would go back to the museum—if for no other reason than to confirm his suspicion that she would never come. His dark imagination had few good things to say for her: perhaps she was a whore, or a belly dancer from an incense-smelling bar, or had rich friends—a person to whom enchanting some poor fool was no more than tossing a candy wrapper into a garbage can rather than let it fall on the street. Perhaps she really was a painter, and lived in a world of art, shut up as tight as a princess in a castle tower. What does she expect of me? he wondered. What right has she to make demands on me? If she wants somebody to talk to, let her keep to her own kind, whatever that might be. If she thinks she's so beautiful, why doesn't she stay at home and look at herself in the mirror? With little effort he could begin to feel hatred.

Yet despite these brooding thoughts, he found he could not toss her out of his mind and hardly an hour would pass when he wasn't trapped between evoking her actual physical presence, her face and smile, the sound of her voice and every word that had passed between them, and berating himself simultaneously for doing it. No, he thought, I'll go back this one last time and when she hasn't come I'll accept that and will just peacefully go to my old ways, no hard feelings or anything like that. I'll just go in, look around once and leave. It will hardly take a half-hour to go over there and return. There's no real point in not doing it. Naturally, it's of little consequence one way or another, but I might as well be done with this once and for all.

In this frame of mind he returned to the museum, calm and unruffled. It was nearly eight o'clock when he arrived. Only an hour remained before closing, and if she were coming at all, she would be there now. He opened the front door with a wide, nearly arrogant swing and stepped inside. The automatic closing mechanism swung the glass door back and fastened it securely with a snap, sealing him in the palatial silence. Immediately he knew she was there, hidden from his view behind one of the many walls. The very air hung with her—a feeling altogether unlike an empty building. His confidence drained from him like water through a dry, cracked rain barrel; he began an infinitely slow and cautious search for her around the labyrinth of partitions.

They met facing each other as he walked into the large, carpeted room where the permanent collection (mostly out of the nineteenth century) was displayed on the walls. He crossed over to her hesitantly.

"Hello," he said, and immediately lapsed into silence, then smiled. He wondered if he might just run away—if that would be something he could finally live down in his memory.

"Hello," she returned. "I thought for a while that you weren't going to come tonight." Then she laughed and it seemed to July like clear-ringing bells. The statement jolted him: it seemed to be so undeniably pregnant with affection; it implied—obviously—that she had been waiting, and *thinking* about him—it seemed almost obscene in its frankness, and he wondered, in horror, if something of the kind were expected of him in return.

She smiled, her teeth gleaming white and straight.

"No . . . here I am." Pause. "I see you're looking at these paintings in this room."

"Yes. What do you think of them?"

"Well, they're . . ." July made a gesture of inevitability. "I don't know. I'm not a painter."

"You have a mind, though, don't you? You have opinions."

"Not really. I mean, sure I do, but they aren't worth much. See, there's very little . . ." His voice trailed away unexpectedly.

"What's your name?"

"What?" he responded, stepping back half a foot.

"What's your name? Mine is Mal Rourke."

"My name is July Montgomery," he said a little too loudly, then added, "I'm twenty-one," as though he were offering an innermost secret, and blushed.

"This one," she said, calling his attention to a painting of a harbor at night with the long brown masts of boats, with lines of light over the water and a solitary figure on the dock, his back facing outward, holding a large pail, foggy and still. (It was one of July's favorites.) "This one is just fantastic. Each time I look at it I notice something else. Did you ever see this cat over here in the corner?" And she pointed to a gray cat no bigger than the tip of a pen.

Back at Mal's apartment, her roommate, Carol, heard the bell ring and, not knowing who it was, pressed the microphone button. "Who is it?" she asked.

"It's Gladys Schmidt," came the returning voice. "And Earl," she added proudly.

Reluctantly, Carol pushed the release button, letting them into the building, waited and met them in the hall.

"This is my brother Earl," said Gladys, looking up at him fondly. "We were wondering if Mal was around. She's been wanting to meet him." Earl stood in perfect military form, excepting the broad, flat smile which he wore whenever being introduced. "This is Carol Pickney."

Carol frowned slightly, wishing to be rid of them both. "She's at the museum. . . . In fact, you might go over there. There's this weirdo who'd been bothering her, and as long as you're looking for her anyway, why don't you go down and make sure he isn't giving her any trouble?"

Earl immediately became intent. "What's this guy like?" he asked quickly.

"Just a creep—some degenerate who keeps forcing himself on her. *I* think he's some kind of pervert."

"Come on," said Earl to his sister in an authoritative tone, as though she were a small troop of men. "We better hurry. Even now we may be too late."

"I never noticed that," said July, and fastened greedily on the little cat as a safe place for his eyes. "I never noticed that!" he exclaimed again. "And look here—here's a box of fish." Then he turned toward her again. "God, you must think I'm a fool."

"You're so nervous," she said. "I guess it makes me feel brave. Then maybe you'd be me and I'd be you," and she laughed.

July's concentration was riddled with holes. Emotions swirled through him like sticks in a flooding creek. Joy and suspicion, openness and aversion. "Would you like to go for a walk?" he asked, looking back at the painting, then remembered an old joke of Bob Reed's, "Or go for a ride on a bus?"

Mal laughed, but looked at him a little oddly, he felt. She seemed to hesitate, then her face resumed her earlier friendliness and she said that, yes, that would be fun. They walked toward the front doors, Mal pulling her coat around her and July nervously zipping and unzipping his jacket and laughing whenever he had the slightest chance. I shouldn't trust her, he thought, then the front door burst open with a loud *bang*, and Earl Schmidt hurled himself into the museum in full officer dress uniform, grabbing July by the front of his shirt and throwing him back toward the entrance with such force that he fell against the bar opening the door and stumbled outside. "Keep away from her, you creep," he heard as the door began to fall back again.

July's mind raced. He got up. A small, dark girl stood on the steps to the museum. The cars along the street were watching him.

He turned back to the glass door and through it saw the uniformed figure staring at him with obvious hatred. Behind him, Mal Rourke seemed to be shouting, but he couldn't hear because the door was closed.

Then it was flung open and the attacker came at him again, moving quickly and hunched over in a kind of fighting stance. The dark girl, in a low, private growl, said, "Get him, Earl." Mal Rourke, now outside, was hurling insults—at whom July didn't know, and thought perhaps at himself. This is serious, he thought. The man in the uniform sank several inches lower and was just about close enough to reach him.

Mal had inadvertently been bumped to the side in the quick shuffle that followed the burst through the door. She was in complete bewilderment when after July Montgomery had been hurled through the door, the uniformed man had called after him to keep away from *her*. She thought that this might well be an old enemy from July's past—something that, so to say, went with him. But when she looked outside she saw Gladys, and remembered she had a brother who wore a uniform and was coming home soon. Seeing through the window that July was completely bewildered, she decided there must have been an error somewhere, and began shouting, "You idiot! What did you do that for!" But by then it was too late.

Though July had completely forgotten Earl Schmidt as surely as if he had never existed at all, Earl Schmidt had not forgotten him. And as soon as he'd turned around and Earl had seen him through the closed glass door, he remembered where he'd seen the face before: in the parking lot . . . the flashlight on his face. Here before him was a phantom from his own imagination, and as though locked in a dream, he filled with private hatred. Mal Rourke, screaming abuses directly behind him, might as well have been in another state. He pushed the door open and went out.

To July it looked as if he'd have no more luck in outrunning him than he would in fair combat. He decided to charge, raised his fists and went toward him in one long lunge. Earl stepped quickly and professionally to one side, easily avoiding the assault, and July in passing, feeling helpless, managed only to kick him in the knee. Then he turned and waited for the inevitable.

"Stop!" yelled Mal, but at this moment Earl was impervious to all sounds. He was overcome with the single-minded confusion of battle. All thoughts, all shades and lines were gone. Only the sensation of the fight. He went forward in blind, destructive joy, but felt himself sinking. Now six feet away stood July. How he wanted to get hold of him! He tried again to take the step, and sank down farther. Then he fell and tried to get up. He couldn't. He couldn't believe it. What had happened? He could get up on his right leg, but the left one wouldn't work. It took a long time for him to figure out that his kneecap had been shattered by that one lucky kick, but even after he knew what had happened he couldn't feel anything. He was speechless with rage.

"What luck," he heard his sister growl.

"Hey," said July, "I'm really sorry. I don't know who you are. Believe me, there's been some mistake." With that he walked away down the steps. Earl hardly heard him. Mal was talking to Gladys, and she ran to catch up with him, the back of her head receiving a look of unforgiving malice from Gladys.

"July," she said when she had reached him, halfway across the street. "July, wait!"

"What?" he said, still walking.

"I don't know him. I've never seen him before. He's a friend's brother. It was all a misunderstanding."

"You can say that again."

"Wait, listen. Believe me, I had nothing to do with it. *Nothing!*"

July stopped and turned abruptly. "That's nice," he said. "But listen, really, I don't know what all this is about. I don't want to. I don't think I can realistically *ever* have anything to do with another person. See, I sort of decided not to."

"Why did you decide that?"

"Because I just don't want any involvement, or attachment. I like being alone. It suits me."

"Oh," she said. It was beginning to get dark. "Well, I'm sorry to've been such a trouble to you." With this she turned to leave. "And I'm sorry about this evening."

There was a long pause.

July said, "Please don't be offended."

"I'm not."

They walked together.

"Listen, meet me in a week . . . not at the museum. Somewhere else," he said cautiously.

"That's a funny thing for a person who's decided to be alone to want to do."

"I know. I must seem like such a fool to you. You . . . Do you have a telephone number?"

She gave it to him and they parted.

July went directly home and sat on his bed looking out the window. He sank into a long period where time seemed fragmented and speeded up, and the remote spots of light, blue and red under the wings of the planes, crossfired in the dark sky. Half awake and half dreaming, his thoughts were no more coherent than swirling waters thick with brown mud. It was a druglike trance and it wasn't until hours later that he finally came out of it and set about fixing himself something to eat in the kitchen while the rest of the boardinghouse slept like cats. But when returning to his room he purposely left the door open. In the hall, right outside, was the black public telephone on the wall; and looking at it made him feel funny. He'd never had anyone to call on it before. Now, if he wanted to, he'd just have to put in a dime, listen for the tone (he knew the phone worked, he'd listened to people making calls on it) and dial the number. Eight five two six nine four eight, listen to the ring, the click as the receiver was picked up, and hear Mal say hello. Or it might be her roommate, and in that case he could just say, "Hi, is Mal there?" as though he used a phone all the time. It all seemed unbelievable and a little frightening: standing right outside his own room where he lived by himself, he could talk to her. Also (and this he dared not even imagine) *she could call him;* the phone could ring, somebody would answer it and say, "Who?" Then pound on his door and say, "Hey, July, it's for you." The very thought made him blush, the receiver hanging from the cable cord . . . "Better hurry. Sounds like a girl."

He fed Butch and went to sleep. For the next week, until Friday, he forced himself not to think about the decision he had to make. Then he bought a packet of file cards on his way home from work. After dinner (canned stew), arguments would come to him and he'd write them down, one per card. All night he did this. Then he read them over to make sure he hadn't written one argument twice, and weeded out any duplications that didn't provide another consideration. For instance, on one card he'd written: *having someone to talk to,* and on another: *being able to communicate ideas and feelings.* But in the case where he had written: *no privacy,* and on another: *not enough time to be alone,* that was OK because there was a difference between them.

He'd taken the following Saturday off (a thing that was a little disturbing in itself; he'd never done it before), and as soon as he got up he made straight for the cards. There were more than forty, one argument on each, and as he read them he wrote either 1 or 2 in the corner, 1 standing for *no I won't take the chance,* and 2 standing for *yes I will.* After he did that he was so nervous he went out and walked around the block before coming back and dividing the 1s and 2s into separate piles. Then, assuring himself a final time that he had been as impartial as he could've been, he entrusted himself completely to the reasoning process and counted them.

Nearing the end, he feared and anticipated the outcome. He'd had a feeling it'd turn out the way it did: the 2s had it, by a majority of one card. It was the argument of the possibility of life everlasting, he thought, that had tipped the scale. Living alone, nice as it was, was bound to get stale if it went on forever. That was the argument that had kept it from being both sides equal, to which there was no reasonable contradiction.

So that job was over. The decision was made. He never once wondered whether he'd made the right choice. It was the only logical thing to do. The problem that lay before him now was the telephone call—and he had to do it.

What if she'd given him the wrong number?

Ring, hello, hello, is Mal there? Mal? Is Mal Rourke there? Listen, buster, somebody's really pulled you through a wringer. There's nobody here by that name, click.

Or what if she'd decided he really wasn't all that she'd cut him out to be, and what did he honestly know about that guy in the uniform? Maybe he'd slipped into the picture somewhere. Maybe he'd been in it all along. Ring, hello (male voice). Hello, can I talk to Mal? Who is this? July. Hey, it's a guy named July! (Laughter in the background.) Sorry, buddy, click. His imagination was reeling.

He went out into the hall, put in a dime, heard the tone and hung up. The next time he dialed the number and listened to the beginning of one ring and hung up. He went back into his room and sat on the bed, sure he would never have the nerve to make another try. This was at ten thirty in the morning. At a little before one o'clock he went outside, ran around the block twice, in the front door, up the stairs, slammed a dime into the slot, dialed the number without listening to the tone, made it through two full rings, heard the snap of the connection being completed and hung the receiver quickly and noisily back into the chrome handle.

Each time the phone rang, Mal's heart turned over. But she sat on the sofa and made herself look as though she had no feelings one way or the other. Her mother and father were going to Cincinnati and she had the whole weekend to herself . . . to wait for the phone.

"Maybe we better call the phone company," she said calmly to Carol, who was standing with the dead receiver still in her hand.

"There's nothing wrong with the phone," she snapped. "I heard some creep hanging up that time."

"Oh well, at least it wasn't an obscene call."

Carol put the receiver down, lifted it again and began to dial.

"Who are you calling?"

"The police. I'll get them to put a tracer on our line. Then let whoever it is try to call again. They can have four squad cars over there before he hangs up. . . . Hello. Yes, this is Carol Pickney, and we just had an obscene phone call. . . . What do you mean, what did he say? He didn't get a chance to say anything this time. . . . Very funny." She hung up. "Wiseacre."

Mal crossed the room to stare at a painting she had half completed on the easel, a sequel to "The Crabs," this one of magpies and giant cicadas among rocks.

"Say, let's go down to Delanie's," said Carol. "It looks like it might begin to rain, and I don't want to be stuck here all day."

"Why don't you go ahead? I think I'll just stay home this afternoon and paint."

"Just for a little while. Come on. I hate going places alone. And besides there's nothing here to eat."

"Nothing?"

"That's right, lazy. You ate all the potato chips last night."

"I did not," she said automatically.

"You did too."

"Well, so what, there was only a half a bag left."

"Half a bag, my eye!"

Then the phone rang. "There he is again!" shouted Carol. "Whatever you do, don't answer it."

"It might be somebody else," Mal said, going for the phone as it rang a second time.

"Leave it alone, Mal."

But Mal kept going toward the phone. It rang again.

"I'll get it," said Carol. She reached over and picked up the receiver and, before Mal could say one word of caution, shouted into it: "Who is this? The police are after you."

There was a long pause at the other end, and a sound like somebody breathing. Then the line went dead.

"Who was it?" asked Mal anxiously.

"How do I know? The creep wouldn't give his name."

"What did he say?"

"Nothing. He just panted."

"Panted?"

"Yes. Trying to make himself sound like an animal."

Mal didn't know what to think. From experience she knew her roommate to be a little quick to jump to conclusions, and a little obstinate about hanging on to those she'd reached, and so with only her to talk to, it would be difficult to get to the bottom of the matter. Probably of no importance. Still, the possibility that July might have been on the other end of the line trying to call her, that Carol'd simply made up the panting part, and that he might never call back again made her angry, and she almost said something she would've regretted later. The weekend of waiting for the phone to ring promised to be long enough, without throwing in an emotional crisis.

"Why don't *you* go down to Delanie's for a while?" said Mal, in a tone that was both friendly and earnest. Carol'd heard the tone before, and had even anticipated it earlier in the day—certain ways Mal betrayed being a little on edge. Like sitting perfectly still when the phone rang, and lighting cigarettes from the glowing ends of used ones. Carol resigned herself to being ignorant of whatever it was that was bothering her—at least for now—put on her blue coat and left.

As soon as she was alone Mal felt some of the pressure of waiting lifted from her. She tried to paint but with no success; it seemed that everything on the canvas was ending up in converging lines, and the color of the rocks continued to creep stroke by stroke toward muddy brown. Shadows were looking like holes, and at one time she became so fed up with herself that she threw her brush (one of her good brushes) against the wall, leaving a greenish-brown smear there and on the carpet. She picked it up, cleaned it with a rag and turpentine, put a piece of plastic over the canvas to keep the oils workable and gave up for the day.

Then there seemed to be nothing that would occupy her. She picked up a book and read the same page four times. As it was Saturday afternoon, there was nothing but middle-aged entertainment and middle-aged advertisements on television. She wasn't hungry and there wasn't anything to eat even if she were. So she made coffee and smoked cigarettes, looking out the window toward South Philly. Finally, at four o'clock there was a movie on television and after that was over she kept the set on and began watching one program after another without bothering to change channels or even see what was on the other stations from *TV Guide*. She wished Carol would come back, but knew from the way she had left that it would be late—half so that Mal might have the opportunity to worry about her and half as a statement of her rights.

At midnight she switched over to UHF. Then the phone rang. Mal turned the set down. It rang a second time. Let him wait, she thought. A third time. She went over to the phone. It rang again. Then she began getting nervous. It rang again. I've got to get it now, she thought. I better do it now. Too late already, maybe. RRIIINNNGGGGGGGG. Then she was overcome with anger. Who does he think he is? Just what does he think I have to do all day? RRIiinn—she picked it up. "Hello," she snapped.

"Hello, is Mal there?" came the voice from the other end and her heart melted.

"This is she."

Pause. "This is July . . . July Montgomery."

"Oh hello. How are you?"

"I'm fine." He laughed. "How are *you?*"

"I'm fine."

He laughed again. "What are you doing now? You're not busy, are you?"

"No. I was just watching television."

"So you're just sitting there now, huh?"

"No, as a matter of fact, I'm standing. Why?"

"I was just trying to picture you there. It seems so unbelievable that I'm talking to you."

"Why?"

"I don't know, it just seems funny. I mean I guess I think you're really great."

"I'm glad," she said.

"Are you?"

"Of course I am."

Pause.

"You're just saying that, huh? Don't you have a chair there?"

"Well, yes," she laughed. "Why, do you want me to sit down?"

"Not if you don't want to."

"What are you doing? Are you sitting down?"

"No. Even if I had a chair I couldn't. The cord's not long enough. It's a steel one. I'm at a pay phone."

"A pay phone! You mean you're out on a corner somewhere?"

"No. Right outside my room."

"Where do you live?"

"On Sampson Street."

"Is it a nice house?"

"Sure. I guess so. Do you think we could sometime get together? . . . I mean, go out or something?"

"Well, I suppose. What do you have in mind?"

"Well, I suppose you've something to do tomorrow."

"When, in the afternoon?"

"Or morning. The morning's fine too."

"Say, really, what's it like over there? Are you really at a phone booth?"

"No, actually it's on the wall. But, yes, it's right here. I know you can't ever be sure, 'cause you can't see it—but here it is, black and squarish with a coin-return empty."

"Say, did you call before today?"

Pause.

"No."

"You have to admit it if you did."

"Why?"

"Just because."

"What time of day?"

"Any time. Did you call any time before?"

"No."

"That's lucky. My roommate thought there was an obscene phoner. She picked up the phone when it rang and shouted, 'Who is this? The police'll get you' at whoever it was. They hung up . . . and who wouldn't?"

"Now that you mention it, I guess I do remember something about that. Is she kind of short?"

"Well, not really. She's kind of heavy, though."

"Yes, I do remember now. I guess I did call at that. Slipped my mind. . . . So how about Sunday?"

"You never decided morning or afternoon."

"Either one."

"Well, what are we going to do?"

"Anything you like."

"Oh, you could just make me shout, as Mother always says."

"All right—I mean don't shout—how about ten a.m.?"

"What are we going to do?"

"One decision's enough for now. Where do you live?"

"In the Rittenhouse Apartments. Number fifty-seven."

"I'll be there. . . . Should I just ring for you . . . or call you before I come?"

"Just come over and ring the bell. I'll come down."

Pause.

"Well, OK. . . . See you then."

"Goodbye."

"Goodbye," he said and tried to climb into the receiver after her voice in that second before she hung up. Then the hissing stillness. He let the cradle down with his finger and fitted the round earpiece into it, disengaging himself from it as though it were a delicate package-bomb. He backed away and stood in the doorway. Then such an excitement started when he turned and looked into his room he could hardly contain himself. For an instant it was as if he could see through things, the bed, the bathroom door and the refrigerator. Butch jumped up on the table to check for butter or butter wrappers, found nothing and sat with serene indifference.

"Say there, you cat," sang out July, coming into his room and shutting the door behind him. "Watch out there. You just don't know whose table you're walking on." Butch looked at him in a way that might say, "Lower your voice, please," and shut his eyes, ending July's first surge of excitement as quickly as it had begun.

He became filled with anxiety and couldn't eat anything. Each hour brought more agitation. During the night the phone rang and he dashed across the room and opened the door before he even realized it, only to come face to face with a young man from upstairs, nearly the same distance from the phone. Both stopped and looked at each other, wondering. July thought he could sense some curiosity over him, the guy who never came out of his room. The telephone rang its loud, clattering ring and the blond youth in his crisp, white shirt came briskly forward, taking control of the situation, and answered it.

"Hello." Pause. "Oh hi, sure. Say, what's going on over there?"

"I thought it might be for me," mumbled July, shutting the door.

No, it couldn't be for me. She doesn't know the number, or where I live. But I told her a little about the room. I said . . . and he began another long, detailed reconstruction of everything that'd been said two hours earlier. But, as before, he wasn't completely satisfied with having remembered it all.

The clock on the windowsill said it was three thirty. Then four. It read five before it even occurred to him that he should try to get some sleep, and he heard the early-morning bells from the church without ever having lost consciousness or strayed from his previous line of thinking.

Footsteps began filling the floors and walls. Running in the water pipes. Toilets flushing. Occasional traffic noise. Doors slamming. The first eight layers of sky were still black, but behind them and especially along the horizon of roofs was some blue.

Inside Mal's apartment building was a panel of buzzers, and without hesitating for even a fraction of a second he pushed the one above ROURKE—PICKNEY 57 and waited. In less time than it would take to fall five flights of stairs, the inside door swung open and there stood Mal wearing a bright red-and-white outfit, the collar and sleeves looking soft and immaculately clean. She smiled and her eyes flashed with a cool, brilliant blue. The warmth in her expression brought July his second thrill, and though he was twenty-six hours without sleep, he had never been more awake or more deeply involved with the present.

"You sure look good," he said.

"Do you like it?" she sang out, twirling around to reveal every inch of her, with movements so light and unaffected that July nearly blushed. "My mother bought it for me. I've never worn it before. Actually I felt a little silly putting it on—it seemed so, well, loud—but then why not? I reasoned. A Sunday morning, after all. I don't think I've ever been out on a Sunday morning. Have you?"

"What?"

"On a Sunday morning. Say, let's go. This makes me nervous standing here in the entrance." They went out onto the sidewalk. A brisk breeze caught the ends of Mal's hair and she pulled a white scarf from some unseen pocket and tied it around her head in a businesslike flurry. "I mean," she began again, taking in huge lungfuls of wet-flavored air, "have you ever had a date on Sunday morning before?"

"No . . . no, I haven't. It's the first one for me."

"And me too. It seems sort of exciting, doesn't it?"

"What?"

"Being out on Sunday morning."

"Yes, it sure does. Say, did you finally decide what we were going to be doing this morning? I guess you know everything's closed now—unless you want to go down to the drugstore."

"I thought you lived over on Sampson Street."

"I do."

"Then how did you know the drugstore was open?"

"I used to live around here, before."

"Oh, where? This seems so exciting. I don't know anything about you—just *nothing*. Why, for all I know, you might've lived almost anywhere. It seems hardly likely that you could've been living around here all these years and I never knew you. I mean, how can it be?"

"It does seem suspicious."

"Where did you say you lived? We can walk by it, that'll give us something to do."

"I don't remember. Somewhere around here. No, closer to City Hall. It was a long time ago."

"Don't you ever go back?"

"What for?"

"See your friends and stuff."

"Not too often."

"Let's walk over there."

"Why?"

"I just think it would be fun to see where you used to live. Also, it's a good day for walking and what else are we going to do? Drugstores aren't my favorite places. And smell the air—doesn't it seem fresh?"

"It's because of the rain."

"Well, are we going or not?"

"Sure. Why not?"

"Oh, good." And they began walking slowly toward Spruce Street. Mal stopped to look in windows and inspect everything along the way. Each time she would turn away provided July with another chance to stare at her, and before they reached Broad Street he was feeling like some smart fellow walking on Sunday morning with his girl, living on the edge of his emotions, chattering lightly back and forth, Mal Rourke's smile bright white and her short bursts of laughter as clean and rapid as running a stick tapping over a row of colored bottles. The churches were letting out, spewing their visitors back onto the street in their best clothes, the lull of the service falling away from them imperceptibly with each step. For a short distance she took hold of his arm as the sidewalk grew crowded, not wishing to be separated, and July (though he realized it was very much unlike himself) was nodding and smiling in recognition of the passing glances he received. They tried to judge from the way people looked what their names might be and what they'd done with most of their lives. At a convenient place July pointed to the top floor of an office building and claimed it was where he used to live.

"That's an office," she said.

"Now. It didn't use to be."

"Did you live here with your folks?"

"For a while . . . well, no, I guess I didn't."

They continued walking. July thought Mal was beginning to tire, but he didn't know what else to do. It seemed sometimes that they had nothing in common, and many of the things she talked about were intoned in such a way that it appeared her whole self was held together with private prejudices and little attitudes about things that she had gained through relationships with other people—relationships that he viewed with hostility. Then they went to a $1.29 steak house.

"I just make more efficient use of my food," he said, when he noticed Mal's eyes watching him pick at his plate. Her appetite seemed enormous and she ate the whole baked potato, salad, steak and milk, and then ate a bowl of ice cream, which, though he had to force it on her, she finished in a matter of seconds. He could tell that the waiter was attracted to her—several times he had caught him looking at her breasts—but he also treated them as being together and his smile was friendly when July would say something. All this, he felt, was lent him by Mal—a generous loan from her abundant personality. She ate with such delicate relish that July was ashamed of his own clumsy use of the fork, which made him more clumsy, and once a slice of meat sprang off his plate and landed on the tablecloth. When they were both able to laugh at it, he wanted to thank her.

A stiff wind had come up while they were eating, and they went back to Mal's apartment building. The closer they came, the more July filled with agitation.

"Come on up and see my apartment."

"No, I don't think I better."

"Why not?—my roommate's there."

"I don't know, it just doesn't seem quite right. Besides, . . . well, I just don't want to." Clearly fixed in his mind was an image, among others, of her roommate making a mockery of him panting on the phone. "But I would like to call you again, do you think that would be all right?"

"Yes. I'd like that."

"Really?"

"Sure."

"And do you think we could go out again?"

"Why not? But why not come up now?"

"No, I've got to be going . . . but when should I call?"

"When? Any time you feel like."

"I mean, when are you most likely to be there?"

"Any time except when I'm working. I work—"

"I know, from noon till six on Wednesday, eight till four-thirty on Thursday and eight till four thirty on Friday." He smiled sheepishly. "But I mean when're you most likely to be there . . . and answer the phone?"

"Oh," said Mal, realizing what was on his mind, but with the discretion not to let him know. "Usually in the evening, between seven thirty and eleven."

"OK. Well, goodbye."

"Goodbye."

The door swung shut, leaving him alone on the sidewalk. *Then* the dark thoughts from the day descended on him and he carried them home in a brown paper bag. Back in his room with Butch, he was so anxious that he returned to a childhood magic he'd devised. He drew a glass of water full to the very top, set it on the table, sat down and said, "Bloodroot," out loud into it. Then picking it up in both hands, being careful not to spill because that would break the spell, brought it to his mouth and drank it all the way down, drinking the word into himself. This done, he would be safe from any tricks of destiny until he heard someone say that word, letting the evil forces loose. He tried to smile at himself because it was such an immature thing to do, but ended up repeating the whole ritual with the word "Glory," which was a more normal word, and if the risk was greater, so was the protection.

"So what was he like?" asked Carol, leaning out from their little kitchen alcove when Mal came in.

"He's very nice. But he's very unique. He's so quiet."

"You mean he doesn't talk?" Carol asked, coming into the living room.

"Well, he talks sort of. But I don't think I know any more about him than I did yesterday. I mean you ask him something about himself and he just kind of doesn't answer. And he looks so serious much of the time. But, boy, he's got a nice smile."

"What else?"

"He's pretty shy. But then at the same time I feel so comfortable with him."

"Did he . . . try anything?"

"No."

"Nothing?"

"Nope."

"What did you talk about?"

"Just nothing. I don't know anything more about him than I did."

The phone rang and Mal answered it.

"Hello, is Mal there?"

"Yes. That's me."

"Oh hi," said July, immediately regaining his natural voice. "I thought that was you, but I couldn't be sure."

"You only left here a few minutes ago."

"I know, but I sort of wanted to call. I'm not bothering anything, am I?"

"No."

"See, I was wondering if . . . well, if you had a nice time today."

"Yes, I did."

"Are you sure?"

"Of course I am. I thought you could tell that."

"Well, I thought so, but when I got to thinking about it I wasn't so sure. I must seem like such a fool to you."

"No."

"I'm sorry if I do."

"You're impossible."

"I know it. Say, I'll call you back later, huh?"

"You're acting pretty strange this afternoon. Have you been drinking?"

"No." Laugh. Pause. "I'll call back. Are you going to be home tonight?"

"Yes."

"Good . . . Say, I don't suppose you want to go to a movie tonight."

"Why didn't you ask me earlier this afternoon?"

"I knew you'd probably have something else planned. Never mind. I'll call back some time when—"

"No, I don't have anything planned and I'd love to go to a movie with you."

"You would?"

"You're going to make me mad."

"I'm sorry. Really, I'm sorry. When do you want to go? What movie do you want to see?"

That night when he'd rung the bell and the door opened moments later, she was wearing a different outfit with a brown coat that came almost to her knees, stockings shining, bright black shoes, and once again the freshness of her spirit nearly knocked him over. She seemed so clean, her clothes, her smell, her hair, teeth, everything about her—the way she treated him and the gay world she lived in—all of it was so exciting and foreign to him that he was almost afraid. It was a world that had never existed for him, but that now was held before him like a carrot before the mule, and each step forward was making more of a fool of him. But sometimes he thought he could trust her and in those times he was the most afraid of all because it was as if the carrot were handed to him as a gift, and his image of himself was one which took nothing from anybody.

They watched a western, and once, at a suspenseful scene, just where a rattlesnake darted out from the rock, Mal squeezed his forearm in a moment of uncontrollable surprise, and he nearly fainted. At a very well-lit place just before the end she burst into a short little laugh and whispered: "You have on red socks." July was completely stunned and thought nervously throughout the rest of the movie, What could be so funny, *or wrong*, with that?

This time, when they returned to her apartment building, she didn't ask him up, which relieved him at first but on his walk home he began to wonder about it, and wondered if it was OK to be in a girl's apartment in the daytime but not at night, or if there was some other reason.

Five days later. "Hello, is Mal there?"

"This is she."

"This is July Montgomery."

"Oh hi. Say, hold on a minute, will you?"

"Sure." He heard the clunk of the phone being put down and he stopped breathing as he listened for her folding into the arms of some man standing beside her. Each second was a month.

"Here I am back again. I had to turn off the water in the sink."

"Are you doing dishes?"

"Well, I was just getting ready to. Carol always complains I don't do my share, and she's gone for the weekend, so I guess I don't have anybody to blame."

"Do you want to do something tomorrow? Go somewhere or something?"

"Well, my parents are coming to visit tomorrow and will probably stay till after dinner. But later that night or Sunday. Where do you want to go?"

"I don't care. We can go anywhere you like."

"Good, then let's go to the shore Sunday morning. I've been wanting to go ever since it started getting warmer."

Pause.

"Where?"

"To Atlantic City."

"OK. Sure." Pause. "How would we get there? Take a bus?"

"We can take my car."

"You have a car? You mean you've got a car *of your own?*"

"Yes. It's a pretty old one, but it runs OK and I like it. It used to be my parents' second car, but they never used it, so they gave it to me. Do you know how to drive?"

"Yes."

"Good, then you can drive. I'll come over and pick you up. Where do you live?"

"No, I'll come over there."

"I can pick you up."

"Well, OK. I live at 921 Sampson Street. Do you know where that is?"

"Pretty much. What time do you want to go?"

"Any time's all right. I suppose we better go early, or not?"

Even though her car was really nothing to shout about, July once again felt trapped in a little drama that was somehow beyond him—participating in another tribe's ritual. The two of them driving down for a day on the beach, in their own car (hers), a picnic basket behind them on the back seat, was almost surreal to him. He had never seen the ocean, but he didn't let on so, and tried to pretend at each new stage of the day's experience that he was completely relaxed and had done it a thousand times. He also began doing something only partially conscious. He began to invade her private world. Each time she would refer to some place she had been, or someone else, he would ask her, "Who? Where was that? When did you say that was, when you were in college at Penn? How long were you there?" And it pleased him that she so obviously enjoyed his attention. Just in the drive up she made several references to places and people he had learned about earlier, and her mystery seemed then to become partially revealed.

Walking down the Boardwalk, they talked lightly back and forth. They cleared the buildings and stepped onto the beach. Mal was talking about an experience she had had and walked along for quite a way before she realized that she was alone. Turning around, she saw July still back at the Boardwalk, dumbstruck, staring at the horizon and the waves along the shore as though in a hypnotic trance.

"July!" she called. *"July!"*

He turned toward her, and smiled, and they walked out across the sand together. But from that moment on for the rest of the afternoon the attention she had received in the car disappeared, and for the most part July just sat and looked out over the water, eating sandwiches and drinking pop and beer in silence, freeing Mal to herself.

The sensation of the clean, hot sun on Mal's skin, and the relentless white sand, the marine horizon and the sea salvage washing in with the waves made her despair that she would ever be a great painter. She imagined she had only the emotional fury of the artist and none of the detachment or dedication. She stretched out on her blanket and put her hands down into the sand to the elbows, brought them up and let the tiny white particles fall through her fingers. She felt a kind of loneliness that was almost a pleasure, and small, insignificant memories of her past yawned open in front of her, inviting her back to when her mother covered her with warm sand, one foot after the other, and when Jimmy Morgan took his three trucks and sank them in the swimming pool behind their house and left them there until his father got mad, and the time she'd run away from home for an afternoon and sat in the tall weeds in back of Jacobsons' garage and was covered with gnat bites. Then she remembered burying things.

"Here's another present to go bury," said her father, handing Mal a quickly wrapped trinket he'd picked up at the university stationery store. She ripped it open, discovering eight cat's-eye marbles and a clear blue bowler. "Thank you," she said, and ran off into her room, where she could look at them in private with the door locked. They were lovely, except for squeaking together horribly when she squeezed them in her hand. Immediately after she examined each individually she felt the desire to bury begin to take hold of her; but she put it off. And waited. The magic could be bad if carelessly prepared. Marbles, for instance, should never be asked to do the job of long, thin things, or be put near them. Long thin things were the most powerful of all, and once when Leslie O. had made her cry, she'd taken a splinter of glass six inches long and buried it beneath the very spot where she'd been standing when Leslie'd said what she did, pointing right at where she'd been, and in two months Leslie had the chicken pox. Then after they'd become friends again, she'd dug it up.

Mal waited for just the right day, and at the end of a slow, lonely evening she put the three yellow cat's eyes in a little triangle pattern, each separated from its neighbors by the same tiny distance, in the very corner of the back yard next to the corner post, exactly four fingers deep. Those were for her grandmother. Three more went to a different place for her dolls; two for her future husband; and the last, the big blue one, right under where the eave pipe let the water onto the lawn, to keep her safe. If any of these was uncovered, no telling what evil might spread.

Then she remembered the two linden trees that stood in front of their house when they lived on Prospect Street. The night wind rattling those giant trees' leaves was like some great voice reading from the pages of her destiny; and though she couldn't decipher the actual words, she could never listen without being sure that something prophetic was happening. The memory of the sound blended with the drone of the ocean and July's talking brought her back into the present.

"The ocean seems very nice today, don't you agree?" he asked, still unable to take his eyes away.

His pretending to have been to the ocean before made Mal want to laugh out loud in merriment. "Yes, it is," she exclaimed. "Let's go swimming," and she jumped up from her towel and ran off toward the water, leaving July to follow at a slower pace, his eyes darting from her to the ocean, back to her, back to the ocean. She jumped right in, swam a couple of strokes, dove under, came up again, swam out farther and turned back to look for July. He stood in his brand-new swimming trunks at the edge of the water, viewing the waves suspiciously. She watched him gather his courage and walk forward to about knee level, then back cautiously out again. But at last he came in up to his shoulders, occasionally dunking his head under and moving several yards one way or another. He doesn't know how to swim, she thought, and went over to him.

Despite all his apprehensions, within a little while July found himself having a good time in the water and laughing freely and watching Mal, who seemed so like a beautiful fish with her long hair streaked flat across her face and the water beading on her skin. This too seemed a feeling that he only participated in—lent to him by her and her world, which except in these few moments of almost illegal pleasure were as different from his real self and *his* world as day and night.

The water was too cold to stay in long and they returned to their towels, dried off and had something to drink. July was so exhilarated by his first successful contact with the ocean that he redoubled his attack on Mal and her private past with an almost obvious lust for detail, only occasionally being drawn back to the spectacle of the sea.

"What kind of paintings do you paint?" "How are they different from one, say, by——?" "Are they all oils?" "How large, would you judge, an average picture of yours was?" "Do you work standing up?" "Do you have a favorite color? Or flower?"

After spending a day with her parents, who generally didn't let her talk at all, this attention was welcome and it made her feel important; but better were the times when they laughed together, and best were the fleeting glimpses she had when he seemed a caricature of himself: because that was when she knew she had loved him from the first moment, as though his soul showed through him like a trapped, cloudy light wanting to come out, wishing for more air, always wanting only a couple of mouthfuls of clean air. It seemed he had somewhere inside him, bottled and smoldering though it might be, more life than in twenty of all the other people she had known. There was simply no telling what he might do next. He was unlike anyone else. His views and opinions when rarely they came out were always completely unexpected. He was always complimenting her.

On the way back to Philadelphia Mal drove. The dashboard panel lights didn't work and they rode along in darkness, only the passing cars' lights illuminating their faces. The open air had made them both a little tired. Talked out, they sat quietly, experiencing the presence of each other unadulterated by expression or appearance. But the silence soon made July uncomfortable, or rather having someone else in it made him uncomfortable, and before long he was back to his questioning. Mal didn't feel like talking about herself any more and her voice betrayed it. July retreated and remained locked in silence for the rest of the way.

Outside his roominghouse in the car, Mal asked him what the other people that lived there were like. "They're all right," answered July.

"Don't you know any of them?"

"No."

"Why not?"

"I just don't, I guess. They don't have anything in common with me."

"How do you know if you don't know them?"

"I know them well enough to know that." Pause. "Mal," he began again, cautiously, "this day was—" Then he abruptly stopped, and it seemed to her that it was emotion that had choked him. She slipped over on the seat and touched his shoulder with her hand. With her other hand she gently turned his face toward her so that in the faint light from the street they could look into each other's eyes, and in July's there were tears. Violently he tore himself away from her, opened the door and slammed it shut and started for the house. In an instant she reached into the back seat, reopened the door and stood beside the car.

"July," she said. "You forgot your towel."

He turned back to her and they stood looking at each other from thirty feet away like two people from different planets. Then he came over, took the towel and kissed her quickly and clumsily.

After he had gone in and Mal had turned around in the street and started back for her apartment, the door to the boarding-house reopened and July came out, still holding his towel, and walked to the middle of the block, watching her drive away.

TEN

Mal Rourke's parents disapproved of him from the start. Though they didn't of course tell him their reasons, they made them plain enough to Mal, and she had occasion to tell him some of them. They drove July crazy. First, it seemed that the objections were well founded and in a way typified all his own fears. Then there was the fact that, no matter what he thought, they should be the ones who knew best and were solely concerned with Mal's welfare.

And, finally, it seemed a losing battle to keep getting to know a person who in the end is bound to turn out like her parents—whom he didn't particularly like.

Through their putting pressure on Mal to stay away from him, she was naturally driven closer . . . closer, he thought, than she would otherwise have been. She was being shoved. He feared there was nothing more solid behind her attraction to him than filial rebellion, which hadn't anything to do with him at all.

Finally, he told her, "You just like me because I flatter you."

"But you do," she said, and laughed.

"I know. I can't help it."

Also, he didn't like continually thinking about himself in relation to someone else. In the many years before, he'd gotten accustomed to thinking about himself alone. A part of him resented all the time she took up. If he wasn't talking to her on the phone or going over to see her, he was thinking about doing one or the other. At work sorting mail he thought about her all the time.

But these thoughts were in his weaker moments. Like most people, he had better times too, and then he was ecstatic. It was as though he'd been born into another person. Before, there'd seemed little to connect him with anything other than the daily pattern of his routine. Now he had the key, and *everything* was in some way concerned with him. Every novel was concerned with emotions identical to his own. Every painting attempted to portray his own feelings. Advertisements on billboards made sense. Where there had been no reasons, now there were. All the self-knowledge he'd believed he had before was comparable to a grammar lesson in understanding language—so intense and clear had his inner psychic forces become since he'd decided with the file cards in favor of not living alone. A purposeful direction seemed to have come into his life, where before there'd been only abandonment. Every week he spent all the money he made. He read as many books as he felt like, one a day even, why not? Sometimes he and Mal would spend the evening reading quietly two feet apart.

With all these revolutionary things going on, it might be imagined that July found little time to think back on his previous life: that he would be completely occupied with the present. But such was not the case (nor was it likely ever to be). Each new emotion that he encountered seemed to be let loose from his past, and the more expansive he became on the one hand, the more groundless he felt on the other, as in flying a kite, the brisker the wind, the easier to get up, but the harder to get down and the more likely to break a stick. Or so it seemed to him. And when a problem would arise between him and Mal, he would think how his parents might have dealt with it in their own lives. He imagined he felt about Mal exactly the way his father had felt about his mother when they first met. His joy they'd had before. His despair they had suffered, as though drinking from the same glass.

His new life was not altogether new. It reminded him of how he used to be in Sharon Center, before the accident, when he'd trusted to his destiny without question. He wasn't so carefree now, not by any estimation, but for the first time since 1953 he had a taste of it—a confident belief in his own well-being: a promise from some silent place outside him said that each week would get better, each year be more than the year before. He felt himself fitting back into a natural current where all people were intended to be, except for those unfortunates who run into such catastrophes that they never recover and at sixty years old can think of nothing but of how they were on the first team in high-school basketball—before it all got bad.

Simply stated, the more he got out of life, the more he demanded of it, and the more intolerable became any conflicts. And as time went on, all the rough spots related directly to one issue: sex. The desire he felt pounding through him and surging up into his throat, and the vibrant quality of Mal's skin when they were alone in his room lying on his bed wrapped in each other's arms, were for all their power, never enough to offset his sense of foreboding about the final naked act.

"Because," he told her, "I've reasoned it out. I asked myself—"

"How can you reason about such a thing! Sometimes I think your heart is made of stone." And with that she turned her face to the wall.

"Be reasonable, Mal."

"I'm not reasonable. That's the difference between you and me. You have reason, I have none. I have feelings, you don't give a nickel for anything."

"That's not true."

"It is."

"It isn't."

"I'm not talking any more. . . . What's wrong with it anyway?"

"Well, nothing really . . . but there sort of is. See, I was thinking, and I decided that everything would be better if the only person I slept with was the person I was married to."

"Well, I like that! Have you got someone else in mind?"

"No, but then the only way I could really be sure it was the right person was if I was already married. Don't you see what I mean?"

"No. And I don't think I want to. You make everything too complicated. Don't you ever just relax and be natural?"

"Don't you see that's what I'm trying to be? But natural in the best way. If the only person I made love to was my wife—and *after* we were married—then she would become a symbol for my own sexuality. I'd never desire another woman because I couldn't imagine it with anyone else. And it'd be the same way for her too."

"Phooey. One can always imagine."

"But fantasizing isn't as bad as contemplating it."

"Oh, July, you make me so that I could just scream. You complicate everything so."

"It isn't me," he shouted suddenly. *"It's your parents."*

A silence fell. It was a truth they didn't enjoy talking about or even admitting. Mal didn't want to get married. Losing her parents' approval (and affection, it appeared) was not something she was willing to do; at least not right away. She'd never had to deny him point-blank, but that was because he'd had the good sense not to ask directly; if he had, she would have thought he was testing her—seeing what she would do for him.

"Besides," he said after a while, standing up from the bed and going over to the window, "my father never slept with anyone but my mother, and I think it's right to be like that."

It was the second time he'd talked about his parents to her and his voice quaked with emotion, fearful that he was taking too great a liberty with his innermost secrets. Mal realized what tender ground he was on, and spoke very cautiously.

"It might be that you had no way of knowing. It wouldn't be likely you'd find out about anything like that."

"I would've known."

"Maybe it happened before—"

"I would've known," he said, with such abruptness that the whole subject sank and the silence instilled itself again.

"Maybe I'm wrong," he said finally.

"Let's not talk about it now."

"I think I'd like to go for a walk. Do you want to come?"

"No. I'll just stay here, if it's all right. I'd like to do some sketching."

"Sure, fine. I'll bring back a pizza."

"And something to drink?"

"And something to drink."

"Do you love me?"

"Well, yes." He smiled and was gone.

Mal was alone. She sat on the bed and listened to the house noises. They were comforting—much more so than the sounds in her own apartment, which always forced her to consider the causes behind them. These noises were nothing more than sounds. They had nothing to do with her. She didn't live here. To her they were sounds from outer space. No one could expect them to be more to her. The responsibility for them belonged somewhere else. She listened, and escaped from the grip of her unresolved passions. Then she got her pad and began to sketch.

Forty-five minutes later she felt a slight chill from the window and, not wishing to stop the breeze and close herself off, she got up and went to July's bureau in search of a sweater. She found the red one in the second drawer from the top, but having a preference for the yellow, she went down one more. Here she not only found the sweater, but, neatly shoved up against a back corner, the chubbiest Bible she'd ever seen, with frayed edges and all the gold lettering chipped away. She took it out and opened it. Immediately a picture sprang up: two people and a child. The man looked a little haggard; his wife was beautiful but dressed old-fashionedly. The boy, she believed, might have been July.

Mal put on the sweater and carried the book to the bed. A hundred pages farther on was another picture. She plucked it out, held it up close and studied it. At that moment the door opened and July came in, carrying a flat box and two cans of Coke. He looked at her and his face turned gray.

"Get away from that," he said, with an anger that cut her to the bone. She quickly set it on the table.

"What's the matter?"

"That's mine."

"Well, I assumed it was."

He put the pizza and Cokes down and took up the book, clutching it with both hands. But once he had it safely within his grasp he didn't know what to do with it; and he didn't know what to say. "That's mine," he repeated.

"I didn't know they were personal. Really, I'm sorry. I've got things like that too. I just thought it was an old book. I keep mine stuck away inside my jewelry box, underneath the lining. I wouldn't show them to anybody for anything."

July sank down into the chair. For the first time in his life he realized that he might not be the only one who had things that were more than special to him, that were neither in the past nor the present, but the future—things that were always just one step beyond, whose importance could never be judged because they were never finally realized . . . things that he was ashamed of because he felt so deeply about them. The idea that Mal had such things too made the realness of her snap a frame closer. Again, he realized, I've made a fool of myself.

"Do you think that you'd ever show them to me?" he asked.

"Maybe sometime."

He crossed to the window and closed it. "Sometime I'll show you these." And he put them back in the drawer. They ate the pizza with great pleasure, July getting all the crusts. Mal took a bus home. Her car was no longer operating.

It was the very day following this that July made the greatest decision of his life. Wednesdays at work were very slow because of being right in the middle of the week. He anticipated this one with the usual quiet dread. Arriving at the post office, he hung up his coat, punched in and waited for the bell to ring. Then he began sorting. By ten o'clock he was so excited that he could hardly make out the most legible handwriting (and he prided himself on being able to read anything; people from all over the building brought scrawled letters to him). By the noon bell there was no possibility of working on. He went to his supervisor, Mr. Anderson.

"I'd like to have the afternoon off, Mr. Anderson."

"Oh, you would, hmmm? Naturally, I would too. Tell me . . . uh, Jason, what seems to be the trouble?"

"No trouble. I'd just like the afternoon off. I'm not getting much done."

"Some days are slow, some aren't. Do your best. Nobody asks more than that."

"I *can't* work any more."

"Listen, Jason, you've got to be more specific. What's the matter, prostate trouble? Infection? Weak liver? Ha ha."

There was a long period of no talking while July looked at the floor.

"What I'd really like to do is quit."

"Quit for good?"

"Yes."

"Better think it over."

"I have."

Anderson shrugged his shoulders. "Up to you."

"Thanks."

"Nothing to me. We'll mail your check to you."

"Fine."

"Goodbye, and thanks."

"Nothing to me."

He grabbed his coat and walked out of the building, feeling as he stepped outside a hundred pounds lighter. His feet barely touched the steps. The corners of a smile crept up into his cheeks, and as fast as he could walk he set off for Mal's apartment.

"July! What are you doing here?"

"Nothing . . . I expected you not to be here. I thought I'd ruffle through your jewelry box."

"I wouldn't put it past you. Come on in and don't stand around in the hall. I just got back from school. Why aren't you at work? Is this some kind of holiday?"

"No. I quit my job."

Mal sat down on the sofa and July sat beside her. She could hear the emotion in his voice and, not knowing what to say, sat quietly until he would find a way to tell her what was obviously burning away inside of him.

"I was thinking," he began, but stopped, folded his hands and started again. "I've decided to go back home." Then a pleased smile came to his face.

"This is very strange. My doorbell rings at one thirty in the afternoon. It's my beloved July. He's not at work. He says he's quit work. Then he says he's going home after just getting here."

"Oh no!" he said, bursting into laughter. "Is that what you thought! Back to my room! Oh no, I'm going back *home.* Back to Iowa. Back to Sharon Center!"

"Where?"

"Forgive me. My head's swirling. See, I was at work sorting, and all of a sudden I thought, 'I'll sort no more'—no, forget that. There's so much I haven't told you. But it's all right now. Everything'll be all right. It's so simple. See, we'll go together, you and me, tonight, as soon as we can get on a train. We can be there in less than twenty hours. We'll just leave a forwarding address at the post office—General Delivery, Iowa City—and we'll take off!"

Mal couldn't sit still. She got up and walked to the kitchen, turned and came back.

"To Iowa?"

"Yes."

"Where's that? Isn't that in the Midwest?"

"Yes. Hurry! Get your things together. I'll go down to the post office and call the station. No! We can call from here."

"Wait a minute. You expect me to just pick up and go with you? Just jump and follow you off somewhere? You really expect me to do that? This is where I live. This is my home. I'm not going chasing off to somewhere . . . You can't ask me to do that. You're testing me. I won't. I have my own life."

July looked as though he'd been struck in the face. "You must understand. See, I'm not trying to test you. That never occurred to me. I'm going. Today. I'm going."

"Be reasonable, July. This isn't something that can be decided like that. It takes time. There's—"

"But I'm going." He got up. "More than anything in the world I want you to come with me. But even if you don't, I'm going. I have to. I don't belong here. I came here to run away. I have to go back. My parents died in an automobile accident when I was ten. Something important went out of my life then, but I can get it back. I want you to come with me. I want you to be with me when I finally become a whole person."

"I can't."

"Mal—"

"I'm sorry. I can't."

"But I thought we—"

"I'm sorry."

"Then . . ." A tear came to his eye and he abruptly turned away to the door. "I'll be going," he said, and left.

The first thing he thought when he stepped from the building onto the street was that he'd run back into it, ring her bell, dash up the stairs, into her arms and forget the whole thing. I'll call down to the post office, tell them it was all a mistake, and tomorrow everything'll be back the way it was. Everybody's allowed to have some bad ideas. He looked up the eleven stories to her window, thinking to see her.

But the window was empty. The truth of his situation revealed itself: he was abandoned. She hadn't chosen against what he'd planned. She'd chosen against him. It was inevitable. There was nothing of July Montgomery that would ever be anything to another person.

It was this very apartment building, he realized, that I came to when I first arrived. I was turned away then and I'm turned away now. He began walking toward the bus stop, caught a bus and went back to the roominghouse. Within a few minutes he packed in a shopping bag everything he cared to take with him: one change of clothes, a piece of cheese, his Bible and pictures, a pistol, a diamond on a white gold chain, a ring of keys. With these and a coat flung over his shoulder, his cat Butch and a little less than one week's wages, he set off for the train station.

"One way to Iowa City, please."

"You don't plan on taking that cat, do you?"

"No, why?"

"Because there's no pets allowed, that's why."

"He belongs to my brother . . . and my brother's not going anywhere on the train."

"That'll be thirty-five seventy-four."

July paid. "When does it leave?"

"Four forty-five. You'll have to make a change in Cleveland and Chicago."

"Fine. Thank you."

He got a box from the station newsstand, poked three holes in one end with his finger and, when the Reading Railroad train arrived, put Butch in it and carried him aboard. He took a seat by a window at the end of the car so no one would be able to sit across from him, and put his luggage on the accompanying seat: the car wasn't crowded and there was no reason for anyone to be forced up against a person who wanted to be alone.

It was a nice car, he noticed, with large, tinted windows, reclining chairs, footrests, head pads and little reading lights. Outside, people walked on the platform and he wondered if he shouldn't have gone to visit his cement room before leaving. No, he thought. It's just as well. He peeked into the box and said hello to frowning Butch, promising to bring him out as soon as it got dark (though they'd be through Cleveland by then). At the other end of the car a conductor came in and began punching tickets and attaching them over the seats. The train began to move, picking up speed in its slow, heavy, lurching way. The conductor steadied himself against a passenger's seat, and July turned back to the window, remembering how when he was little he'd always thought those men were so daring to be standing up when the train was accelerating, with their completely relaxed, almost bored look—tempting fate at every second turn. Then he heard the door bang closed. "Say, miss, please stay in your seat until we're moving."

"I'm sorry," said a voice and July swallowed an icicle, "but I'm looking for someone," and as he looked up he saw Mal with two big suitcases and a box, bumping her way down the aisle, her mouth set in a determined, grim manner.

"Mal!" he cried, and nearly upset Butch in his hiding place. "Over here!"

With all her luggage, she wedged herself quickly toward him. He put the shopping bag in the rack overhead, then her two suitcases. She fell into the seat beside him.

"I thought I'd never find you," she sighed, and blew out a long puff of exhausted air.

"I don't doubt it. Are you really coming? I can hardly believe it. It's too good to be true."

"I called your house and they said you weren't there. So I called the station and hardly had time to get down here. The train was moving when I got on it!"

"What can I say?" said July.

When the conductor reached them, they handed their tickets over, and as he punched the small holes he looked at them suspiciously, then went on to the next car. July opened up the box on his lap and showed Mal Butch, his eyes green in the dark.

"What made you come?" he asked.

"I guess I'm just a fool for you. But just in case anything ever happens like this again, I brought enough to come back. It'll be my *escape* money. I've never ridden on a train overnight. This is pretty nice."

"I know. It's the only way to travel without getting a headache." July could sense that Mal was uneasy—that if the train had still been at the Philadelphia station she might have excused herself to the bathroom and never returned. But the decision was made, the train was moving flat out, stopping for nothing, and even if he himself might have wished differently it would have been of no matter. They talked easily back and forth, then Mal closed her eyes and kept them closed all the way to Cleveland, where they bought sandwiches and changed trains.

She was afraid. Most of her wished she'd never come. Something ominous hung in the air, a kind of impersonal dread. She tried to displace these feelings by stuffing them into her mind's image of July so that he would become bigger, larger than her family, her school friends, her ambition to be a great painter, Carol and the apartment. But the more she tried to do this, the more July's image resisted and stayed small and measly. She didn't know that much about him, and now they were going to *Iowa* together. Of course there was *some* reason to come. She did like him a lot. He was nice to be with *most* of the time. He had a capacity for understanding her and never playing games. He was good-looking, and a conscientious listener. She was getting tired of school. Her roommate depressed her because her whole life was getting up, going to work, coming home, talking about her friends, and Mal was afraid her own life would become like that. And besides, a true painter would be able to work anywhere, and one whole suitcase was filled with her oils, brushes and sacred art books. She also desired adventure. There *was* reason for coming.

So it was back and forth all the way to Cleveland. But then the bad thoughts took the upper hand, and one hour into Ohio, with July talking quietly in the dark to his cat who sat on his lap, Mal decided that at the next stop she'd get off and go back. The decision brought her a great release.

As she sat there, eyes closed, content with her decision and running over how much money she could get back by exchanging the unused part of her ticket, she noticed July was becoming restless. He changed positions constantly, put Butch back in the box, took him out again, went to the bathroom, came back, went for a drink of water from the water fountain, put Butch back, bought a paper, turned on the light, then turned it off.

"Say," he asked when a porter passed by, finding his way in the blue overhead nightlights, "how far is it to Chicago?"

"About four hours."

"How far from there?"

"Depends on where you're going, boss."

"Iowa City."

"This train don't go to Iowa City. We're headed for Milwaukee and Minnesota." He talked in a perfectly intelligible, practiced murmur. Mal continued to keep her eyes closed, sustaining the myth that she was asleep.

"Well, how far would you guess it was to Iowa City?"

"From here?"

"No, from Chicago. I don't care, either one."

"Are you going to Chicago or Iowa City?" asked the porter, and Mal smiled in the dark, recognizing the tone of humor in the man's voice, knowing that July wouldn't know he was being teased. He's so serious, she thought.

"We're going to Iowa City."

"Oh, then you'll have to change trains in Chicago."

"I know that. I wonder how far it is to Iowa City from there?"

"You mean you want me to make a guess?—'cause it would have to be a guess . . . this train's goin' to Minnesota."

"A guess, then. How far?"

"Five and a half hours."

"Five and a half . . . I figured closer to six."

"You might be right, boss."

"Well, thank you."

"You betcha," and he went silently on down the aisle, his white coat a little bluish from the light.

"So ten hours," July told his cat, "ten hours." Then he got up, clambered over Mal and went to the bathroom again, came back, tried to read the paper, put it down and woke Butch up to play with him. The cat jumped down and got into the box. July cupped his hands and looked out the window.

"It's a shame," he murmured, "for it to be so dark." Mal was astonished. He talked to himself! She'd never known anyone who talked to himself. *First sign of insanity,* the saying went, but now that she'd finally heard someone she was sure it wasn't true. July could be a hundred things she could never imagine, but not insane. His problem, she thought, was that he was too sane. There was a solidity to him that could never be shaken. She felt safe with him. She stretched, turned toward him and opened her eyes, thinking there would come a time between then and Chicago when she could tell him that she was going back.

"Oh hi," said July. "Have a nice sleep?"

"Pretty good. Once you get used to the motion and the sound, it relaxes you."

"Yes. We're less than four hours from Chicago, and between five and a half and six to Iowa City from there. I'm so nervous. It seems we couldn't be there fast enough and at the same time we're getting there too fast and I wish I had time to get ready. I'm really glad you're awake."

"Well, good."

"I wonder if we should go to the house first thing."

"What house?"

"My house, in Sharon Center, just across the street from the garage."

"I don't know."

"I wonder if anyone's living there now."

"I'm sure I don't know. What does it look like?"

"It's white, and not too big. There's a three-wire clothesline in the front yard and two big cottonwoods. It sits on the northeast corner of an intersection, the blacktop to Hills and old Highway 1. Three bird feeders, one up against a kitchen window in back. The porch has a swing and Dad used to sit in it even in winter and Mom would open the door and tell him to come in for dinner. Snow could come in through the screen and lie on the cement floor and it would blow when the door opened. My father had a red Ford, a real old one that used to sit in the shed in front, and on rainy Saturday afternoons I'd sit in it and pretend I was going somewhere. This must be terribly boring to you."

"Not at all."

"Think of it, each second we're getting closer, a foot at a time, eighty miles an hour. It seems somehow amazing."

"What does?"

"Things like old Sehr's house. It's probably still there, all of it. The summers feel the same probably. Soon the corn will be dead in the fields, the beans brown. The limbs from the cottonwoods are probably still falling off into the yard. The highway commission wanted them taken down. 'Trash trees,' they called them. 'Too much trash falling off into the road.'

" 'When you see some,' Dad told them, 'come tell me and I'll clean it up, because nobody's going to touch those trees.' He had a black walnut in back and someone from the lumber yard offered him five hundred dollars for it and he wouldn't sell it. Mom gave him a little grief about that, but he argued that if the time ever came when we needed five hundred dollars and couldn't get it any other way, *then* we could sell it—the price of lumber wasn't likely to go down. So if we kept the tree, then we had it *and* the money, where if we sold it we had just the money."

"And were they really killed in an accident?"

"Yes. Just outside of Iowa City."

"Whose fault was it?"

"It was an accident."

"I know, but who was to blame?"

"Some guy who was twenty-six and drunk . . . but it doesn't matter."

"What happened to him?"

"I don't know. Oh, I wish I could see out of this window!"

Without their having noticed him before, a conductor was standing beside them. "Keep it down here, folks," he whispered, friendly. "People's tryin' to sleep," then slipped on out of the car and they could hear the banging rails for a moment before the door closed.

"I wonder if we could go out there," July said quietly.

"I don't think so."

"It's just all so hard to believe. First I was in Iowa, then I was in Philadelphia and now I'm going back to Iowa—like three different people. And you're with me. Only it seems like—no it doesn't."

"What?"

"Nothing. I'm just babbling. I wonder how long we'll have to wait in Chicago."

"You keep asking me questions I can't answer. Just try to go to sleep. When you get to Iowa City you'll be there. Thinking about it won't bring it any closer. Is it Iowa City or Sharon Center you're going to?"

"Sharon Center . . . but there's nothing there. It's just a little community I guess you'd call it. It's about eight or ten miles from town."

"Town being Iowa City."

"Right."

"How big's that?"

"Not big. There's a university there. That's nearly as big as the whole town."

"Oh. Well, let's see, what time do you suppose it is?" She tried to distinguish the hands of her watch in the bluish darkness. "Nine thirty, I think."

"Then we'll be in Chicago by one."

"These trains are nice, roaring through the countryside with one light, on its own track, away from busses and cars and people. Just this thing with us inside and everyone else safe."

"Safe?"

"Yes. At this very second everyone's safe. Don't you think?"

"Well, I suppose. I wonder if anyone changed my old room around, or if the garage is being used, or if someone broke in and stole all the tools. It used to be that when Dad'd leave for lunch he'd just walk across the street and in the house without bothering to lock up and never lost anything to people stealing. He loaned out tools, of course, and sometimes it'd be months before he'd get 'em back—but that's just laziness more'n anything else. Of course, things change. The men used to joke that there wouldn't be any use to come there and steal 'cause you could never find anything. The wind blowing through the cottonwoods! I can remember that sound. Mal, you should've heard it when blowing would come up in the night and Grandma and I'd sit on the front porch while Mom and Dad were asleep—it sounded like nothing else in this world. We sat with the lights out and those old branches'd wave and glitter . . . then the lonely sounds of the cars coming through and moving out of hearing, popping bits of gravel with their tires."

"How old were you when you left?"

"About ten, why?"

"Just that your memory seems pretty good for it being that long ago."

"I had occasion to go all over it quite a few times, and I guess it kind of made it clearer for that reason. Sometimes I'd lie at night and just try to remember as far back as I could."

"I've done that. It doesn't work very well."

"I know. You have to use the memories to get at the time. It won't work the other way around."

"It must've been pretty terrible, your folks getting killed."

"It's a horror that never seemed to realize itself. Just when I'd think I had it under control, bang, and I'd know it was worse than that. I kept getting it into my imagination—not consciously, understand—that they weren't *dead,* they were just gone for a while. And let me tell you, you pay for those things."

"What did you do then?"

"Lived alone. Do you remember that apartment I showed you?"

"The one in the office building?"

"Yes. Well, I never lived there."

"I knew it! I just knew it!"

"Shhh," came from somewhere in the car.

"I lived underneath City Hall, under a subway platform, there at the Broad Street terminal," he whispered.

"Not really."

"Yes. I lived there for four years, selling newspapers."

"You *told* me you sold newspapers."

"Then I worked for Franklin Carroll and lived in the furniture store—Carroll's Furniture."

"I remember that place. It's not open any more."

"I know. Carroll shot himself."

"Really? . . . You didn't see him do it, did you?"

"No."

"He was your boss, huh?"

"Yep. What time is it now?"

"We'll be there soon enough," she whispered and touched his arm. "Why didn't you ever tell me any of these things before?"

"I don't know. It seems so melodramatic, I guess."

They were quiet for a long way, July feeling the motion of the train through every inch of him. They held hands. An old woman wandered by and went to the bathroom.

"Mal," he said softly.

"What?"

"If you want to go back, that's OK."

"Is it?"

"Well, of course it isn't all right with me, but as far as my life's concerned it's fine, if you know what I mean. For the first time I feel like maybe I'm getting out from under some ugly things. I'm so excited about coming home. If I was rich, I'd buy the trains."

"Well, you probably wouldn't. Rich people don't buy things like trains. They make *investments*. . . . I *was* thinking about going back."

"I thought so. In Chicago?"

"I don't know. But you have to promise that if I decide to, you won't say anything."

"Not even 'Oh heck'?"

"Nothing. Promise that you'll never say anything."

"I promise."

"Good. Now I'm going to take a nap." And she closed her eyes and fell asleep, noticing that she was much more comfortable than she had been before, and that her mental image of July was now bigger than a peanut.

They got to Chicago and learned, much to July's dismay, that the layover would be eight hours. The prospect of sitting in the transit station all that time wasn't appealing. The dark walls and windows were gloomy. And July could tell Mal was very tired, despite all the sleep she'd had. The trip was taking her emotional strength away as fast as she could build it up. He wanted to leave quickly, because any moment she might decide to go back, march off into a black metal train and be gone forever.

"We'll go to a hotel," he said, "get something to eat, catch six hours of sleep and come back." They walked uptown. At the first place, July wrote them down as man and wife to save money and was given a key. Mal was too tired to eat and they went right up to their room.

July had an unexpectedly pleasant sensation locking the door and hanging the chain. The little room was light green with a single window and Mal seemed to wake up as soon as they went into it.

"I'll take a shower," she announced on peeking into the bathroom, and hurried to open one of the suitcases for her nightgown and toothbrush and toothpaste and a bottle of perfume which she picked up so July couldn't see it and dashed off into the bathroom, clicking the door shut behind her without locking it.

As soon as July heard the water turned on in the other room he realized what a spot he was in. He looked at the bed, which had a red cover and was only barely big enough to be called double, and wondered how it'd happened. There was nothing else in the room except one chair that looked as if it had never been sat on, and there was barely room for it to fit between the bed and the window. He was tired, his defenses were down and he had a strange sense that something was going to happen. His desire was beginning to rise. He took Butch out of the box and Butch immediately ran under the bed and wouldn't be coaxed out. The shower was turned off and the shower curtain pulled open and he sat down on the bed. Fears of personal inadequacy were his last hold on the thinking world. He heard the sink faucet turned on and off, and on and off, then an indefinite period of absolute silence and muffled clothes sounds and the door swung open. Mal stepped out onto the carpet, her skin glowing from the heat of the shower, her hair wet and hanging over her shoulders, her nightgown holding her in like a cloud, and smiled self-consciously. From then until about an hour later, as he lay looking out the opened window listening to two o'clock being rung out of some cast-iron bell, Mal's steady, deep breathing beside him, July never had a coherent thought. As the ability began to return to him he was simultaneously filled with dread and joy: dread because he might in some way be held accountable for having such weak ideals, and joy in feeling that he'd finally penetrated his own terrible isolation. Mal turned over, half woke and, speaking heavily through her throat, said, "Come to sleep," closed her eyes and lapsed back away from him.

Naturally, there was no way he could do that. With the excited warmth he felt inside him, the memory of Mal Rourke saying "I love you" and the ever recurring realization that tomorrow he'd be in Iowa made sleeping impossible.

They made love once again in the morning and got Butch out from underneath the bed.

They boarded the Rock Island Line, heading west, and Mal said: "You worry too much. You shouldn't worry so much."

"Worrying keeps me safe," he said. "I wouldn't do it if it didn't help any."

But his excitement was just beginning. It was late morning when they crossed the Mississippi River and he felt that if the windows were open he'd surely jump out into it and let its thick, muddy water carry him downstream. The Rock Island Line went on through Dubuque and into the flat plains beyond the rolling riverland, into Iowa. Farmers were in the fields picking yellow corn, inching along with dogs following beside the giant back wheels, and his soul seemed to be ripping from his body, trying to get out the window and into the air and dirt, let the dying leaves on the trees dry it up and the sweet sounds of the earth carry it on forever. Memories came flooding over him so fast that he couldn't take time to tell them to Mal. He wanted to eat a watermelon, roast pumpkin seeds in the oven, lie in a white-clover field, have a pet crow, swing on a rope swing, go fishing along the English River and get his line snarled up in the bank weeds and yellowbirds, buy penny candy in a one-room store, fry up a mess of catfish, split rails out of oak and ash, listen to bullfrogs and spring peepers, lie out under the night sky and let Orion swirl above him, his sword slitting the membrane of reality, bleeding it into the surrealism of Iowa.

They stepped off the train in Iowa City and put their luggage in a quarter locker. Butch finally had his freedom and drank a half-carton of cold milk that July poured into a plastic dish he found in a wastebasket. Mal clung to his arm and spoke in a worried voice, looking around at their destination. "What are we going to do here, July? How are we going to live?"

"Don't worry about that," he said. "Just wait. Everything will work out." Then he added an aside to himself: "I'm finally here," and half expected one of the few people they saw at the station to come running over and say *Aren't you July Montgomery from Sharon? My God, you've been gone a long time. Tell us, where've you been? What've you been doing?* But he knew it wouldn't happen. It was more likely no one'd remember him at all. Which would be OK, he reasoned.

They put Butch in a locker with another dish of milk and an apology, walked to Wardway Plaza and caught a ride down to the blacktop. Then they walked nearly a mile until they were given another ride in a blue van heading for the cheese factory.

"I always come this way," the man explained. "If there's one thing I can't stand, it's traffic. Where you kids heading?"

"Sharon Center," said July. "Do you live around here?"

"About six or seven miles that way," and he gestured off to the east.

"You a farmer?"

"Heavens, no. Do I look like one!" He laughed. "No, my family and I just live on an acreage. I work in Iowa City at P and G."

"I used to live in Sharon Center," announced July.

"Oh, you did. Hmmm. I take it you don't live there any more."

"Maybe yes and maybe no. Hard to say. Well, it depends on the house. By rights I think the house that used to belong to my father now belongs to me. Doesn't that seem right to you?"

"Oh, no you don't," the man sang out cheerfully. "You're not about to get me involved in some family affair—some squabble over who gets what. I've seen too much of it myself."

"It isn't. I wouldn't have anything to do with something like that. Besides, there's nobody really to contest—The cottonwoods are down!" he cried as the van came up over the rise that brought the little cluster of houses into view.

"How long you been away?" asked the man.

"Twelve years," said Mal.

"The bird feeders are gone, the walnut's gone. The house was never repainted."

They pulled up and the van stopped. "Here you go," the man said. "Good luck." He let them out and drove on. Five men stepped out of the garage and stared at them. Both the side door and the front door were open and someone was welding inside with a loud *pzzzz*. July stood still and looked around.

Mal took hold of his arm and whispered under the inquisitive eyes of the men: "July, what are we going to do now? Somebody lives there."

His parents' house did look occupied.

"Don't worry. Everything'll be all right. Just because some of the things are different doesn't really mean anything. . . . The garage is open. Come on, let's go talk to them first."

"No, let's don't go over there."

"Sure, come on. They'll be friendly. They're just a little shy."

"They don't look shy to me. They're staring!"

"Come on." And July marched over to the garage with Mal walking gingerly behind him.

"Hello there," he said.

"Hello," said one of the men dryly, talking for them all. The man using the arc welder stopped and cocked back his hood.

"My name's July Montgomery." Recognition jumped into the faces of three of them, but before they could respond he went on, "My father, John Montgomery, used to own this, and the house across the street. Do you by any chance know who's living there now?"

"You're July Montgomery?"

"Yes."

"What'd he say?" asked an old man who couldn't hear very well, stooping over insistently.

"He said his name's July Montgomery," the man next to him shouted in his ear.

The old face wrinkled in thought, the brows knit together; then a toothless smile opened on his face and he turned his blue eyes on July in pure delight. "July, July Montgomery! You're the grandson of Della and Wilson."

"That's right," said July, then added, *"That's right."*

"You're John's boy, the one who run away."

July nodded.

"And now you're back. Ho ho," he laughed. "And now you're back. You're John's boy and now you're back. Ain't that something, Glen?" he said, turning to the man with the black hood above his head, and without any sense of what's proper and polite, which had disappeared with his hearing, went on, "That's

July Montgomery. That's prob'ly his welder you got there. This whole buildin' prob'ly belongs to him. Ain't that somethin! Old Frunt says you was dead. Your uncle he is, ain't he? But the relation ain't through him, is it? It's through her."

July nodded. "Who lives across the street?"

"Well, I guess *he* does," spoke up one of the men in overalls, happy to have a part in the conversation. "Perry Frunt . . . and the missus. Lived there for years."

"Well, good," said July. "I was afraid there might be someone I didn't know," and turning toward Mal, added, "See, I told you everything'd be all right. Say, can we get some pop out of the machine?"

"Sure," said Glen, still holding the brazing iron; and, managing to get July a little away from the rest while making change for a dollar, said in nearly a whisper, "Say, you know Frunt sold all this to me, and a dear price he had'ave too. I tole 'im it wasn't worth it all quite—that 'e had my back up agin the wall what with my shop in Kalona being closed down and out a work. On good faith 'e sold to me. I got the receipt in the house if you ever—"

July shook his head. He'd come back to regain himself, not to repossess. "I'm glad someone I know lives in the house. I was afraid there might be strangers there."

The man took the hood from his head and nudged him with it in a gesture of extended friendship and said in a between-you-and-me tone of voice: "I'd say you might be better off if it *was* strangers. If it wasn't for the nature of your aunt, that house'd be viewed sourly by everyone who goes past it. You'll not be expectin' to get much out a that fellow."

July moved with the two root beers over to rescue Mal from the unrelenting eyes of the farmers.

"Do you suppose my uncle's home now?" he asked.

"What's that? What did he say?"

"He wondered if his uncle would be home now!"

"Wondered if he'd be home! I'd say he gets more use out a that house than any man alive. Never comes outside a it even to mow the lawn. Sets his wife to doin' that along with workin' for 'im. No, if he ain't in there and most likely swillin' from a quart bottle of beer, he's out to the tavern in Hills, lookin' for someone'd buy that old Ford a your dad's offen him—thinkin' it'd be worth twice what it is."

"Well, we better be getting over there," July said to Mal. "Can we bring these bottles back later?"

"Sure," said Glen.

The two crossed the road. Back at the garage, July heard the old man cackle. "Ain't quite as big as 'is pa, is he? But golly, wouldn't it be right for old Wilson to be here—he'd know what to make of 'im. He'd always judge a fella right down where they was from. A person'd wonder how anybody'd get along livin' on his own, I mean that young, without, well . . . you know."

"They're hateful," said Mal.

"No they're not. There used to be a bird feeder right here"—he pointed to a place in the lawn—"on a thin metal pole the squirrels couldn't climb up." They looked into the unpainted shed where the old Ford stood outfitted with twelve years of cobwebs and rust.

"Do we have to go here?" she asked, looking toward the house.

"This is where I used to live," said July, a little in wonder that Mal would think they might just go away. They went up, rapped on the door, waited and rapped again. It opened an inch and a little more until the chain caught it. A piercing gray eye peered around into the crack.

"Hello," July began.

"Get away from here," snapped a voice behind the eye. "Go beg somewhere else." The door slammed shut.

"Let's leave," said Mal. "Think of Butch all cooped up in that little place."

"Nonsense." He pounded again, and called out, "Uncle Perry! Hey, Uncle Perry!" Across the street everyone from the garage was outside watching them. "Let me in."

The door cracked open a second time.

"What's this? Who are you? Go away."

"I'm July Montgomery. Open up."

A smell of cigarette smoke and old beer came from inside. He watched his uncle's hand go to the wall to steady himself. The eye came back just above the chain latch.

"July Montgomery's dead. Get on away from here."

"Look at me."

"He didn't look anything like you. His hair was much lighter. He wasn't nearly so tall . . . very short, in fact." The eye kept up its constant assessment of him. Behind the yellow flesh in his cheek, July could see the muscles trembling. "Now, beat it before I have the law down on you. Go on, git!"

"Where's Aunt Becky? I hope she's back soon," he said, perfectly at ease. "I hope you've kept the rooms as they used to be. I don't suppose the old furnace Dad took out is still down in the basement, or the boat he was building."

"Anyone can look through a basement window. Take that little hussy and get away from here. July Montgomery's dead. He drowned himself in the river."

"No I didn't. I've been living in Philadelphia. And I noticed you took down the bird feeders and the cottonwoods. Oh yes, here, look at this." And he drew out one of his photographs and handed it through the narrow opening into a yellow hand. The door closed, but no sounds came to indicate that the lock might be being dismantled. Obviously he was standing, looking at the pictures and thinking. "Oh, by the way, Uncle, you can keep that one—I've got a whole lot more." The silence continued. July looked toward the garage, where the figure of the stooping old man waved to him from the crowd of onlookers.

Realizing that there was no way out of it, Perry Frunt opened the door. "Come in, come in. It's so good to see you. Why, we'd surely given you up for lost, son. Your poor Aunt Becky nearly died a thousand times since you first was gone and we found your little bed empty in the morning. Come in, come in. Wait till your aunt gets home. What a blessing. How did you ever manage to . . ." and as he continued July and Mal came inside, Mal wishing the door could be left open for air. Newspapers and magazines with black and white naked women on the covers littered the floor and couch, a half-drunk quart bottle of beer sat wedged between two cushions. The television was on and turned down low, the fuzzy picture barely bright enough to see. Wallpaper torn and peeling from the ceiling. The curtains were drawn and as the door shut she noticed that all the lights were burning. An ashtray was spilling cigar and cigarette butts onto the table. She felt sorry for July and turned, expecting to see him saddened by the spectacle, but he seemed oblivious to it as he stood and stared at the woodwork. He saw the thermostat control on the wall and ran over to it, from that to the knob of the front door, examining it in rapture, extracting from it every second of past it held silently within it.

"That's the old television!" he exclaimed. "And the table!"

"We've tried to keep them," said Perry, "just in the least hope that you'd come back."

"Can we go upstairs?"

"Sure, sure, July. This way."

"I know the way!" he exclaimed and, dragging Mal by the hand, ran upstairs and flung open the door to his room. It was filled with boxes, old clothes, old farm implements from his grandfather's barn—things Perry had thought would someday be worth something as antiques and had been afraid someone'd steal if he left them in the barn. But in the closet he found some of his things—his red shirt and in the bureau drawer underneath a loose stack of magazines was his junk box.

What had been his parents' room was locked. The guest bedroom was obviously what Frunt and his wife used now; one single bed pushed up against the window with a little picture of Christ above it was made and clean, but the rest of the room was in complete disarray and smelled like wet rags.

"Let's get out of here," whispered Mal, hearing Frunt's soft, slow footsteps coming up the stairs. In the back of her mind was the rising dread that any minute Mrs. Frunt would come home, and a woman who lived in the kind of house they were in was someone she didn't want to meet, and would be a little frightened to. Three large rust spots in the hall ceiling marked where water had leaked down from the roof.

"You see, we kept most of your things. Your poor aunt was told by all her friends, 'Just throw 'em out. There's no chance of him ever comin' back.' But just in the case—" He seemed nearly exhausted after the climb, and stood for a moment panting. "You'll have to excuse this up here, its not being real tidy, but with poor Becky working her fingers nearly to the bone ten, twelve hours a day, and with losing our only daughter to what I'd have to call a no-good, though I usually don't hold by any name-calling, and me in the physical shape I am, well, there's hardly wonder we get by as well as we do."

Then they went downstairs so July could look at the kitchen and Mal saw how Mrs. Frunt lived there. She'd built her world in the kitchen. Not one thing was out of place. The floor was spotlessly clean and shining, a special bracket for each set of utensils hanging on the wall, a dark walnut shelf reserved for cookbooks, braided hot pads, a neat row of little spice jars, the stove and oven immaculate and gleaming. The light blue curtains were pulled back and tied with a delicate white cord. Plants bloomed on the sill, carefully pruned and dusted. There was one wet spot on the countertop where Perry had opened a quart from the refrigerator, but generally, as you could tell, he respected this refuge—and she held to it with the passion of a saint. He'd put the opener away.

"Make yourselves to home," said Perry. "If there's something in the refrigerator that strikes you, just go ahead and take it. We don't have much, what with the little Becky can make and what I scrape together God knows how, and the price of even the most meager foods—though I suppose we wouldn't know what to do if we had better. When you have so little esteem for yourself I guess it doesn't really matter; bread and coffee are good enough for the likes of me. But if you can find anything, you're welcome to what we have."

July was staring out the kitchen window. "See what's in there," he said to Mal.

She came over to him and whispered: "*You* see what's in there. I'll have a sandwich and potato salad if you can find it."

"That would be good," whispered July and they gave a short muffled laugh.

Perry smiled, though nothing in his face, even his eyes, showed good will. They sat at the chrome-and-formica table with their half-drunk root beers and waited for Becky to come home. Perry pulled up a chair beside them and lit a cigar he'd taken from the pocket of his pants which he'd already been chewing on earlier that day. The television was still playing in the other room.

"Things haven't been easy," whined Perry. "I guess it's no use my telling you, for maybe you've been in a position to know yourself. Why, trying to get someone to run that nice little place of your grandfolks—not more'n thirty acres it is, and what these cheatin' farmers have to have to plant a few seeds once a year's enough to scare a person. Why, the taxes alone, not to mention the upkeep. Have you got any idea what the taxes were on this place when you left?" and he pressed his insistent gray eyes toward July and Mal (who was exactly across from him—as far away as she could be).

July shook his head.

"Well, I'd wondered. When you run off I wondered. Your poor aunt and I nearly died from worry. Why, she even called the police! But I wondered when I learned that the burden was likely to fall on me to try and take care of this place—there bein' no more responsibility in this world than you can shake a stick at, it came upon me to look into what the taxes were and I had a thought then that maybe you'd run away to get out from under this terrible burden of the taxes. Oh, they were terrific. Higher'n I'd ever seen before. But I took it on me that we'd stay and try to hold on to the place. And do you know, them blasted crooks at the tax bureau has more'n doubled the taxes—doubled 'em! Why, it's unbelievable. So while you was off carryin' on in—where'd you say?—Philadelphia, one of the finer cities in the East, and maybe you had a rough lot of it and maybe you didn't, that ain't for me to know; it was my lot to be here, scratchin' and savin' and trying to keep the place from going back to the state. Do you know how much we've paid?" He did some invisible calculations on the top of the table, moving the end of his finger around like a pencil stub. "It comes to a little over, for the two places, a little over fifteen thousand, closer to sixteen thousand."

"That seems like quite a bit," said July.

"Well, I would hope to shout it does. Course I've got to admit I had my hopes—foolish things, ain't they, hopes?" He addressed this to Mal, pointing the mouth end of his cigar, and she curled up inside herself with a little external shiver. "Your aunt and I, heart-sick and poor as we are, we always hoped against hope, you might say, that someday you'd be back safe and sound and in good health, which I can see you are. Ah! To be young again. An' though I'd tell her that it wasn't to no end, frettin' and carryin' on, her comfortin' me and me comfortin' her, takin' turns, so to say, still she thought that maybe, even above all else, that maybe if and when that great day were to come, and thank God that it has, that there might be some small reward for the caretakers . . . a reimbursement, so to say . . . what was rightfully owed to us." And with that he turned one of his piercing eyes on July, who, though he had followed most of what he'd been saying, had some time back been distracted by the view out the back door toward the horizon.

Finding Perry had stopped talking and was looking intently at him as though he should respond, he said, "Well, good, good," and looked uncomfortably at his folded hands in his lap.

Frunt murmured something and went off into the living room.

"He said he wants you to pay him sixteen thousand dollars," whispered Mal.

"No he doesn't. You must have misunderstood him."

"He does. He thinks you owe it to him, for the taxes."

"Surely not. Besides, I don't have anywhere near that."

"I think what he's trying to say is that if you want to take the house back, then you'll have to pay it. He doesn't want us here, July."

"Sure he does. He just seems a little gruff. It's his way. . . . This kitchen's a lot different, but somehow the character's still the same. Oh, Mal, I'm so glad to be back. I'm so sorry I wasn't more charitable toward your relationship with your folks."

"I'm glad to hear that," she said. A car pulled into the driveway. "Let's get out of here, July. We're not welcome."

"No, no, I heard a car pull in. It must be Aunt Becky."

The front door opened and Perry's voice began in quick, slurred words, indistinguishable from the kitchen, followed by the cry *"Praise be to heaven!"* "Now wait," said Perry, raising his voice, "there's a way if we play it right—" "Out of my way, you old fool. Out of my way." Something crashed and Aunt Becky ran into the kitchen, tears flowing unchecked down her large, round face. She looked at him, and when he lifted his eyes she let out a wail that filled the whole house, ran over and put her arms around his neck, fairly pulling him up out of his chair. "July, July," she said as she cried. "In my lifetime if I see no more miracles than this, it's enough. Give praise to the Lord. You've got the look of your father in you. Oh, July, July!" And she abandoned herself to deep sobbing, standing by the table, holding her face in her hands, her large breasts shaking.

"Don't cry," said July.

"I ain't only crying for myself," she sobbed. "I'm cryin' for your folks. I'm cryin' for your grandfolks. I'm cryin' for the last twelve years come autumn." And as soon as the sponge inside her dried up, she rushed to Mal and took both of her hands up in her own. "Forgive me, dear. I'm carrying on like an old fool and you must think I didn't even notice you here. But aren't you pretty, though. Are you a friend of July's?"

"Yes, I guess I am," and she laughed.

"Then you're as welcome here as Santa Claus himself. And no doubt it's partially because of you that July came back—for having someone to care for a person makes things work out where normally they'd just be giving up. God bless you." She gave her hands an extra hard squeeze and gently let them go, stood up and looked at July again, drinking him into her, holding both the image of him and her memory's picture, not caring for the moment to learn any of the details, only to be overjoyed.

"Now you must be fairly starved. Let me get you something to eat. I'm a little hungry myself. And over dinner we can talk about what you've been doing these years." She flew to the refrigerator and began hauling out dishes and putting them on the counter.

"He's been in Philadelphia," said Perry from the doorway.

"Go back in and watch television," Becky snapped without looking at him. "We have things to talk over here. Don't worry, you'll be called for dinner." And being so dismissed, Perry receded. Becky set two large dishes of strawberries before them. "Eat this now. It might be some time before we can get along to the regular meal. So have this and perhaps a glass of milk, and begin with the evening when you disappeared and tell it all up to here without leaving anything important out."

So July told her nearly everything he could remember, and she listened intently while paring the potatos and throwing together a salad, sifting flour over the biscuit batter, lifting pans from the wall, adjusting the four flames on the stove, peeking through the small window in the oven, chopping up green onions, pounding meat, breaking eggs into a round silver pan and doing dishes whenever she had a spare moment. July came to the part where he'd decided to come back—how he'd felt only half a person, and how he'd gotten on the train alone, but Mal had come—when she turned from the sink with the flour sifter in her hand.

"You'll be wanting this house," she announced. "You can stay up in your room until we've got all our things out of here."

"We have no intention of putting you out, Aunt Becky. I was just curious to see the place. I hope I can come back sometimes."

Perry Frunt had returned to the doorway.

"No, you'll be wanting the house," she said. "Of course you will. John and I felt the same way about the house across the street—but there was nothing we could ever do about that."

"No, no. This is what I did have in mind—if it's all right—that is, I hoped we'd do—anyway, is there anyone living in Grandma's house?"

"Well . . . no."

"Then I propose Mal and I live there."

"But that old house hasn't been lived in for years. It isn't even modern. There were some Amish there for a couple of years and they just tore out everything. And that was five or six years ago. I tell you, I don't think it's fit for a person to live in at all."

"Is it that bad?"

"Yes."

"Well, I'm sure it's not all that bad. I've had my heart set on it."

"It's not so bad," said Frunt. "We've tried to keep it up."

"And the old Ford. I did sort of hope that I might have Dad's old Ford."

"Of course, July. Don't you understand—all of this belongs to you—legally. It's all yours."

"*Legally* speaking," said Frunt. "Down on paper it all comes under your name. Your poor aunt's name and mine appear nowhere. But then there's never such provisions. Thank goodness there's such a thing as decency, though that seems to be going out in this new day and age."

"Enough, you old fool. Get out of the kitchen until we call you."

Perry obediently slunk away.

"And I was wondering if I could have the bird feeder that Dad was making in the basement—if it's still there."

"Of course you can."

"It's yours, stupid," said Mal.

"The taxes," Perry mumbled that night before he went to bed. "I suppose you'll be wanting to pay the taxes from now on."

July was so excited that he couldn't possibly wait until tomorrow to see his grandparents' old house.

"Oh, it's ghastly, and it'd look so much more fearful at night," said his Aunt Becky. "I just don't think it's fit for a person to live in."

"Come on, take us out there, please."

"We can wait till tomorrow, July."

"No we can't. Bring a flashlight if you have one. We'll go without if you don't."

Perry was in bed. The three of them drove the five miles out into the country and parked in the overgrown driveway. In the moonlight they could see several broken windows in front. A brief flurry of wind moved the windmill blades around sixty degrees and the shaft groaned.

"Let's go back," said Mal, but July had already disappeared into the high weeds in the yard. "Come on," he said. "It's only a little ways."

"There might be chiggers in there," warned Aunt Becky.

"What're chiggers?" asked Mal.

"The porch swing's still here!" sang out July. "Hurry, bring the flashlight."

Both of them dutifully set off into the weeds and, reaching the steps at the same time, collapsed the bottom board with their combined weight. Mal gave a little scream.

"I tell you," whispered Becky, "I just don't think this place is fit to be lived in."

Then July called from inside for the light and they went in.

"Isn't this something!" he exclaimed to Mal once he had the flashlight in his hand. "Look at that magnolia wallpaper! Look at the woodwork."

"It's awful," said Mal.

"No it isn't. Look at these light switches . . . see, you turn them like this. See that? I'll bet you don't know what that is."

"So what?"

"It's an air control for the furnace. All manual, but it acts like a heat control—it *is* a heat control."

They went into the kitchen.

"Is there any water in the house?" asked Mal.

"No," said Becky from the living room. "The Amish who lived here tore it out."

"Well, I can see not using it. But why did they have to tear it out?"

"I suppose somehow it got in the way."

I'm not living in a house with no water, Mal assured herself. If I'm expected to do that, I'm going back home. If there's no water, no me.

The idea of going back East made her less anxious. After all, she reasoned—whenever I decide to, just leave. Simple. Much of the wood was rotten where the counter was attached to the wall. Rot was in the windowsills, and cobwebs covered the dark ceilings. July saw a grate overhead he could remember dropping marbles down, watching, on hands and knees in the room above the tops of people's heads. One could clearly tell that as far as he was concerned, he'd found his place.

"Isn't brownstone a little uncommon in the country?" Mal said to Becky as July stamped about upstairs and they stood still, not wanting to go in any direction without a light for fear of bumping into something or falling into a hole.

"Naturally," said Becky. "That's what we kids always thought. No one seems to know exactly how it happened. It's a much older house than any others around. Even when Dad bought it, July's grandfather Wilson, no one knew how it'd come to be here. The man he bought it from could show who he bought it from, and that man was dead. The record of deeds showed who *he* bought it from and nobody knew him, or'd heard of his family. The farm'd originally been homesteaded by a man with an odd last name . . . let me see, some kind of animal or something . . . wait—Kingbird. No, Kingfisher, that was it, Kingfisher, who'd homesteaded it back in the early eighteen hundreds. But how or why it came to be made out of brownstone is a mystery not likely to ever be turned over."

"And no one ever knew anything about Kingfisher?"

"Well, not really. John, July's father, was real interested in it for a while and he looked up all the old records he could find of a famous outlaw named Kingfisher, and it was his contention that it could've been the same one. But Dad, like the rest of us, thought it was a little far-fetched—especially because Kingfisher lived mostly farther west and south, and he would've had to've been in his eighties—and it showed that he kept it ten years."

"Does sound a little suspicious."

"Hey, come up here!" called July.

"We haven't got a l-i-g-h-t," called Mal.

"Oh, be right down."

July wanted to spend the night sleeping in the barn watching for owls, but he was coaxed back to the house in Sharon Center by way of going first to Iowa City and picking up Butch and their suitcases. Early the next morning he was outside, clearing away the cobwebs from the Ford, inflating the tires and throwing out the bird nests. The morning grew older. Not knowing much about mechanics, he was always running across the street for advice and tools, a battery, oil and gasoline. Late that evening it started and everyone but Perry took a ride around the block; they used the headlights on the last stretch of the road.

Mal simply waited. Though usually not good at biding her time, she found herself content just to wait until what was going to happen began to show itself. All decisions were off until then. She found sitting in the yard so pleasant and whole afternoons sped by with such quickness that when it would seem she'd just come out, the sun would begin sinking toward the horizon, once noticed go faster, until the chill of the evening and Becky's call to dinner forced her in. It's good for color composition, she rationalized, not sure exactly how it would work, but convinced that because nature could blend colors so well, she would learn it simply by exposure. More than anything she missed having a place to paint without fear of being too obvious. Artists aren't performers, she thought. They don't like to be watched. But then actors were artists, weren't they, sort of? Yes, but they were *performing* artists: a big difference.

July told her that Becky had cornered him about being married and he'd had to tell her the truth: they weren't. Then the pressure seemed to be on; waiting was interminable. Twice Mal was sure that comments were aimed at her like barbed hooks, to go in easy but catch and rip, and she was just ready to tell July the time had come to take her back to the depot when he decided to move to the country house, and then they were alone.

At first it was too much to believe. Surely she wasn't really living out in the middle of Iowa, more than fifteen miles from the nearest town over two thousand, in a house that leaked when it rained, with a piston-type water pump that July'd put in that had to be turned on by inching one's way down into the damp basement and sticking a screwdriver into a little metal box at just the right place to snap the switch—for water that left rust spots when it sat overnight. There wasn't a blade of grass in the yard. All giant weeds. After they'd cut them down with a sickle, they found an unpainted picket fence. Then the drain line plugged up and the basement began to fill with little splushes every time the toilet flushed, so they had to go out to the barn and sit on a rail when they wanted to go to the bathroom. "You'll have to dig up the septic tank," they were told, after a coiled wire they'd rented hadn't been able to penetrate from the basement, six inches deep with brown water alive with bits of toilet paper and chunks of floating feces, to where the problem was. "It'll be OK," said July, "as soon as we know where to dig." The broken windows still needed to be replaced. There were no storm windows, large cracks in the foundation, and winter was officially a month and a half away.

Mal simply couldn't believe it.

July learned from one of the men at the garage that the septic tank had been taken out—that there was nothing down there but a straight line of four-inch clay tile, nothing else. So six feet from the house July began to dig.

"How deep does it have to be?" asked Mal.

"It depends on how big the tank is. Anyway, it's seven feet down to the basement, add another foot and the height of the tank and you have it."

"July?"

"What?" Another shovelful of dirt flew up out of the three-foot hole.

"We aren't really going to live here, are we? We don't know anybody—anybody our age. I feel like people must think we're—well, that we're sort of degenerates living here. They all stare when they drive by—I can see them."

"Nonsense. By next spring we'll have the place in shape."

"We can only do so much. You can. I'm almost no help at all. We're going to have to get jobs, and we can't depend on *that* car"—referring to the old Ford. "We don't have driver's licenses for this state. Becky said it was against the law to put in a septic tank without a permit. The yard'll never be a yard. It's all weeds. We won't have time to fix the roof before it snows, the nights are cold and I just feel so weighted down all the time—oh, forget it," and she burst into tears and ran inside.

July sat down in his hole and felt a pocket of nervous energy swelling up in his throat. Everything Mal had said was true . . . except about the yard. He was sure grass would eventually take over if you kept mowing everything down. Maybe I'm idealistic, he thought. Maybe it won't be as easy as I'd hoped.

Maybe I'm just a fool.

Then he checked his impulse to run back into the house immediately: it was always better to take time and think things out before rushing ahead. Whenever other problems had sprung up between them and he hadn't taken time to think, he'd ended up saying things he regretted and making a bad situation worse. Mal could always think much faster in a tense situation and whatever he said she could shoot holes through. This time he would let things settle before deciding on how to deal with them.

The first realistic thought he had was that she might be right—it might be just the stupidest thing to be living out here. It might be completely obvious to everyone else that it couldn't be done, without unhappiness. So what Mal had taken to be staring from the slow cars that drove by in front (and he'd seen them too) was in actuality looks of astonished wonder: *How could anyone be so stupid as to try to live there ? Is it some kind of experiment? I wonder how long the girl'll hold out.*

He reconsidered. No, it isn't that way at all. They're looking because they're curious—*generally* curious—and Mal's upset. This coincided with the facts as well, and had a better feel. It was more hopeful.

What was Mal upset about? (Be careful, this one's tricky—you've been fooled before.) Start with what she said: complaints about the house.

Then it came to him. She didn't like it here! He mentally shuddered. It wasn't that she was in a bad mood, or mad at something he'd done, like the time he'd not really listened to what she'd said and had forgotten all about it—important things about painting; and it wasn't that she just didn't know what to do with herself—like not being in school or working. *She didn't want to live here!* Nothing could be more awful. All along . . . he could see that from the very beginning she'd not wanted to stay. She was unhappy just *being* in this place. He'd brought her 967 miles to be in an unhappy place. He leaped out of the hole, throwing down his shovel, and ran into the house, tracking black mud across the thin red rug they'd bought at an auction for a dollar and talked all night about how it added just the perfect color to the room.

"Mal, Mal!" He found her in the dining room, sitting beside the window, ran to her and took her by the shoulders, turning her toward him. "I'm sorry. We'll go back to Philadelphia this minute. We'll pack right now. We'll drive the Ford. Hurry. I guess I never really thought you didn't like it here—basically. A few annoyances was all, I thought. Come on, we'll pack right now." He was pulling her up.

"Stop touching me!" she yelled, and shook herself free. Then after a period of red silence said, "The Ford wouldn't get that far."

"Sure it would."

"It breaks down every other day. It'd never make it."

"Then I'll take you to the train and *I'll* drive it out. Two days. Only two days and we'll be together again. I care about you much more than living here. Never forget that. Come on."

"We can't."

"Why not?"

"Because I spent all the money!" she said, just before bursting into tears and burying her face in her hands. July picked up her purse from the table, took out the little leather pouch where he knew she kept the "money to the East," and opened it. A single dollar bill was all that was left, after it had been raided now and then for groceries or materials to fix up the house. He held it as a proof against him, undeniable evidence of his own selfishness. He put it down and tried to think. Mal continued to cry.

"Oh, it makes me so *mad!*" she screamed, and slammed her fists down on the tabletop.

July jumped back. "What?" he said.

"Crying. I hate it!"

"I do too. But wait—I have it!" and he ran upstairs, across the ceiling, back again and down.

"Here!" he said. "Here!" And dangling from a delicate white-gold chain was a diamond as big as the buttons on her blue dress. "All the money we'll need."

He put it into Mal's hand. It seemed for an instant as if it were alive, the little chain quivering like a thin fish.

"It's beautiful," she said. "Where'd you get it?"

"I bought it a long time ago."

"Is it real?"

"Sure it is. I bought it at Snells' Jewelry, remember that place?"

"It's real nice."

"It'll give us enough money to go back East and get a place and take a nice long vacation—say, through the winter."

Mal carried the necklace to the mirror in the kitchen and put it on. Looking into her own eyes and admiring the reflection, she thought: Now I must decide to stay or leave. She thought very hard, trying to be as fair as possible, realizing that staying had to mean more now than waiting, and leaving meant forever.

July came into the kitchen and stood diffidently close to the refrigerator. Her time was up. Whatever she said would be what she decided.

"I'm not going. But you have to promise that we can be more *practical.*"

July agreed in an instant. But in the last ten minutes something had changed between them. He wasn't sure what it was, or exactly what new conditions would be likely to grow from it. Yet something different was in the air. And he noted it.

They spent all of that evening planning, making lists on a piece of paper, adding figures that represented amounts of money, and taking each other's clothes off, safe and happy that there was no one for miles, nothing to break their inchoate web of closeness. The diamond was too important, they decided, to sell outright, and they'd look for a place to borrow money on it. Then, with a reliable car and the things they had to have before winter set in, they could buy it back at a little each month. Because most of the work on the house would have to be done by July, Mal took it upon herself to find a job—part time if possible—something where she could earn the $185 they'd figured out they would need each month. One of the upstairs rooms was to become a studio, and July would put another window in the north wall to catch the reflected light. After they got a better car they could take the driving test in Iowa City.

But the septic tank remained foremost in July's urgent thoughts, and after they obtained a loan and bought a new car (or at least a newer one than the Ford), a green Chrysler, and Mal was off looking for work, July dug as though he were possessed. He dug the six-foot round hole through the top two feet of black dirt, past a six-inch layer of small rocks, down to a sandier, browner soil, and into clay, which presented such a problem he was finally forced to stop. The clay was so wet and sticky that it wouldn't come off his shovel when he threw it up out of the hole (now nearly seven feet deep) and it was easier to break away chunks and throw them out. This worked well enough for another six inches, but as the clay became more moist the pieces didn't stay together as well, and by the time he pulled himself up with the rope fastened to a window frame of the house, he was nearly exhausted with anger and frustration. When Mal came home he had a bucket tied to a rope and they dug the next several feet together: July filling the bucket with his hands and helping her pull it up the first seven feet, and Mal taking it the rest of the way to the oak two-by-twelve laid across the top—and from there to the side where the mixture of clay and water could be dug out and the bucket lowered back down. The rope grew slippery with the clay. Darkness finally sent them tired and hungry back into the house, where they ate a silent meal of pot pies and milk and went straight to bed.

The following morning brought with it a great setback. During the night the water had resumed its natural level, two feet from where they'd stopped digging. Essentially they had dug a small well. So the first job was to take the water out by bucket. Great slabs of clay fell from the sides of the hole, splashing into the water, making the cavity swell out at the bottom like a bell. "I think it's too dangerous down there," called Mal. "If something were to happen I could never get you out."

"There's no danger. Besides, we're almost deep enough."

On they went until noon, jumped into their Chrysler and drove into Iowa City and bought a black treated-metal septic tank for $40.75, the shape of a giant bean can with a lid over the top, five and a half feet in diameter, five feet high, 250 pounds in weight, put it with help on top of their car and drove home at ten miles per hour.

From the bottom of the tank to the inlet opening measured thirty-nine inches. All the instruction booklet said was to make it level. They had another foot to go. Three hours later they lowered the round cylinder with a fence stretcher from a scaffolding of oil drums and lumber. It fitted into the mud hole as snugly as if it'd already been lying there twenty years. The inlet and outlet were right in place—lined up both vertically and horizontally with the tile. They cemented the connections with ready-mix, and ran laughing upstairs to take a bath as the piston pump banged away.

They ate a long dinner, complete with a bottle of wine, and woke the next morning in horror to find that the water in the ground had forced the tank upward, breaking it away from the tile and raising it a foot higher. July began to swear and throw clods of dirt down on the lid.

"Can't we just fill it with water?" asked Mal. "That'll make it sink down again."

"No we can't!" screamed July as though the whole thing were her fault. "Because more clay's probably fallen off underneath. It won't fit right. Now we have to take all that water out, pull up the tank, take the water out from the ground and dig another foot down. Jesus, I'd've thought we ran enough water in there. Wouldn't you think that? God damn it!"

"Well, obviously we didn't."

Taking off the lid proved to be extremely difficult, there being nothing to grab hold of except the thin edge of the inch overhang—and of course one couldn't stand on the very lid he was trying to lift up. The hole was not any larger than it had to be to fit the tank. Old pieces of pipe, metal fenceposts, many other things were tried to probe down with, grab and lift, before they came upon the idea of using a garden hoe and got the lid up out of the hole.

The next difficulty after getting the water out was that, though the tank had floated upward, it was nevertheless still a foot and a half down into well-packed mud and clay, and their little scaffolding collapsed under the unbelievable strain of the fence stretcher, to which July had attached a longer rope so he could pull it from a second-story window in order to get the right leverage angle when the rope was let into the ratchet holder. The plank lurched to the side. The middle frame piece and the glass from both windows flew out into the yard with a great crash, the tower of oil barrels tumbled, Mal was nearly crushed by the falling two-by-twelve, and the tank eased down another inch into the clay.

"I said to hold it!" yelled July.

"I couldn't!" yelled back Mal. "This is one of the stupidest ideas I ever heard of! Putting in a septic tank!"

She's right, thought July, clumping down the stairs. Absolutely right. The broken window casing was a terrible thing to look at up close. The very house seemed to scream at him, *Hey, watch it, will you!*

"You were right," he said. "It was a stupid idea: I should've had the bigger oil drum on the bottom. I knew it would be more stable that way, but it seemed like they fit better the other way around."

"No, no! The whole thing was stupid. Nobody does this kind of work with the tools we have. People have *equipment* for this kind of thing." She walked out to the barn. The Chrysler's motor roared and she drove out, heading for the road.

"Hey, where are you going?" shouted July.

"Somewhere to take a shower. If I have to break in a house or rent a motel room, *I'll do it.* Come if you want to."

"No, I better think this out. Don't go now."

"Sorry. I'll be back in an hour—then we can do anything you want to." And she was gone in a cloud of dust and gravel. July found a cigarette inside, smoked it and tried to figure out how he'd make the scaffolding stronger. Then an idea flashed to him: if he hurried and worked as fast and skillfully as he possibly could, he might be able to piece the windows back in—everything except the glass, of course—before she came home. And he could assure her that glass wasn't very expensive and could be gotten easily and she wouldn't feel so bad about everything. While he was working he could think up a way to make the scaffolding stronger. Perhaps *she* could pull from the second floor and *he* could hold.

When Mal returned she found him working on the windows and very irritable because, as he said, it was like Murphy's law—if something *could* go wrong, it *would.*

But their mood improved with the afternoon, a few chances fell to their favor, and the exhilaration they felt when the tank was finally cemented in place again and they could hear water pouring into it from the house was twice that of the night before. Sitting with their dinner on the porch as the cool sun set in the distance, they smelled the air, noticed the great naked trees that lived behind the barn, a faraway barking of dogs and a windless November hush.

"We're lucky," said July. "It could be a lot colder now."

"I know," said Mal peacefully, as though she knew far more than she cared to express.

"We should take more time to notice things," he continued. "We should look and be open to more—because the better feelings aren't the ones that come naturally. They have to be worked for. They come when everything else is shut out." Nature looked as if it were dead. Leaves lay carpet thick on the ground. The plant stalks had turned gray and brown. The realness of the crisp air was overpowering. The silence was broken only by the wind, cardinals, woodpeckers, sparrows and jays—the rest of the birds having left silently in the night, great groups of them leaving at some incomprehensible whisper from their souls, passing through the dark air like spirits along the ghost trails. The other animals, raucous before, had turned inward. July felt this fall stir through him with feelings deeper than even his memory could claim. "I know," said Mal.

The next week brought the first snowfall, but the wet ground absorbed it and nothing remained by mid-afternoon. July bought two bundles of wood shingles and a gallon of plastic tar, and patched the roof. The cracks in the foundation were filled with calking compound and mortar; they set the picket fence upright and painted it. The small oil burner in the living room worked better than they could have hoped, and they came upon storm windows while cleaning out a shed for the second car. With weather stripping here and there the wind was completely shut out. A new control switch and the water pump could turn on and off by itself. The glass for the windows was cut at a hardware store in Kalona, and for nearly a whole week they worked on the inside of the kitchen, laying linoleum, painting the walls and shelves, taking out the rotted wood along the counter and replacing it with boards from the barn.

Mal found a job as a salesgirl at "Things and Things" in Iowa City, four days a week through New Year's. She took her driving test, got a license and had a set of snow tires put on the Chrysler.

July was filled with the Christmas spirit, and set up a tree three weeks before the twenty-fifth, with colored lights that would either blink or burn constantly. The pleasure he felt when for the first time Mal saw the big wrapped package he'd put under the tree for her was almost impossible to contain, and he nearly said, "Go ahead, open it," when she pleaded to know what it was. But he didn't, and said she'd have to wait. Finally, a snowstorm came and the snow remained on the ground.

Mal put two packages under the tree for him, one small and heavy and the other larger but weightless, both perfectly wrapped with ribbons and bows and delicately folded name cards with *To July, from Mal* and *To July, from Santa* written inside, done with her infallible sense of taste in small things. July's package for her looked crude by comparison, and he resolved to do one as well as he could, and not give in to the urge to get it done and put under the tree. He felt small beside her. She knows, he thought, how important those things are—that peacefulness is a matter of small things done well—that the foundations of well-being, love and motherhood rest on them. Where could she have learned that? Does she realize that everything she does brings me closer to her? Or does she do them without thinking?

They bought scented candles and had a time each evening after dinner and dishes (Mal would never leave the kitchen in disarray for even five minutes) when they burned them.

By Christmas Eve there was one more present for July and three more for Mal. There was one for Butch too, though he didn't show much interest in it. Dinner was by candlelight and they were both so excited and happy they could hardly eat. In their minds the little living room with the tree and lights and candles burning, the red rug, the secondhand overstuffed furniture, two paintings of Mal's and the dark oak woodwork was as nice as the Sistine Chapel. They took baths separately in the chilly upstairs bathroom, dressed in their flannel pajamas and slippers; and with the knowledge that each other's clean, warm skin was only a couple of frail snaps away—drawing this sensation out by touching each other only lightly—they went downstairs and sat next to the tree.

"Now Butch first," said Mal, drawing the large cat up and putting his present in front of him. He touched it once with his paw and started away. July caught him and held him. Mal opened the red package for him; it turned out to be a toy mouse that would squeak when pinched. July took it from Mal and held it very close to Butch's face and squeezed. In an instant he was out of the room and up the stairs.

"Cats are so hard to buy presents for," said Mal.

"That's true. So are you. Hurry up and open one of your presents. Here, this one."

"No, you have to open first."

"Oh no. You have three presents here. Naturally, you open first. Fair's fair."

"Well, I have one for you that couldn't be wrapped. So you have three too."

"Couldn't be wrapped, you say. Too big?"

"No. And no more hints."

"Here. This one. You open this one," said July, and set one of the two smaller packages in Mal's lap, unable to resist giving her knee a little caress as he drew back his hand. The smell of the candles and the tree filled the room. He was ashamed of how crude the wrapping seemed, with edges of tape and paper sticking out from the corners. She opened it and discovered a white knitted hat with a ball on top where the yarn converged; there was no elastic band, but when she put it on it fitted snugly at whatever angle she set it. Jumping up from the floor, she ran into the kitchen to admire herself in it. There seemed to be no such hat that she'd ever seen before. It made her look beautiful, she thought. But I must be careful not to wear it in the rain, for it would shrink, I bet.

"Oh, how did you know just the right size?" she sang out, coming back.

The desire July felt for her after seeing her run off into the kitchen, her round buttocks moving beneath the pajamas, was just getting settled down when it seemed he was forced to observe her coming toward him, her face beaming with happiness, her breasts rising and falling with her steps.

"Come here and I'll show you," he said and reached out for her as she came closer, his senses able to feel with anticipation.

Mal laughed and dashed to the side to avoid his grab. "Oh no, none of that now. Remember we decided to wait. Remember?"

"Rules are made to be broken."

"No, no. Besides, you have to open a present now." She handed him the small, heavy, oblong one and sat down.

"Why can't I have the big one first?"

"Nope. Big one last."

"Do you like that hat?"

"Oh yes! It's simply beautiful, adorable, and I'll wear it every chance I get. See, I'm wearing it now . . . so open yours."

July did, trying to take the gift apart without ripping the paper, but having a hard time of it.

"You have to just tear them," said Mal. "You can never really save very well. The paper's never the same afterward. I know, I used to too. It seemed such a waste—such wanton destruction. But it's just one of those things that aren't made to last. That's part of what makes them so nice."

"I feel so shallow when you talk sometimes."

"Why?"

"Because I would've never thought that much about it. I would've just simply felt bad that something beautiful was spoiled—and that would've been the end of it."

"Oh, surely not. But hurry and open it."

Within the box and under a layer of cotton was a pocket knife with three blades. The smallest blade was fat and curved quickly, a particularly good shape for shaving and paring. The second, a half-inch longer with a flat edge, opened to a slightly closer perpendicular position to the handle, an aid in drawing a long cut toward you. The third, bigger than the other two combined, running nearly a full three and a half inches to a very sharp point, seemed massive and at the same time elegant. The handle was dark bone locked in place with brass rivets. He appreciated it with the devotion that only a person who loves having things in his pockets can appreciate: a knife to be truly proud of, a functional size without being either pretentiously masculine or weightless.

"Thank you."

"Promise you like it. I was so afraid you wouldn't. I thought you'd probably want a bigger one, but I wasn't sure."

"It's perfect. Did you sharpen it? It surely didn't come from the store this sharp."

"Oh good! I hoped you'd notice that. Now I know you like it. Yes, I sharpened it. Not bad, huh?"

"Not bad! It's as sharp as a razor. Only professionals can sharpen knives like this."

"Silly. Now you have to hurry. I have another one for you in the summer kitchen."

"No. You're next. Here, open this!" And he gave her the heavy, large present, this one better wrapped because it'd been done for him at the store, but it was still way shy, he felt, of having the sensitivity of Mal's.

"It's a book," she said immediately.

"Well, it's pretty hard to disguise a book."

The package contained an art book filled from one end to the other with color prints, with almost no attempt made to explain how the paintings worked or what they stood for, only brief autobiographical sketches of the artists and an occasional note referring to some aspect of their technique, beautifully designed and with reproductions of such quality that Mal said they were as good as a dusty painting. She only looked at a couple, quickly, then closed it.

"It's wonderful!" she exclaimed. "But I don't want to look at it now. I want to save it for tomorrow morning when I can see it in the light and give myself to it completely. A book like this shouldn't be just skimmed over."

"Look at it now! We'll look at it together."

"No, we'll look at it tomorrow. Not now. Oh, July, I'm afraid you've spent too much. We can't afford it."

"No I didn't!" shouted July, obviously very proud of himself. "Look at it closely—the corner and the bindings. It's used!"

"It isn't." But looking at it more closely, she could see the tiny traces of age, the slight discoloration of the edges of the paper where fingers had been turning, and the ease with which it opened—signs of previous ownership by someone who'd had great regard for it and knew how to take care of a valuable book. This seemed to enhance its value for Mal, first because she didn't need to feel guilty in having something reserved for only the well-to-do, and secondly because it was already experienced, which made the plates more like real paintings.

"Now come," she insisted, and led him through the kitchen and into the summer kitchen (or back porch, depending on whether she or July was addressing it). "In there." And she pointed to a large cardboard box.

July opened the top and jumped back, surprised by an unexpected activity down inside it. Then going toward it again and looking down, he stooped and lifted a white-and-brown puppy, larger than Butch, out of the box. The dog squirmed and barked once. July set it on the floor and it scampered around in a circle and attacked a pile of paint rags in the corner, growling and shaking its furry head. July immediately sank down to the wooden floor and began talking and playing with it, almost as though Mal weren't there at all.

"Her one leg is shorter," she said. "The man at the pound said nobody was likely to take a dog with a deformity and she'd probably have to be put to sleep. But he said she'd be a big dog."

July didn't seem to be listening. "Hey there," he said to the puppy. "Keep away from those rags. They have turpentine on them. Here, look at this, look at this. Whoa, what a bite. Look out there."

Mal stood back in the warmth of the kitchen, reviewing for herself the decision she'd made before getting the pup. She was well aware of July's devotional love of animals, so much so that in Philadelphia and sometimes here in Iowa she had felt herself hating the relationship he had with his cat because she was so completely shut out of it, and sometimes when she returned from work her jealousy would rise up because of the knowledge that for the whole day Butch had shared July's company and in the course of fixing up the house little dramas had been played out that she was doomed forever to have no knowledge of. So her decision to get the dog had been made understanding that she'd be in some way tested. There was never a chance that the short leg would make any difference. She might have brought a blind rat home (or up from the basement, for that matter, as July'd trap them but wouldn't put poison down, and very soon they were too smart to be trapped). And now she checked herself to see how her decision was working out—if she was going to be able to feel safe enough with this relationship which had been of her own creating.

At first it seemed as if she'd failed and the threshold of her jealousy was being tried. But it was tried with the wrong key and held fast. She watched him pick up the dog, put it on his lap and hold its shortened foot—"Getting a little hungry no doubt"—and she could see that she'd made the right choice. She had the safety of the onlooker. She knew he would be safe from her jealousy, and she could also hear herself in the tone of his voice as he talked. Usually the beloved, now she held the power of the lover. And more than that. In several minutes, when he did look up at her, he knew right away what'd been dared by the gift, stood up and rushed over to her.

"I love you," he said.

"I know," she answered, and realized only then that the art book had been the same kind of decision for him and she hadn't known it, and felt a great admiration and love for his understanding.

Her next present—the small one—enclosed a little card on which he'd written *To Mal from the selfish fool* and contained the old photographs from inside the fat Bible.

Such a symbolic gift was hard to respond to properly, as are all symbolic things, which seem to demand a particular kind of emotional response for which no physical expression is possible. To embrace him would deny the seriousness of the feeling, and to embrace him "seriously" or to try to explain that she understood the importance of it would be both melodramatic and pedestrian. Also, everything she might want to express was already assumed in the very act of giving the gift. It was unnecessary. But still a response seemed to be demanded and she was left hoping only that he would *know* exactly what she was feeling.

Despite the importance of the situation, she felt her skin beneath her pajamas flush in expectation of being touched.

The last was the large, weightless package for July, and with the help of the puppy July tore into it, only to find it empty but for a small piece of paper on which she'd written in crayon with large, clumsy letters, making it look as though a second-grader had made it at school, *Will you marry me?*

Whatever might have been Mal's confusion over the proper response to the pictures was magnified and confounded a thousand times now for July. He'd wished for nothing more ever since the museum in Philadelphia, but had resigned himself to living with the possibility of her eventual departure; and because they'd grown closer, that possibility had become small, and he'd found it easier to live with and almost never thought about it at all. But now he realized how real those old desires still were, and the sensation of seeing them come true—to possess her forever and never fear living even a single day without her—was something he would've traded a lifetime for, if that choice could have been clearly stated so that he understood it.

Surprisingly, he was also a little afraid, and curled back from such a total bond, as it seemed to imply more than he could fully grasp. Maybe I'm not ready for this, he thought. Really. It was always a kind of fantasy before. But as he looked up at her, he knew that the same fear was in her eyes, perhaps more so, and that in reality it was only the containing, protective shell of an experience so much more vital than either of them had any comprehension of that to attempt to explain it was foolish.

"Soon?" he asked.

"As soon as you want."

These few spoken words seemed to clear the air of all the inhibitions of seriousness that had thrived in the silence. All July could think was of Mal's body. Mal filled with the frantic realization that her skin was about to be ravaged, and felt him coming toward her before he ever moved.

Mal wrote to her parents explaining that they had decided to be married, implored them to forgive her for all she might have done which they believed compromised them (and her) and, if they couldn't come out to the wedding, at least to participate in her happiness. A week passed, during which time her job expired, and each day she was sure a letter from them would be delivered. Another week went by. Then came a short, cryptic note from her father, typed on his office typewriter on college stationery, explaining his moral outrage and belief that everything she'd done in the last ten months was misguided, strongly urging her to abandon her infatuation and return to the East, ending with a firm though grandiose pledge to pay for any emergencies which might come up involving her health. Two days later a letter came from her mother in which she wished her happiness, as though a kind of degenerate, pale happiness was all that would be possible for her now—well-being, comfort, respectability, self-esteem and spiritual harmony being forever out of her reach.

When July saw the letters he became very upset. He knew how much Mal had hoped for a reconciliation.

"I'm sorry."

"Well, so am I," she said with a brave smile and stuffed the letter into the crowded living-room wastebasket. "But I guess it's just tradition—the girl leaves her family for the family of her husband. It can't be helped."

Their marriage ceremony was short and uncomplicated. Two people were asked in off the streets of Iowa City to be witnesses. In the brief private talk before the words were read, the pastor's only concern was that Mal and July hadn't been married before and that they shouldn't ever be married again, because in his mind that was the most damnable of all sins. Then the little ritual was acted out, their vows were spoken aloud and rings exchanged, and *at this moment you are man and wife* tied them together legally, morally and with the full blessing of society. Mr. and Mrs. July Montgomery shook hands with their witnesses and departed in their green Chrysler, now half belonging to Mal, through the snow back to the country.

Through one of the girls she met at "Things and Things," Mal found another job, this one as a waitress in a restaurant. It was mostly evening work and, though basically very unpleasant, left the morning and early afternoon free for painting, which is the only time in the middle of winter.

The thrill of knowing throughout the whole day that he was married made the rest of February fly by with unbelievable ease. Even when the water pipes froze, and the wind ripped all the storm windows from the north side of the house and dashed them to the ground, and the cars wouldn't start, he still kept on the right side of things. But by the middle of March he knew he'd have to give up on the house for a while, let the upstairs go without paint and the front porch last as it somehow had for many years, and find a job.

Cabin fever, he told himself. Not good to stay in the house so much.

The usual terrors of job hunting were considerably lessened by being able to identify himself as a married man and circle that place in the questionnaires. It seemed he was now entitled to all the respect due a real citizen. He felt he'd joined the status quo. The American tradition was for once behind him and he was encouraged not to go *begging* for a job, but merely search one out as had all the great majority before him. And with this added sense of personal courage he ventured forth and a week later began working as a taxi-cab driver in Iowa City.

He bought another old car.

By dint of their different work schedules there remained no more than two or three days a week when they had any real time to be together, and these would drift by so quickly in comparison to the other days that it seemed more as if they *never* had any time together. The winter continued to wear away at them and one night when July'd fallen asleep waiting for Mal to come home on a Friday night he woke up and had a terrifying moment in which he completely lost touch with what he was doing. Now, what was I trying to accomplish? he asked himself. Exactly why did I come out here? What *precisely* is the reason for living here as opposed to any other place? He reached for answers which had been so close to him before and which his every movement and thought had seemed to embody—but found only the gloomy, cold, hostile walls of their bedroom. Outside, the snow lay at cat's-eye level twenty degrees below zero.

The kitchen clock said it was after one, and the house itself knew it was late. Turning on a light in an empty room seemed to be an intrusion. The radio had a faraway, demonic sound as though coming from the deep recesses of a cave, heavy and thick, with dark, meaningless voices. The silences were alive: the dog, Holmes, was sleeping somewhere in the barn, and July decided to walk out and find her. It was a pretense to listen for Mal turning off the highway onto the gravel two miles away, but on a still winter night with the roads cleared it was as unmistakable as something could be. He dressed warmly.

Leaving the light on in the living room and carrying a weak flashlight, he went out. Around his eyes he could feel the searing cold. The path to the barn was easy enough to see by the starlight. He stopped and listened. The refrigerator turned off in the house. He strained to hear better. She's been late before, he told himself. They have a lot of business on Friday night. People stay till all hours. The place simply gets jammed. Then stick around afterward and clean up. A wonder she gets home as quickly as she usually does . . . usually before midnight . . . an hour and a half late so far.

He heard a distant, jumbled sound and his senses quickened. It might be an echo of the tires' noise, still on the highway. Then he heard it again, and again, but no closer. Only wind in the trees, he thought. When you really hear her turn the corner, there won't be any doubt, you'll know it can't be anything else. Only the *false* sounds make vague promises.

He felt as though he had been standing there a long time. His face was beginning to numb. He was also letting his anxiety get out of control and had begun playing the subconscious game of *If I can hear her, then in three minutes she'll be home,* putting aside all attempts to rationalize how she might have come to be so late. He conferred with his better reasoning.

Now look, if something's happened, *somehow* they'd've gotten in touch. Because I don't have a phone doesn't warrant *this* kind of worry. And be it as it may, until she drives in the driveway she won't be here, listening or no listening. So go find Holmes.

He flipped on the flashlight and went into the barn. The faint ball of orange light hardly illuminated the loose hay covering the floor, and it was distinguishable only by shade from the rough wooden walls. He walked ahead very slowly, feeling along the wall for the opening. Holmes usually slept back against a manger, underneath the ladder to the mow. July turned and went down the aisle between the stanchions, hearing his muted footsteps and breaking the peaceful spell of the barn. A mouse rustled out of his way. He shined the light ahead, stretching it out as far as it would reach, playing it along the sides of the mangers, not allowing himself to speak until he caught the glint of Holmes' eyes.

"Hi, Holmes," he whispered, as though the big barn were a cathedral and the darkness were the cloud. The dog came toward him. "No, don't get up. I just thought I'd come out and see what you were doing."

He sat down in the hay and took the dog's head in his lap, turning off the flashlight. "So how's it going, old Holmes?" and he felt along her back, sinking his fingers deeply into it. The dog's spirit seemed to leap out to him. "Don't worry, Holmes, there's no sense for you being upset. It's probably not even two o'clock yet. It's a half-hour, maybe forty-five-minute drive from here. Having a coke or sandwich before she left would make it about 12:45; then figuring on cleaning up after a busy night, washing the tables off, sweeping the floor, especially if one of the girls was sick, makes it after midnight when the last customers left. Why, I've left plenty of restaurants myself at midnight. So there's nothing for you to be worried about. Just go back to sleep." He put her head back down in the hay and carefully stood up. "Go back to sleep," he urged again and began making his way outside where he could hear better. It was becoming harder and harder to keep his imagination from running over what it might be like to get into his car and drive into town looking for her, see some flashing red lights ahead, see the tangled fender of a brown station wagon, then the—

He reached the door. Every fiber of his being was wired to his eardrums, ready to devour the first little tremble. It was of comfort to be listening again, involved in some way in the activity of her coming, as though listening would bring her closer. He stood with the barn to his back, thinking that because of its huge size it would reflect any noise that might escape him directly from the source.

Then he heard something, so faint that he couldn't be sure it wasn't his own desire. The sound disappeared too quickly to be tested. No, that was her, he thought—still on the highway, just before the hill. Then a faint wind came through the oaks in back, the brown, clinging leaves rattling against each other like giant, flat insects. Damn that wind, thought July, and despite it he tried to pick out Mal turning the corner, knowing the sound would last only a little longer than five seconds before the first hill tucked it away and she'd be hidden from his hearing until she reached the top, where he'd get another chance to hear her before she reached the next hill, and at this one—if he was standing out front in the road—he could see the headlights! He ran through the snow, making a fresh trail in the crusted surface. Holmes followed behind him. The sound of their running made the second chance to hear her null and void. They got into the tire tracks and reached the gravel.

He looked off into the distance and watched with wild, flashing eyes for the halo of approaching car lights to climb the crest of the faraway hill. First that, then as the halo grew brighter and bigger, at the same time the sound would come reaching toward him, the two lights would pop into view, suspended like handheld beacons in the darkness, and come bobbing and roaring toward him. What time must it be? he thought. It's too clear for the light to reflect off the atmosphere. I won't see it until just that moment. His eyes were trying to leave his body. The dog sat silently beside him, her breathing not even stirring the air, locked in animal concentration.

All of a sudden he believed he could see the line between the dark surface of the road and the sky, at just the top edge of the distant hill, a little clearer. It seemed at that point he could tell just exactly where one left off and the other began, more so than anywhere else on the horizon. He looked a little to the side, sharpening his vision, his heart collapsed upon itself. Then it became unmistakable—a thin white halo crowned the top of the hill, growing in a slow, nearly transparent explosion. Then the headlights popped above the horizon, accompanied by the caressing, hard sound of the tires on the gravel, and the line between earth and sky was obliterated; all that now existed was total darkness and the two parallel white lights.

July shivered. Joy mixed with relief. He berated himself for worrying and forgave himself immediately. It seemed the life-and-death game had been played, with his destiny coming up all sixes. He felt as though he were not only spared but blessed. I'll never worry again, he told himself. As the sound came closer he recognized the exhaust system of the Chrysler, removing that last tiny doubt that with everything else it might be another car. He was truly saved. Holmes was running excitedly back and forth on her three legs, knowing the sound as well.

Then he filled with a different emotion, quickly and with no warning. This one almost like fear. Holmes sensed it and looked at him curiously. He was ashamed. He didn't want her to know what he'd gone through. It seemed it would be unfair for her to know—after all, there was nothing to worry about really. It wasn't proof of his caring for her so much as a betrayal of his weaknesses, a burden she didn't need. He turned and dashed toward the house. Holmes followed, picking up *in sense* July's desire to be hidden, and was let into the house.

Mal came in, finding him in the rocking chair reading. "Phew, what a night!"

"You're pretty late," said July calmly. "I was beginning to get worried."

"That's silly. But look at this!" She sat on the sofa and one at a time took dollar bills out of her purse—tip money. July counted them off: ". . . three, four, five, six! . . . Fifteen! That's really good!"

"Phew." Mal took off her shoes and stretched out. July looked at her and thought wordlessly, *If you ever could know how much I love you, you'd be frightened.*

The never ending winter was a trial for both of them. Their house seemed not able to withstand it, and in the middle of the living room they could feel cold, moving air on their faces. The water pipes froze again and again, cracking and bursting the lines. Mal was in a painting slump. It was too cold in her studio upstairs, and even if she could take it bundled up in a heavy coat, the paints didn't act properly. A few days of melting weather turned the barnyard into a mud hole and twice July had to walk down to the neighbor's to get him to come with his tractor and pull their car out. So they learned to park on the road. (July hated this. A person's car should be next to his house.) In April they were able to get their diamond back and that helped to revive their sense of accomplishment and purpose. They made a couple of friends they could, on occasion, go visit. July rediscovered his love of reading novels by the Russians Dostoevski and Tolstoy. They were true winter-breakers. He was even able to persuade Mal to read *The Brothers,* and for many nights they worried over Alyosha's character. July feared he might loose Mal to Dimitri and reminded her of their contract.

"You're the only one I'll ever love," said Mal. "But wouldn't it be something to run into somebody like that!"

"It's just the criminal element you crave."

"No! And he isn't a criminal. He's possessed with life!"

"He's possessed by his emotions."

"Life without emotions is nothing."

"He's simply mad."

The miserable weather improved. Melting from underneath, the levels of snow ran into the swirling and thick streams. Water oozed from everywhere. Scorpio began his climb in the south, splashing his tail down below the horizon. Mayapples and jack-in-the-pulpits began to come up through the snow with single-minded, wonderful lust for the warm air. The red-scaled buds of the maple tree beside the fence puffed up with a sense of awareness and caution. The grass reclaimed its rightful pigment and the bleak ground erupted in tempting, wild smells. Driving to work, July couldn't go slow enough. He seemed always to be missing something. Every day brought too many changes to keep up with, and he wondered if it was better to linger over several instead of trying to catch them all—the question of questions.

Mal found painting on the open porch inspiring. She had never painted outside much and it was as enjoyable as drawing had been to her when she was little. Surround yourself with real color, she decided, then paint.

The first meadowlark to sit on the wire by the barn and announce the beginning of spring brought back the answers to July. What was he doing here? He was living here. Why here? Because this was where he was born. This was where his father was born. This was where his grandparents Della and Wilson had elected to stay. Why? Because there was something about it—the land and the weather and the *feel* of it—that had made them happy and at ease. He felt the same way. Why had he brought Mal? Because if she could love him, then she could love it too.

Their house felt much better now that the space heater wasn't running continuously, and the lights weren't always on, and the hot-water heater didn't have to work so hard, and there was no more snow to be heavy on the roof, and the rats had left for the fields, and the smudgy storm windows were gone; fresh air in the living room, singing birds perching along the eaves, goldfinches waiting for the dandelions to come up, robins grabbing grubs, and the pleasant sound of the back screen door as it banged.

Before, it had seemed to Mal that the house tried to eject them, having been alone so long that it had become distrustful of people; but now it opened up to them, outstretched enfolding arms and was eager to be preened and fussed over and made "homey."

Planting a garden was like something from outer space. The seeds were so small, so perfectly inert-looking (with the exception of beans) and the idea that one could follow the little instruction booklet that she'd found in a newspaper—planting this one so far down, so many inches apart, this other one another way, cover them all up and of their own accord they'd start growing into huge plants bearing fruits you could eat—seemed almost too much to believe, like the most exciting, well-thought-out sales pitch that could possibly be imagined. On top of that, the seeds—if they did one one-hundredth of what was claimed—were cheap. And for what reason? Because of warmth, water and length of days. Ridiculous.

"Of course it'll work," said July. "How do you think farmers grow—"

"I know that!" she exclaimed, a little hurt that he'd not been able to see what she meant. "Just it's so hard to believe it will work. Of course it *will* work. But the idea seems so impossible—I mean, why should it?"

"Evolution."

"Oh, you're hopeless. Now keep making the trench with your hoe."

"We've got enough beans."

"You can never have enough beans, or pumpkins."

"That guy should've done a better job plowing this. There's weeds here."

"Well then, you'll just have to hoe them out."

"Get away from there, Holmes."

Butch, like the house, had taken a while to adjust. Right away he'd decided he didn't like Holmes, and kept being amazed that day after day she stayed around, annoying as she was. When the inevitable realization came that, for all her unpleasant and rough mannerisms, Holmes was here forever, Butch decided the best thing to do was completely ignore it.

Each month seemed to double the size of the brute; but as she grew, her mannerisms became more predictable and mellow, and though she was clearly of a threatening size with teeth a whole inch long, Butch had less and less cause to be afraid of her. In fact, he began to enjoy her company—especially when they'd lie together on the porch, he on the little railing and Holmes at the top of the step. And every noisy car that went by, every unsettling sound brought her up on her big feet, bristling with her instinctual protectiveness, which made Butch feel very safe, and he spent many afternoons sitting in the warm sun smiling and feeling like an old king. Then sometimes they'd walk about the barnyard together, looking things over and messing about in the hay.

Mal needed little urging to quit her job. The first time July mentioned that they might take a month or two off and enjoy the spring and early summer, she agreed wholeheartedly. The restaurant was more upset to learn of Mal leaving than was the cab company, which let July go the very second he voiced his desire. Mal finished out the week at The Ranch and said she would probably be back looking for work at the beginning of fall—maybe even before. (She wasn't as optimistic as July about how cheaply they could live in the summer.)

The days drew out longer. Little speckles of lettuce popped up through the ground. Their secondhand lawnmower chopped through the weeds in the yard, and grass *did* seem to take hold, even though the rough stalks of the burdock, chicory and buttonweeds never seemed to give up. On the first good sunny day (the ground wet and soft from rain the night before) they dressed in their bathing suits and began digging and pulling them out. A thankless job it seemed, but a little color came into their skin and they had to admit when they were through that they felt better about the yard. July hung a swing from the maple tree and they painted the fence and mowed around the barn. Day lilies grew in the ditch in front. They built a large window box just off the porch and planted cosmos. Mal finished a painting that seemed to be a turning point.

"I don't understand," said July.

"What I mean is that now I can *sense* better what composition means. It's interest. Composition means interest. Of course converging lines should be avoided, along with things cut in half, but that's because they're uninteresting. I guess what I'm trying to say is that there *is* no way, right or wrong. All painting is an attempt—no, that's wrong—is made up of individual attempts to create interest."

"But some kinds of interest are better than others."

"Naturally." On Mal's easel was a red dog sitting in a green yard with yellow dandelions bigger than life size and an unpainted fence and a broken window with blue inside. It reminded July of her crab painting, but he didn't say so. He liked it quite a lot and urged her to put it up in the living room. "It's not finished," she said happily and began adding more colors to the grass.

July went for a walk down behind the barn into the oaks. Squirrels chattered at him from their leaf nests. He saw a bird in a mulberry tree stretching its wings and fanning out its tail, displaying its brilliant orange and white feathers, like a great butterfly. Not knowing, however, what kind of bird it was, he resolved to get a bird book and learn them all. There's no excuse for ignorance, he thought—ignorance of natural things. And because there're so many things to learn is all the more reason. His negative self tried to argue that just having fun was more important than learning, but he amazed himself with how easily he could push that begging objection aside. He was getting stronger, he felt. It was easier to decide on doing things—easier to deny the opiate of inactivity. His restful moments lately had been filled with laying the foundations for more projects.

But just as he was settling down with his back to a large rock with moss and lichen growing on it, with a feeling of pleasant self-contentedness, he remembered that he felt left out: Mal had her painting and there was no denying how absorbing and forward-moving it was. It was work, learning and enjoyment all at once. And what did he have? He could no more paint than fly to the moon.

Perhaps I could learn to play a musical instrument, he thought. But the idea of making squawking noises off by himself in some room was very disheartening. I'd never be any good, he complained. Sure, I like music well enough, but people who're good at something—who have it in them—don't start out when they're twenty-two; by then they're well on their way.

Wait a minute, he thought. The world wasn't created only for artists. Others belong in it just as rightfully, and there was nothing that stood in his way any more than in anyone else's which kept him from extracting its full pleasures. There *was* an obstacle but wasn't it the same for everyone? Inactivity, stagnation and the unwillingness to delve into experiences for understanding. He resolved to get a book about trees as well, decided to build a lean-to so that they could sleep outside overnight and set about gathering poles to make it with and finding stones to lay in a circle for a fireplace—not rocks from the creek because those might explode.

Later that afternoon Mal came down the hill looking for him and he had an opportunity to watch her unobserved as she walked along, concealed behind a small thicket of hawthorn. Her expression and movements were much less animated, as he imagined his were when he was alone. She stopped and looked at something on the ground and examined it seriously, then stood up and looked around for him. He called out, and together they finished piling the brush onto the lean-to and sat inside when it was finished.

They went back to the house to eat dinner and get matches, returned, had a fire and listened to the whippoorwills and night insects. The yellow flames subsided, leaving only the redness of the glowing coals. The sky grew brighter. The wildness of their little woods seemed to surround them. They lay together without speaking, but July could sense Mal was ready to talk; something was bothering her—not to the degree of worry, but enough to keep her from the silent participation he was enjoying. He sat up and put on some more wood, giving her the opportunity to break the silence.

"I was wondering," she began. "I don't know if I can find just the right words to say what I mean, but is this all there is?"

"Is what?"

"Our lives. I mean is this all there is to it, just working and keeping the house fixed up and having pets and sometimes enjoying things and sometimes not for this reason or another—is that all?"

"Wow. Really, I don't understand what you mean—or maybe I'm afraid to. Whenever I try to think about what you're saying, it seems like something terrible."

"I knew you'd think that. It's not that way. All I mean is that I feel sometimes that there should be *more*—something that we would always be working towards. What we're doing now, is that what everybody else does, and is it the same thing for them, so on blah blah? Doesn't it seem that somehow there *must* be more? Because this can't be *really* living. *Really* living must be something else entirely. But maybe there isn't such a thing as that—oh, I hope you're understanding all this in the right way. Maybe there isn't such a thing as *really living* at all, only *just being alive.*"

"Maybe," said July sorrowfully, looking down into the fire.

"Oh no, silly. This isn't anything against you or against the way we live. Can't you understand that? It's not really *against* anything. Here, let me ask you this: do you think we're *normal* people?"

"Sure."

"What do you mean, sure?"

"Sure—of course we are—if the other choice is abnormal. We're physically and mentally all here, therefore normal."

"Is that all normal means to you?"

"What else can it mean?" There was a defensive tone to his voice, but at least, thought Mal, he's arguing.

"I've always thought we were sort of special."

"In what way?"

"Very individual and one of a kind. Worthy of admiration just for what we are."

"That's just the way you think of yourself."

"No, both of us. We're together. But what I was trying to say is that I used to think we were special, and now I see us sometimes as being ordinary—just another couple living in the country, getting by—"

"Do you mean we should have financial careers, or see more of the world and have more friends, or have children, or what?"

"None of those things—they'd just be more of the same."

"Somehow I can't help thinking that what you're saying is very snobbish."

"But it's not!"

"You'd probably like to live around more painters."

"You're the one who feels snobby about painting, not me. I just like to do it. You think it's so important."

"I *was* thinking about it today," admitted July, "and wondered for a while if I shouldn't learn how to play a banjo—so I could have something. But I decided to learn more and do more instead. I'm going to get some books on birds and trees."

"You always think so constructively," laughed Mal. "I guess that's my trouble. I always tend to blame things outside myself instead of finding something to do about bad feelings. . . . Why *not* learn how to play the banjo?"

"Because it isn't something that interests me. I only thought it up to have something *artful* to do."

"That's nonsense."

"I know."

"It's just sometimes I get afraid that I'll become bored with everything, and that nothing will be able to satisfy me. You must feel like that at times."

"I did some in the winter. But not now."

"I was thinking that earlier tonight." She put her arms around him. "But I don't now. You don't pay enough attention to me, I guess."

Then she added, "If we weren't together, what do you think would be different about you?"

"I'd be miserable and stupid."

"No, I mean *objectively.*"

"I'd probably still have three cars, but I wouldn't take the time to mow the yard." Then their clothes came off and the evening fell away to libertine delights and sensations well beyond any regard for efficiency, a shameless display of even their most hidden, wanton desires.

ELEVEN

July's idea was that he'd work as a farmhand for their neighbors, baling hay, cultivating and such. He had a keen interest in knowing exactly how each phase of the farming operation was carried out, as well as a belief in the possibility that the way the men lived their lives might offer him an insight into a better way to live his own. So while he was driving their tractors he'd also be stealing glimpses into their souls.

Mal accused him of a kind of elitism. "You imagine yourself mingling with the common people, or thinking of them as being very quaint."

"I don't."

"Then how can you take that kind of interest in them? Why should you care at all for seeing into their homes?"

"I'm interested. I want to know what they're like."

"Why do you think they're not just like everybody else? What could possibly be different with them?"

"They're more isolated—and a lot of them always have been."

"That's it. You think of them like children. You suppose them to be nobly simple."

"Nothing of the sort. I'm just interested. I wonder if I could get a job with some of the Amish."

"See!"

"See what? You must admit they've probably got the right idea. If we just would live like that, we'd be better off."

"But they can't be said to be 'in society.' They've merely retreated from it."

"There's no way you can escape being in society, unless, I suppose, you lived by yourself in a submarine. Look, no automobiles, no electricity, no television, no movies, no smoking, no drinking or taking drugs, plain-dress code and a community to live in. Reduce the number of anxiety-producing elements and you reduce the anxiety level."

"They live with plenty of anxiety, you can bet on that. That much isolation breeds anxiety."

"You can't say that. You don't have any way of knowing."

"They can only live the way they do because there's the rest of the world to take care of what they don't do."

"Which just proves they're in society."

"Well, if everybody lived like them—they just couldn't. For one, there's not enough land. There'd be no jobs."

"Now you're asking them to live in a way nobody can be asked—to live in a way where if everyone else were just like them the world would be better. Certainly we're no models ourselves."

"We make no pretensions."

"Who said they do?"

"Well, they just seem to imply it, by being so . . . different, and pious."

"That's just because their living code is a little stricter than ours."

"A little! Besides, you couldn't ever give up listening to music, or reading—reading, how would you like to be told what you could read and what you couldn't?"

"Who said they do that?"

"I'll bet they do."

"I didn't say I believed in all their personal religious beliefs—only that their basic way of life was good."

"Way of life, can't be separated from the beliefs that give rise to it."

"Now you're just arguing to be arguing, Mal."

"I guess you're right. But I do want to go to the movies tonight."

"All right. But I think we should fix up a wood-burning heater to burn some of these dead elms . . . to save on the fuel bill."

July's first job was with a baling crew, consisting of fourteen or fifteen boys mostly his own age or younger and two older overseers. They accepted him immediately but with great reserve, and only murmured pleasantries like probing fingers whenever he was around. There was never an introduction of any kind, and he had merely been told by the boss on his first day, "You work with them," indicating five of the boys who were getting into a one-ton truck. And although it seemed everyone knew his name already and where he lived and that he was married, it was left up to him to listen for their names as they spoke together, because, as he guessed, it was assumed that he knew theirs.

Right away there was a keen sense of challenge. Several of the boys were clearly bigger and tossed bulky bales about with an obvious disregard for their weight, and though no hostility was ever shown and it was obvious that allowances were to be made for his lack of experience, still he felt that even the man on the tractor was anxious to see how he would work out and if he was just a weakling.

"Here, use these," said one of the boys beside him on the wagon, and handed him a pair of thin leather gloves. July looked quickly around, suspecting a special advantage had been turned his way, and noticed that the rest were wearing gloves and that his own hands were cut mercilessly from the rope and the clover ends. He soon discovered it wasn't the weight of the bales so much as their bulky shape that made them hard to handle and exhausted him to such a degree. Three-fourths of his energy was working against itself. Also, he discovered arms could do very little work as compared to legs and back. By the beginning of the afternoon he could manage the bales with the rest of them, but his very bones seemed to ache, and at lunchtime he wished desperately for a place to catch fifteen minutes' sleep. The other boys played baseball, and, finishing his sandwich, he got up and joined them.

The air was so thick with hazy moisture that afternoon that it was like sticking your head into a hot, sticky pond and trying to breathe. The direct sun was almost unbearable and the backs of his arms ached from exposure. Some of the boys worked with their shirts off and were as brown as nuts with hard, lean stomach muscles.

When the others came back from the barn with another empty wagon, they asked for someone else to come up in the mow. July could see that it must be a disagreeable job because no one volunteered, but he thought at least it would be out of the sun and went along with them.

It turned out to be worse than anything he could ever have imagined. If it was a hundred degrees in the sun, it was an extra twenty or thirty in the barn, where there was no circulation of air whatsoever and the dark roof had had all morning to fry it. As for the humidity, there was simply no comparison. Out in the field was like a cool desert. Two other boys stood with him and waited, talking gloomily; one explained to the other the bad luck he'd been having with girls for the last three years. When July saw what was going to happen, his heart nearly folded up. Lifted by a pulley system pulled by a tractor, suspended from four large hooks, a bundle of eight bales came up, filling the upper door; it caught on the runners and moved into the loft, coming toward them, maybe twelve feet overhead. It came closer until it was almost directly above, then one of the boys beside him called, *"Now,"* and someone outside pulled the trip rope, releasing the hooks and letting the bales fall. A tremendous cloud of hay dust filled the entire barn, sticking to the sweat on their arms and faces and, except for the hairs in their noses, would have layered their lungs. The two boys rushed forward into the densest part of this cloud, dragging the bales away from where they'd fallen and stacking them along the sides of the barn. July followed suit and managed to get two of them at the expense of nearly twisting his ankle in a hole between two loosely stacked bales, as they were of course walking on layers of already stacked hay. No sooner had he pulled the two bales over to where the other boys had stacked theirs than one of them yelled, *"Now,"* and almost from nowhere there appeared eight more, which fell into the same places, and they rushed forward again to clear them away before the next bundle.

"It gets better," said one of them to July, his face almost completely black with gobs of the tiny pieces of leaf hanging from his nostrils, "when we get the level up so the bales don't have to fall so far." July looked. The mow was maybe fifty feet wide, and a third again that long. To go up only three and a half feet would take two layers of bales, 24,500 cubic feet of hay. They had just enough time, working as fast and hard as they could, nearly choking on the dust, to clear away the eight bales before another load fell down. July had made up his mind that each time he would carry three bales back, but there were many times when Jack and Bonesy would get the extra ones and he was thankful for that when it happened.

After an unimaginably long time there came a shout from outside, telling them that the wagon was empty. It meant a ten-minute break while waiting for the next, and they scrambled down the ladder and outside. In the pump house they washed with the hose and drank long, deep mouthfuls, running the water through their hair and over the backs of their necks. Then they sat in the shade of the pump-house wall and July felt as though he'd never known real relief before. He also felt a great sense of comradeship with his two fellow workers and imagined they felt the same—which wasn't actually true, he noticed later; when they talked together, it was different from when they talked with him. Furthermore, it was just another day for them.

July found that reflection upon any subject was impossible with such fatigue; that in itself was a novelty, and he indulged in having no thoughts and seeing the world through the eyes of an ox. That night he was almost too tired to eat and fell asleep in the rocking chair at eight o'clock. Getting up in the morning was unbearable, even at nine, but he managed it. The hay was still too wet from the dew to bale in the early morning.

Three days later the work was as easy as that kind of work could ever be, and even working up in the barn with black dust hanging from his nose, he could think convoluted thoughts and daydream as regularly as when he was sitting on the back porch. He fitted into the schedule of staying up late and getting up just before rushing out of the house.

They finished at the one farm and moved on to another. The crew felt more comfortable with him, and included him in the crudely intimate discussions of women, money, gadgetry, ambition and sports. Mal once asked him, "What do you talk about while you work? Give me an example of one of your conversations."

"What time of day? It depends a lot on what time it is."

"Why?"

"Well, first thing in the morning nobody says much of anything, and even despite Jack and Bonesy, who're especially noisy then, there's a general sluggishness and irritability—usually centered around the weather or the particular difficulties of the day ahead—the heat, working for such and such who might be hard to get along with, and for the most part composed of short, biting comments. Everybody's as a rule thinking about sleeping. But nobody talks of it because that makes the day get longer.

"Then later on, when the noise of the machinery and tossing a few bales around has had a chance to jar you into being awake, nearing eleven, they all seem to want to talk out what happened the night before, and even the less memorable events get told—some at length, some only scantily, depending on who's talking and their own bent for that kind of thing. A lot of interest seems to be focused on sex at this time, but it never gets really bawdy until the afternoon.

"By lunchtime the talk is more about our cars and movies, famous basketball players or what a person might do if he had a lot of money. Lunchtime itself is pretty solemn—at least the first quarter of the hour; then it loosens up and everyone's truly gregarious—even more so than just before quitting, which is friendly but a little selfish too, because all you can think about is getting home or wherever you're going.

"If there's ever any trouble or arguments it's always in the middle of the afternoon—say around three or four o'clock. Swearing and general hostility seems to be able to slip in naturally, 'fuckin' this,' and talk of perverts and minority groups, and 'that son of a bitch couldn't figure his way out of a grocery store.' It also tends toward a more vulgar view of the relationship between men and women, and gives way to that considerably. I guess it's usually the hottest and most miserable then, and it's difficult to get up the emotional energy to be charitable. It's during these times that I always think of all the other things I should be doing with my life and how I need to read more and get among a better class of people: that's my own way of participating in the mood.

"Then as we can feel the air get cooler, and see the boss is beginning to think about calling it a day and getting into some more comfortable shoes and sitting under his elm tree at home with a breeze blowing on his face, drinking ice tea made by leaving glass jars with tea bags and water in the sun—then a surge of vitality and good-heartedness begins to come. We start thinking about how close we are to being done if we can finish up a particular field, what entertainment the night holds, and a long-range excitement seems to take over: joy in being alive—pride in working—that sort of thing. Then it's all waving and shouting and roaring the engines of our cars when we leave. The drive home is an unbelievable merriment, usually speeding, and with no regard for any seriousness but the immediate sensation of well-being."

"But what do you talk about just before you leave? No, don't drop your head now, I'm almost finished."

July reorganized himself and Mal continued to sketch him against the porch railing.

"Well, for instance, Bonesy might say to me—supposing we were working behind the baler at the time, and about every fifteen or twenty seconds another bale comes issuing out of the gate, 'So, how do you like being married, July?' And I might answer, 'Oh, it's all right if you like that kind of thing.'

"'We all like that kind of thing,' he continues, 'It's the matter of the same kind of thing day in day out that some don't agree on.'

"I suppose.'

"I really thought Jack and MacLean was going to get into it yesterday, didn't you?'

"'No. Jack ain't one for fighting, I don't think.'

"'He looked pretty mad.'

"'That's a whole lot different thing. You ever been inside that tavern in Kalona?'

"'A couple times. It ain't much of a place. Closes at six o'clock. Too many old geezers in there. Why?'

"'Just wondered.'

"'Didn't you say you had a '32 Ford?'

"'I still have it. Everything in it's original.'

"'Did you do it yourself?'

"'No. My dad did it.'

"'Boy, I really like old cars.'

"'So do I.'

"'They're just so much better than the newer ones. There seems to be so much more sense to them—everything is so obvious as to what it's for. You should've seen this old Cadillac I had once. Man, driving that down the road really made you feel like something. Steel gray mine was, and I got some of those real wide white-walls and put them on, and a big old spotlight just outside the vent for bushwhacking.'

"Then we might talk a bit about going fishing somewhere or buying a motorcycle, drinking beer, the fact that marijuana grows wild but is illegal, what drug fiends must be like, or the loose morals of hippies living in overcrowded houses with mattresses on the floor, or the government. As it gets later, both of us might start feeling pretty good about each other and make plans to go swimming together at the reservoir, or go to a drive-in with you and his wife. But we sort of know even when we're talking that we won't."

"There, all finished," she said, and turned her pad so he could see his own likeness in it.

When the baling crew moved on toward Hills, July quit, spent a whole week around the house with Mal, sleeping outside nearly every night, and hired himself out to help cultivate, driving the fat-tired tractors down between the rows of corn and beans and digging up the weeds with curved, flat metal fingers.

This job was altogether different from haying, and being entirely alone for long, long stretches at a time reminded him of something out of his distant youth in Philadelphia, and before. The ability to be with oneself, he decided, was something that reached further back than anything else. Each person must have his own way, for better or worse, but the ease with which it can be tolerated can only depreciate from lack of practice, and never improve beyond what it was originally meant to be.

The thoughts that accompanied July's solitude were, he felt, almost like no thoughts at all—like being dumbly aware of awareness itself—consciousness at its lowest level. This was something of a revelation to him, as he'd always thought before of mere consciousness being more closely associated with entertainment than thinking, and seeing now that these two were somehow one and the same thing, working in and out of each other mysteriously and irrevocably, he felt he was just about to burst upon a new level of understanding. But when he talked about it with Mal that evening he couldn't make himself completely understood, and where he'd been able to see the distinctions so clearly before, now all his thoughts, in words, seemed meaningless and foolish. It was then he realized, though he didn't try to communicate it, that he had come to an even greater understanding than he'd at first thought: mere consciousness was the very act of putting things together in one's mind. Making sense of something was the act of sensing itself.

He worked at cultivating for several weeks and then helped Isaac Bontrager build fence. It looked as if in the summertime he wouldn't ever have to go out looking for work again, because he'd become known as a friendly, good worker and the farmers would stop over occasionally if they needed help, and if they didn't he stayed at home and read or went swimming with Mal, or sat on the back porch with Holmes and Butch, watching the rain and trying to experience the sort of things he imagined the Indians back in the seventeen hundreds might have when the oaks and prairies were an endless, inviting expanse of uninterrupted nature.

Mal went back to work at the restaurant in late August. The baling crew came through the Sharon Center area for the second cutting of hay and July got on it again.

They had a list of thirty-eight different birds they'd seen during the summer, and could identify most of the trees along the roads and down the hill behind their barn. Mal was getting together twelve paintings which she'd decided to take around to the shops in Iowa City and see if they would display them.

Wally, Leonard and his half-brother Billy Joe sat in the front of their Mercury sedan eating slices of peaches from a can Billy Joe, the mute, had stolen in a grocery store along the Coralville Strip. Wally, the driver, was twenty-six; Leonard was from a little town along the Mississippi and was wanted for burglary and assault in Cedar Rapids, and was twenty. Between them, Billy Joe, released one month ago from the state reformatory in Eldora, was almost seventeen, and had shared the same mother as Leonard. The parking lot in the Wardway Plaza was hot, but they had the windows rolled up to keep out the flies.

"God damn it, Billy Joe, don't spill none a that on the pictures!" said Leonard, and pulled the *Zap* comic book away from the peach syrup dripping from his hands.

"Slobbing bastard," said Wally. "Hold it over here closer," and he pulled the comic book closer to him. "And fuck, don't eat all of 'em, I only got two so far."

"Billy Joe got 'em," said Leonard carefully, not wanting to anger the older, bigger boy, but wanting to plead his half-brother's right to at least an equal share of the sweetened peaches. "An' you already read it once."

"God damn it, get your fuckin' finger out a there!" And Wally hit Billy Joe's arm, causing peach juice to spill onto his lap and the pictures and making him begin crying with sucking sounds.

"You di'n' need ta hit 'im!" shouted Leonard.

"Fuck if I di'n'. Son-of-a-bitch keeps puttin' his finger into the rip in the dashboard 'n' tears out all the packin'." He bent the torn corner back to hide the hole and tried to smooth it over.

"You di'n' need ta hit 'im."

"Do more'n that too if he don' cut it out. Slobby bastard. We should never've brought him along."

"He don't hurt none. Got the peaches, di'n' he?"

"Fuck peaches."

Billy Joe had stopped crying and tried to wipe the pages off with his pants.

"Careful," said Leonard, and took it from him. "Pages break easy if you got 'em wet."

"Shit. We got to get us some money." And Wally pounded the steering wheel. "We ain't got but a quarter-tank of gas."

"I thought you said we'd just make it down to your friend's place. Didn't he say we could stay there?"

"That's what I said, di'n' I? And that's what I meant. But we can't go down there flat broke. Hell, ain't you got no class at all? Don't you got no style? We got to give him somethin'. *Shit,* if I wasn't with you little punks, I'd do me somethin'."

"What?"

"I don't know. But I'd do me somethin'. There's always ways ta get a little coin together, or snatch, I might get me some snatch. There's plenty a cunt in this town for a guy who knows how to do it."

"What're we goin' a do, Wally? Son-of-a-bitch, there's a patrol car! He's comin' over here!"

"For Christ sakes, try to be cool. Jesus, what a couple of punks. Don' go lookin' like that or he'll know somethin's up, you dumb fuck. Just sit there. Can't no cop do nothin' to ya if you're just sittin' there." The police car drove by and Wally sneered at the men inside it from the corners of his eyes, his mouth curled at one edge, as though daring them not to stop. They went by.

"What're we goin' ta do, Wally?"

"First we got to get some more food—then we think. Send Billy Joe back in for somethin' else, an' no more fuckin' fruit. Get some ice cream."

"He went the last time."

"Well, he's got a do somethin'. We di'n' have to bring 'im."

"I'll go myself," said Leonard, and got out of the car. He pawed through the trash barrel in front of the grocery store, took out a discarded green bag from the drugstore and entered through the automatic doors. Billy Joe slid over and sat next to the window sharpening his knife.

"Here, let me see it," said Wally. "Hell, this ain't sharp at all. They ain't sharp unless you c'n lay 'em up against your thumbnail like this here . . . and without pressing on it, if it'll keep from slippin' off when you tilt it forward, then it's sharp. If it won't, then it ain't worth a shit for anything. This is cheap steel." He tossed it back. "I wouldn't never carry a blade so dull as that'n, not if I had me a knife. Automatics is more my style. Always has been." And he stared out of the window as though reviewing all the numerous wild things he had done in his life. Leonard came back with three ice-cream bars and a tin of sardines. They were eating them when Mal walked out the large automatic doors and past their car carrying a small bag of groceries and wearing her waitress uniform. She climbed into the old Chrysler and pulled slowly out of the parking lot.

Without saying anything, Wally started the Mercury and got onto Highway 1, heading out into the country behind her.

"Hey, where you goin'?" asked Leonard.

"Di'n' you see that waitress? Hell, they've always got a lot of money lyin' around. We'll just check it out where she lives. Most of 'em works at night. Probably get a hundred or maybe two."

"Waitresses don't have any money."

"Shit they don't. Hell, where you been anyway? You talk like you haven't been around. Sure they got bread. Most of 'em fuckin' whores 'n' shack up with their bosses. Jesus, don't you know nothin'? There ain't hardly a waitress that ain't a whore."

"She probably lives out here on some farm with 'er folks, I bet. Can't nobody break into a farmhouse. They got dogs, 'n'—"

"I just said we'd check it out. We got nothin' better right now. We already sat almost all afternoon in the parkin' lot."

"It wasn't such a bad place."

"Cops get suspicious after a while. Besides, who c'n tell, we might be on ta somethin'."

The green Chrysler made a lefthand turn onto a gravel road and they followed from a quarter-mile back.

"You think she fucks, Wally? Could you tell by lookin' at 'er?"

"I could tell. It's the way they walk, sort of loose like. She's a whore, you c'n bet."

"You're gettin' too close."

"Shut up."

"Put that away, Billy Joe. We'll hit a hole in the road and you'll rip open your finger."

Mal pulled the Chrysler into the driveway. They slowly stopped, opened the trunk, took out the jack and lifted the back bumper—Leonard's idea to look as though they had a flat while inspecting the house. The girl was inside. A three-legged dog began to bark at them from the corner of the yard.

"See?" said Leonard. "Come on, let's get out a here." But no sooner did he say this than the waitress stuck her head out of the front door of the house and hollered at the dog to stop. And when it kept on she came out, grabbed it by the fur around its neck and dragged it off toward the house, around the side and put it in the basement. Then she went back inside.

"There's other people livin' there," said Leonard. "Let's go back to the parkin' lot an' you'll think of somethin' else. We c'n get us a gas station tonight. This place gives me the creeps."

"There ain't no way we c'n know for sure. What we should do is go on up there to the door—hell, dumb bitch put the dog in the basement—'n' pretend we wanna use the phone 'cause we got a flat 'n' no spare. Then, see, we get a chance to look around, 'n' if there ain't nobody there but her, then we c'n wait until she gets off to work 'n' go in then."

"But she'll let the dog go again. He's big."

"Dogs c'n be handled with . . . 'n' maybe she'll leave it down in the basement anyway."

"No girl'd be livin' out here alone."

"I just said we'd check it out, you jackass."

There was an anxious silence while all three of them stared at the house.

"OK, let's go," said Leonard. "Billy Joe 'n' I will stay behind you."

At this point Wally seemed to freeze from the center of his eyes outward and he turned his head. Leonard and Billy Joe had already stepped forward and were waiting for him in the middle of the road. His pale hands shook and curled up unconsciously.

"You fools," he said, in a fast, whining voice. "You fools, we can't all go in. Only one or two got to go in. It wouldn't seem right all of us goin' in."

"Then you go," said Leonard.

"You dumb fuck, how smart do you think that would be? The cops drive by and you're in the car, so they get out and ask you some questions while they call in your description on the radio. Go ahead, try to answer as if I was a cop. 'Where're you goin'? What're you doin' here, kid? Let me see the registration for this car. Where's your license?' "

"There's no police goin' a come way out here."

"You want to take a chance? You want to? Now get going. Take Billy Joe with you if you want to."

"What'll we say, I mean for using the phone?"

"Just say you want to call to a station, dial some phony number and pretend to talk."

"Then what'll I say?"

"Then I don't know. Say something."

Wally got into the car, though the jack still held the back tire off the ground.

"Why don't you come up then and say you got it fixed? Then we c'n leave."

"Sure, sure. Go ahead." He gripped the steering wheel to calm his hands.

The two half-brothers went up to the house. Wally watched them knock on the door, then step inside. His stomach knotted up like an old tree. Breathing through his mouth, he stared up and down the gravel road and threw the wet comic book into the ditch. Three or four minutes later Leonard came out with something in his hand. He carried it through the yard and came to the car. It was a glass of ice tea.

"She give us some tea and says ta come inside to wait for her husband to come home. They ain't got no phone."

Together they went to the house.

TWELVE

July was just getting off work. He rode in the back of the truck with four others, bumping along toward where their cars were parked. Though not actively engaged in any conversation, he listened to Jack and Bonesy and the Bontrager kid talking. "They say you can eat 'em. Pull 'em in the fall. The Indians used burdock roots as a potato substitute."

"Couldn't've been a substitute, 'cause they never had potatoes. Potatoes come from Ireland."

"Don't be too sure of that."

"Well, I guess I'm not, but those Indians could make use of about anything. They made paint from bloodroot, I know."

July felt an uneasiness stir within him, but he couldn't identify it and tried to push it out of his mind.

"We used to rub that all over us when we was kids," Jack continued, "and pretend to chop off our fingers."

"Can't you find something better to talk about?" said July.

"Boy, but ain't you touchy today." Then they went on talking about race-car drivers. "I'd like to have one of those Ferraris. You know, if you buy one of those, take it out and it won't run two hundred miles an hour, you can take it back and they'll give you another one."

"Some of those guys can make nearly a million dollars a year driving in races across the country."

"They've got races all over the world."

"It'd be the glory I'd want rather than the money," said Bonesy.

Despite all his power over his emotions, July turned yellow with dread. All his rationality told him that today was like any other. There was no cause to be alarmed about anything. It was a long time ago that he'd played that foolish game. He was much older now.

But his key would hardly fit into the ignition because it shook so much, and he nearly collided with a milk truck because of fish-tailing around a loose corner. The Chrysler was in the driveway, but Holmes wasn't anywhere to be seen. Oh God, he thought. Something's happened to Holmes. He sat in the car trying to prepare himself for how he would respond when Mal told him, made a solemn promise to himself that if he'd imagined everything and the dog was all right, then he'd never worry again, ever, got slowly out of the car and went into the house.

Mal was on the sofa, one hand dangling down to the floor. She was dead. Her fingers had begun to stiffen. There was blood everywhere.

As he began to go into shock July imagined that he was having no reaction at all; he seemed to himself to be perfectly adequate, perfectly numb. At one time he noticed he was sitting down holding a piece of the waitress uniform that was ripped away from her collar and was saying out loud, "Nothing could be farther from the truth. No." He didn't know how long he'd been there or how much else he'd already said. Or what he was talking about. The sound of the voice was without any emphasis: dream language. Then it was as if his senses would black out at different times, reviving for an instant here and there and he would be completely aware of the sound of the clock—nothing but the regular sound of the clock. The little ceramic pot on the table was all that he saw for a long time. The hours in between were filled, so far as he could tell, with nothing. Later he could remember thinking, *I've got to . . . I've got to . . .* but he couldn't quite grasp what it was. Then he heard the dog bark in the basement, and though it took him nearly ten minutes to walk outside because of the porch swing grabbing his unpredictable attention with its little chains to the ceiling and holding it long after he wanted to get away, he went around to let her out into the yard. Together they wandered aimlessly beyond the fence and onto the gravel road. In the ditch he picked up a comic book. On the cover was stamped *Property of Riverview Courts.* He carried it down the middle of the road, then threw it away. He walked until it was almost dark and someone took hold of his arm and said they'd been honking at him and was he all right and he said, "Call the police," and kept walking, going off into a large hayfield, not having any idea where he was, who he'd spoken to or what he'd said.

The only presence he was at all aware of was his dog.

Long after dark he'd gotten back onto the road, and that's where the patrolmen found him and coaxed him into the car and back to the house.

"I know what's in there," he told them when they pulled into the driveway. "Don't think you'll be showing me anything. You think perhaps that I'm just coming home now for the first time. You think I was walking home from work and now this is the first time. But, see, I already know what's in there."

And he climbed out of the car.

As they came in the police photographers were still taking pictures, though Mal's body had been covered over. As the ambulance men began to pick her up July wondered if he might rush forward and push them away—telling them not to touch her. It seemed that he might and might not at the same time. He didn't, and acknowledged in not doing so the fact that since he'd first seen her lifeless form on the couch there had never been even a suspicion that its ugliness and vulgarity could represent his wife; and though at one time it had had a great deal to do with her and been very much involved with even his own feelings for her, it was still such a minor part that when the other, larger part had gone, there was no resemblance. He was glad to have it out of the house.

As they carried her past him, he noticed that he was answering questions put to him by a sympathetic yet persistent young lieutenant.

"Now, when was it you said you came home?"

"I don't remember. I got off work and came home. About six or six thirty, I guess."

"Only a few more questions if you don't mind. I'm sorry about having to do this all now, but it saves us from having to keep bothering you later. Say, do you have some family you want me to call and get over here?"

"No."

"Then why don't you come with me? We can talk on the way to town. I think we better get you to a doctor, or somewhere you can be looked after."

"No."

"Of course it's up to you, but if I were you I don't think I'd want to stay alone. Christ, man, you don't even have a phone out here."

"It doesn't matter."

"OK, now just a few more questions. When you left this morning—"

July's memory stopped recording here, and three hours later, according to the clock, he found himself alone with all the lights in the house on, sitting on a kitchen chair in the middle of the dining room. He reviewed his circumstance and then forgot everything until the beginning of the next afternoon, when he was in the barn lying in the hay. Through a crack in the side he could see his Aunt Becky's car, and so ascertained that he must be hiding from her and kept doing it until her car was gone.

He promised himself that in the morning he would eat something, and found that promise written out to himself and taped to the refrigerator, signed. He ate a fried egg and threw up; but he did feed the dog and cat.

Within a week he was suffering no more blackouts, and could think as clearly and bitterly as his grief would allow.

With all the powers of his rational mind, he resolved, *I'll not accept this. I won't stand for it. I refuse to accept it.*

He was consumed with thoughts of violence and imagined the things about him exploding. When he could sleep he dreamed of people and buildings blowing up, of his arm swelling up without warning and popping.

It's this death business, he thought. *All along it's been this death business. I'd've been all right if it wasn't for this death business.* But then as the days drew out into weeks, it wasn't that so much as the violence of it—the bitter resentment he felt about there having been persons who *caused* it. It wasn't necessary, or natural, or even a quirk of fate. It was *caused.*

The lieutenant visited him every several days, and at one time said, "We've got some people who we suspect. At least we'd like to find them to talk to them about it."

"What'll you do to them?"

"That'd be up to the judge."

July wasn't satisfied with that at all. He had no regard for his own life, and his only thought was that he might take a long, sweet, bitter revenge. The experience of losing her had boiled him, so to say, and for immediate fears—he had none, and would as soon fight a whole army as go outside and mow the lawn. Each second was drawn out unendurably by imagining into its tiny space the whole infinity of loneliness to come. Each first snowflake of entering winter.

"What are their names?" asked July, cutting off the words at the ends of his teeth. But the policeman wouldn't tell him.

That night he prayed to God that He make Himself known. He implored that heaven help him. *In the name of the Father, the Son and the Holy Ghost, my parents, and at the very cost of my own soul,* GIVE ME THOSE NAMES. But the sky was as dark and unyielding as ever, and July, in an act of total abandonment and renunciation, took his Bible and fired all the bullets from his mother's pistol through it, poured gasoline over it, burned it in the road and covered the ashes with gravel.

THIRTEEN

One morning July told himself he had to go to work. The baling crew would be just finishing up at Bonderman's farm and he *must* go over there and try to get back into some kind of living routine. It seemed like such a futile effort, he nearly talked himself out of it. But at the last minute he went.

He arrived a little late, and parked in the uneven line of cars along the road. The others were already walking out through the barnyard toward the machines and stopped as though a single body to turn and look at him as he came up carrying a second shirt and gloves, grief like old wounds covering his face. The foreman, Lyle Hogue, and Bonesy came forward to meet him, hanging their heads in shame at not being more at ease. The others stood and watched.

"Hello, July," said Lyle. "It's good to have you back again. All of us, we're . . . " His voice trailed away.

"We feel awful," said Bonesy, and added, "We feel awful."

"So do I," said July and motioned with his eyes, by looking away, that the interview was over. The three of them walked together into the larger crowd, who clung to July and offered short, uncomfortable condolences. But in some the interest of horror gleamed in their eyes and questioned him without words: What was it really like? I know what the newspapers said, but what was it really like? Go through it again, from the time you first came home. What exactly did they do to her?

Immediately he wanted nothing to do with them—any of them.

Lyle Hogue gave him the job of driving the tractor, pulling the baler and a hay wagon. Bonesy and Jack came with him to grab the bales as they issued from the chute, and they rode in the wagon down the lane to the field. The motor roared in July's ears.

It was a mild, calm morning. Clouds like moored ships wandered to the left and right, tethered to long ropes in the sky. A pale, pale silver moon four days from nothing hung suspended from a nylon fishing line bank-fastened to the flashing river of heaven. Here and there, diamonds of moisture twinkled underneath the leaves. The heads of the long, thin millet grasses along the fence rows, in the pastures and bunched sparingly in with the clover were red with seeds and, like old men with drooping beards, nodded and bowed to the gentle push from the ground breeze—spirits moving along the ghost trails. The color of the sky itself was blue, blue-air blue. The horizon was adorned with trees, toadstool miniatures that puffed out in animal-shaped balloons at the top. Redwing blackbirds landed on fencepoles both feet first, their black-cloaked wings and tails fanning out in a gesture of a magician flourishing his cape and singing their rolling chirp, a single wavering note played endlessly, the red and greenish blue on their shoulder like a club badge. Wrens, the witch birds, chattered from the thickets. Rabbits scurried out of their way, and pheasants in their oriental plumage haughtily viewed them from afar. July drove, caring for nothing.

The field they worked in was the lower half of an eighty-acre section, the other half planted in winter wheat. The highest place in the hayfield was right in the middle, and from there July could see a house nearly three quarters of a mile away, standing by itself at the end of a short lane. Two small bushes grew in front. He drove in slow circles, feeding the cut hay into the baler, which chewed it and spat it back out in oblong cubes, tied with coarse unbraided hemp, into the hands of Bonesy and Jack, who stacked it up.

Each time July went over the middle he would look toward the house. It held his attention. He saw someone come out of it carrying a loaded basket, set it down and begin hanging laundry from an invisible wire. Shirts and pants, towels, underwear and socks dangled like pleasant memories against the green background. This sight was soothing and each time one of his round sweeps of the field would reach the several-acre mound in the middle, he would be straining his eyes to see it lift into view in the distance, and each time more laundry would be drying. Finally, two long lines of it hung there, and the picture it gave him was like having a friend. He lived in it when he couldn't see it and talked to the woman about clothespins, drying time and the little drama of her life.

Then the woman went back into the house and there was only the laundry; and abandoned to him, the pleasant memories turned sour and hung like the truth. He became more and more depressed. Another tractor came out to take away the full wagon and leave him an empty one. He stopped when he could see the house, and Bonesy and Jack climbed down to pull the pin. It was wedged tight and they called to him to back up a little to take the pressure off.

But at that time someone else came out of the little house and stood against the white side, holding something, then walked forward to the clothesline and sat in the grass. All July could see was her long brown hair.

"Hey, back up, July," said Jack. But he paid them no attention, as if in a trance. They looked at each other and wondered what to do. Bonesy began to climb up on the back of the tractor, but all of a sudden July slammed it into gear and lurched forward, throwing Bonesy off and nearly running over him with the hay baler. "Hey!" they both yelled accusingly. July shifted into a higher gear and pulled the throttle open all the way, heading for the small white house in the distance. Jack and Bonesy ran behind him for a way, bales bouncing off the wagon and the baler banging and clanking in the ruts. He was going too fast to catch. But they continued running, thinking that they'd repossess the tractor when he stopped at the fence. But the fence didn't stop him. He went through it as if it were made of crepe paper and began tearing through the standing corn, ripping out a strip as wide as the wagon. The next fence didn't stop him either and he broke off the wooden posts like popsicle sticks. Then there was a small creek, and he went over that as well, leaving the wagon in it, the tongue dangling behind him. A wheel fell off the baler and he half pulled and half dragged it through the last remaining field before the house.

Betsy Hammond, three years old, sat in the yard holding her doll and saw the tractor coming. She remained sitting as it came closer, right up to the yard and halfway into it. Then she stood up and backed toward the house. The young man climbed from the smoking machine and stood next to the far clothesline pole, staring at her. He didn't talk, smile or make a gesture of any kind, just continued to stare at her. Then came closer.

Her mother came out of the house and ran over to her, taking her by the shoulders and putting her protectively behind her leg, silently squaring off against the man from the tractor.

"I'm sorry," he said. "I thought for a moment"—pause—"that she was someone else."

"Go away," the woman said. He turned back to the tractor, then to the hanging clothes. The mother hesitated. "Say, you're July Montgomery," she said, and immediately her face became compassionate and she even took a step closer to him. But he backed away.

"I only look like him," he mumbled.

Lyle Hogue's car roared into the driveway and Lyle and two others jumped out and ran over to him. At the same time Jack and Bonesy came running through the great swipe in the beanfield. Jack climbed up on the tractor and drove it back out of the yard. Lyle took July by the arm and gently but cautiously led him to the car. The others went to see about the wagon and the baler's wheel.

They drove the whole way back to July's car without talking; when they had stopped and it was time for July to climb out and leave, Lyle began: "Look, July, take some time off. Go somewhere and just take it easy for a while. Get yourself straightened around." July opened the door and stepped out onto the gravel. Lyle got out of the other side. July started to talk, but Lyle cut him off. "Forget about it. Accidents happen. Nobody was hurt. Forget it. Just try to get yourself together. . . . And, July, I don't know if this will sound right, and maybe it won't, but for what it's worth, I'm sure glad that it wasn't me what happened to you." July looked at him with completely vacant eyes, climbed in his car and drove away.

He went back home, parked in the mud and looked in the mailbox. There was a flyer from a hardware store in Iowa City with a recurring little cartoon man who pointed, smiling, to the red-hot specials and buy-the-second-for-only-one-penny deals. He put it back inside and closed the flap door. As an afterthought, he put up the flag, then wondered who he would ever send a letter to. He went to the porch, got a hammer that was lying there on the floor, went back to the road and tore off the flag and threw it into the ditch. Then he took off the box and jumped on it until it was flat. He went inside and read for a second time the note to himself on the refrigerator and fell into a chair at the table, putting his head in his hands.

July slept on the sofa, afraid to go upstairs with her things in the bedroom and bathroom, her shoes in front of the bed. In the morning his neighbor drove by, slowly, he thought, wishing to see in. He closed all the curtains and turned on the lights.

Around noon his Aunt Becky came into the drive and got out of her car. He had hidden from her before. He wanted nothing to do with her now. He despised her. The sight of her walking into his yard, dressed in her clean, fresh-smelling clothes, her hair arranged just so on top of her head, her brown gloves, and that look of anxious concern on her face as she looked around, hoping to see him and offer him comfort, drove him nearly mad with fear, resentment and rage. He carefully reclosed the curtain and went down into the basement to crouch in the moist darkness with his back to the cement foundation. He heard her knock kindly on the front door, wait, knock again and walk back and forth on the porch, then down the steps and a minute later he could hear her knocking at the back door.

This time she let herself in. Holmes' feet danced in the kitchen as she met her like an old friend. It made July's fists draw together the way she talked to the animals, kindly, softly, putting food down for them in case he might have forgotten. The door slammed and he thought she was going. He looked through the basement window. She went to her car, but returned with a box, went back to the kitchen and July could hear her putting things in the refrigerator. Then she went into the living room and parked herself like a century.

A half-hour later a van pulled into the drive and a man got out. His aunt let him in. They talked in murmurs. He returned to the van, brought back a black telephone and was gone again within ten minutes. His aunt waited another two hours, then finally he heard her walk out of the house and watched her get in her car and leave. Then he went upstairs. On the small table before the sofa was a telephone. Next to it was a note: *I've put this in, July, so that you might call me. Please do. Becky.* He read it without touching it, and turned down the dial on the bottom so that he would not be able to hear the ring if someone called him, thereby nullifying in his own mind all that she had tried to do.

He sat on the porch looking out toward the road in front for a long time, noticing that his outlook was becoming increasingly morbid and grim. His terror of living was exceeded only by his terror of death, which kept him trapped forever between despair and misery. He felt the demon of catatonia tighten its grip on his will. His physical sense of himself was weak, pale and impotent. He sat nearly all the rest of the day without moving, got up, went into the house and wandered through the rooms, finally coming to a rest in the bathroom, where he sat looking at the three inches of cold water he'd run into the tub two days before. Its clearness attracted him.

Mal . . . Mal . . . Mal.

The following day brought him another visitor, this one from the police department. It was the young lieutenant. As before, July hid in the basement. The policeman knocked twice, briskly, then came in and went into all the rooms downstairs, checking the closets as well, and then went upstairs. After five minutes he came down, and from the basement window July watched him go into the barn and return to the house after lifting the hoods of the cars to see if the motors were warm. Twice he called out July's name, opened the basement door, turned on the light, came halfway down the stairs for a quick check and went back up.

July heard him dialing the phone.

"Billy, this is Lester. Get me Snider, will you?"

Pause.

"Snider? Right. I'm over at the house now."

Pause.

"There's a phone here now. Somebody put it in for him. There's a note here."

Pause.

"No. Can't find him anywhere."

Pause.

"There're three cars out front. . . . Listen, what have you got from—" Pause. "Oh, never mind, then. I don't know what to do. Wait, I guess. Get a hold of Muscatine."

Pause.

"I'm sure he'll turn up."

Pause.

"No I haven't. What did you say? '66? Mercury?"

Pause.

"All three? What makes you think—"

Pause.

"Maybe so. I'll be back in tomorrow morning. Talk to you then. I'll be here another hour or so. Call if you need me. The number's three eight six nine eight seven three."

He hung up, but remained sitting on the sofa. He stayed in the house for another half-hour, then went outside and July saw him picking around in the driveway and road, inspecting the flattened mailbox and discarded flag. He came back to the house for a moment and left.

The note on the door said. *Dear July, stopped by to see how you were. If you have the time, why don't you come in and we'll have lunch together. Call me 383-6464. Lieutenant Lester Helm.* July opened the door and it fell onto the porch floor, where he left it.

But something was working away at him, and he tried to go over the telephone conversation—that much of it that he had heard. He tried to think, but it was almost as if he couldn't. His grief had stunted him and hollow shouting was all he could manage before coming to rest once again at the foundation of madness, where hatred was his only rationality.

The following morning the back door of the house banged closed, announcing July's entrance into the yard. He wore no coat and held his arms close to him with his hands in his pockets. Long, thin puffs of frozen breath, flared at the ends, came from his nostrils. He walked to the white fence and stood beside it for a long time, letting his hand slide gently over the tops of the wooden pickets. Then with no warning he yanked off one, wrenching the nails from the upper and lower rails, threw it out beyond the drive and kicked through several more. Then he walked around the house several times, beginning to shiver. Before he started to wander toward the barn, he recovered the picket, pounded it back in place with a chunk of brick, fitted the others together where they were broken, and backed away from the fence to see how far away one had to be not to notice.

He entered the barn and stood shivering in the doorway, his hands back in his pockets. His clothes looked a size too large for him. His face was thin and pale. Dark gray shadows hung beneath his red eyes. He went all the way in and closed the double doors. Immediately the inside of the barn darkened. Then he began pacing back and forth in front of the mangers, looking at the dirt floor under his feet.

He stopped to listen as a car went by in front, hearing it slow down, but continue on—thinking at first that it might be his aunt again. Then he opened the larger set of doors and drove the Chrysler in and reclosed the barn, in this way hiding it so that if she were to stop by she would think he wasn't home and not wait around so long, or even get out of her car. For a long time he sat in the driver's seat of the car looking at the dashboard, then started it and shut it off; then started it again, almost turned it off, but then, with his hand on the ignition key, slammed the foot pedal to the floor and ran it for several minutes wide open, the motor screaming. Then shut it off, got out, went up into the loft and lay in the hay looking at the cracks between the boards, which grew darker as the afternoon wore on. The hard core of light gone, he fell into the deepest despair and his thoughts became the color of old black rubber. In the middle of the night, shivering like a leaf, he stumbled slowly out of the haymow and went to the house and sat with his animals.

The next day, after having fought its way through layers and layers of cold sorrow and hatred, an idea came to him. He went out of the house and walked down the road, searched along in the ditch and found the comic book he had thrown there. As he had noticed before, on the back was stamped *Property of Riverview Courts.*

He drove to Iowa City and went to the library. There, in the Muscatine telephone directory was the name of a trailer court: Riverview Courts. It seemed quite a coincidence. Of course, there might be a thousand Riverview Courts across the country, but it did seem strange that there would be one in the only town he had overheard the lieutenant mention. Now, if there was in that trailer court another coincidence, a 1966 Mercury, it would be truly an odd set of circumstances.

July took the pocket knife Mal had given him for Christmas, sharpened to a razor's edge, and left for Muscatine, driving at a steady forty miles an hour, having hardly the presence of mind to refill the gasoline tank or stop for stop signs. He shoved a ten-dollar bill out of the window to pay for four dollars and sixty -three cents worth of gas and then drove off without waiting for the change, not because he was in such a hurry, but because he'd forgotten, picturing all the number of ways he might take his vengeance with such clarity and resolve that without the automatic habit of driving the car would've meandered off the road and into the ditch.

"Tell me where the trailer court is," he demanded of the first person he saw on the streets, and received directions. At exactly three a.m. he drove in among the long trailers, parked the car and walked along in the dark looking for a Mercury. He knew it was there. He found it hidden in a metal garage, and in the trailer beside it there was a light on. Also the sound of a radio and loud talking.

He slipped between two other trailers and came around in back. Two cinder blocks carefully piled upon each other brought him up to the level of the window in the bedroom, where he could look through the opened door along the whole length of the trailer.

Two young men were sitting at the small kitchen table. The other, a boy, sat on the sofa next to the radio. The two at the table were drinking beer out of bottles.

"What're we going to do, Wally?"

"Don't ask me that again. Don't ever ask me that again. I'm sick of it, fucker. Use your own head for a while."

"Murder. That's the worst of all things. They could hang us for that."

"Shut up. You think I don't know that?"

"Maybe somebody seen us in the parkin' lot 'n' wrote down the license plate. They'll be the FBI, Wally."

"Shut up, you stupid jackass."

July could hear the sucking noises of the younger boy, and could see him crying. The older boy stood up and shouted at him to be quiet, then hit him in the face. Blood ran down from around his eye and the gasping noise grew louder.

"Shut up, fucker!"

"Don't hit him again," yelled the other boy, getting up from the table, knocking over the empty and half-filled bottles.

"You want to try me, mother?"

"Just don't hit 'im again."

"It's his fault, you dumb bastard! You said to bring him along and now we're here 'n' wondering if we won't be hung."

"He didn't mean to. He just got scared."

"They don't want me for nothin'. I could leave you sons of bitches right now—you know that, don't you? They ain't getting anythin' on me."

"It was your idea to go out there, 'n' you was the one who started pushin' 'er."

"Nobody'd believe I had nothin' to do with it. I ain't never been in trouble before. It'd be your word against mine."

"He just got scared."

"Scared of a girl." The sucking noises grew louder. "Shut up!" And he raised his fist as though to hit the boy again.

"Don't, Wally. No more hittin'."

"Then make 'im shut up. It's like being in the room with a sick horse or somethin'."

"What're we goin' ta do?"

"I told you never to ask that again, fucker. Next time you get it. We got to think. There's plenty a smart ways a gettin' outa a thing like this. Shit, they don't catch but one hundreth of murders. We just got ta have a good story up, in case we was asked by somebody."

"We could say we just never left the parkin' lot."

"Then they'd say real fast, 'What was you boys doin' in the parking lot?' Go ahead, you try to answer, like you would if you was being asked by a detective."

"I can't think, Wally. God, I'm scared."

"I know you are, punk. That's why we got all three of us to stay here until you guys get your cool back. Course they got nothin' on me—you remember that."

"Don't leave, Wally, please."

"Just remember that, 'n' get him to shut up. God damn, why don't they have no TV shows when you need 'em? Get me a beer."

Leonard went to the refrigerator and brought one back.

"How many more we got?"

"That's the last one."

"Shit. I seen me a show once where these two guys killed a guy. They was tryin' to be smart, of course, but what give it away was that one of'em left somethin' behind at the crime which later was traced to them—a pair of glasses. Now, we di'n't do nothin' like that, see. An' no fingerprints 'cause we wiped everythin' off. Now we got to get us an alibi—some place where we was."

"We can say we was fuckin' some girls."

"That ain't no good. They'd just ask who."

"We'd say they was whores we picked up, that they didn't give us no names or nothin', and we c'n tell how each other's looked an' all agree."

"Then they'd say 'Where?' 'n' 'When?' If we said we was in a hotel, we'd have to prove—"

"We could a been in the car . . . out in the country somewhere."

"Oh no, never mention nothin' like as to remind them of somethin' connected to the crime. They'd go, 'Ah, so you guys were out in the country, huh? What car?' Then maybe they get the idea to ask that cop in the parkin' lot if he remembers a red Mercury, kind of jazzy-lookin', 'n' he probably would. No, we c'n say we was here."

"But we wasn't. There's too many people around. Donnie was here before."

"He's a down guy, hell. He'd say we was here. I was here all last week. Jesus, can't you keep 'im from doin' that?"

July opened his knife and stepped down from the cinder blocks. Looking at it in the faint light from the window, he knew he wouldn't be able to use it. A shiver of deep regret passed through him. He'd stayed too long looking in the window.

At first he thought that Mal's betrayed spirit must be crying out in utter misery and shame as it lay unavenged, but he then recognized that feeling for what it truly was—his own sense of pride and loss begging him in the pretended voice of his wife. He sat down on the cinder blocks and thought.

If I kill them, then how am I better off?

You'd still feel bad, but you'd feel better about it. If you don't want to kill them all, just get the big one.

How's that any different? One, none or all—I don't see where it makes any difference.

At least you'd know you weren't a coward.

That's ridiculous. And, anyway, what's bravery got to do with it? It's a matter of making them pay for what they did to her.

Pay who?

Her.

She's dead. It would be nice, granted. But it can't be. If she was still alive, do you suppose she'd say: JULY, GO KILL THOSE MISERABLE KIDS, AND EXPLAIN TO THEM EXACTLY HOW MUCH THEY HURT US BEFORE YOU DO IT?

I don't suppose. Of course she wouldn't say that—and that's the reason. What right did they have to take someone's life like that?

They didn't have any right. What's that got to do with it?

If they didn't have any right, but did it anyway, they can expect nothing better.

And probably don't. But if they didn't have any right, then neither do you.

Damn it, I simply want to for myself.

Good, now we're getting down to basics at least. Do you think that'll make you feel better?

Yes. Better about everything except Mal being gone. Her absence'll be the only pain.

Only!!! What other pain is there?

Hatred.

That's a joy compared to Mal being gone.

I know it.

July went to the police station and told them who he was and that there were some murderers over in Riverview Courts, number 27, gave them a description of the car and the plate number. They wrote down the information carefully and asked for the spelling of his name, which he told them, along with his address. Then they told him that they'd already known the boys were somewhere in the area, and it'd've been only a matter of time before they were picked up anyway. It was a simple procedure of pulling out files on likely types and looking around and talking to people, and thanked him for the information.

"I was going to kill them," he confessed solemnly.

"Don't worry, Mr. Montgomery."

At this point July cast all thoughts of them out of his head, and with the bang of his car door closing behind him, his involvement with them ended. The long journey back to his lonely house began.

Now that he was not protected from his grief by outrage and fantasies of revenge, the very *fact* of his aloneness made itself clearly felt for the first time. He was overwhelmed with dread. It seemed there was no place to which he could turn for comfort. Behind him was regret, and the alluring desire to go over that day and find ways of altering the events so what had happened wouldn't have. He might have come home for lunch. Mal might have gone to work that afternoon instead of waiting for the evening. He might have been sick and stayed home. He might have thought to leave the gun where she could get it, and taught her how to use it. These and countless other circumstances were alternative ways that day could just've easily gone, and there was no *reason* that it hadn't.

To his left was the commonness—the almost mundane statistic of it: people get killed. In any large city hundreds of people were killed every year. Everyone knew that each day you managed to get through with yourself and your family alive and unharmed was quite a treasure—and you should thank your lucky stars for it. People get killed sometimes. It's the way of the world—something that an introspective person should have conceded from the very beginning of his conscious thought: an undeniable rottenness to living itself.

To his right was nature, which was the closest thing he had to a religion, and in it he noted the same grim statistics—death and killing, almost as frequently as life and growth. No, it wasn't all like that, bees, seed-eating birds and the like had little participation in the horrors of it—but they were preyed upon by winter, predators, pesticides, food shortages and adaptation difficulties. There was no comfort for him here.

And in front of him, toward which he was driving steadily, were the empty house and the drawing Mal had made of him hanging above the sofa, about which one of the policemen had commented, "A sort of an artist, wasn't she." He remembered wondering what he had when she had her painting, sitting down in the timber below the barn, and only now was he aware of the answer, which came screaming at him from all around: he had her. *Oh, why didn't I realize how happy I was then?* The picture above the sofa was a good one, capturing him just as he had been, a little smug, self-righteous and proud of the mere situation that he was who he was and considering that quite a virtue—completely unaware of how he owed everything he had to her. To have her back he would gladly give *anything.*

Yes, all along it had been this death business. Everyone he had ever loved had been taken from him, past that impenetrable barrier: his grandmother by nature, his parents by accident, Carroll (whom at least he'd liked a lot) by his own choice and, most terribly, Mal by human ignorance and malevolence. No, that wasn't right. The distinctions weren't that clear. All of them in a way had been within nature, and couldn't escape being. All had been accidents, even his grandmother's—there was no reason *not* to keep living. As his father had long ago said, it isn't age that kills anyone. It's always some malfunction. Just as much an accident with Mal as with Carroll—even to decide to take one's own life is an accident. And what could be more rightly attributed to ignorance and malevolence than a traffic accident? Wasn't there malevolence in his grandmother's death too? He thought there was.

It was light when he returned home, and he sat in the living room staring at his own image above the sofa, drawn with a broken piece of charcoal and sprayed with a thin fixative to keep the tiny grains of black dust from falling off. He looked at it and thought he would rather be dead.

In the trailer, Wally Cobb thought he heard something and went over to the side window. A solitary figure was walking by in front, moving with caution, and he watched him get into an old car and drive out of the court.

"Come on," he said. "Hurry." And all three of them got into the Mercury, backed out of the garage and went after the moving tail-lights.

"What you suppose he wanted, Wally? Maybe he didn't have nothin' to do with us. Do you s'pose he was a cop?"

"I don't know, but we better find out for sure."

They followed him to the police station and watched him walk inside.

"He must be a cop. Let's get out of here."

"No, I don't think so. If he was, we'd be caught now. No, he ain't a cop."

"You think he maybe didn't have nothin' to do with us—maybe it's somethin' else? Did you really see him up close to the trailer?"

"No. We got to just wait."

A short time later he came out of the station, got into his car and drove off. They followed him from a careful distance behind. Hours later, back in the Iowa City area, they began to get nervous. Then, when they continued to follow and he led them back to the brown-stone house, they began to panic.

"He must be her husband, Wally. How did he know—"

"I don' know. I don' know."

"How could he know we was—"

"I don' know."

"God, what're we goin' a do? They're goin' a get us, Wally. They already—"

"Shut up. We ain't caught yet. First we got to get rid of this car."

"Then what?"

"Then we c'n go see my cousin Ollie. He'll know what to do. He's been in plenty of trouble before. He'll know what to do." Staying on the back roads, they headed for Kalona, where they hoped to be able to steal a car and drive to Illinois.

The Shamrock Hotel and Bar had rooms for $2.50 a night, and sold bottled beer at thirty cents. There was one common bathroom on the second floor. At about four o'clock in the afternoon the low, hoarse sounds of arguing and cursing began to flood out onto the street. The prostitutes came in at seven, and when one least expected it a woman's cry from an upstairs room would disturb the night lull of the traffic. By midnight, dark, stooping figures from inside began to spill out onto the sidewalk, where they lay intermittently sleeping and cursing at imagined audiences. Pushers met addicts and suppliers here and made dealings across the tables along the wall. Black-marketeers sat at the bar selling as freely as vacuum -cleaner salesmen. Only a few of the girls lived there. The rest went home at 3:30 a.m., walking past the warehouses and abandoned office buildings. It was a retirement home for the morally destitute.

Today was Friday. The official weekend had been ushered in just moments earlier, when M. Beshamp came back from work, went into his room, ordered his wife to undress and lie across the bed, took off his belt and beat her with it before they made love, as they did at the same time each week.

Two young men were talking in the hallway on the third floor. One was Ollie Parrott, twenty-nine, who stood six feet three, with the build of a 314-pound refrigerator, long blond hair, nearly white skin and red, red lips, hips like a woman—a monster who had already left five men lifeless on the street after pulling their billfolds from them and digging out the change from their front pockets with his huge fingers. His brutal eyes were light blue, as though filled with faintly colored water. The other was Earl Schmidt, dishonorably discharged from the Army for striking a superior officer, living now with Ollie by what they could steal. Though only twenty-three, he appeared to be fifty and stood bent and leaning against the hallway wall as though he could not support his own weight. They talked of money in soft, secretive voices, and went down the corridor to their room to eat plain bread and coffee.

Through the front door downstairs came three boys, one larger than the other two, and the desk clerk, from behind his newspaper, watched them approach. "Ollie Parrott," one of them said very nervously.

"Ollie Parrott what?" said the clerk insidiously.

"His room. Which is his room?"

"Thirty-six. Third floor." He went back to his newspaper.

Ollie opened the door, and immediately Wally Cobb greeted him by name, in the same breath explaining who he was in case Ollie had forgotten. Obviously he had. Ollie leveled his cold stare at them, still holding the door as though to slam it shut at any unexpected second. Earl Schmidt sat at the little table and looked at them with abstract contempt. In his pocket the safety was off his automatic.

"What do you want?" snapped Ollie. "We're busy."

Wally stammered.

Leonard Brown blurted out, "We're in trouble. God, we're in trouble. Help us."

"We're in trouble," added Wally.

"What's that got to do with me?"

"We thought maybe you could help us. You've been in trouble before."

"Tell 'em to say what they want or get out," said Earl.

"I've never been in trouble," put in Ollie. "OK, punks, come on in and tell us what you want." They came in and Ollie shut the door. In bits and pieces, unrelated to sequence or importance, from both Leonard and Wally, they explained their situation. Their story fell upon unsympathetic ears. Ollie opened the window and spat out of it, turned back and said: "So what am I supposed to do? You can't stay here, if that's what you're getting at."

"Throw 'em out," said Earl.

"Just tell us what to do," pleaded Wally. "That guy—the husband—somehow he knows us. He can identify us."

"It's quite a problem, all right. I hope you get out of it." Ollie opened the door for them to leave.

"Wait. Here, look." From inside his jacket Wally took a crumpled newspaper and unfolded it. "Here, look," he repeated and handed it to Ollie. It was the write-up of the killing. It told how her husband had come home, what he had found, the absence of clues, statements by the police, and the assumption that, whatever the motive was, it hadn't been money, because there remained $300 in an upstairs drawer and a diamond valued at over $2000. Ollie read it and closed the door slowly, handing the paper over to Earl, who spread it before him on the table and, chewing on a piece of bread, began to read. He read the name twice before his eyes came back to it. *July Montgomery.* He stopped breathing, and he turned the safety of the pistol on for fear his nerves would pull the trigger of their own accord and shoot a hole through his leg.

"Now, what's this place like?" Ollie was asking. "You say he lives there alone—in the middle of the country? And *already* once you punks been there but didn't take anything?"

Ollie talked to them for the next three hours while Earl sat staring down into the newspaper. The only time he spoke was when Ollie asked him, "Earl, hey, Earl! You want to do it?" and he looked up and answered in a breathless whisper, "Yes."

"It'll be a week or more," said Ollie to the boys. "Time for us to get down there and look around. It's perfect. Now, the thing for you guys to do is find yourself a place to stay—hide out, I mean—but where some people can see you. Not around here. That way you'll have an alibi. Me and Earl, see, we already got one if we're picked up 'cause we was here. They'd have to think the two murders was associated, and if you didn't do one and we didn't do another, then there's no worry. Just don't stay anywhere around here. Get into another state."

It was dark when the boys left the hotel, and before the next morning they had driven over five hundred miles of back roads and county blacktops, back into Iowa, heading for Omaha, where Leonard knew some people from reform school living in a house. They were hungry and the money they'd gotten from Wally's friend in the trailer court was almost gone.

FOURTEEN

July was sleeping upstairs now; not on his side of the bed, but hers. It seemed warmer there. In fact, he avoided his own side away from the window as if it didn't exist, so much so that when he arranged the twisted blankets (he used no sheets and slept fully clothed except for his shoes) he even avoided placing any over there. He had taken all of Mal's clothes and put them in the closet, where they lived like spirits in the dark, waiting for him to have to look at them again, some of them laughing, some of them crying and some of them staring and never asleep. His dreams became more and more terrifying and it was increasingly difficult to get out of them when he was awake.

He no longer had those times when he would forget—fall back into his former habit of knowing that when she was out of sight she was just in the next room: now he no longer thought about anything else at all. Her death and memory had his undivided attention. Horror draped the walls. Every light in the house burned without rest.

Saturday afternoon he went outside. Wind blew and it was a little cold. He walked into the yard with his dog and cat, and later went into the garden. Round orange and green pumpkins had puffed up on the snaking vines. The summer squash was knotted and hard. Tomatoes were ripe and rotting and the rats had gnawed holes into others. The beans were nearly dried on the brown stalks. The sunflowers curled over at the head like hanged men. There were several big green-and-white-striped watermelons.

A person could save some of this, he thought. Freeze the beans and . . .

He felt an urge to do a little work and went into the barn to get a hoe. Something in his step seemed to infect the animals and Holmes began running around all over the place and Butch scurried about in the hay after invisible mice. The wooden handle felt good in his hands and he advanced with it toward the garden, the hatred of weeds rising up at each step. He began to tear away at them, but within several minutes the cat and dog sat dolefully and stared at him from the fence. He stood there inert, leaning on the hoe, his eyes completely vacant. With an air of futility he took another couple of swipes with the hoe, and stopped again. Who cares? he thought. Weeds or no weeds, what's the difference? Why hate weeds? Why not hate everything?

Once more he tried to go ahead and do more hoeing. But he couldn't. Then unexpectedly he whirled and began smashing the watermelons and pumpkins, splitting them open with the blade of his hoe, swinging it down from over his head, blow after blow after blow. He chopped at the bean plants, and hacked down the standing yellow stalks of corn, crying and cursing.

That night he began to hear his own death calling to him. It didn't have a voice as such, and its communication was more direct. It talked through his feelings. It *was* his feelings, in a way.

A deep morbidity would come over him, so scrambling his senses that he began to believe it was the ugliness of things he saw around him rather than his own distorted view of them. His memories were all of the same kind, and when he remembered, he remembered bitterly. He pictured himself small and having to get away. And the only place to go was there—in that feeling: his own death-dark womb to hide in.

That night was blacker than pitch. A northeast wind blew across the roof in long, sagging groans. The old house trembled. The window sashes banged. Down in the woods the dead elms split and howled. July went out onto the porch. The wind grew wet, drawing the rain with it. The storm seemed enormous, as though it must cover the whole world—coming from some furious place in space. A lightning bolt ripped across the sky, tearing the black cloth back to the brilliant light on the other side of it, then sealing itself up like an instantly healing wound, bathing the ground in a cold blue light. July looked and thought how ugly it was.

As quickly as it had begun, the storm abated. Within ten minutes the land was covered with a piercing silence. Not even a breeze stirred the leaves on the oaks. It was as though he could hear for thousands of miles and everywhere there was nothing. The moon rose flat and blue-green out of a dark cloud and its eerie light froze the stillness harder. Then far in the distance July heard something. It sounded like the beating of his heart and blended with it perfectly . . . but it continued to get louder. It was hoofbeats, fast, then slower, over hard ground and soft. They came from miles away. He heard them strike the surface of the blacktop and keep coming. It's not on the road, thought July. It's coming through the fields. He strained his eyes off toward the horizon and saw something mount the most distant hill, then disappear down into the following scoop of land, moving with unbelievable speed. The air itself was poised now, and when the shape, no larger than an ant, came into view over the crest of the near hill, it began to tremble. A gray horse, tall, long and thin, a white mane and tail, his eyes green, the steel nailed to his hoofs flashing blue in the light of the moon, his feet striking the ground only once or twice in ten yards, jumping fences by merely altering his strides, coming toward him. And he carried someone whom July recognized at once though he had never seen him before. Perched like a sparrow on the neck of a hawk, leaning forward as though breathing down into the giant stallion's ear, the wet blade of a knife in his teeth, his dark coat cut and streaming out behind him in ribbons, his legs gripping the sides of the beast and curled beneath him, a handful of the white mane in his right hand, urging him on with his barking voice, his teeth silver and gold, a rifle and its broken and splintered stock stuck under his arm, the smell of burning powder in the air, rode the great Kingfisher. July knew him in an instant, as quickly as he might pick himself out of a crowd, and he felt his jaws tighten as though gripping the cold blade of the knife to keep it from falling. They rode like the wind, the stallion's nostrils wide, sucking air, his mouth opened in a grimace of excitement, the old outlaw's black eyes wild and cruel.

Then popping into view on the horizon—a line of them like an army of ants—came his pursuers. They disappeared into the scoop of land and when they re-emerged July could see them more clearly. A whole herd of them, gray, huge hogs but running like dogs. Their feet didn't seem to touch the ground and they snorted and spit and howled after the running horse. The bushes, trees and grass recoiled from them in revulsion.

The outlaw and horse cleared another fence and were in the field next to the yard, still heading toward him. Halfway through and the hellhounds were in it too, each of their dark howls like some mad cry from an animal's imagination.

In one long bound the horse and rider entered the yard and July could see the old outlaw's face. A scar stretched from beneath his left eye all the way to his chin, and July remembered that long ago three men had held him down while another beat him with a deer foot severed eight inches above the hoof. Left for dead, he'd crawled and rolled down from the hills, down to the ocean, where he'd submerged his head in the salt water, come up, and felt the searing burn of the wounds ignite again the terrible strength he had been born with. Later he'd killed them all. There was a bullet hole in one of his hands, made by a rifle from three hundred yards. His life was one catastrophe after another. The Devil had him then, and liked his name—the kingfisher of men . . . but he was loose now.

His face and hands, neck and as much of his chest as July could see where his coat was ripped away were covered with wounds, new wounds on top of old, old on top of older, as though his body had originally been ironed together, a man who in his whole life had never had a friend, or wanted one; as far as people were concerned, he had no favorites, to whom women were only an evening's entertainment and the morning's regret. His home was the stars. All the good thoughts he ever had stayed in him: his exterior was as rough and crude as he could make it. His spirit was greater than his mind, and it swung him like a whip around the whipman's arm. Trapped under a fallen tree, he once went five days without water or help. In a Mexican jail he had dug himself out with just his hands. Though not the best fighter, or runner, or lifter, or shooter, or swimmer, or thinker, or even that much braver then the next guy, he simply *never* gave up, and *refused* to accept that he was beaten. It was the simple, unimpeded drive to stay alive at whatever cost, for no great purpose or need that he could understand because it wasn't to be understood, that burned in him like a comet, and it wasn't joy that lit his face now but an expression that July almost couldn't fathom: he was at once grim, determined and frightened. (This was his last chance: they had all been last chances.)

Coming by the porch, both horse and rider turned their eyes on July and he backed against the side of the house. From both, the look was the same: compassionless strength—the quick, naked bones of survival. When all else was torn away, there was only this to carry on, and it worked well enough. In the next instant they were gone from the yard, over the wooden picket fence, beyond the barn and out of sight. Then the gray creatures were in the yard and all of them as they ran turned to face July. It was the ugliest moment in his life, but with the cold eye of the legendary outlaw in him, he glared back at them and thought, *Get me now, you blood demons, the chance won't come again.* They passed on and were gone as quickly as they had come. The storm folded back over the house, barn and fields. The rain fell like silence. July prayed, *Dear God, why must we live alone?*

FIFTEEN

Halfway through Iowa, just off Highway 6 outside of Des Moines, Wally Cobb, Leonard Brown and Billy Joe Brighton pulled into a hamburger stand, went inside the glassed-in partition and ordered sandwiches, fries and Cokes. Billy Joe had an orange drink. They ate at a little table and watched across the street where several men were trying to start a white Oldsmobile, jumping it from another car's battery.

They were out of money now and a kind of tension seemed to hold them together. When Leonard, after finishing half his Coke, went over to the water fountain and poured in an inch of water to make more, he couldn't free himself from it and moved stiffly and self-consciously. The manager watched them from behind the stainless-steel counter with suspicion.

"You sure you know the address?" said Wally.

"Fourteen ninety-one Edgeway."

"Why can't you give them a call?"

"They don't have a phone. But they *got* to be there."

"Now, my idea is that we stay for a couple days, no longer than a week, and move on to . . ." Wally saw Billy Joe's face turn white and he whirled quickly around. Two policemen stood in the doorway. Two others were outside.

"All right, boys, take it easy. You're under arrest. Slowly now, stand up. Keep your hands on the table."

"Let me go," said Wally. "Please let me go. I've never been in any trouble before. I didn't have anything to do with it."

"With what?" said the nearest policeman, holding out the opened handcuffs. They took them outside and put them in the back seat of the patrol car parked at the side of the building.

From the time the three boys had left the hotel to when Ollie was ready to leave two days later, Earl had hardly left their small room. Once he'd gone down to the barroom below and sat by himself at one of the far back tables, eating, chewing the tough meat automatically and without enjoyment as he stared into the dark tabletop, as though hypnotized by a swinging pendulum inside his mind, not looking up even when called to from the bar. Betty May, an old prostitute who lived in the Shamrock, came silently to his table, pulled up a chair and began to be friendly.

"Hey, Earl, I seen you from across the room and wondered to myself why of Earl was sittin' way back here in the dark, so I come over, 'n', hey, somethin' the matter, Earl?"

He lifted his head and let his blank eyes fall on her face as though she were no more than one of his own thoughts.

"Hey, Earl, you don' look so good. Maybe you need a drink. Let me get Bobby to bring you over one. What's the matter? Tell ol' Betty May about it. You know we always been good friends as can be."

Earl's expression hadn't changed, and he automatically cut off another corner of meat and chewed it. Betty May became a little frightened, and decided it would be best to go back to the bar—after one more try. She reached out and took hold of his shoulder.

"Hey," she said softly. "Earl, it's Betty May. You all right? You remember me. We done a lot of tricks together. We was together that night—"

"Who are you?" said Earl, looking at her now with a fierce intensity, and she quickly took her hand back and moved to the edge of her chair, ready to jump, knowing that if she were caught back here in the corner she could scream for all she was worth and no one would come but to watch. There was no recognition in his eyes, only a bitter hostility at being interrupted.

"It's Betty May," she said. "You know me."

He stood up and put a dollar bill on the table. "I *don't* know you," he said flatly, and wandered through the bar and into the lobby, where he mounted the stairs, stepping slowly and deliberately, each step an individual decision, like one possessed. At the window at the end of the hall on the third floor he stopped to stare outside and remained standing there for over an hour, then continued down the hall and into his room. Neglecting to close the door, he fell into a chair next to the table and stared at the floor.

They left for Iowa in Ollie's Pontiac.

"There's the house," said Ollie, indicating a lonely structure just off the road, with two miserable-looking automobiles sitting in the mud in front. Earl looked out his window and felt a shiver go through him.

"Easy," said Ollie behind the wheel. "It'll be easy. We'll have to sort of check around for a while, of course."

Earl's fingers wrapped around the arm of his door in an involuntary, convulsive grip, still staring out the window, not recognizing anything but a blur of muted browns and grays from the ditch, hearing far away Ollie's excited voice.

"Come on, Earl, snap out of it. We can turn around up here, make a sweep back. Hell, who knows what he got on 'im? Hey, what do you think?"

"Sure," said Earl absently.

"There, down there along the creek it winds all the way back up to the barn. Hey, does that look OK to you?"

"Sure."

Ollie looked at him with anger, but let it pass. "Boy, you've been queer lately," he said and drove around the block to take another look at the house. They met an old pickup and the driver waved at them.

"Friendly bastards around here," said Ollie.

Earl had taken the bullets from his .45 Army automatic and was intermittently cocking it and firing it dry, making little snapping noises.

July sat in his bedroom and felt like a plant with its roots cut. From his bed he looked at the partially opened closet door and thought over his life and what if any opportunities lay before him. Days passed like ugly, slow-moving trucks. He thought about Mal and he thought on and on. Some of it was incomprehensible. He would repeat things over and over—he would begin a thought with "We used to come home and . . ." and would lose track of the rest and begin it again: "We used to come home and . . ." and still not be able to finish, and would start it again, but stop, abandoned in the same narcotic image. He knew that what he was doing was wrong. Some things were clearer than they had been. He saw that he was not succeeding in resurrecting Mal, but only her death—making *it* a living occurrence that happened again and again. He knew in his right mind that he must divorce her from his mental image of her—because *he was killing her now*—he was making her into what she never was. The light of his life, he was chaining her to himself and making her drag him through the mud. He knew it was wrong, but it was his grief thinking for him, because if he gave her up there would be nothing left of him—a small peanut of a person, wrinkled and unable to live in the world. There were three relationships that he was concerned with: Mal when she was alone with herself; himself alone; and the relationship they had between them. Now, with her gone, two thirds of his life was missing.

There was a talking voice in him that insisted at different times that he *knew* what he was *supposed* to do. He knew he should give her up—that is, forget about her and go on normally, make new contacts and get into some different thoughts and experiences and let them work on him like health specialists. That would be the *mature*, gentlemanly way to go about his affairs with that sickening, stoic, smiling bravery. But he just didn't think he could do that. It seemed that moral indignation itself would crucify him if he tried it.

No, it was not that he had loved her once that was causing him so much grief. It was that he must love her twice: once when she was alive and once when she was dead. He must love her *more* now, because it was only through his love that she could be alive, as it was only she in his life that brought him happiness. She was the key. Without her the whole world lived in misery. So it wasn't the first time that he had loved her (in which he was guilty of not having realized how uproariously happy he was) that tortured him now and threatened to snap him like a stick. It was the second time. It was loving her dead. But then his mind cried out unexpectedly, louder than his grief: You fool, love her once, love her alive. You participated in happiness *with* her: life gave it to you both: her death changes nothing finally. Cut her loose. The dead aren't dead. Love her living, not death.

But I can't, he thought. I just don't think I can do that. I only understand things emotionally. My habits and feelings have the power over me. Coward! cried his conscience.

Going to sleep seemed to be impossible. He got up and went downstairs. Sitting on the sofa, he felt an urge to make something with wood. Bringing up several boards, a hammer and two jars of nails from the basement, he dumped them on the floor and gave up the project as quickly as he had conceived it because of not being able to think of anything to make. Returning to the sofa, he sat and stared at a slender red clay vase on the table in front of him, the dried stalks of wildflowers wilted and bent now like burned lizards. He looked at it for a long time without really realizing what it was, then remembered Mal had picked those flowers, had snipped them off and put them in there with several inches of water to prolong their flush petals and fragrance, but they were dead now. Even if he wanted to replace them with others, he couldn't. All the flowers were dead now. Winter had almost arrived. No more until next year. The little vase itself was something he had brought back from the Goodwill store in Iowa City and it seemed a curious object when isolated from the table and room. It seemed odd to him that the purpose of something could be to display (for appreciation) another thing that was alive but doomed—that what it was to contain was of more importance than itself, but much, much more fragile.

He went into the kitchen and stood next to the table. Butch came in and stepped on his foot. He filled the dog and cat bowls with dry food mixed with water, and sat watching them while they ate.

They seemed to enjoy eating. Holmes hardly chewed at all and July remembered once when his mother had criticized his father for eating so rapidly and he had responded, "Can't taste it otherwise," and laughed. But July'd noticed that he slowed down after that.

Then he thought of his grandfather Wilson and remembered that the only thing anyone had ever really said against him (as far as July knew anyway) was that he maybe spent too much time with his dogs, and when somebody told him that, *he* thought it was a compliment, because *he* didn't think a person *could* spend too much time with dogs. July smiled at the thought and the smile was so completely unexpected that he was startled right out of it. He hadn't thought there were any of that kind left to him. He pictured his entire emotional makeup as being so many electrical circuits—a huge network of tiny passages capable of conducting his charged thoughts through them, with countless thousands of different courses. A single thought would start moving and come to a junction where four alternative paths existed; when it had fallen into one of them, another four or five directions would open up, and so on, cutting across other circuits and every which way. This unbelievably complex system was made even more complex by each small segment of line having its own particular emotional value, ranging from very good, through nonfeeling, to very bad.

As the days wore on, he had felt his possibilities contracting. Coming to an intersection, he could see that one and sometimes two of the four channels were slowly being sealed up, like doorways being cemented over, and that it wasn't easy to get into them any more. Before long it would be impossible. He knew very clearly the substance that was sealing these avenues, knew how it was getting there, but had no idea how to stop it. Invariably, it was the channels containing the *good* feelings which were being closed. He had seen also that the beginning work on the *bad* had started, and that the future held almost exclusively nonfeeling channels, when his thoughts would roll straight through his mind like a bowling ball down a narrow alley and, deviating just the slightest bit, would fall into the gutter, slide all the way to the end and drop into the machine to be returned. He was powerless against it. Watching it happening, understanding it and at the same time not having any influence over it filled him with a hopeless, bitter rage (which was quickly becoming a constant mood, and he began to feel friendly toward it). The quality of his thoughts was being drained from them. But one of those channels was open. He had just been in it. Something inside him was tearing down those walls, opening him back up. He sat down and held on to the table to steady himself. Holmes turned and looked at him. Butch licked a paw and rubbed it over his whiskers. They didn't seem so sad. Yes, he thought, he could imagine how someday maybe there might be some times ahead when they might go out into the yard, lie in the sun and not have to think about Mal, but just be happy. He could imagine how, after a while, some of those moments might be possible. It was the first glimmer of joy that he'd had since Mal was murdered, and though it lasted only several seconds, still it filled him with a tenacious hope, and for the first time he took up the task of deciding what he was going to do. He had to start getting away from home. Get rid of her clothes. Perhaps he could leave altogether. He needed to find a job; there wasn't much money left and he wasn't going to live off Aunt Becky. The issues quickly became too much for him to handle, and the weight of infinity pressed down on him with gloomy, unresolved riddles, but with a courage that astonished him he pushed them from his mind and thought, *I'm tired. First rest, then think,* and he went upstairs and fell into a deep, dreamless sleep—this time on his own side of the bed.

SIXTEEN

Lieutenant Lester Helm was talking to Leonard and Billy Joe in his office from behind a gray steel desk. There was no real doubt that they had killed the girl. It was written all over them. There was even blood on their clothes. But they were remaining very close-mouthed and refused to say anything other than blatant denials. They couldn't remember what they were doing three weeks ago, or much before that. Leonard had readily confessed to being wanted in Cedar Rapids for armed robbery and seemed anxious to be sent there for a hearing so he could get it off his conscience. Billy Joe Brighton followed his brother like a pet and always appeared to be studying his face. There were bloodstains on the walls of his right pants pocket, where he'd put his unclean knife away before getting rid of it. The other one, Wally Cobb, had faint fingernail scratches on his face and was so frightened that they'd have the story from him probably before the night was out. But what interested Helm was something Leonard had said after they were first brought in: "We didn't do it. You'll see we didn't."

Helm also wondered where they had gone after July saw them in Muscatine. The car they had been in had been stolen in Illinois, yet they said they'd never left Iowa. He had an interest in knowing everything. He decided to call July and have him come in and look at them. (He also wanted the comic book.) He picked up the telephone and dialed with the eyes of the two boys on him. It rang five times. He hung up and called again, let it ring eight times and closed the receiver.

Moving quickly and silently, Ollie and Earl entered the barn from the back. The day was beginning to clear, and within a half-hour there would be direct sunlight. Ollie stood in the safety of the darkness inside and looked through the partially opened double doors. He inspected the yard and house with no more excitement than a county tax assessor, noticing that all the lights were on and the back door was wide open, with only a screen between the yard and kitchen. No movement of any kind inside.

Ollie took out the silencer and fastened it to the end of his pistol; it obstructed his front sights, but that wouldn't matter at such close range and would eliminate that faintest chance that they might be apprehended before they could get back to the car and onto the highway.

"You don't suppose that guy would be gone, do you?" he whispered, as though he were talking about a family of rats. He was neutral to murder. Another's life meant no more to him than a ball of dust from underneath a sofa.

Obtaining no answer, he turned back to Earl, meeting a pair of dark, glowing eyes that looked past him to the house with primeval concentration and malice.

"Come on," Ollie whispered. "Let's go. You take the back door. He's probably upstairs asleep." And he moved out across the barnyard, stopped, listened and returned to the barn, taking hold of Earl's arm.

"Earl, hey, c'm'on. Get it together. Jesus, what's the matter with you?"

"OK, OK," muttered Earl and went out of the barn behind Ollie, moving unsteadily, halting and starting, haunted by his own thoughts. Far in the distance Ollie heard a truck on the highway. The summer insects were gone, and when the murmur of the diesel died away, perfect stillness pressed down. They went through the little gate and entered the yard, walking on the long, wet grass.

Ollie was in the house first, and except for the sudden hum of the refrigerator, it was as quiet as outside. The living room was in shambles. A broken plate with old food lay in a small heap next to the wall covering the staircase, and the brown stain dripping down to it revealed where it had first hit, several days ago. Torn bits of paper shredded to the size of match heads lay in an irregular circle in front of the red upholstered chair. A hammer, some boards and two jars of rusted nails were in the middle of the floor. Stuffing had been pulled from a rip in the arm of the sofa. The picture above it had had the eyes cut out with a knife, leaving square holes which exposed the cream-colored wall beyond. On the table were a twenty-dollar bill and a note written in a neat, bold hand: *Dear July, I've had this put in* . . . What a cruddy place, thought Ollie, putting the bill in his shirt pocket. Earl entered the kitchen just as the refrigerator shut off, and Ollie watched him involuntarily jump backward and stare at it anxiously, his unsilenced automatic in his hand, as though he couldn't convince himself of the impossibility of there being someone inside it. Ollie shook his head, and for the second time that day began thinking about going to California alone.

Ollie carefully checked the dining room and went to the staircase. Moving with extreme caution, the safety lever of his pistol moved to the off position, he mounted the steps. All the lights were on. As he came, he noted that there were three bedrooms and one bath. The doors to all of them were open. As he reached the landing, Ollie looked into the first room at the sleeping shape of July Montgomery, fully dressed, with a corner of the blanket pulled around him. Ollie stepped out of the stairwell onto the floor, and in the same instant realized two things. First, there was the dull footfall of Earl at the bottom of the stairs. Secondly, a large, three-legged dog had materialized from the other side of the double bed and was halfway across the room, running in a silent, swift attack.

Ollie fired his pistol twice, both times hitting the beast, but not halting its deadly progress, his bullets having only the effect of bringing out a cry of pain and ferocity. The dog leaped and Ollie threw up his arms to protect his neck and face, and fell backward, unable to break his fall in any way, and unable, after landing full on his back on the sharp wooden stairs, to defend himself from the relentless ripping attack of the snarling dog on top of him.

"Earl!" he yelled as he fell down another five stairs. "Earl!" And Earl, moving unsurely, like someone in a dream, took the safety off his automatic and shot the dog. The explosion was magnified by the narrow staircase. Holmes tried to leave Ollie and come toward Earl, but after another loud bark of the pistol she moved no more.

"Earl . . . Earl, I can't move. Earl, come get me up."

But Earl didn't hear, and was looking into the eyes of July Montgomery, who stood at the top of the stairs, unarmed, sleep hanging heavily from his face with an expression of total bewilderment. But no fear. As though his own personal life at that moment meant nothing to him.

Earl had been telling himself for several weeks that sooner or later he was going to snap out of it. Sooner or later this dream state wherein his emotions and his thoughts were held captive, roiling about in utter confusion, would play itself out, and he would rightfully take command of his life again. In his own unreasoning way, he was able to see that his imagination was out of control, and he was, *at best,* only partially conscious. On one hand was the sweet idea of killing July—the lucky coward—on the other he was confronted with an unexplainable fear. Unlike Ollie, Earl had never murdered, and the idea of it caused him to run wild with terror and horror. The act seemed like only the tip of the iceberg—the rest remained underwater where he couldn't see it. Was it really going to happen? And when he stepped into the house, Earl'd asked himself again, Does this mean it will *really* happen? Surely, when the time comes, I'll snap out of this.

He had shot twice at the dog, with no more than a dreamer's confidence that his gun would have any effect—half expecting the bullets to roll down the barrel and onto the ground like soft peas. The noise and jolt of the report surprised him and gave him more confidence. Then, when he was just starting to make some sense out of what had happened, to understand exactly what it meant, he'd looked up into July's face. Instantly he realized, Now! Now's the time. Now I must snap out of it. But he couldn't. His reactions were slow. They refused to agree with his willful thoughts, and by the time he'd raised his gun and fired, July had dashed out of view and one of the bedroom doors had slammed. Earl went up the stairs over the dog, past Ollie, who pleaded once more to be stood up on his feet, and toward the closed door. From inside he heard noises. He hesitated, hearing Ollie descending the stairs, letting himself down with one arm and shoulder to the living room. He waited almost a minute, then turned the knob and swung open the door.

The light was no longer on and the room was as dark as a well. He stood in the doorway for several seconds, then moved to the wall, waiting for July to make some noise to give himself away. Finding a light switch, he flipped it on, but nothing happened. The bulb had been taken. Slowly his eyes began to adapt. The wallpaper of great magnolia flowers frightened him. They appeared to be faces, or no, if they couldn't be faces, what then? Pale, round, faceless heads.

Cautiously, he began to work his way around the room. But there seemed to be so many places a person could hide. He continued to think he heard noises. Clothes strewn all over the floor and furniture seemed to jump at him.

Then the door slammed, sealing him in total darkness. He wheeled around and just before he fired aimlessly and the red-and-blue flame spat out of his hand, he heard a key turn in the lock. Feeling himself becoming more confused, he opened the curtains, letting a thin wash of gray light in from the morning, crossed to the door and found himself imprisoned.

He must have Ollie's gun, he thought, and immediately saw his own imminent death rise up in front of him.

He could hear no noise from the hall. His only thought now was of escape. But wasn't July waiting just outside? With Ollie's gun trained on the door from the stairwell? What chance was that?

The window! He ran to it and looked out. Yes, this was the way July'd gotten out of the room, by hanging from the sill and dropping eight feet to the ground. But just as likely he was outside now, waiting; and crawling from the window would make a target no one could miss. The other possibility was to jump straight out and fall, and he pictured himself receiving the deadly shots while groveling on the ground, both legs broken.

He sat on the bed and tried to think. He weighed his fears. To stay in the room and not move meant capture. Or did it? Might it not mean death? Death was imminent. July meant only to kill him, and would wait him out, however long it took. No food or water. This was the country, after all. Or he might have called his friends, and any second six pickups would pull into the drive, loaded with men who hoped to catch him alive.

No, July'll call the police. Of course he will. But why should he?

Mustering all his courage, he got off the bed and crossed to the door, stood back several feet and fired a clip of bullets into the lock. With his back to the wall, he tried to force the door open from the side, reloaded, fired twice more and pulled it open. Now all he needed was to pick a moment and fly out into the hall, firing as he came. It was a chance.

"July," he called. "July. Hey, let's make a deal. July!" But there was no answer.

He's going to kill me, he thought, then heard the sound of someone hammering somewhere.

Now! he decided, and jumped into the hallway, his automatic ready to fire. But the hall and stairs were empty. The hammering continued, from the bottom of the stairs. He heard three nails driven deep into wood. Slowly he crept down past the dead dog. The hammering stopped and he heard footsteps going farther off into the house.

The door at the bottom was nailed shut. It was too stout to break.

The only escape would be from an upstairs window to the ground. But now he had more windows to choose from.

He went up and checked the other windows (turning the lights off as he went). Ten altogether, all of them virtually the same distance from the ground. He took off his shoes and, carrying them, he walked from room to room opening all the windows. Now he was really trapped. July could sit calmly in the living room, listening for him scrabbling down the side of the house, and shoot him at his leisure.

Looking through a front window in a room completely bare of any furniture—three suitcases and an armload of empty cardboard boxes—he saw the patrol car arrive. The morning was brighter now. The motor was shut off, and the lights dimmed. One of them got out; the other remained talking into the microphone in quick, hushed tones. A cracked, spitting voice came from the dash speaker. They came toward the house together, unfastening the snaps on their holsters, but conscientiously not removing their pistols.

Captured. Relief overwhelmed him. In his whole life, it was the best feeling he'd ever had.

A little later a highway-patrol car arrived, then two more. He could hear them below, prying the door open, and one of them came into the yard and called up to him with a loudspeaker to give himself up. They carried Ollie out on a stretcher, but he wasn't dead. No sirens. Tossing his gun out the window, Earl went back to the hall, put on his shoes and sat on the stairs until they opened the door. Only one of them had a drawn gun. They didn't push him around, but let him walk downstairs with dignity, accept the handcuffs and go out to the back seat of one of the cars. He thought they respected him.

SEVENTEEN

It was after seven thirty before they were all gone. Several of the men had stayed and helped July bury his dog in back of the garden. Lieutenant Helm was there. "It seems someone wants to do you harm," he said. "Do you have any idea why?"

July didn't. His life seemed completely out of his own hands, and a hard core of violence lay, like a cinder, in his heart. At the age of twenty-two years it seemed he was cursed to go on living. It would be better, he thought, if I had never been born.

He watched them leave, and went into the house. The walls retained the sense of violence, like a captured scream, just beyond the painted surface. He sat in the living room and tried to think.

There seemed nothing he could do about the swelling personal horror, and as he tried to form an encasement which would contain it, the pressure became as bad as the growing.

You must do something *quick,* he told himself. The cream-colored walls stared at him through the two square holes in the charcoal drawing. They watched him walk to the window and look out, then cross the room to the kitchen where he stood running water into the sink. He went into the living room and sat on the sofa and looked at the red clay vase and the hardened and brittle wildflowers. Mal had picked them in the last week of July. He lifted the receiver of the phone on the table before him and dialed.

It rang twice and the crisp, friendly voice of his Aunt Becky met him on the other end.

"Hello," she said. "Hello . . . Hello, who is this? . . . July, is it you? . . . July?"

"It's me," he said. "I guess I sort of, well, need someone to talk to."

"Oh, July," she cried, bursting into tears which were as clear to him as if they'd fallen on his hands. "I'll come right over. Wait where you are and I'll be right over."

"Well, if you don't mind, I think I'd rather come over there. I mean there's been some things going on over here . . . and I'd rather not stay." He could tell his voice frightened her. It was too cautious.

"I'll be here. Don't you worry. Come right over. Will your cars drive?"

"Yes. I'll come right over."

And as he hung up, just before he took away the earpiece, he heard her say to herself as though with the phone crushed to her breast, "Praise the Lord."

July went upstairs, looked in all the rooms of his house once more before closing the doors and clasping the windows. Downstairs in the basement, he turned off the electricity, turned off the water, the heat, and closed the valve from the gas tank. Then ran the water from the lines. He locked the house and placed the key in his pocket, put Butch in a box, started the Chrysler and drove away.

On the road he tried only to keep his mind on driving, but something called to him in an old but not-forgotten voice. And as he drove, it began to soothe him with its sound. He reached the blacktop and turned right, heading for Sharon Center. By the time he reached the four-way stop sign at the intersection with the black sunken-pebble highway to Hills, he was willingly giving himself to it, forming himself to a shadow of what he was, and instead of turning in, he continued on.

His aunt saw him from the kitchen window, and immediately put on her hat. She hurried outside, climbed into her car, backed out of the garage and started after him as he disappeared around the first corner a mile away. She lost sight of him again on Highway 1 when a truck pulled in front of her, saw him make a lefthand turn onto Riverside Drive into Iowa City and then lost him again. She drove from block to block looking, with no success. A half-hour later she had an idea and drove to the old train station. There in the lot was the green Chrysler, empty. She hung her head, closed her eyes, folded her hands and thought in prayer: "Keep yourself headed forward. There's nothing easy in this world—and to give up is to lose everything. Do what you feel you have to, but do it in order to *improve* yourself. No running. Learn how to suffer and nothing will ever be able to hurt you. Reach as far as you possibly can, without pride. Be more than you are able."

In lurching slow motion, gaining speed, the Rock Island Line pulled out of the freight yard, headed southwest, toward Kansas City, Coffeyville, Scottsdale, Spring Valley and Moline.

Photo by Lewis Koch

As a young man, DAVID RHODES worked in fields, hospitals, and factories across Iowa. After receiving an MFA degree from the University of Iowa Writers' Workshop in 1971, he published three novels in rapid succession: *The Last Fair Deal Going Down* (Atlantic/Little, Brown, 1972), *The Easter House* (Harper & Row, 1974), and *Rock Island Line* (Harper & Row, 1975). In 1977 a motorcycle accident left him paralyzed from the chest down. He lives with his wife, Edna, in rural Wonewoc, Wisconsin.

More Fiction from Milkweed Editions

Visigoth
Gary Amdahl

I Am Death
Gary Amdahl

The Farther Shore
Mathew Eck

Crossing Bully Creek
Margaret Erhart

Thirst
Ken Kalfus

Ordinary Wolves
Seth Kantner

Roofwalker
Susan Power

Sky Bridge
Laura Pritchett

Cracking India
Bapsi Sidhwa

Water
Bapsi Sidhwa

Aquaboogie
Susan Straight

Gardenias
Faith Sullivan

The Blue Sky
Galsan Tschinag

Montana 1948
Larry Watson

Milkweed Editions

Founded in 1979, Milkweed Editions is one of the largest independent, nonprofit literary publishers in the United States. Milkweed publishes with the intention of making a humane impact on society, in the belief that good writing can transform the human heart and spirit.

Join Us

Milkweed depends on the generosity of foundations and individuals like you, in addition to the sales of its books. In an increasingly consolidated and bottom-line-driven publishing world, your support allows us to select and publish books on the basis of their literary quality and the depth of their message. Please visit our Web site (www.milkweed.org) or contact us at (800) 520-6455 to learn more about our donor program.

Milkweed Editions, a nonprofit publisher, gratefully acknowledges sustaining support from Anonymous; Emilie and Henry Buchwald; the Bush Foundation; the Patrick and Aimee Butler Family Foundation; the Dougherty Family Foundation; the Ecolab Foundation; the General Mills Foundation; the Claire Giannini Fund; John and Joanne Gordon; William and Jeanne Grandy; the Jerome Foundation; the Lerner Foundation; the McKnight Foundation; Mid-Continent Engineering; a grant from the Minnesota State Arts Board, through an appropriation by the Minnesota State Legislature, a grant from the National Endowment for the Arts, and private funders; Kelly Morrison and John Willoughby; an award from the National Endowment for the Arts, which believes that a great nation deserves great art; the Navarre Corporation; the Starbucks Foundation; the St. Paul Travelers Foundation; Ellen and Sheldon Sturgis; the James R. Thorpe Foundation; the Toro Foundation; Moira and John Turner; United Parcel Service; U. S. Trust Company; Joanne and Phil Von Blon; Kathleen and Bill Wanner; Serene and Christopher Warren; and the W. M. Foundation.

Interior design by Wendy Holdman
Typeset in ITC New Baskerville by BookMobile
Design and Publishing Services, Minneapolis, Minnesota.
Printed on acid-free, recycled (100 percent postconsumer
waste) Rolland Enviro paper by Friesens Corporation.